From Grandeville – A Tale – Tale 12.

Braidna

Being The Second Tale of Mythology. Of A Sort.

George R. Mead

E-Cat Worlds Press

Comments and questions? –> gmead01@gmail.com

Briadna

Everything is fiction, nothing more, nothing less. No real people are in these tales nor do any real life clones of the characters exist.

LCCN 2011941172

Mead, George R.
/Briadna. Being The Second Tale of Mythology. Of A Sort.
George R. Mead.
p. cm. – (From Grandeville, a tale; Tale 12)
ISBN-13 978-0-9817446-4-3
1. Fantasy. I. Title. II. Series.

E-Cat Worlds established its publishing program as a reaction to the large commercial publishing houses currently dominating the book industry and the smaller intellectual clones. It is interested in publishing works of fiction and non-fiction that are often deemed insufficiently profitable or commercial or that are not necessarily reflective of literary trends and fads.

E-Cat Worlds, 57744 Foothill Road, La Grande OR 97850
www.ecatworldspress.com
SAN 255-6383

In the middle of nowhere - Creativity.

First Edition:
Printed in the United States of America

From Grandeville.

Portal
Lair
Search
Not Again
And Again.
Magiwitch
Rebirth
Offspring
Holiday
Treasure
E'Nilt
Briadna

A Tale of the Feyra

Jonathon and Dee
Dee of The Fontala

Nonfiction

A History of Union County
The Ethnobotany of the California Indians
A History of the Chinese in The West: 1848-1880.

It was night.
As dark as night can be.
No moon.

Just a soft, hovering layer of clouds.
Capping the wide, round valley.

Dark and quiet.
Late at night.
Very late at night.

He sat and muttered to himself.

May You Live In Interesting Times

Grandeville. Not Too Far From Greater Downtown.

"Well, Partner, what do you think?"

"I think that you have been shot."

Red took his hand away from his left shoulder and looked at the stain on his hand. The one on his chest, on his shirt was a darker blue than the shirt itself. On his hand it was just a bright, sorta, red. He nodded. "What I thought. Not much though."

He was leaning back against their Black & White, wondering how he was going to explain this to his wife, Sandy. And to The Chief. He figured that The Chief would be easier to handle.

Green walked over to the crumpled form lying in the dirt of the alley, slumped against the back of the garage. "I called for medical help."

"The Chief is really going to be unhappy."

Green nodded. "Lot's of paper work."

They had just come on shift and had just driven down into the main drag of greater downtown Grandeville when they saw this fellow run from *Dave's Soup and Salad Bar*, pistol in hand, and dart down the alley.

>>>> 1 <<<<

So they had driven around the block, parked, jumped out and ran around and through a front yard before cutting back into the alley. The police car sat blocking one mouth of the narrow alley. They were going to have to pay Sally Sellerman for her flowers, and the wrecked flowerbed.

And there he stood, looking surprised, gun in hand.

"Police," stated Green. "Just stand there, quiet, and drop that gun!"

The owner of the gun fired as Red leaped one way, Green the other. Red grunted. Green charged up to the shooter, grabbed the hand holding the gun, and wrapped both inside his large hand. The man screamed. And screamed. And then went very quiet. Green had let go and punched him.

And now they were waiting.

But not for long.

The ambulance raced up the alley from the other end, the free end, and Charley Jurgen, leaped out with his two helpers. Charley checked Red while his helpers checked the body on the ground.

"Damn, Red," observed Charley, "you've been shot."

Red nodded and let Charley lead him over to and into the ambulance. "Just be a few minutes," said Charley.

He helped his assistants load the gurney and shove it into the ambulance. "This guy is a mess," he snapped. "Tell E.R. to get ready."

The ambulance raced away.

Green walked around Sally's quiet house, thought that she was probably off playing bingo, left a note under her doorknob, walked over and got into their squad car, and drove over to Red's house. To tell Sandy what had happened. It was Saturday, she would be at home. Then he'd go back to the station and start on the paperwork. Later he'd go up and visit with Red in the hospital, if they kept him that long.

Grandeville. Red and Sandy's House.

The door opened at the first ring. Sandy opened the door, sheaf of paper in her free hand. She was a very busy attorney. She looked past him at the empty car. And sucked in a quick breath. "Green?"

"Red is all right," he rumbled, all deep base tones. "He just got shot. A little."

"WHAT?"

"Got any coffee?"

"Sure. Shot a little?" She hurried toward the kitchen, Green right behind her. She stared at him as he filled a cup, and took a sip. He touched his left chest high near the shoulder. "Right about here. Almost missed."

Then he told her the phone number of the emergency room operator. He leaned against the counter while she asked questions in her crisp lawyer way of asking crisp questions to whoever was on the other end of the conversation.

Banging down the telephone, she spun around and demanded, "What exactly were you two doing, this time?"

Green shrugged. "How about I let Red tell you. He is going to be home for a few days, I suspect." He set the cup on the countertop and headed for the front door. "Thanks. Gotta go tell The Chief, do paperwork."

Grandeville. River View Hospital.

"Dumb cop," she said when she picked him up, just outside the Emergency Entrance, hugging as much of him as she could. He was huge. So was Green.

"Almost missed." Red smiled at her when she looked up. "I got lots of pills to eat. And all of next week off."

As they walked through the parking lot toward their car, she said, "All right, tell me everything." It was her addressing the court room voice.

"Yes, Counselor."

Grandeville P.D.

Two days later, Green stood in The Chief's tiny office, filling a goodly portion of the available space in front of the Chief's desk.

"Red is my partner!"

"This," replied The Chief, "is your new partner. Until Red comes back to work. It is only for a few days. You are not working alone. Correct?"

Green just looked at him.

Then at her.

She was just five feet tall, probably weighed around a hundred pounds and was on the slender side. Not skinny, just slender in the way Chinese often were.

"This," stated The Chief, "is Braidna Chin Lee, the daughter of Chen's cook."

"The number one cook," added Braidna.

"Ummm, yes," agreed The Chief. "Ms. Lee comes with very good recommendations."

"From?" asked Green.

"Training," answered The Chief.

Green nodded, knowing that he was stuck, dug around in his pocket and handed her the keys. "You drive. Know the area?"

"Grew up here." She looked up at his face. "Watched you and Red play college football."

"Let's go . . . partner."

Grandeville. Red and Sandy's House.

"This is Braidna Chin Lee. How ya doing, Red?"

"Suffering. Happily." Red smiled at Braidna.

"We are on duty," stated Braidna, frowning at Green.

"Shhhh, Officer." Green nodded at Red. "Just stopped by to see how you are doing."

"Back in a week."

"Good. Let's go, Lee!"

Red walked them out to the squad car. "Sandy said that it took three hours to fix the perp's hand. Only minor damage to his jaw."

Green shrugged.

"Shifty Sam is claiming excessive force."

Green shrugged again and settled into the passenger seat. "I suppose I could have shot him."

Red slammed the door. "See ya, partner." And bent low so he could peer past Green at Braidna. "Listen to Green."

She drove them away.

"Shyster lawyer," rumbled Green.

"Was it excessive force?" She looked over at the hulk filling that half of the car seat.

"Nope." He pointed. "Let's go get some doughnuts. Might as well start your on-the-job training right."

Grandeville. Greater Downtown. The Evening Hours.

They walked into The Railroad Bar and Grill, most often called "The Rail" by most folk, a favorite hangout for the rowdier segment of the bar society, such as it is in Greater Downtown Grandeville. The bartender had phoned in, calling for help.

Green nodded to his partner after they entered the establishment. "Your turn. The big guy at the end of the bar in the bright green checkered shirt."

Braidna nodded back at him and walked down the bar. "Roger Randle?" she asked.

The big man straightened up and looked down at her. "Oh golly gee whiz, a toy cop."

He slammed his hand flat on the bar top. "Gimme another beer, Zig!"

Zig the bartender shook his head. "Go home, Randle."

"Do I have to crawl over there and do it myself?"

Braidna stepped back. "Mr. Randle, you are disturbing the peace. Come along quietly. Please?"

Randle the Rowdy laughed. And saw Green. "I am gonna mash up your helper, Green."

Green crossed his arms over his chest. "Go ahead. She is in training."

"If you attack me," stated Braidna very calmly. "I shall have to use force."

Randle decided he would just toss her over the bar top and then go peacefully with Green. He grabbed her.

Almost.

He hit the floor, on his face, hard. And felt his arms yanked around his back and his wrists cuffed.

Green walked over and lifted him to his feet. "Let's go, Randle." And yanked their prisoner toward the door. "Nice move, partner."

Later, as they cruised the late night dark streets, Green said, "Well?"

"My father made me study with Master Chen."

"You know Tinker?"

She shook her head. "Only heard about him."

"Just wondered." He held out the bag. "Have a doughnut."

Grandeville. Tinker's Place.

They stood on the rear deck in the late afternoon, on a pleasant Saturday, carefully not staring at one of their visitors.

"Braidna Chin Lee," explained the small Chinese man. "This is my worthless nephew." Chen bowed to each of them as they watched Braidna. And beamed at Tinker. "Take her into the dojo and see if you can beat her up. I will sit out here and drink tea and speak with the lovely ones." He sat and allowed Chicken to fill his cup.

Tinker nodded and led Braidna away, to the dojo.

Chen smiled at everyone. "Introduce me," he said to Chantal. "Explain the changes in personnel, please."

So Chantal did.

And they all sat and talked.

And drank tea.

Chen glanced at his watch. "One hour is enough."

Smoke nodded and walked down the deck and over

the door to the dojo, swung it open and called inside, "Time!"

Tinker walked out.

Braidna followed him out, hobbling. One eye was puffing up.

Tinker sat next to Chen and took the filled cup that was offered. "She is very good."

Chen nodded and watched Braidna ease herself onto the wood bench next to the picnic table where they sat. "You will come up here for one hour every Saturday."

She nodded.

He looked at Tinker. "You were too gentle. Next time do not be gentle."

Tinker nodded.

Braidna smiled a crooked smile at Tinker, one lip was puffing up also. "I am a fast learner."

"Have some tea," said Chen.

Chantal poured.

Some time had passed, some time later, they all walked out to the driveway and waved goodbye as Chen drove back into town, taking Braidna with him.

"Very pretty," said Messenger.

"Tough cookie," stated Tinker.

"Seems nice," added Chantal.

"Wonder what Chen is up to," mumbled Tinker.

"Very quiet," said Sgenn.

"Strong pouncer." Smoke smiled at him.

"Most slim a'figure," added Chicken, giving him a sly wink.

"Knock it off, you guys," he growled, spinning and

heading toward the house. "Gonna take a shower."

"Could have invited her to stay for dinner," called Fair Morn at his back.

Everyone thought that it was a good joke.

Except Tinker.

He was starting to worry.

Next Saturday, she drove herself to her appointment.

Thirty minutes later, he yanked the door open and leaned out. "SMOKE!" And pointed at the crumpled body as she hurried in. "Is she all right?"

Smoke knelt next to Braidna and nodded.

"She missed the block," he explained.

Smoke lifted the limp form in her arms and stared at him.

"Talk to Chen," he snarled and stomped away, into the house, into the shower, and then to change clothes.

When he stepped back onto the rear deck, he looked around. "Where is she?"

"Chantal drove her home. Messenger took the van." Fair Morn handed him a cup of coffee. "Slugger."

"Don't start!"

"We did tell her to shower here." Chicken smiled at him. "No need to wait."

He frowned at her. "And don't you even think to start hatching plots, sneaky pete."

When Chantal and Messenger returned he grumbled at them as well. "She is a cop with G.P.D. Chen thinks that she needs more training. She is the daughter of his number one cook."

Chantal sat, poured herself a cup of coffee, took a sip, and growled back at him. "You have to punch her lights out to do that?"

"An accident. It happens sometimes." He held out his cup. She refilled it and got frowned at.

Grandeville. The Bowl and Go.

They were bowling. It was the third day off for Red. They were sipping from their pitchers and watching their opponents carefully not winning the second game.

"Tinker has been whomping on your babe partner, partner."

Green pointed at the taller woman. "That's my babe. Lee is just my partner pro tem." He took another sip. "Partner."

It was the last frame of the game, and they won by one point. Their opponents came back to the table laughing and smiling at something.

"Good losers." Red looked at Green as he stood up.

"Right." Green set his pitcher down as they headed for their lanes to start the last game.

"Hold it, Moose Meat." Janine stepped in front of them.

"What?" asked Green looking over the top of her head at Red. "Don't we start first?"

"Sure," said Red.

"Down here," she ordered.

Green looked down.

"How come your buddy Tinker is beating up your cute partner?"

"Red is my partner," he rumbled. "And I don't think

that he is cute."

"Ms. Lee," interjected Sandy, smiling at Red. "I think that you are cute."

"Thanks, babe," rasped Red.

Green picked up Janine and set her out of the way. "You wanna know, go ask. She and Chen are down there in the far lane. Let's go, partner."

As the two gigantic men went down to abuse the bowling alley Sandy poked Janine in the side. "Cool it, Streak. Those two never pry into what they think is someone's private business. And don't start acting jealous with Green either. He won't stand for it."

Janine nodded and headed for the far side of the bowing alley.

When she returned, it was their turn to bowl.

"Well?" asked Sandy as she lifted her bowling ball from the rack and eyed the pins.

"She said that it was none of my business."

Sandy laughed and rolled a strike.

Grandeville. Tinker's Place. Saturday.

She hit the floor, rolling, sprang to her feet, and was knocked stumbling back against a wall. He watched. And bowed. "Time's up."

She walked over to the door and picked up her bag. "Chantal said that you had a great shower. I'm ready for that." Sweat made lines down her face and dripped onto the floor.

"Getting better," he stated, leading her down the rear deck toward the side door.

"One of these days."

"What?"

She laughed. "You're going to get it."

He opened the side door. "Straight in. You can't miss it." As she walked inside, he spun around and walked over and sat at one of the several wooden tables and drank a large glass of orange juice. And glanced sideways at Chantal. "Don't say it."

In the driveway they heard a car pull up, the door slam.

"Master Chen," said Smoke.

"Checking up, I suppose," mumbled Tinker.

Chen walked down the deck to them, looked at Tinker, then his watch, and sat down.

Smoke pushed a filled glass in his direction.

"Thank you, Wise One." He smiled at her. Then at Tinker. "Nephew, we have serious business."

Tinker stared at him. This was unlike Chen. The rest filtered onto the deck where they could see first hand and listen directly. They had all felt Tinker's sudden concern.

Chantal sat next to him. "Relax, Cowboy."

"Umm?"

"Most clearly stated," said Chen. He looked at his watch and nodded.

"What ho, Sire!"

Prince Goose and Lady Chen walked around the end of the house and started down the deck toward them. They had walked over from their place to visit at Lady Chen's suggestion. She had been called by Master Chen.

Lady Chen bowed to Tinker and to Master Chen. Then she sat next to Goose who had already plopped down next to Chantal.

"I have trained you well," said Chen to Tinker. "And Braidna Chin Lee not too badly."

Tinker nodded.

Fair Morn hurried toward the far end of the rear deck. "I'll bring coffee and cups."

Master Chen sipped at his juice. "My honorary niece is pretty, is she not?"

Tinker nodded.

"She is twenty eight years old." He smiled at Chantal. "Surprise, isn't it?"

"Certainly is." Chantal smiled back. "She looks like a college freshman." She winked at Tinker. "At least John isn't beating up a child."

Master Chen looked at Tinker. "Still?"

"She is getting better all the time. It took a full hour today."

Chen nodded. "Good." And waved one hand. "This is a large house, a very large house."

Tinker's brows began to furrow.

Chen laughed. "She will behave." And then he looked very serious at Goose. "I am truly sorry, Prince, but I must have my dragon back. For awhile." He beckoned to Lady Chen. "Come here."

She stood and smiled gently at Goose. "Fear not, White Warrior." She stepped around the table to stand next to Master Chen.

He touched her with one fingertip, and handed the thin golden chain with the dragon amulet dangling from it to Tinker. "Wear this until I say otherwise."

Goose sat stunned, staring across the table at them.

"She will come back, Prince." Chen tapped Tinker's shoulder. "Now, Nephew." And watched as Tinker slipped the chain over his head.

From all sides Tinker could feel the sudden wariness, the sudden dancing thoughts of mayhem, coming from the rest of himself. "What's going on?"

Master Chen sat straight and looked from face to face and watched as Fair Morn returned carrying a large tray with pots and cups.

"Great danger swirls around Braidna Chin Lee. She will live here until it passes." He smiled at Tinker. "She is very pretty so you will not mind. Her Father and I have talked. She will obey as all dutiful daughters do."

The side door of the house opened and she walked out, dressed in faded jeans, sandals, and a t-shirt emblazoned *Chen's Chinese*. Behind the black outlined red letters soared a golden dragon.

"Nice t-shirt," stated Master Chen. "I am sponsoring a little league baseball team."

Tinker sighed. "I don't like this."

"You will do it!"

"Sure."

Braidna stopped three paces away. "Grandfather, have you talked?" She smiled at Tinker. "Great shower! That is really a great shower and the largest hot tub that I have ever seen anywhere."

Chen nodded at her. "I have talked with him. Chantal will show you to your room and explain . . . things."

He stared at Braidna. "They do not like visitors, or strangers, being imposed upon them. You will be most polite, unobtrusive, quiet, and obey them in all things."

She bowed to him. "Of course, Grandfather. I will cause no concern to you or to my Father."

"Good." Chen bounced to his feet. "Time to go. Come with me, Prince." He headed for his car, talking softly to Goose as they walked.

"Oh my," gasped Messenger, looking from Braidna to Tinker to Smoke. "Oh my gosh!"

Tinker sighed. And sagged. "Not again? Merde."

Braidna looked at him, frowning. "'I am sorry. I didn't want to do this. But Father and Master Chen insisted." She looked at Chantal as she rose to her feet. "I really don't need to be baby-sat."

"Come on," said Chantal. "Let's get you settled. John will be all right in awhile." They headed into the house.

He looked across the table. "Smoke?"

"She doesn't know anything. She is just obeying her Father and Grandfather. Master Chen was very guarded. Goose is very upset. And Chantal just went upstairs to get her gun."

"Oh dear." Messenger looked all round eyes at Smoke. "Is she going to shoot Braidna?"

"Nope."

"Braidna's a cop," said Tinker.

Smoke shrugged. "Nothing wrong with that. There is nothing in your laws, here in this elseplace, that says that Chantal can't carry her gun at home if she wishes to do that."

He fingered the golden amulet hanging from the thin chain around his neck. "I wonder why he did that to Lady Chen?"

"Can't lose her, that way," suggested Smoke.

"And we don't have the foggiest idea of what's going on this time, do we?"

Chantal returned, gun belt on, holster strapped in a cross-draw style. The long barreled revolver gleamed soft blue in the sunlight. "Next."

Fair Morn headed into the house. "Taking no chances."

He sighed heavily.

"The lady cop is carrying her things from her car," explained Chantal. "I put her in the central guest bedroom and gave her a quick tour of the house."

He nodded. "Well, you guys are gonna have to behave now that we have a house guest. Especially one that is a cop."

"We do all be most behaved well," snorted Chicken.

"Sure."

"Damn right we are," growled Chantal. "And that goes for you too, Cowboy!"

"Huh?"

"No messing around with skinny butt."

"She do be slim, nay skinny," stated Chicken, who was also quite slender.

"Don't start that kind of nonsense!" he growled at Chantal.

"Hum," hummed Szart, rolling a black wand back and forth between her palms.

"And I do not want to see magic wands out when she is around, either." He frowned at her and at Sha'gar. And then at Sgenn. "Or hear things growling around under our feet!"

Sgenn nodded.

Fair Morn rejoined them, her weapon in its sheath

strapped to the outside of her right thigh, covering it from the edge of her hip to just above the knee. "Ta dah!"

"And no wing flapping when she is home."

Fair Morn grinned at him. "You could just claim that I am a strange looking kite. I could hold one end of the kite string."

Braidna stepped from the house, dressed all in blue. "Time to go to work." She smiled at them. "And I am really sorry to become such a bother." She carefully didn't stare at the weapons she could see especially the thing on Fair Morn's thigh. "Do I need a house key?"

"Nope," said Chantal. "The door is always open."

Braidna nodded and headed for her car.

Grandeville. Greater Downtown.

Janine looked over the top of her cup as she and her boss took a break. "Did you know that cop is now living up at his place?"

Sandy laughed. "Wonderfully obscure sentence, Streak. Which cop? Whose place?"

"That Chinese person. Tinker's."

"She is?"

"Uh huh."

Sandy stared at her. "Wonder what's going on? This time."

"Me too."

Sandy refilled their tea cups. "Well, that is certainly a safe place to live."

"They ever tell you about Mar? What happened to her?"

"No!" Sandy stared at the tabletop. "She was from out

there." She shook her head. "I don't really want to know about those places or persons."

"Yeah. I still have bad dreams. Once in awhile about it."

They stood in the clatter, the din, and the steam of the hard working kitchen at Chen's Chinese.

Braidna stood next to a shorter, somewhat bowlegged man wearing a white t-shirt, white pants, and a white apron. Everything he wore was badly stained. He was beaming at Chen who was holding the camera and taking pictures of the pair, father and daughter. Father was easily twice as wide as his daughter.

Standing next to Chen was a much larger policeman looking uncomfortable. He was a foot taller than Braidna and weighed at least twice as much.

"You also," ordered Chen.

"Come on, Alex," said Braidna.

So Alexander Jasna stepped around and dwarfed both of them.

"Many thanks," said Chen. "I shall hang this one by the front door."

He escorted the pair of cops to the entrance of the restaurant. "They hire large people," he observed to Braidna.

She laughed. "I was the only female to apply."

Then the two cops headed down the sidewalk, a walking foot patrol. It was the first assignment of new officers on their own. As they strolled along, in and out of various of the businesses, in the late evening, it being a special Nite Sale for the downtown merchants, Alex asked her about her week riding with Green.

"Different," she replied. She smiled at Alex. "If you ever get to work with him or with Red, you better like doughnuts." She pointed at the narrow passageway between two of the buildings. "Let's cut through here. The Chief said he heard a rumor that some high school kids were planning on decorating the parking lot back there."

Alex nodded, and followed her in.

Grandeville. Tinker's Place.

They were sitting in the large living room, reading a book.

Actually, he was reading the book. And they were listening, mentally listening.

Earlier in the evening after sitting where ever each had thought was comfortable, they had merged together, into a single entity, and had become the story, each personality and personal background adding to the experience.

He sat slumped in one of the couches. Messenger was curled against one side. Szart had claimed the other side.

Smoke lay on the floor, flat on her back, eyes open, seeing the ceiling and their collective imaginations.

Sha'gar was sprawled on another of the couches, her head in her sister Sgenn's lap.

Chicken and Chantal sat in their favorite chairs.

Fair Morn lay at an angle to Smoke using Smoke's stomach as a pillow.

It was a really tense moment in the story. The monster was creeping up on the heroine. The thing had already removed several minor female characters from the story in grossly erotic ways. Smoke had chosen the book from the description on the flyleaf, read to her by Chantal.

Szart suppressed her laughter. She thought that these kinds of stories were comedies.

Messenger tightened her arm around his waist. Events were really getting very intense, for her.

The secret door in the wall behind the heroine slowly, silently began to slide open.

And she walked in.

"You have anything stronger than coffee?"

She stopped and stared at them as heads suddenly jerked in her direction, as they became themselves.

"What happened to you?" snapped Chantal.

Braidna shrugged. "Some sort of wild animal." Her left sleeve was ripped open as was the left side of her sturdy blue blouse. She wore a bandage on the back of her left hand, a bandage around her left forearm, and a band-aid on her left check.

"Alex beat it with his baton and it ran away. It was too dark to see what it was."

Chicken stood. "Sit. We will fetch you coffee and Irish."

Braidna dropped into a vacant chair. "Thanks. Got off early." And smiled at them, just a little. "Ummm, sorry about interrupting. The Chief told me to go home early."

"We were just reading," explained Tinker. "You sure you are all right?" He looked at Smoke.

Fine. She is just fine, said Smoke, mind to mind. She had already checked.

Braidna looked at the book he held. He had closed it over one finger, marking the place. The house had been totally silent when she walked into the house and then into the large living room. Yet he had said 'we' were just reading.

Chicken returned and handed a large mug to Braidna. "Most hot. Most delicious."

"Thank you again." Braidna looked at Tinker. "I really am all right. Just require a new blouse." She laughed. "I have several spare ones."

She looked around and wondered why Chantal and Fair Morn were still wearing guns. She assumed that the thing Fair Morn had was some kind of gun.

Then she saw the sword in its sheath leaning against the chair where Chicken sat. This was really starting to look like a rather strange bunch. But they certainly didn't look or seem like the usual paranoid, quasi-military groups that were afraid that the government was about to attack them. Certainly Master Chen wouldn't have put her among such a group.

Chicken stretched out her legs, her pant legs pulling up, exposing the tops of her boots. A knife handle poked up alongside the outside of her right leg, from inside the boot.

Braidna took a sip from her cup. "Hot." And took another sip. "Pretty good."

Tinker looked at Smoke, now sitting up and staring at Braidna.

She didn't see enough for me to tell. Smoke shrugged.

"I don't like this," he grumbled,

"Really, I am all right." Braidna emptied her mug. "I am all right. It was really nothing to get excited about." She stood. "Mind if I take a shower? After that drink, and a shower, I think that I will just go to bed."

"Go ahead," said Chantal. "Won't bother us." And

watched Braidna head for the kitchen to set her mug down. "Maybe that's all it was. Nothing."

"Bad coincidence," he mumbled.

Messenger poked him in the side as she sat up. "What are we going to do?"

"About?"

"Braidna."

"Umm, I don't know." His eyes jumped from face to face. "Wait and see?"

A sea of blank faces stared back at him.

"Can't follow her around all the time, can we?" Somehow he had slumped even deeper into the couch. "Any of you tricky types have an invisible guardian we could put on her?"

"No," replied Sha'gar.

"Nope," added Szart.

Sgenn frowned and thought. Then she shook her head.

"So much for that idea." He sighed from deep inside the couch, at least as deep in the couch as he had managed to slump.

"John," said Chantal. "We do have something like that."

He looked at her. "We do?"

"You are wearing it."

"What?"

"The amulet. Lady Chen. She is sorta invisible."

He sighed. Heavily he sighed, and began to wonder how Chen had managed to tangle them up in whatever was going on, this time. "We'd have to tell her."

Smoke poured calm into him.

"I know that, lover. Any better ideas?" Chantal looked at all the other parts of herself. "Well?"

They began to break into clusters, talking inside.

"I could loan her my cannon," suggested Fair Morn.

"No way." Tinker glared at her. "Bad enough that she even sees that thing."

Sgenn looked at him. "I could send a . . . servant to follow her around."

"How are we gonna explain something grumbling underneath her feet all the time?"

"Me'Lord," stated Chicken, "do give most fair Braidna, Lady Chen. And do let us explain most clearly." She smiled at him. "Thee do be best in such endeavors."

"Gosh," gulped Messenger, eye growing rounder and rounder. "Are we adding her?" She nudged him in the side. "Certainly fast, really really."

"No! We are not!" He glared at her. "Doing that!"

"I didn't think so. We don't have any more room in The Chamber." Then she smiled at him. "But she is pretty, really really."

"Coming down the hall," interrupted Smoke.

"Shower's free," said Braidna as she passed the hall doorway, wearing one of the thick, white robes. There was always a stack of them next to the shower door and in the hot tub room. "Night all."

"Ms. Lee," called Tinker. "Could we speak with you for a few minutes?"

She halted and leaned back through the opening, looking into the large living room. "Oh, sure." She stepped in. Her skin glowed, soft golden tones. A large white towel was wrapped around her head and her hair.

She sat in a chair facing him and tugged the robe closed at her throat, and then around her legs. "Braidna, please?" And smiled. "I know, not very Chinese. Father made it up because I am American, not Chinese. Even if my upbringing was very, very Chinese correct."

"Ummmmm."

"Yes?"

He jerked the amulet from inside his shirt and slipped the fine golden chain up and over his head, handed it to her. "Here."

She took and examined it. "A Chinese dragon. This is very well done."

"Ahh, we want you to wear it."

"At all times," added Chantal.

Braidna shook her head. "I can't take this. It is too valuable."

"It is an amulet," explained Tinker. "It will protect you."

She laughed. And quickly composed her face. "Sorry. You sounded just like my Father telling me about Water Turtle."

"This," he growled, "happens to be true."

Braidna shook her head. "I know that you mean well. And I know how much Master Chen means to you. But I am not wearing magical charms." She started to stand.

"Sit down!" he snapped.

She dropped, sat straight, and set her face. And readied herself. He was the only one she was worried about.

He sat up and leaned forward. "I want you to just sit

there and not do anything. Smoke?"

She nodded.

Tinker held up the chain and stared at the amulet. "O.K., Chen, show yourself, the Lady Chen."

Braidna stared at him. This was really a group of crazies, after all.

"Get out here," he snarled.

A small cloud formed, filling the central spot of the room. And quickly faded.

The woman dressed in ornate, heavily brocaded robes, bowed deeply to him, arms tucked inside her sleeves. "Master Chen will be very unhappy, Noble Master."

"We will worry about that later." He pointed. "This is Braidna Chin Lee, his number one cook's daughter. Master Chen and her Father sent her up here for protection. She won't wear the amulet. So we decided to try and convince her."

Braidna clenched the arms of the chair tightly. She recognized the designs on the woman's robe, Royal Dragon figures. The woman turned in her direction and bowed.

"Lovely One, I am Chen Gum Lung, the Golden Dragon of the House of Chen, the amulet." She bowed again. "Do what you are told."

Braidna stared past her at Tinker. "How did you do that?"

He sighed, and looked around the room. "O.K., now what?"

"Outside," said Smoke.

"Oh, aye, Me'Lord. This one do have head most hard." Chicken stood. "Outside, wench!" It was a Royal command.

Tinker stood. "Please?"

Braidna rose to her feet and carefully walked to the front door, and outside onto the front deck. She had decided that it would just be best to humor them, then go to bed. Tomorrow she would move. Whether her Father or Master Chen liked it or not.

After they had all gathered in the large parking area beyond their vehicle, Tinker pointed. "O.K., Lady Chen, out there, the dragon self."

Lady Chen stepped off the deck and walked out into the large open space. "Asss you wish." She disappeared in a swirling cloud. It slowly dissipated.

"Oh my god!" gasped Braidna.

The great head lowered and looked at her. "Have no fear, it isss I, Chen Gum Lung!"

Braidna looked from her to Tinker. "I am either going crazy or you and my Father and Master Chen have an awful lot of explaining to do."

"Not crazy, not your father," he grumbled. "Let's go back into the house."

They did. Moments later, Lady Chen walked inside.

"Now," asked Tinker, as all regained their former places. "You ready to do what I asked?"

Braidna shook her head. "You explain first."

He sighed. "Back to the amulet, Lady Chen, please?" She nodded.

He reached down, picked up the chain, and held it out toward Braidna. "The only explanation you get is what you saw. Wear it!" He smiled. "Please?"

Slowly she reached out and took the chain. Yanking the towel away, she carefully slipped the chain over her head.

And nodded. The amulet disappeared just below the hollow at the base of her throat. "May I go to bed, now?"

"Sure. It is time for all of us."

Fair Morn stood and walked along with him as he headed for the hallway. She waggled the hand wearing the large ornate ring.

Braidna headed for her room, And decided that this was all stranger than she wanted to admit.

Smoke watched her and wondered why she seemed so calm and accepting. There was something else going on.

It was just after lunch, an hour of so, when Braidna walked out onto the rear deck carrying a small gym bag. She was wearing one of Chen's t-shirts, jeans, and sandals. "Going in early." She waved and hurried to her car.

"Hum," said Szart.

Sha'gar nodded. "Hum."

"Tight," observed Sgenn.

Tinker looked up from the stack of papers that he was reading. "What?"

"Braidna's t-shirt, Cowboy." Chantal refilled his coffee Cup. "You missed it."

"Oh."

Grandeville. Chen's Chinese.

She walked in and stood next to the cash register while he made change and talked with some happy customers. As soon as they left, he turned and bowed slightly. "Lovely Niece." And recognized the fine golden chain hanging around her neck.

She returned his bow. "Grandfather, we must talk."

Chen clapped his hands together. Once. A surprisingly loud sound. The number one waitress hurried up.

"Stay here," he told her. "We will be in the Numba One Private Booth." He headed that way, Braidna right on his heels.

After pouring tea, he sipped his, and looked at her.

"I am not a child, Grandfather!"

He looked at her t-shirt. "Obviously. A pretty young woman."

"What is he, your Nephew?"

"A friend, an author, a martial artist of some skill."

She fished out the chain and dangling amulet. "And this?"

"The Golden Dragon of the House of Chen."

She waggled it at him. "No tricks?"

"No." He reached out and touched it with one fingertip. "My chosen Nephew continues to amaze me. He is a very private person and yet he gave you my dragon. Events twist around you, Braidna Chin Lee."

She poured tea into their cups. "Explain, please?"

Chen nodded, and told her about the family dragon. When Braidna smiled, he reached out and touched the amulet gently.

She sat there, hands held in her lap. "Grandfather Chen?"

"My Honorable Niece With The Shocked Face is uneasy at learning of your existence. And I suspect that my Honorable Nephew wasn't too helpful in explaining, either. Has he added Lee Chin to them?"

Braidna stared at him.

"No," replied Lady Chen. "My Master, the Great Warrior, merely wishes that the beautiful and proper Lee Chin to be protected at all times." She bowed her head. "He tries to do what you asked of him. To protect her."

She looked sideways at Braidna. "She has already been attacked while she was on duty. He felt that she would not accept a constant guard."

Braidna stared from one to the other. "This is crazy! Grandfather?"

"No, it is not! You will wear my dragon amulet. You will continue to live up there. I promised your father." His eyes fastened on Braidna's. "Shall we tell him no?"

"No." She felt a slight tingle from the chain as it appeared around her neck. She hastily pushed the amulet inside the neck of her t-shirt. "I will do as you say, Grandfather."

"Good." Master Chen smiled. "Have you hit him yet?"

She shook her head. "Not yet."

"Keep trying. It is good training. For you."

And Then Some

Rogesau.

    It was night.
        As dark as night can be.
    No moon.

    Just a soft, hovering layer of clouds.
        Capping the wide, round valley.

    Dark and quiet.
        Late at night.
            Very late at night.

    He sat and muttered to himself.

    Dark things moved and wiggled, slithered and crept and crawled all around him. But, not too close. Never too close.

    He was dressed in soft clothes of a light grey color and sat slumped, one of his legs tossed casually over one arm of the chair. The leg ticked back and forth as he sat deep in the chair and deep in thought. Nothing, no thing, would dare interrupt him when he sat deep in thought. He nodded to himself And sat up. "Heh."

    He stared at all the warped creatures. He sighed. What he wouldn't give to have some really intelligent help. Someone he could talk to, talk with someone who could talk, someone who would understand.

Someone human. He shrugged. Well, at least, someone who looked human, regardless of their race. Of course, and he admitted to himself that he was just a wee bit biased, he really did prefer humans for company, real humans. "Heh! More or less."

He nodded. Again. To himself. It would just take time. And he had that. All the time that there was.

He waved them all away. It was a nice sunny day. He'd rather admire the grass, the trees, and the flowers than all those things. Standing, stretching, he walked out onto the meadow. And chuckled. This was really a nice elseplace. He was glad that he had taken it.

Grandeville. Tinker's Place. Late Evening.

The movie was just finishing.

It had been a musical. Messenger had chosen it. She was sharing the couch with him. They were both propped up with large pillows behind their backs. Popcorn bowls, all empty, sat here and there. She wore a large, ornate ring on one thumb.

Braidna wandered into the large living room, coffee cup in her hand, eyes rapidly scanning the room, taking a very close look at them. "Good movie?" And sat in a chair.

Smoke waggled one hand at her.

"Yep," replied Messenger. "Really really."

Smoke looked at Braidna, great orange gold eyes seeming to grow larger and larger.

Braidna sucked in a quick breath. She hadn't noticed the pupils of Smoke's eyes before. They were vertical, mostly dilated in the low light of the room, but still obviously vertical.

"What?" asked Smoke.

Braidna tugged her tie loose and popped the top button of her service blouse loose. "Grandfather told me about you. Is it true?"

"WHAT?" Tinker jerked upright.

Messenger scrambled out of his way. "Gosh."

"Chen did what?" Tinker swiveled around and stared at Braidna. "'He did what?"

Everyone was staring at her. Her eyes darted from face to face. "It is true. I can see it." She laughed.

"Damn that Chen," snarled Chantal.

Tinker flopped back. "Now what's going on?"

Sgenn looked over at him. "He shouldn't have done that." Deep down, something growled.

"Sister," cautioned Sha'gar. Braidna was staring at the floor. Sgenn nodded. The sound stopped. Szart looked at Tinker.

"NO!" he snapped.

"It was a laugh of relief," hastily explained Braidna. "This is all so fairy tale stuff."

"Fairies are kak ptar kak," grumbled Szart. "Little pootak pests."

"Hum." Sha'gar looked at her.

"Pootak," repeated Szart. "Pests."

Sha'gar shrugged.

Braidna stared at them.

"Get used to it," grumbled Tinker at Braidna.

"It is hard to." She exhaled loudly. "I thought that I was going crazy. Hallucinating."

He nodded. "Welcome to the club."

"They eat holes in your clothes," hissed Szart at Sha'gar. Braidna shook her head.

"What?"

Her face flushed. "Grandfather also told me about, ummm, the rest of, ummm, yourself." She glanced at the ring on Messenger's thumb.

"Damn big mouth," growled Chantal. "For a little person."

Anger flashed across Braidna's face. "It was only told to me so I could know how to properly behave around you. So I would not, ummm, disturb you by being here." She stood. "Good evening." She headed toward her room.

"Certainly would like to know what's going on," he muttered. "This time. HOLD IT, BRAIDNA! You don't get off that easily."

She walked back, watching them, watching him, carefully. "What?"

"You know about us. Tell us about yourself."

She sat in the chair she had just vacated. "All right, fair enough." And leaned back. "My Father, the youngest son of his family, left home and wandered the world. Somewhere, he never said where, he met my mother. I was born in Central Oregon. My Mother died when I was six years old shortly after we moved to Grandeville. My Father did not take it well. And eventually, Grandfather Chen found us, hired Father, and we have been here ever since." She smiled at Tinker. "I was raised traditional Chinese and very American also. So, I honor my Father's, and my Grandfather's wishes. A foot in each camp, in a manner of speaking." She stood. "Not much to know, is there?" And headed for her room again. "Good night. Again."

He sighed. "So much for that." He stood and headed for his bedroom, one arm swung over Messenger's shoulders.

Chantal looked at Smoke. "Think if we asked Chen, he'd tell us anything else?"

Smoke shrugged.

Nar Danda. Warm and Sunny.

Hand'l looked at his companion, Izar the Wth. "Why do we always get these jobs?"

Izar looked down at his companion, Hand'l the Seart. "The Dir-Chief knows we are good?"

Hand'l nodded. He hadn't wanted an answer, not at all. But Izar would answer any question Hand'l asked. Subtle was not a Wth's strong point. Strong was. The Wth had always been loyal to the Artgld Sector. It had always been this way.

Hand'l and Izar had been working together for many, many turns. They were always given the difficult assignments. A matter of pride to Hand'l. A matter of indifference to the Wth. It was just the way they were, the Wth.

Hand'l read the message disc again. "Not much. Less than any other time. We shall be a long time out, this time." Izar didn't wiggle a whisker.

The pair walked into the many-walled tower and stood on the exact spot. And were sent.

Fran's Dance. Overcast Day.

Hand'l lightly touched Izar to show that he had seen it also. It was a Seek Beast slipping from shadow to shadow. The Wth nodded and slipped around the building next to them.

Hand'l stood and waited. Something hissed and went suddenly silent in the crackle of crushing skeletal material.

Hand'l nodded. And walked that way. Wondering why that thing had been here.

Park's Flower.

"Are you all right, Dear?"

They had been strolling along the main street of the town of Green Tvid, named after a local blossom, when three Red Guards had thrown him aside, crashing into the wall of the nearby building, and had grabbed her. The Green and Black Guards had stared at the action.

Acrid fumes, dust, and smoke, drifted through the open space which hadn't been there before. A large piece of the town of Green Tvid was gone. Along with the three Red Guards.

He sat on the ground, his back against the building he had been blown against. His right hand clenched a long black wand. She stood next to him, concern on her face, frowning slightly.

He nodded. "Duff?"

"I don't know, Dear. Put that thing away, please."

Shoving himself to his feet, he stuffed the long black wand up his left sleeve. And looked around at the wreckage. And then at the Green and Black Guard.

The Qart of the Green walked over. And bowed slightly. And hissed politely. "The Red are too impulsive."

The Qart of the Black stomped over. "Who pays? Those persons shouldn't have done that!"

"The Red will answer," said the Qart of the Green, waving one arm at Plum Duff and the $1.98 Magician. "Come with me."

Duff nodded. And tugged $1.98 into motion after the Qart of the Green. The Qart of the Black made notes on his wilt.

Space. 66.29.09.22, In Ship's Notation.

The great sphere sailed along, metal walls glistening softly in the faint light. Taking a short cut through this sector of mostly empty.

He strolled into one of the cavernous workshops and wiped the sweat from his face. He had just finished the proscribed workout, carefully monitored by Gyre, the silver skinned woman walking by his side. Standing by the railing, he looked down and beamed. At the weapon the MechBots were working on. "It is beautiful." He almost purred.

"All signs back to normal," stated Gyre. "You are very healthy."

He slid his arm around her waist. "Because of you."

"We are Macabre's." She jerked. "Emergency."

He felt the ship shift under his feet. "What?"

"An emergency signal, asking for help. Not far. All defenses up. All weapons ready."

His eyes twinkled. "Trouble?"

"Just beyond scan sight."

Ho, ho, ho, ho, ho, ho." He tugged her toward a door hissing open. "Let's get properly dressed, have something to eat, and see what it is."

Grandeville. Tinker's Place. Late Evening.

It had been an unusually hot day for this time of year, late summer, normally a rather pleasant warm not hot time of the year. Even at night the heat radiated up from the streets and the pavement.

The house was quiet. Most were sleeping. She walked

into the house rather unhappy at The Chief for having to wear a hot, dark blue uniform. As she passed the shower room she could hear water cascading. "Who's in there?"

"Just me," answered Smoke. "Just back from my run. Come on in, the water's fine." She laughed

"You don't mind?"

"Nope."

Braidna hurried to her room, rapidly peeled off her soggy clothes, grabbed her robe, slipped it on, and hurried back down the hall. Hanging the robe on a hook, she slipped inside the large room, water banging onto her from all sides, from the many nozzles. "This is wonderful." She slowly turned, searching for the soap.

"Here." Smoke shoved one hand at her, holding the bar. Her eyes were clenched tight as soap suds ran from her hair down her face.

Braidna took the soap and stepped close to one of the nozzles as Smoke bent forward, water blasting into her hair, rinsing off. "Be in the hot tub," she said.

And in a little while, Braidna walked from the shower room, and slipped into the great hot tub, and smiled at Smoke. "Pure luxury."

Smoke nodded. "We like it." And looked sharply at Braidna.

"What?"

"Stand up."

Braidna stepped onto a seat and did.

"Interesting tattoo," observed Smoke, sinking down in the water until it lapped just under her chin.

Braidna looked down. Three parallel lines, snake

wiggled around the soft swelling of her right breast. She traced her finger from the outside to the inside, following the lines. And stepped down and sank deep into the hot water. "Had it forever. Mother did it. When I was little." She smiled. "Before I grew. She seemed to know just where to put them."

Smoke winked at her. "Very nice."

"The tattoo?"

"What it is decorating."

Braidna sank up to her chin. "Thank you, Smoke. You are lovely also. All of you are."

"Did Master Chen tell you anything, umm, about what he thought that the danger was?"

"No. Just a feeling. Smoke?"

"What?"

"He did tell me all about all of you. Is it really true? Or just more fairy tales of some sort?"

"Probably true."' She smiled. "I don't think that he would make things up."

"Why did he, John, get so upset when I told you that?"

Smoke smiled. "He is a very private person and doesn't like people knowing about us. He doesn't think that the culture here could understand." She surged from the tub, picked up one of the heavy white robes and tugged it on, the thick material absorbing the water drops on her body. "And he just worries a lot."

"I won't tell anyone."

Smoke held out another of the robes. "Here." She turned away as Braidna shrugged on the robe. "You can cut through here into the hall." And opened the door for Braidna to The Chamber. And stepped inside, and pointed. "That way." Braidna nodded and went that way.

Suddenly a loud sizzling thunder rocked the house. Something screamed injured rage agony. The explosion banged and echoed off the forested slopes.

Everyone leaped from their beds, grabbing their weapon of choice and hurtled out into the open space of the Chamber.

Braidna ran back in from the hallway. "What was that?"

Tinker charged from his bedroom, tugging his robe on. And jerked to a halt, he had seen Braidna. "Oooops." He wasn't wearing pajamas. "Sorry." He hastily tugged the robe closed, flapping the belt around and into a tight loop.

Szart ran from his bedroom, wearing her pajama bottoms, a sparkling silver wand clenched in her right hand. "Spell ward! Something large. Demon ugly."

Chicken raced in, blade flashing in the dim light. "My Lord?"

Then the rest poured into the space. And looked at Szart.

"Something unwanted," she explained. "Tried to enter." She headed out the door, headed outside. "Look for parts."

They scattered, turning on all the outside lights, grabbing flashlights and lanterns from a hall closet.

"Damn early in the evening for things like this," grumbled Chantal heading for the kitchen to start making cocoa. "Or early morning."

Braidna ran to her bedroom, grabbed her pistol and flashlight and hurried out the front door and began to search.

Out in the first pasture, Fair Morn waggled her lantern. "Found something. Ugly."

Szart hurried over to check it. Fair Morn pointed. "Looks like a fragment of a wing."

Szart knelt and poked at the black leather piece with her wand. And nodded. "Demon wing."

"Winged demon?" Fair Morn peered over Szart's head at the thing.

"Yesssssssssssssss."

"We never met any with wings before."

"Zak tak kak ugly," sizzled the short witch.

Fair Morn straightened up. "Well, it is good to know that the ward worked."

Two shots banged out, and echoed from the nearby forested slope. They had come from the front side of the house.

Smoke was the first to charge around the end of the house. Braidna stood, pistol pointing at something near one of the lilac bushes. Her eyes were wide, staring. But her pistol was rock steady.

Sha'gar ran from one direction, Sgenn from another. Something, large and dark, hovered behind Sgenn. Red eyes looked at Braidna. It licked its lips.

"No," commanded Sgenn. "Friend." The red eyes looked elsewhere.

"By George, tis most ugly a'thing." Chicken poked at the stuff on the ground with the tip of her blade.

"I need to sit down." Braidna spun around and walked over and sat on the edge of the front deck.

Messenger hurried over, brows furrowed. "Are you going to urp?"

"Kitten," warned Tinker as he hurried over to them. He had cut through the house. He jumped down to the lawn and looked at Braidna. "You all right?"

She nodded. "Yes. Fine. Just a little woozy for a moment."

Sha'gar stared down at the thing. Hissing angrily she slashed at it with a flaming red wand and leaped back as it flowed into dust. "Snar worm."

Tinker looked over. "What?"

Messenger leaned close to Braidna. "Better tug your robe closed, there is an awful lot of you showing."

"Snar worm," growled Sha'gar. "Hate things demon sent." Her eyes darted here and there, seeking another of them. "Suck you dry."

Braidna yanked the top of her robe together. "Thanks."

"No problemo, dudette," giggled Messenger.

"Smoke?" He looked at them.

"Everyone is fine. And I do not feel anything around here except us and Braidna." She winked at him. "She is fine, also."

"Three yums at least," whispered Messenger to Braidna.

"I think that she killed it, mate'mer." Sha'gar indicated Braidna.

"Let's go back to bed." He turned and headed back inside.

"What is that?" asked Braidna, looking at Messenger.

"Your, ummmmm, chest," giggled Messenger. "On a scale of one to five. Fair Morn is a five."

"Oh." Braidna yanked her robe closed at the neck. It was already closed. "Welllllll, thank you. I suppose." She stood and headed inside after the others.

And then they all wandered back to their bedrooms,

stashing weapons, settling back down.

And in the early morning hours when the moon was just kissing the ridge on the west edge of their lands, she softly, gently, appeared in a quiet lilac fog. Standing on the rear deck, she reached out, located the one that she sought, and slipped on silent feet into the house.

Smoke's eyes popped open, pupils dilating, soaking up all the available light.

The figure bent and kissed her. "First Greetings, Smoke."

"First Greetings, Tinlee, the Adept. Why are you here?"

"I came to visit, as you said, when you were last with us."

Smoke yawned. "It is early. We were up late." She flopped the covers back. "Crawl in, it's a large nest."

Tinlee did.

Smoke dragged the covers back into order.

Tinlee rolled onto her side and slid one hand inside Smoke's pajama top. *I came to learn more.*

Go to sleep. Smoke yawned again. And did.

Tinlee kissed Smoke's shoulder. *Yes.* And did

Dol Spar. Bright and Sunny.

Mirf burst into her office, momentarily startling her two clerks. Fred and Quan just looked at her. They were used to the erratic behavior of their boss. Rema and Nema were not quite used to her. Yet.

"So?" boomed Mirf. "Everyone is ready to travel, right." She nodded. "Of course right!" She looked from blank face to blank face. "Ho boy, such enthusiasm this is!" And sat on the edge of her desk.

"Where?" asked Rema.

"S'good question. Glad that I thought of it." Mirf stood. "We are going to, ready for this?" And looked from blank face to blank face, again. "Rim Din Din!" She laughed loudly. "Don't blame me! I didn't name it."

Estar Nal. A Rather Pleasant Looking Place.

The core pair of the Green Plain Set gathered the Prime Males together and sent fringe females running to the adjoining two sets requesting a contada to speak of a temporary merge.

Fringe females of the three sets had taken edge males from each other for generations. The Core Pair talked with the Prime Males and hoped that the fringe females would survive long enough to deliver the message. The threat was so strong that an extreme repattern was necessary. The Core Pair's eyes glowed brighter red as they talked. The Prime Males shifted uneasy and smiled no-threat, displaying black, pointed shark teeth.

And it was decided.

They would hunt raid deep until the threat was eliminated. Barking orders, the Core Pair sent the Prime Males running to prepare the set. Except for the two borne to the floor.

Hahn Dohr Kahn. Warm Sunny Day. E'Nilt's Town.

"Princess, take some men with you."

"I do not require any." She strolled out of the village, a short figure wearing gleaming, golden scale armor, a golden sword hanging from her belt.

Once out on the open plain, she turned and looked back.

The central structure was now complete, totally rebuilt. As were two of the outer structures. All of the rest were nearing completion. The gem mines were open and working. Workmen's houses were up. Everything was flowing smoothly under the capable direction of her Chief.

Just not so long ago she had given him his instructions and had told that she would be gone for an unknown length of time. There was something that she had to do. So she had started off, knowing that all would continue to proceed smoothly until she returned. Even if she didn't return.

Spinning on her heels, she headed straight for the gigantic black cone named M'Ban's Mount. Following the newly constructed road that connected her village with Wurm and Spa and eventually the Royal City, she strode toward it in an even ground eating walk.

Days later, she was striding down one of the many tunnels inside the volcano, torch held high, seeking the one that she knew lived in here. Far ahead she saw the soft red glow of the great inner chamber. A monstrous black form blocked a goodly portion of all available space.

As she approached, two green eyes popped open and watched the tiny figure stop and stare upward.

"M'Ban, I am E'Nilt, Princess to the court of Queen Lurin. I beg help and information."

The Great Black dragon lowered her head until it rested on the smooth stone floor, one gigantic eye not too far from the face of this tiny creature.

"Griz, griz, griz," laughed M'Ban. Dragons thought most things having to do with non-dragons were funny. She blinked. "I knew of a Princess with that name eons ago. Are you related?"

"NO! I am that E'Nilt."

M'Ban huffed green smoke surprise. It billowed over E'Nilt. She coughed and snapped, "Stop that!"

M'Ban gently blew. The wind whistled around E'Nilt and dispersed the smoke. "I didn't think that Hephira lived so long."

"A long story," replied E'Nilt. "But I am not that old."

"Griz, griz, griz." M'Ban slid an enormous paw under her chin. For her there were no really long stories. "Tell me your story, tiny Princess E'Nilt."

And E'Nilt, knowing a little about dragons, knew that she would have to, or she would never get to the business that she wished to discuss with this mountain of a beast. So, she sat on one dragon toe and began her story.

Grandeville. Tinker's Place.

The house was filling with light, the soft light of early morning. East facing windows were about to let the first rays of the almost above the far ridge sun slide into the rooms.

She slipped on silent bare feet up to the door, yanking the belt of her robe tight, and gently knocked.

"Ummmmmmmm?"

Tapping gently again, she eased the door open and whispered through the narrow gap, "Are you alone?"

"Whozit?" he mumbled.

"Briadna."

"Go away."

"I brought cups and a coffee pot."

Smoke slipped past her, accompanied by a woman Braidna hadn't seen before. Smoke wore black pajamas, her companion filmy lilac garments. "He is alone," said Smoke to Braidna. "Kitchen is this way," she said to Tinlee.

Braidna carefully pushed the door open and peered inside. His bed was king-sized and set flush with the floor. It was covered by an equally large puffy down comforter. "You in there? Somewhere?"

A hand popped out one side and waggled. "What do you want?" Then his head appeared as he flapped the comforter away. And glared up at her.

Walking over, she sat on the floor, pulled a small table over and set the pot and coffee cups on it. She filled the cups and handed him one. "Talk."

"Urm," he grumbled, lurching upright and backwards to thump against the wall. He pulled the comforter higher with one hand and took a sip from the cup in the other.

She waited.

"O.K.," he said eventually. "What?" And held out the cup for a refill. "Please?"

She refilled it, then her own. And sipped. "What is happening?"

"Dun'know." He slumped a little, eyes partially closing. "I don't like it."

His eyes opened. "Me neither."

"What was that thing, those things?"

"You heard."

She looked at him, her face a perfectly composed mask.

"Yes, I did. John?"

"What?"

"Tell me about them, your women."

His eyes studied her's, ever so carefully. "Chen really didn't tell you very much, did he?"

"No."

"What do you want to know?"

"What are they?"

He sighed.

Go ahead, MindMate. She needs to know.

He nodded.

She noticed that just for an instance, he had seemed to be somewhere else.

"O.K," he said. "What do you want to know?"

"Are they human?"

"Sure." He smiled, a little. "Sorta."

"You have to do better than that. Start with Smoke. And her friend."

He sat straight and held his cup out again. And watched while she poured, carefully clenching her robe at the neck as she leaned forward.

"What friend?"

Tinlee, the Adept, of The Vander, explained Smoke in his mind. *She came to learn from me. You are safe.* Smoke laughed.

"Oh?" He nodded as his eyes refocused on her's. "O.K., we will start with Smoke. But no interruptions."

He began.

In the kitchen, Smoke began making breakfast for three. Fair Morn had joined her and Tinlee.

Fair Morn opened the refrigerator and began to take out more ingredients.

Tinlee watched them. "What are you doing?"

Smoke shoved the hash browns around in one of the large cast iron skillets with a wooden spoon. "Cooking. Breakfast."

Tinlee stepped close to her side, bent over and peered into the pan. "Very different."

He finished and held out his cup. She refilled it. "All true?" She watched his face.

"Yep."

Braidna touched the gold chain around her neck. "Even after this, it is hard to believe."

"Understandable."

"John?"

"Ummmm?"

"You are just human, Grandeville human, right?"

He nodded. "So is Chantal."

"They all don't look any different, ahh, other than Smoke's eyes."

He nodded. Again. "Breakfast is almost ready. I'll be right there."

She stood, taking the pot and the cups. "I'll wait."

"Ummmmm, I gotta put on my pajamas."

"Oh!" She spun and hurried from the room. And wondered how anyone living the way he did could be so, so shy.

As Braidna joined them at the dining room table, Smoke smiled and said, "This is Tinlee. She is visiting. That is Braidna.

She is also visiting."

Fair Morn took a large measure of the hash browns and shoved the platter toward Braidna.

Tinlee smiled at Braidna. "Very pretty."

"Thank you. Pass the toast, please."

Smoke handed Tinlee the plate. "This."

Taking a piece, Tinlee handed the plate to Fair Morn who gave it to Braidna as Tinker walked in and dropped into his chair. Smoke shoved a pot in his direction.

As he filled his cup, Tinlee stood, walked around, bent, and kissed him. "First Greetings, Lord." And returned to her chair.

Braidna carefully held her face blank.

From the kitchen came the rattle of pots on the range. It was Chicken. Fair Morn jumped up. "I better help her. Or she will make a big mess, a bigger mess."

Soon they were all there, around the dining room table, eating, and holding a number of small conversations.

Chantal hastily finished and headed for the back door. She was the only one not wearing pajamas and robes. "Sick horse to see. Then I'll be at my sister's place to check their new livestock. Be home for dinner." She banged outside.

Moments later, they heard her small car roar down the driveway.

"Veterinarian," explained Smoke to Braidna. "Let's take a walk," she said to Tinlee. And to the rest of herself, *We will be beyond the first pasture, down in the Great Hollow.*

Then they began to disperse to various activities and chores that needed doing.

Braidna halted Fair Morn as the dining room emptied.

"What?" asked Fair Morn.

"May I see them?"

Fair Morn stared at her. And shrugged. "Wellll, I suppose." And reached up and began to unbutton her pajama top.

"Your wings!"

Fair Morn laughed. "Thought that it was a strange request. Let's go outside, the front lawn. Not enough room in here."

Braidna followed her into the large living room and out onto the front lawn. And watched Fair Morn as she stepped away and turned to face her. And began to unfold and unfold and unfold her great butterfly wings.

"Ahhhh," she sighed. "That sun feels so good." The great wings pulsated slowly, the iridescent scales reflecting spots of color over everything as the wing patterns seemed to shift and change as the wings waggled.

Braidna stood and stared.

"You feel all right?"

Braidna nodded. "Yes." She stepped close. "They are beautiful." And walked around Fair Morn. "How do they do that, just pass through your pajamas like that?"

"Don't know. It is just the way that I was made."

Braidna stopped in front of her. "I thought that John was just pulling my leg."

Fair Morn grinned at her. "He might. Nice legs."

"May I touch them?" She laughed. "Your wings?"

"Sure." One wing curled around as Braidna reached out.

"They are warm. And so smooth, like suede." Her hand gently stroked over the surface of the wing. "Can you really fly?"

"Yep. Stand back." The great wings began to beat.

Braidna stepped back.

Fair Morn lifted off and soared up and over the roof and then came swooping around the end of the house to settle gently on the grass in front of Braidna. "Have to be careful. Don't want people seeing me doing that." She grinned. "I usually fly at night."

"Thank you for showing me." Braidna smiled at her.

Fair Morn winked and began to fold and fold and fold her wings.

"Where do they go?"

Fair Morn shrugged. "'Don't know. Just the way that I was made." She stepped close and gently hugged Braidna. "Don't look so unhappy. I was just Big Red's magical jest, a pinup babe with butterfly wings. Just a temporary joke to play on him."

"Him? Temporary?"

"John." Fair Morn headed for the house. "Messenger broke the magical bonds and took me with her. Breaking the bonds made me real."

Braidna gasped. "She did what? That happy, bubbling, ahhh, young woman, did what?"

"Broke the magical bonds linking me to Big Red. One word of wisdom, if I may?" Fair Morn halted them in the hallway.

"Of course."

"Don't assume that they are all what they look like."

"Like you and your wings."

"Yep." Fair Morn spun away. "See you later. Chores to

do."

Braidna shut the door to her bedroom, sat on the edge of the bed, and stared at the wall, trying to put everything she had learned into some semblance of reality. And wondered what on earth Chen was doing, putting her in such a household

It Never Stops, Does It?

S'Pos Best'l. Late In the Day.

They came down onto the sand, rock, and brittle brush at a flat place on the ridge.

M'Ban had agreed to help E'Nilt in return for E'Nilt doing something for her in return. Dragons could slip in and out of the inbetween with the greatest of ease but they often required help in other matters. Traveling through the inbetween wasn't something they really had to think about, they just did it. It was all in their dragon nature.

The great black dragon opened one clenched front paw, allowing E'Nilt to step free. Just in front of them stood a stone tower, tall to E'Nilt, not very tall to M'Ban. The tower was the entrance to the village, one of the entrances. The village was deep below the surface, escaping the heat of the long summers of this elseplace.

Down there lived The Imfarla. E'Nilt had to convince them to give her the Mar Lak. M'Ban wanted it for some purpose and E'Nilt had agreed to do this in exchange for help. She had old debts to repay and absolutely required the aid of this immense beast.

"I will wait." M'Ban tucked her legs underneath, curling her tail around, beginning to look more and more like a great black hill that had suddenly grown from the ridge.

E'Nilt stepped through the door and started down the

spiral stairs. The door was only about one-and-a-half times her height so she assumed that the Imfarla were not all that much larger than herself.

The light was dim but adequate. She had never heard of this elseplace or this race and wondered what they would be like.

Estur Nal. A Very Pleasant Appearing Place.

The Core Pair watched as their set moved and shifted in small movements as the near set, The Green Hill Set, approached and touched, edge to edge. The Prime Males and the Core Pair shifted into an attack wedge as the other Core Pair and their Prime Males walked from the Green Hill Set and into and through and slowly approached. The fringe female that had carried the message wobbled from side to side as she staggered from the Green Hill Set, her garments hanging in tatters. She staggered into the middle band, alive, status elevated.

The Core Pair watched the others approach, their Prime Males staying close to their sides and back, moving nervous around them. It was daring to enter another set this way. It was often terminal.

Ahamaezur barked a command. Her core-sister did the same. Their Prime Males slipped backward, making space, flashing jet black shark teeth in nervous smiles. Their hands lightly touched weapons as they continually adjusted their positions relative to the small group approaching.

Ahamaezur and Amamaedur sat on the bare soil, eyes glowing red, watching.

Dapemargur and Datemaeiur stepped away from their Prime Males and sat, eyes glowing red. Their knees almost touched other knees.

Grunting greetings, Ahamaezur and Amamaedur handed Dapemargur and Datemaeiur each a small sack.

Carefully wiggling a finger in the sack, Dapemargur fished out the pale blue object and quickly returned it, and stuffed the sack into her garment. Datemaeiur did the same. The pairs moved closer together.

The conversation began. All around them the two sets blurred together as fringe females and middle females eyed the new males. Here and there, one sprang, dragging down her choice. It was normal behavior for the Tark Demons.

The sets had merged.

Fran's Dance.

They were in one of the places where information could be acquired. Especially when one had a few gold coins to lay in certain outstretched palms. Hand'l sat at one corner table speaking softly to the one that they had sought. Iztar stood close by.

"A seek beast!" One Down looked doubtful. No one knew his real name, or even how he had come by the label he was now known by.

Hand'l nodded, and slid a coin across the table top using the tip of one finger. "Iztar put the remains in the sewer. You may go and look for yourself, if you wish."

One Down shook his head. And slipped the gold coin into a pocket. "Why here?"

"That is our question," replied Hand'l.

"Horrid creatures controlled by horrid beings. Watch your backs. And all around."

Hand'l nodded. Another coin fingered its way across

the table top. "Let me tell you what we seek." Hand'l leaned forward, forearms on the table top, and began speaking ever so low, telling everything that they knew.

Rim Din Din.

They stepped into the lobby of the small detachment of Monetary Control, mostly filling the available space.

"Ho boy, such a place this is."

A clerk hurried through the only door that led into the interior spaces. "May I assist?"

"Certainly." Mirf handed her a slip of paper. "I want to see this file."

The clerk look the slip and read it. Her eyes snapped up and quickly checked the insignia patch that each of them was wearing on their left breast pocket. She blanched and gasped. "Ahhh, doo gab!" Hastily clapping her hand over her mouth, she spun, and ran from the room.

"Sooooooooo," said Mirf. "Shall we wait?" She looked from helper to helper. And nodded at them. "So O.K., we will give a wait." She sat on the edge of the small desk.

"Mirf?" Rema nudged her sister. She had been staring out the front window.

"Vat?"

"Why did we come here?"

"Rumor control. M.C. heard one." Mirf laughed, loudly. "Such an understatement that is." She crossed her arms over her chest. "A very careful magical guild has begun seeking something that they lost. We want to know what they seek, why they lost it, and where they think that it might have gotten to. That bunch stirring around is worrisome. To us." Her arms flew wide. "Ta dah! So here we are."

S'Pos Best'l.

Finally, after many, many steps down, she walked from the bottom landing, through the only opening, and out into open space. The chamber was large, artfully carved, creating a feeling of being outdoors. Not too far away stood a cluster of round buildings. She followed the well-paved path in that direction, watching carefully, noting movements in that cluster. The inhabitants obviously were aware of her presence.

With a confident stride she headed down that passage between the structures. And around the first sharp bend.

Strong hands grabbed her.

Estur Nal. A Pleasant Appearing Place.

Each Core Pair had gifted the other a brace of Prime Males. Now they were all sitting very close together and talking. About hunting. About this favorite hunting spot and that one.

One edge of the merged sets began to undulate. The four looked toward the disturbance. Coming down the slope, flowing in soft waves, the third set approached. The Green Hollow Set. The Core Pair of that set and their Prime Males strode through the layers toward them. One large Prime Male dropped the body he was carrying at the feet of the correct Core Pair.

It was the fringe female that they had sent to carry the message. The third set had just returned from a hunt and many had been still highly agitated when she had run up. Racing toward the core pair, she had managed to scream out the message as she was grabbed. But it had been to fast to prevent.

In offer, the five responsible were to be permanently attached to the set of Ahamaezur and Amamaedur.

Panamaeaur and Pahamaesur barked the orders. Far to one side the five sidled over and joined the furthest edge away from their new Core Pair.

The three Core Pair sat. Ahamaerzur and Amamaedur gave Panamaeaur and Pahamaesur each a small sack. After they had examined the sacks and had hastily stuffed them inside their clothing, the talk began.

Finally, after more gifting, the merged set was over enlarged. On the next light they would trend toward the opening. When they reached the opening they sought, after the few days walk, the minor set in that area, the Edge Hill Set, would either allow them to pass or disappear.

Ahamaezur and Amamaedur invited the other Core Pairs and their selected Prime Males into their dwelling. Pausing at the door, Ahamaerzur looked out over the gently moving mass as it spread out, settling in for the dark. Fringe females, enjoying a special freedom, dragged down new choices.

She turned, said something, and all Core Pair laughed, black shark teeth gleaming in the light. They would eat and talk. And then enjoy their gifts,

Space. 66.29.09.35, In Ship's Notation.

They sat, finishing their meal, and looked at the object. The view screen slowly magnified the thing. He sat comfortably incased in his battle armor. Ship's defenses were up, all necessary weapons focused on the other vessel.

"Sensors indicate something alive in there," stated Gyre.

"Something?"

"Searching data banks."

His eyes rapidly took in the details as the image grew

larger and sharper. Whatever had happened, that vessel out there was badly holed. "Not much usable," he observed. And watched as the sensor missile shot from Ship, rapidly covering the distance between the two space craft. It plunged through the outer hull and stuck, half inside, half outside.

"Connecting," said Gyre. "Computer linked. Searching for log. Log remnant connected."

The image on another screen on the wall jittered, the picture broken into erratic flashes and splashes of color. A voice gasped, "Vessel losing all drive power. Survivors withdrawing into interior emergency space. We have sufficient supplies to last two five harda. All area emergency pulse for help sent."

"Remnant?"

"Yes. That computer is badly damaged. Most records destroyed." Her eyes looked at him, refocusing. "One survivor."

"Anything around?"

"Not alive." She indicated another screen. "Dead bodies."

He peered at it as the screen magnified. "What is that thing?" A piece of wreckage drifted past. "And that?"

"The other vessel and crew."

"Two unknown races that tried to kill each other?"

"Yes."

He stood. "I'll take the Sparkling Tigers with me." Punching a button he said something all soft gurgle, and then headed for the appropriate passageway. "They don't mind the vacuum of space." The door hissed open.

Deep in a hold, Ship readied the Portal, the last

surviving Portal in the universe of universes.

Rim Din Din.

The Section Heads hurried into the room, a husband and wife team. She carried a thin folder. He looked from face to face. "Mirf?"

Mirf smiled at them. They blanched. The woman hastily shoved the folder at Mirf. "Chief Inspector."

"Special Investigator," said Mirf taking the folder and sitting back on the edge of the desk. "New job, new title. So do a relax. I just want to read this." She began to thrash her way through the folder, and finally handed the badly battered thing back to the woman. "So tell me what else you know."

The woman stared at the mangled remains she held. "What else?"

"You bet your booties what else! There is always what else not written down." Mirf waggled one hand loosely at them. It appeared to be badly connected to her arm. "So whisper in my ears, delicate as they are."

The man cleared his throat. "Come to our office, please."

The pair turned and led Mirf and her crew into the small staff space that was M.C. on this rather isolated elseplace. All eyes watched the procession. And many wondered what was going to happen to their station if not to their station heads.

They all fit into the office space without too much struggling. The Station Section head, Aamle, looked embarrassed. His wife was still staring at the tattered thing that she held. She had never seen anyone read and destroy a folder in that fashion before. It seemed that maybe the tales that they had heard of The Mirf were true.

"So," said Mirf, slipping into a chair. "I'm all ears.

Once."

The Station Head set the remains of the report on the desk top and looked at Mirf. "Not much to tell, all rumor, not solid enough for a file entry."

The man cleared his throat and told them.

Dol Spar.

They thumped and banged back into Mirf's office. Actually everyone walked rather quietly except for Mirf, who thumped and banged. Flopping into her chair behind the desk she looked at her clerks. "So, find me something on The Wizards of Trefil. Machen schnell!"

Rema and Nema ran from the room.

"Ho boy, do we have a puzzle or do we have a puzzle?" Mirf looked at Fred and Quan. And nodded at them. "So I know, it's a puzzle."

Park's Flower.

The Qart of the Green ushered them into the presence of the Grey Erml. They stared at each other. The Grey Erml down from the top of the pedestal it curled upon. Duff and $1.98 up from the audience spot.

"You are magic using folk things?" hissed the Grey Erml.

"We are," replied Duff, clenching $1.98's hand, a warning to not do anything sudden.

The Qart of the Black stepped forward, hissing ever so politely. And explained what had happened. The Qart of the Red gurgled unhappy.

The Grey Erml looked at the Qart of the Red. "The Red martra will answer," it hissed, waving the Red away. "Magic using things do not come here. We greet you arnal."

The Qart of the Black and the Qart of the Green bowed low to Duff and $1.98.

"Many thanks," replied Duff.

"We heard of you here and asked your presence. The Red are too impulsive."

"Yes." She released $1.98's hand. He tucked his arms inside his sleeves.

"What do you want?" he asked the Grey Erml.

The Grey Erml hissed, uncoiled, and slithered to the floor. "A special favor."

Then it explained.

Grandeville. Tinker's Place.

It had been a very quiet three weeks. And everyone was very relaxed on this mild but sunny Saturday.

He and she were in the dojo. They had been there for about an hour and a half, training time having been lengthened at Chen's suggestion.

He stood, a very relaxed, alert person, hands and arms floating lightly in front of his chest.

She stood, just beyond reach, eyes fastened on his eyes, flowing slightly to the left.

Suddenly she jumped in, fist snapping at his face.

He slipped sideways, slightly, just enough, turning one hand, deflecting her arm, pushing her off balance. Then he was behind her, the other hand hooking over her left shoulder, under her chin, yanking her backwards, slamming her to the floor. Dropping to one knee, his other leg pressing into her mid-section, his fist flashed down. It stopped, just touching the tip of her nose. "Gotcha!"

"One of these times," she said.

"Sure." He stood up and stepped back.

Bounding to her feet, she twisted, leg snapping around in a high side kick.

He stepped in, hooking his arm under her thigh, and grabbed her gi, the top of her uniform, spun and tossed her back to the floor. And stopped. "Ooops. Sorry."

She looked up at him.

"You all right?"

"Yes." She stood and dragged her gi back up and over her shoulders and yanked it shut.

"Maybe you ought to wear a t-shirt."

"Perhaps." Her foot caught him in the chest and drove him backwards. As she lunged in, he dropped and swept her legs out from under her, and jumped sideways. And punched as she leaped up and at him.

She stumbled back, bent over, gasping.

On the rear deck, at one of the wooden tables, Smoke poured tall glasses full of fruit juice.

"They are going to need this."

The pair walked from the dojo. She was in front, rubbing her middle gently.

"Go take a shower," he said as he handed her a glass.

"Thanks." Braidna emptied the glass and headed into the house.

"Pretty nice." Smoke grinned at him.

"Don't start!" he grumbled, refilling his glass.

"New type of literature."

"What?"

"Gi ripper." She laughed as he frowned and sat on the

bench. "Well?"

He nodded. "O.K., anything to end this topic of conversation. Pretty nice." And half emptied his glass. "She ought to wear a t-shirt."

"Didn't seem to mind."

He frowned at her. "Then what are you going on about?"

Smoke sat next to him. "There is something different about her."

"In what way?"

"Very calm given all the not usual for this culture stuff that she has been exposed to." And nudged him gently in the ribs. "Including you ogling her, ahh, chest."

"Perhaps she just takes things as they come along. And I did not ogle her chest!"

Smoke nodded. "Not perhaps. She does." And leaned against him, just a little. "I want to take a peek, a very careful peek."

"Oh no you don't." He jerked upright. "Every time you do that this group gets bigger."

"Any more orange juice." Braidna came from the house wearing one of the thick white robes, all the buttons fastened, the belt looped tight. Her hair was wet and slicked back, a shining cap. It gave her an exotic, regal appearance.

"Lots," replied Smoke, filling the glass that Braidna had left behind.

"Shower's free," said Braidna, taking the glass and walking over to the edge of the deck to stand looking out over the flower beds and at the far forested slope.

"Remember what I said," he grumbled as he headed

into the house.

Smoke smiled. She stepped over to stand beside Braidna. "Why are you so calm?"

"About?"

"The Golden Dragon, us, John ripping your clothes half off."

Braidna smiled. "I was raised on Chinese fairy tales. And you are a very comfortable group to be around. Quite calm feeling, actually. And he really didn't do anything. Except frown." She laughed. "I could have been a guy for all the reaction that I got." And looked at Smoke. "Maybe he gets excited over more, ahhh, fuller, physiques."

"Chicken is as slim as you are." Smoke grinned. "He gets pretty excited about her."

Braidna shrugged. "Guess that I just don't get excited."

Smoke nodded. "Makes you as strange as us."

Braidna shoved her glass over. "Please?"

Smoke filled it.

Estur Nal. A Very Pleasant Appearing Place.

Tirimarpur and Tidimarfur stared across the soft valley at the far slope. A set larger than any known was pouring over the crest and flowing in open waves down the gentle slope, heading in their direction. Tirimarpur barked orders, calling their set close, making it small, compact. Tidimarfur ordered all to sit. Only the Core Pair stood.

All eyes, glowing soft red, watched the far slope alive with figures walking slow, no more than a fast pace. From that they knew that it was not a hunt. As the lower edge touched the bottom of the valley, they saw the center of the set. Three Core Pair, walking close, strolled over the crest and down.

Tirimarpur touched Tidimarfur on the shoulder. Even from this distance their predator sharp eyes recognized the Core Pairs, they were all from Hamatanar, The Green Holdings, a many prowl from here. Most knew never to hunt way over there, in that territory. Tirimarpur and Tidimarfur had taken their small set to this space, a sparse land, mostly not visited by others. It was a good place to slowly build a set with only an occasional visit to another set.

The lower edge flowed out and touched them, fringe females and secondary males edging around, eyeing them. Tirimarpur and Tidimarfur stared at them. Minor details in costume told them that the three Green sets had merged, intermingled. They barked low, soft orders, reading their set. They doubted that any would survive the assault.

In front of them a space formed and the three Core Pair strode out and into this minor set, ignoring the fringe females and secondary males, all eyes focused on the center, the Core Pair, standing, watching their approach. Tirimarpur shifted one way, Tidimarfur the other, attack ready. Then they stared. The three Core Pair had sat down and were beckoning them to join them and talk. In total confusion, they did.

Space. 66.29.09.35, In Ship's Notation.

Macabre drifted in through a great gap in the side of the vessel following the map projected on his visor. Two horse-sized objects followed him, bright shafts of light flashing in all directions, striking everything, except Macabre.

Soon, he stood at the end of the shattered interior corridor, looking at a hatch. A series of lights flashed across the top of the hatch, flickered and blinked.

"One," said Gyre in his ear piece, "still alive."

"Can you contact it?"

"Trying."

"Contact."

"Message sent and understood."

The lights began to pulsate.

Macabre snatched some lethal thing from his belt and stepped to one side. "Don't kill it," he ordered the Sparkling Tigers. And watched as the hatch, slid open, exposing the entry chamber.

The three of them barely fit inside. He rapped on the inner door with the grip of his weapon, just to signal that he was inside.

The outer door slid shut, interior atmosphere hissed into the chamber, and the inner door slipped open. Soft blue green light flooded the entry chamber and the interior space.

S'Pos Best'l.

"Release me!"

Her wrists were held in one large hand, her arms held straight over her head. The other hand was clamped firmly around her ankles. She could barely wiggle.

The Imfarla were large blocky creatures. The one in front had plucked at her shirt with two claws and had grunted when the shirt had ripped away. One finger was now poking at her. The creature seemed to be puzzled by her shape and form.

"Stop doing that!"

"Emmmmmm," it hummed, holding her head with two fingers, turning it back and forth. It released her and squinted. "Two skins." And plucked at her trousers. They ripped.

"STOP DOING THAT!"

"Emmm. What are you, bent warped small thing?"

"I am E'Nilt, The Princess E'Nilt."

"Emmmmmmmm." It tugged at her braid.

"OUCH!"

"What where race is an E'Nilt two skin?" And pinched a fold of skin on her side and tugged.

"STOP!"

"Emmmmmmmmmmm." It did. And watched the liquid slowly spreading down her side. "It weeps. Emmmmmm." It turned and slid away. Followed by its companion, still tightly holding its captive.

Estur Nal. A Very Pleasant Appearing Place.

Hastily stuffing their gift pouches into their upper garments, Tirimarpur and Tidimarfur nodded agreement. And received a Prime Male from each of the Core Pair and gave one to each Core Pair in exchange. The single Prime Male exchange was a tacit recognition of the small size of their set, the Edge Hill set.

Then the sets merged and intermingled. And settled in place for the rest of the day.

The decision had been made.

They would raid deep.

Through the gateway.

The decision was to eliminate the threat.

Totally.

And then close that gateway.

Forever.

All around the Core Pairs, in the soft constant motion of the many merged set, weapons were readied, sharpened and resharpened.

Fringe and secondary females prowled at ease, making new choices. All were safe to do this rare thing.

At first light they would pour through the gateway, full hunt possession released. Anything not one of them would be fair game.

S'Pos Best'l.

"Amtran! Amtran!"

The man pointed and snapped, "Dar ta mda!"

E'Nilt was dropped onto the large bed. The two large creatures slid from the room followed by the man, who quickly returned, set things on a small table, and began to wash and bandage her side. When he finished, he sat back and stared at her.

"They meant no harm. It was curiosity. What are you?"

"Hephira."

He nodded. "Interesting." And poked her with one finger. "These make you a female of your kind, is that not so?"

"Yes. Stop doing that!"

"Interesting texture."

"OUCH!"

"Emmmmmmmmm." He sat back. "The other gender as small? There are only two?"

"Yes and yes. What are you?"

"Thin Imfarla." He stood. E'Nilt judged him to be at least one and a half times as tall as the Princess Lurin. "You must feed to heal," he stated. And slid from the room.

She tried to sit up. All she could manage was to roll slightly to one side.

He returned, sat next to her, lifted her up, and shoved a mug under her nose. "Feed. To heal." And poured the grey stuff into her mouth.

Choking and gasping, she twisted her head to one side. Grey stuff slopped down her chest. "Not so fast!" she snapped.

"Emmmmmm. Not used to little things." He tilted more of the stuff into her mouth.

Fran's Dance.

One Down looked from Hand'l to Iztar and back again. And shook his head. "A long past event."

"How long?"

One Down's fingers flashed. "It seems that such an event happened here. But hard to learn much so long after."

Hand'l nodded and slowly slid another gold coin across the table.

One Down watched its slow approach. And cleared his throat. "If it were more given the job, I would seek on Tell Used." He slipped the coin into his pocket. "Long ago. It was a short event. Here." And stood. "But on Ten Used maybe longer and not so long ago. Perhaps."

Hand'l watched him slip from the room. And stood. "This trail is beginning to twist. Not good, not good." He headed outside followed by Iztar.

S'Pos Best'l.

Her eyes popped open. Suddenly awake. Surprised.

"Emmmmmmmm." He yanked the covering away and removed her bandages. And bent close to peer at her side. "Emmmmmmmmm. Just a small mark." As soon as he straightened up, she sat up. And realized that there was no pain. She felt well rested, full of energy.

"You are done well."

"Thank you." Crawling to one side of the bed, she sat on the edge, legs dangling. "How long did I sleep?"

"Some."

"May I have some clothes? Mine were pulled apart."

"Emmmmmmmmm. No. We do not have things that small." He sat next to her. "Would you like something else?"

"My sword."

He plucked it from a table and handed it to her. "Were you planning on hurting us?" Two-thirds of the blade was snapped off.

E'Nilt fastened her belt around her waist. And realized that she still wore her boots and trousers, what was left of her trousers. "No."

"Why did you come here?"

"To fetch an artifact."

"Emmmmmmmmmmmmmm. We have many."

E'Nilt threw the sword remains on the bed. "A thing called Mar Lak."

"You can not have it. It belongs to a Cankle. All the Imfarla would cease to be if we gave it to you. Emmmmmmm, emmmmmm, emmmmmmmm."

"What's a Cankle?"

"Greater than vast. Blacker than the inside of dark." He stared at her. "Nothing could done well you if the Cankle got you."

E'Nilt pointed at the ceiling and made a wild guess. "The Cankle is up there waiting for me to bring her the Mar Lak."

He shot upright and slid rapidly from the room.

Zar. Grey and Green.

They poured through the gateway.
And spread outward.

The formation was a great curve, the outer points thrusting forward, ever widening. As they raced across the countryside small groups roiled and thrashed as things were run down, dragged down, ripped, and shredded.

Wider and wider spread the great hunting set. The Core Pairs, all the Core Pairs, had released the bonds. Everything was game to be taken.

A small group danced nervous around the gateway, watching the enlarged set as it disappeared over the far rise, running swift on silent feet. Nothing between the advancing set and those guarding the gateway moved. Just a slight breeze. The secondary males twitch smiled at the secondary and fringe females as they jerked and moved, short quick moves, hunt possessed moves.

All eyes glowed kill red, black shark teeth glittered in the light.

Far to one side they saw it, hurtling toward the gateway. Something had survived, had managed to elude the set, and was trying to escape.

The group faded, space shifting, seeming to be where they were not.

On it came, seeing only the gateway, and the figures standing far to the side. It came leaping in great arcs. One arm was gone, one wing dragged tatters in the grey dust.

They hit it, all hunt fury energy. It didn't have time to scream.

Looking up from the remains, the Senior Secondary female, from the Green Plain set, licked her lips clean, stood, stretched, muscles rippling, joints popping, preening for the Secondary male, from the Green Hill set, she had chosen. Arching her back, she eyed him.

Stepping nervous, he eyed her in return, admiring her strength and feral beauty. She was near Core Pair ready and had taken the name Ferumaetur. He soft slipped, carefully inspecting the other females. Her sister half couldn't be any of those present.

The small group settled, guarding the gateway, watching for survivors.

S'Pos Best'l.

She stomped across the ground and viciously booted her in the nose.

The great eyes popped open.

"You farz norz!" snarled E'Nilt. "I almost died, my clothes are mostly gone, and I lost my sword." She kicked the great dragon again. And struck her on the side of her snout with the Mar Lak.

"Ouch," said M'Ban, just trying to be polite. All she could feel was the lightest of feather soft taps.

E'Nilt leaned close to one of the enormous eyes and glowered into it. The eye was larger than her head. "The next time you had better well tell me what to expect."

M'Ban blinked. And lifted her head from her forelegs and peered down at the tiny figure. "You can get clothes on Izalna One Over." She picked up the still angry Hephira, her claws curling around, making a hollow cage, and lifted into the air.

Grandeville. Tinker's Place.

He held her in his arms, hands clasped together in the small of her back "Pretty nice."

She leaned back against his hands and smiled at him. "I bet that you say that to all of them."

His eyes flew open, staring into the dark night of his bedroom space. "Nooooooooo." The cry echoed through their minds. "Noooooooooooo!"

Smoke grabbed him, her minds clamping down. "MindMate, what it is?" His bedroom door banged open as they charged inside.

Chantal was first, snapping on the ceiling light. The air crackled angrily as Szart and Sha'gar ran in. Dark terror rose from the deep below just behind them as Sgenn stepped quietly in and off to one side, dark grey eyes carefully searching the room.

Chicken charged in. "My Lord!" Followed by Fair Morn, then Messenger.

He shoved at Smoke. "Off. Lemme up!"

She sat up and watched him as he sat up, squirming back until he could lean against the wall.

Chantal knelt by the side of his bed, easing the hammer of her long-barreled revolver back down. "John?"

"Something is really wrong." His eyes swiveled around and looked at Smoke. "Better take a look."

She nodded. And smiled.

"Don't start!" he growled.

Smoke passed his dream to the others.

"Lech," grumbled Chantal.

"That shouldn't have happened," he snarled back.

"Especially when I am in the bed." Smoke leered at

him.

"He is just insatiable." Fair Morn sat at the end of the bed and dropped her cannon onto it. Tinker glared at her.

Messenger stuffed her wand into her hair. "Maybe he needs some vitamins and minerals?"

"He needs someone to explain what's going on this time?" he grumbled at Smoke. "And send that thing away," he rumbled at Sgenn. "And calm down," he snapped at Szart and Sha'gar.

"Testy, testy," mumbled Chantal. "Calm yourself down, Cowboy. You are bothering us all, damn it."

He sucked in a deep breath. and did. Calm down. He knew that his emotions affected the entire group of interlinked minds. And looked at her. "Better?"

"Yep." Chantal looked at Smoke.

Smoke shrugged. "Hard to tell. His reaction was so violent that it jumbled things." She smiled at him. "Next time just enjoy it. Then maybe we will be able to find something."

"Merde," he observed.

"You just let us do the damn worrying, grumble butt," snapped Chantal. "Or we will never get any rest."

"O.K." He nodded. "Go back to bed." And slipped back down and into and under the covers.

Smoke tickled him. "Maybe I ought to go to my room and not distract you." She grinned at him.

"Smoke!"

Fair Morn turned, as the last one to leave the room, and snapped off the light. And laughed. "Sweet dreams." She closed the door.

"Not funny," he grumbled into the darkness.

"Go to sleep, MindMate. We have to find out." Smoke merged with him, and waited as he slowly drifted to sleep.

Search and Discovery

Midi Rope Stud.

He looked at her. "You really think that we should be doing this?"

"Yes, Dear, I do."

"Duff, we are magicians. We do not know anything about finding people. And they weren't even people." He waggled one hand, indicating where they had just come from.

"Yes, Dear."

They were strolling along a wide track through a rather open and pleasant forest. This elseplace was where the Grey Erml had told them was the place to start. And to visit the town not far from where they had just appeared.

"Do you know anything about The Wizards of Trefil? I have never heard of them."

"No, Dear."

He sat on a handy downed tree trunk. and stared at her. "Duff."

She stopped in front of him and looked into his eyes, seeing the worry and concern there, for her. "I know. But we will be careful. Very, very careful." She held out her hand, the shining starburst gleaming energy soft glow soft blue cloud halfway up to her elbow. "And we have this."

He nodded. And watched as she put it somewhere. "Is it safe? That thing it gave to you?"

She grinned. "Safer than some red jewels we know, or knew. Just a little touch tingle."

"You are sure?"

"Yes, Dear." She reached over and slid her palm over his cheek. "See?"

"All right."

"Let's go to town, Dear."

He stood and they strolled off.

Space. 66.29.09.35, In Ship's Notation.

The survivor was short and wide, brown and lumpy.

Macabre carefully watched it as it looked at him and the pulsating masses that were the Sparkling Tigers. Their claws had clattered on the metallic floor when they had entered the chamber. It watched them more than it watched Macabre.

"I am Ard," gurgled the creature, all liquid bubble. "You heard my help cry?"

"I did."

"Are any of the Akin still out there?"

"No. All that could be seen was wreckage and bodies, parts of bodies."

"Akle akle," bubbled Ard. "It is good to know that."

Macabre waved one hand, the hand not resting ever so lightly on one of the weapons on his belt. "Not much left."

Ard gurgled. "More than the Akin." It pointed. "What are those?"

"They are called Sparkling Tigers. Do you have any knowledge of them?"

"No. And you?"

"I am Macabre."

Ard made low popping sounds. "That Which

Removes?"

"Haven't heard that one before. "

Ard waggled fingers, toes, and long whiskers. "We is untooled."

"Yes." Macabre gestured vaguely. "Your ship is no longer usable. May I take you someplace?"

"Remain end here."

"I can fit a room for you."

"Final here." Ard touched something, a panel in one wall opened. A long shaft, all midnight blue pulsed soft light.

"We this to Chimera Icide taking. The Akin not wanted our duty." It looked at Macabre. "Do our duty. All your's else." It sagged closer to the floor. "Do?"

"A long journey," said Gyre in one ear piece. She had already checked Ship's data bases. "A far hidden corner. A dark spot."

Macabre walked over to the opening and carefully inspected the artifact. It was very unusual. He shrugged. He had seen hundreds of unusual artifacts. "Is there anything in this scrap heap we can use?"

"Nothing," replied Gyre.

He took the thing from its fastenings. "I will deliver this. Who gets it?"

Ard gurgled and stopped making noises.

"Vital signs ceased," reported Gyre.

"Coming back." He turned and blew away the chamber door. And made a great hole in the outer hull from this spot.

Grandeville. Tinker's Place.

It had been a quiet week.

A week of peace and quiet.

And untroubled sleep.

So, they decided to plan a picnic.
After watching a movie.

She walked in just as the film ended. And dropped heavily into a chair. "I am losing my mind!"

Smoke glanced over. "You are very healthy."

Braidna took a handful of popcorn from the bowl just handed to her by Fair Morn. "Thanks."

Chantal took the tape from the VCR and rewound it. "So what's the problem?" And dropped back onto the couch. Next to Messenger who was carefully looking at Braidna. "I don't see anything," she whispered.

Braidna yanked off her boots. "Someone talked to me." And sat up. "Only no one was there."

"What did they say?" Tinker sat up, a little. Szart was sitting with her legs thrown across his lap.

"I don't know. It was a foreign language."

"Pretty strange," he observed.

"Hum," added Szart.

"It was strange," agreed Braidna. She looked at Chantal. "And I do not use illegal substances either."

"Imagination?" asked Chicken.

"No. It was definitely a voice. I was in the middle of the **Blue Goose Grocery** parking lot. Not a car or pedestrian in sight. And this woman spoke to me." She took some more popcorn from Fair Morn's bowl.

"First time?" asked Tinker.

"Yes."

"Don't think that I'd start worrying until it happens a bunch." He tickled one of Szart's knees.

She wacked his hand.

"Spoil sport."

"Hum hum," she said, twisting the ornate ring she wore on one finger.

He winked at her, and tickled her again.

And shortly thereafter, they all headed for bed.

He held her in his arms, hands clasped together in the small of her back. "Pretty nice." She leaned back against his hands and smiled at him. "I'll bet that you say that to all of them." And tugged the heavy blue uniform blouse loose and began to unbutton it, starting at the bottom button.

He smiled. "Lovely skin."

"China Gold," she said, shrugging the garment from her shoulders. The blouse draped over his hands, sleeves brushing the floor.

Shouldn't be doing this."

"Kaldor e'ent ti dier guar en'en'ita."

Jolting awake he stared into the darkness.

Soft glow illuminated the room as Szart sat up.

"Damn dream again," he grumbled. And sighed loudly. *Smoke?*

Got it, MindMate.

Well?

Relax.

He tried. Szart yanked the covers back into order and slid back under, gently sliding her arm across his chest.

Go to sleep, MindMate. We will talk in the morning.

"Merde," he grumbled.

Szart hitched higher and breathed soft warm at him. "I could cast a black rikter on her."

"No! Whatever that is."

"The Faan do not allow their's to be trifled with," she growled softly.

"We don't know what is going on." He felt the others listening. *Goes for you too,* he said to Sgenn and Sha'gar.

Kar ptar pak do, grumbled Sha'gar as she called back the spell.

Braidna stared up at the ceiling in her room and watched the red glow fade away and wondered what that had been. She didn't notice the black shadow thing in the far corner sink back into the down below.

Midi Rope Stud.

The town was neither small nor large. It was just a rather medium sized place sitting not far from the edge of the forest. And not too far from the town the grass ended and the landscape became all bare rock and sand and boulders. It was a startling and sudden transition from green to grey and brown and light tan. The barren land broke sharply downhill and fell steep slope to sprawling, twisting canyon lands.

"Different," observed $1.98.

"Yes, Dear. Let's find somewhere to eat."

They had walked a good part of the day, here in this elseplace. The sun was leaning far to one side of the sky as they strolled into the town. The inhabitants, a tall thin folk, stared at these two strangers, but kept to their business, whatever it was.

Three blocks and two turns later, he halted them. And pointed at an open doorway. The cooking smells seemed to be coming from inside there.

Duff headed over and into the building. He followed. And tried to watch everywhere at the same time.

The room had three tables. Each table had three chairs. Two of the tables had occupants. They sat at the remaining one.

A tall, thin individual wearing a coat of green and orange patches hurried over, bent and stared at them with soft green eyes.

"We'd like to get something to eat," said $1.98.

The green eyes looked at her.

"We are hungry," she said.

"One gold," hissed the individual. "Four nandler."

She set one gold coin on the table. Snatching the coin, the individual hurried away. And returned to set two square plates in front of them, four bowls filled with steaming foodstuffs, each different, mugs, and a large purple jug.

"Smells good." Duff ladled some of each onto his plate, then her own. He filled their mugs from the jug. And yawned.

She nodded. "It was tiring, speaking with those . . . beings."

He looked around the room and leaned close to her. "Why would anyone come here?"

"Perhaps because no one would want to?"

He indicated the others in the room with subtle signs. "Should be easy to find out. From what we were told she should have been obviously not from this elseplace."

She dumped more food onto his plate. "In the morning,

Dear. There is no hurry."

Izalna One Over.

They came down into an immense field next to the village.

This field was a special place. It had been a special place as far back as memory could recall. All knew that it was a special place. All knew that one did not ever venture out into that special place, that special vastness. Of course, in the dead of night, young folk sometimes did. But they never told anyone about doing that. No one knew why it was a special place. It just was. And always had been.

But, now, on the sun filled day, slightly past straight up, all knew why this was a special place. They poured from town to stand along one edge and stare. So and so, they said, one to the other, that is why.

E'Nilt peered around one great paw and called at the gawking crowd, "Is there someone among you that sells clothes? I require some clothes."

A tall woman stepped forward, one hesitant step. "I do such."

"Bring me a shirt, a small shirt, please?"

The tall woman bobbled her head and hurried into town. And wondered what manner of wakal that small being was. And what manner of beast it was that loomed over it like a great hill.

"Griz, griz, griz," laughed M'Ban.

"Not funny," snapped E'Nilt, watching for the tall woman to return. At least this place was warm. "Who are these folk?"

"Underlan."

"And what do I do with this?" She waggled the Mar Lak at one gigantic eye.

"Show it to the merchant who now approaches."

E'Nilt spun around and watched as the tall woman carefully approached, one hand clenching a garment. She stopped and looked down. "I size guessed." And handed it to E'Nilt.

E'Nilt took the garment, shook it out, and looked at it. It was a baggy smock-like thing. She tugged it over her head and shoved her arms through the sleeves. The garment was about two sizes too large.

"What manner of wakal are you?"

"I am Daish a'an'Nald ca E'Nilt, Princess of the Realm of the Dragon, Hahn Dohr Kahn." She drew herself up to her full height. "Who are you?" And looked up.

"Uderlan Cubres, garment maker." She stared at E'Nilt's ears. "What are you, wakal with the long name?"

"I am Hephira." She shoved one hand from a sleeve and folded back the material into a thick cuff. And held up the Mar Lak. "Do you recognize this?"

Cubres rocked backward, eyes flying wide, mouth falling open. "Oooo."

E'Nilt spun around and glared at M'Ban's eye.

"Griz, griz, griz," laughed the dragon, lifting her head from the paw where she had been resting it.

"Come with me," stammered Cubres. "I will take you to Sphere Kack." She turned and headed for the town.

"Bring me what you find," hissed M'Ban at E'Nilt.

Ten Used.

They walked down the wide street that led through this

large urban center. This place was a major crossroads for trade and travel in this sector. Many body shapes and forms mingled in the throngs here. No one looked at them. No one paid them any mind.

"Looks promising," observed Hand'l.

Iztar grunted.

So they wandered, looking for the right place, admiring the buildings, the lush settings. Stopping at an outdoor place, they ordered a meal. And were served, without a glance.

"Very promising," said Hand'l.

Iztar nodded.

They headed into an area of narrow streets, where everything wasn't as polished and clean. If anything, the population here was even more varied than where they had been walking.

Selecting a likely place, Hand'l walked inside, over to the server, ordered and sipped, and said, "Where would one find information about things lost? Is there a one who could, who would, aid us?" He slipped a gold coin over the counter top. The sever took the coin, carefully inspected it, and indicated with a flick of his eyes, a corner table and its solitary occupant, a large, burly, more or less human appearing individual. "Ziptik."

Hand'l turned and watched the room for some time before wandering over to the correct table. Rusty red eyes looked up at him.

"It is told," said Hand'l. "That Ziptik might aid us in finding something lost."

"Ibta," grunted Ziptik. "Sit."

Hand'l did. Iztar stood nearby.

Ziptik shrugged one ear. "Nipta."

Hand'l slid a small stack of coins in Ziptik's direction. "May I describe that which we seek?"

"Ibta. Do."

So Hand'l did. Ziptik sat quiet, listening carefully, the stack of coins untouched. The correct amount would be removed, if and when.

Ziptik took the stack. "There was such a one. Arrived furtive nervous. Stayed look. Left calm confident."

Hand'l nodded. "Much better," he said to Iztar. Iztar shifted its feet. "Did this person have a name?" asked Hand'l, shifting another stack in the correction direction.

Ziptik took that stack. "Arrived Arnal. Stayed Daral. Left Mornal."

Iztar puffed out its cheeks.

Hand'l nodded, and shifted yet another stack. "Is there one who knows where this trio went?"

Ziptik removed two coins. "Renmel the Doorta. A special skill for those who need." Two more coins disappeared. Instructions were offered on how one went about finding Renmel the Doorta. It was on the far side of the city.

"Many many," said Hand'l as he stood.

"Ibta."

Hand'l and Iztar headed outside to make their long walk across this large city.

Medi Rope Stud.

"Oona the Light Skin," stated Nan'dril the Wise.

$1.98 and Duff had finally been directed to this person.

"She stayed short. Came to hide, greatly agitated." Nan'dril laughed and waved one hand at all the folk in the room. "Poor thought." All the inhabitants skin tones were dark. Dark red, dark blue, dark brown. Regardless of the chosen color, all were deep, dark tones. Nan'dril held a gleaming gold coin in a shaft of light. The coin glowed. "Among us this is obvious." And laughed again.

Duff nodded.

Nan'dril reached out and gently touched $1.98. "This size." And then touched Duff. "This kind."

$1.98 pointed at the coin. "She was that color?"

"Light," stated Nan'dril.

$1.98 nodded. "Where did this person go?"

"Abner's Hole. All light skins." Nan'dril's face folded in down folds. "The creature was in help need. Ask Pok'l. A light skin, maredan to us." He nodded and handed the gold coin back to $1.98.

"Gift," stated Duff, standing.

Nan'dril's face lifted. He handed her a green square. "Pok'l." And merged back, quiet still.

"Come, Dear, we have to go to Abner's Hole." $1.98 stood and followed her from the room.

Nan'dril hoped those creatures could aid Light Oona.

Ester Nal. A Fairly Pleasant Place.

The great combined set poured back through the. gateway. They carried the dead and the dying and those too badly injured to walk. On the other side nothing lived. Every nest had been destroyed. Every egg crushed. The winged ones had ceased to exist.

Then they closed the gateway, sealing it forever.

The great set filled all sides of the valley, slowly settling down, burying the dead, tending the wounded.

All the Core Pair settled to the ground, knee touching knee to talk, and to decide. Barking orders, they sent the Prime Males to pull Fringe Females and Males, to the middle, making adjustments, honoring this one, or that one.

Then the eight stood, turned in unison and looked at her standing, watching. Amamaedur crooked a finger, eyes glittering red, ordered Ferumaetur over. And watched her step quiet soft and stand ready, to accept her fate. To stand and hear their decision. They told her.

Spinning away, Ferumaetur scanned the ever moving set, her eyes glittering. Then she pointed at a tall female with a great gash running from her hair line, across the side of her face, and down across her torso. Prime Males side slipped and urged her forward. Ferumaetur handed her one of the two small sacks she had been given and gave this one the chosen name, Fezumaedur. And acknowledged her as a forever sister. Then each Core Pair donated to them.

The Green Plain Set, the Green Hill Set, the Green Hollow Set, and a few from the Edge Hill Set. The three Green Set sent additions to the Edge Hill Set until they were larger than the newly created set, named the Grey Wood Set.

Then all the Core Pair sat and discussed matters of importance. Recognizing that they now had special bonds between them, they reallocated territories until all were nodding agreement.

All around them, the members sat motionless, eyes fastened upon the Core Pair, listening intently. And it was decided. In two turns the sets would reform and disperse. Then the combined set began to move, outward settling into this form and that form. Here and there, a Fringe Female, unable, or unwilling, to wait, dragged down her choice.

Ferumaetur and Fezumaedur walked shoulder close to shoulder, inspecting, seeking, and then choosing the four, their Prime Males. Flashing black shark teeth nervous smiles, the chosen four eyed each other and admired the strength and feral beauty of this new core pair. And grunted soft comments to each other. The new Core Pair had selected one male from each of the other four sets.

Grandeville. Tinker's Place.

They were part way into breakfast, talking quietly. He was mostly awake. Soft sunlight washed in through the dining room windows. It looked like it was going to be a nice day. For late summer.

Braidna joined them, dropping into her chair. "Day off."

Fair Morn shoved the large baking pan across the table at her. "Eggs with green chilies."

"Thanks."

Then they were done and beginning to talk about things that needed doing today.

Smoke leaned across the table and said to Braidna, "Kardor e'ent ti dier quar en'en'ita."

Braidna gasped. Her coffee mug bounced off the table top, splashing coffee in all directions. "What?" She stared at Smoke. "What . . . did . . . you . . . say?"

"Kardor e'ent ti dier quar en'en'ita."

"Oh my," gasped Messenger, staring at Braidna as she sagged in her chair, eyes jerking wildly. "You don't look so good, really really."

"That," gasped Braidna, "is what that voice that I heard

said." Lurching upright, she glared at Smoke and demanded, "Was that you?"

"No. It was you that said that is his dream." Smoke's eyes seemed to swell larger and larger. "What do you hide?"

Braidna's hand slammed flat on the table top. "STOP IT!" She started to rise and found that something was keeping her pinned in her chair.

"Stop that," snapped Tinker.

Szart nodded.

Braidna felt it go away.

Smoke looked at him. "We have to know."

"Indeed, My Lord." Chicken stared at Braidna. "Master Chen did feel something."

"Kardor e'ent ti dier quar en'en'ita," softly stated Smoke, her minds pushing at Braidna.

"An edo d'ant ta pn'ita," mumbled Braidna, eyes rolling up as she sagged in her chair.

Sha'gar grabbed her before she could topple to the floor.

"Now what's going on?" He looked at Smoke.

She shrugged.

Space. 22.29.10.44, In Ship's Notation.

She stood next to him, a silver woman, and watched as he carefully inspected the object.

The thing lay on a work bench, all midnight blue shaft, pulsating soft internal light.

MechBots had scurried away, back into their slots, all data neatly packed away in Ship's brain.

He held one end of the shaft close to his face. And nodded. To himself. To her.

"Certainly looks like something attaches there." Which

is exactly what the MechBots had reported.

"It is part of something," stated Gyre.

"What?"

"No data."

He checked the other end of the shaft.

"Ship," added Gyre, "has no record of any artifact like it. From anywhere."

He set the thing back on the bench top and looked over at the wall. She had a map placed there, glowing soft tones. A red dot, representing Ship, indicated their position relative to their destination.

"A long way."

"6.2835 days," she replied.

"Looks fairly empty."

"A great hole containing few stars."

He nodded.

"The Ard ship data bank indicated that its destination was there. Ship brain agreed that Chimera Icide is in there. It is a primitive place."

"Like John's?"

"No. Worse."

He slipped one arm around her waist. "Let's go to deck 4A."

"Doughnuts will be ready by the time we arrive."

A door hissed open in a nearby wall.

Zar. Grey and Green.

It stepped from the ruins of the structure and headed for a secret place through which it could flee this place. It had been tossed on the floor of a tall tower exposed to the sky by the winged terrors that had grabbed it on Par Tak. After beating and mauling it, the things had flown away. Shortly thereafter, after it had recovered enough energy and strength to heave itself to its feet, it had peered over the edge of the low wall. And it had seen them.

A wave of them. Then another wave followed by yet another wave, running swift and silent, eyes glowing red bright, dragging down everything they met.

Still as the stone that it leaned against it carefully peered out and down and watched the unending slaughter, some groups flowing into the structure and then out again. Finally they were gone leaving behind great stains and silence. And bits and pieces, uneaten bits and pieces. Every now and then, a wounded member staggered back from the direction they had run.

Finally, it realized that nothing lived anywhere near the tower, so it ever so carefully eased itself over the edge of the low wall, and crept down the outside of the wall, finding small places for fingers and toes. It was very adept at this. There was no other way to get down.

On the ground, after carefully scanning the area, it had staggered away. It had to find the place that it sought. A place to escape through.

Dol Spar. An Office in Monetary Control.
"So, vat do we know?"
It was a rhetorical question.
Asked by Mirf.
So, she answered it.
"Bubkes, that's vat!" She looked at her assistants and her clerks. "Soooo, kinderleh, give a suggestion, do me a help. How do we find out what these messugeners are up to?"

Gesturing violently at the badly mangled folders and papers on her desk, she hissed, "These sneaky-butt Wizards of Trefil are giving me such a heartburn that I could dissolve horseshoes." Then she explained to her puzzled assistants and clerks what horseshoes were.

Suddenly her eyes squinted into narrow glittering slits as she stared at something only she could see. Quan looked at Fred who indicated to him that this was not a good sign. Quan leaped to his feet and hurried off to the armory beckoning the two clerks to come along.

"HO HA!" Mirf stared around the suddenly empty room, mostly empty room. "Such a thought that was!" She leaned forward and peered at Fred. "So, glitter-eyes, where's the rest of my help?"

"Chirp."

"Vunderbar ! Better not take too long."

It didn't.

Quan hurried back into the room, handed Fred her three stilettoes, and nodded at Mirf. "Ready." Fred fastened each of her weapons to her left upper arms.

Rema and Nema each walked in wearing a long blade and sheath on their belts.

Mirf headed for the door waving one seemingly disjoined arm wildly. "So don't just stand there smiling, let's hit the road and give a go!"

Bahn Duhr Tohr. The Royal City.

"So it's hard to believe that I am doing this."

Mirf looked up and down the street and headed her group up the slight slope toward the castle looming over the town. And as they strolled along, she explained where they were to her two clerks. Fred and Quan had recognized the place.

Up the grade, around a corner, and through the open gateway they went. Mirf waved regally at the startled gate guards. "I know the way! Stand your post, Soldiers!" And herded everyone through the great doors and up the correct staircase.

Eventually they stopped in front of a rather non-descript door in the middle of a long hall, a number of floors above the main courtyard. Mirf rapped on the door with one knuckle. "Better be home," she grumbled.

"Go away," something snarled from the other side.

"Sounds like the right place to me." She kicked the door. "Open up!"

It did.

The door slowly eased itself open.

And it peered out and down at them.

"Dinner?" gurgled the monster, running a thick tongue over even thicker lips.

"Dinner schminner," snapped Mirf, pushing past the thing into the room. "Nuff messuggener tricks. I came seeking help."

The monster disappeared.

Hanred smiled at her. And smiled even wider at Rema and Nema.

A door banged open and Ripple stalked into the room, stuffing her blouse into her trousers. "What do you want?"

"A drink." Mirf dropped into a chair at the table. "This is Rema and that is Nema, my clerks. You already know Fred and Quan." She winked at Hanred, as she indicated her clerks.

"Pretty nice, huh?"

Ripple sat, frowned at Hanred, who was still eyeing the clerks, and held out her mug. He hastily filled it. And sat. Next to her. "Clerks?"

"Hum hum," said Ripple to Hanred. "Speak!" she demanded of Mirf.

Mirf shrugged. "So, things are normal I see. Still a pain-in-the-buttsky." Mirf emptied her cup, poked it in Hanred's direction, and ignored the ever-darkening look she was getting from Ripple.

Hanred refilled the cup, then Ripple's, then his own, suppressing his smile.

"Mirf," growled Ripple, reaching in a thin green wand that glowed fire at its tips.

"Nice sparkler," observed Mirf. "So I really need some information." And waggled her hand. "And before you should ask let me tell you. Our files are mostly empty." She nodded at Ripple. "And you probably know what I need to know." She shoved her once again empty mug toward Hanred. "I will owe you, Faan witch Ripple."

"Hum," said Ripple, throwing the wand somewhere.

"A deal?" asked Mirf, sitting straighter, watching the witch face staring at her.

"Yeessssssssssssssss."

"Ho Boy!" Mirf's eyes glittered hob-goblin delight. "A deal's a deal!"

Ripple nodded.

Mirf winked at Hanred. And leaned back in her chair. "So tell me, tell us, everything you know about the Wizards of Trefil and The Guarded Lands."

Ripple stared at her. Hanred stared at Ripple. He had never seen her sit so still or stare with that intensity of concentration, unless she was planning some truly devastating action. It was something to be very carefully worried about.

Mirf stared back, at Ripple. "That bad, huh?"

Ripple tapped the table top with one fingertip, the pointed nail rapping. Small puffs of smoke rose from the tiny holes she was making in the wood.

They were suddenly in the highest room in the northwest tower of the castle. The room with no doors. Only a large open, floor to ceiling window. And a large balcony.

"Worse and worse," mumbled Mirf, looking around.

Ripple had relocated them all, including the table and chairs, jugs and mugs. Under the table, her hand squeezed Hanred's thigh.

"The Wizards of Trefil," she began. "Are a mage guild that wishes to be left alone. The Guarded Lands are what they call their elseplace. Few visit. The few who do mostly do not survive. They wish to keep to themselves."

"Well," said Mirf. "Well, well, well."

"Do not bother them."

Mirf propped her head in her hand.

"You will die."

Mirf winked at her.

Ripple glared back and spoke to Hanred, "You speak to her."

"Why?" asked Mirf, "are the Wizards of Trefil stirring into the elseplaces?"

Ripple gasped. Black filled the room.

"Ouch!" Hanred twitched as her fingers dug deeper into

his thigh.

Ripple waved the air clear and released him. "They are doing what?"

So Mirf told her everything that she had learned. And shrugged one shoulder which wobbled in a very broken way. "So it's not much but that's why I came here. So tell me."

Ripple did.

Iztak One Over.

Sphere Kack was a room, a thing, and a person.

The person spoke. "What do you want, wakal?"

He was taller than Cubres and eyed this small creature in the poorly fitting costume with a disdainful expression.

"You may address me as Princess E'Nilt," snapped E'Nilt.

"She has the object," stammered Cubres.

"This?" gasped Kack, taking one step back and then another look at their small visitor.

"It is so." Cubres waved one arm. "This wakal came with the h'wakal that fills the special field. And has the object."

Kack backed further away and dropped heavily onto a tall stool. "Agh flagh!" And mumbled, "This is very hard to believe or to accept." His eyes jumped over to Cubres.

"Black as nothing, larger than all," stated Cubres. "This wakal travels . . . " Her face flushed, her eyes looked at a wall. "Undraped," she gurgled. And covered her face with her hands.

"I do not," growled E'Nilt. "That was an accident." She snatched the Mar Lak from a deep pocket and held it out and toward Kack. "You want this?"

Kack slid from the stool and dropped to his knees. "It is

the Arba Stone, as written, as described, as illustrated." He wobbled from side to side. "It was told, many many, that the Arba Stone would return to us. And all the Uderlan would rejoice."

E'Nilt walked over to him, her head now on the same level as his. "Take it. I was told to give it to you and to take what I found."

She dropped the Mar Lak in front of Kack and turned, her eyes scanning the room, searching for something that she could take. The only object that was obvious was the large globe sitting on a pedestal in the center of the room. She doubted that she could even pick that thing up. There was nothing else, other than the rather ordinary looking furniture.

"Gaaaz that dragon," she growled to herself, as she continued to look around the room, the circular room.

Grey Ghost. Once A Fairly Pleasant Place.

He leaped from the large, circular, raised stone platform, and stomped back and forth along one edge. Things fled in all directions.

"How dare they do that! Those were such wonderfully horrible, heh, things, heh, with wings."

Nothing dared respond. It was a rhetorical question after all.

He jumped back up and sat on the edge of the platform and kicked his legs back and forth, deep in thought. And mumbled, mostly to himself, "Might have been a little deficient in the brain department. Heh. Maybe the wings had something to do with that. Heh. Wellllllll, guess we will just leave those Tark alone. Wouldn't do to have them racing through here, causing problems, eating all my helpers."

He stared blankly into somewhere, pondering what to do next, what to use next. He required something better anyway. Those winged demons had no effect.

"Heh," he said, pondering what to use. Next.

"Heh," he said, smiling broadly.

"Heh."

Abner's Hole.

They stood in the small square of the small village and looked at it.

"Let's try to find the inn, first, Dear." She pointed. He nodded and they headed that way.

"Pleasant appearing place," observed $1.98. "Wonder if she is still alive?"

"I wonder why she flees in such a twisted path." Duff pushed open the door and led him inside.

The innkeeper, a large and round fellow, beamed happily at them as they sat. And at the gold coin that Duff set in the center of the table. "Most welcome here," he boomed. And then suggested the specialty of the house, neglecting to mention that it was the only dish prepared by his establishment. At their agreement, he hurried away and quickly returned, shoving large bowls in front of them along with the proper utensils as well as goblets and a large jug.

"Do see not many travelers in Abner's Hole." He stared, peering at their faces from beneath bushy eyebrows. "Not ever. Almost."

Duff indicated the empty chair and set another gold coin on the table top.

He sat. "Hamptor," he said by way of introduction. "What?"

So, while they ate, Duff explained. And finished. Her story. And her meal. And tapped the coin. "With skin that color."

"Ahhhhhhhh dub," nodded Hamptor. "Danced sideways out. You her not-hurt?"

"Yes," said Duff. "We do not want to cause harm to her. Just talk."

"Ahhh dub."

$1.98 pushed his bowl to one side. "Do you know to where she, ahh, danced sideways?"

"And her name?" added Duff.

"Irla," stated Hamptor. "Ahhhh dub."

$1.98 exhaled, a long soft sigh.

"Never mind, Dear." Duff patted his thigh. And said to Hamptor, "Can you take us to the place, where Irla danced sideways?"

"Ahhhhh dub." Hamptor stood and headed for the door to the outside.

Duff set another gold coin on the table. Then followed Hamptor. Outside. And found him standing in the middle of the street. He pointed down, at the street, at a spot on street.

"Here?" $1. 98 stared at the inn keeper.

"Ahhhh dub." Hamptor pointed again and left them, returning to his inn.

"Check carefully, Dear. Whatever she did, she apparently did it here."

Mumbling softly to himself and something else, $1.98 began to walk around and around and around and around the spot. Now and then a small puff of orange smoke popped into existence and floated away on the slight breeze.

Around and around.

    Puff Puff.

      Puff.

By the time he had finished his inspection of the area, the air was hazy. Duff watched him, holding a wadded piece of blue cloth over her nose and mouth. And tried not to cough.

"Can you take us, Dear?"

He nodded.

    And did.

A Small Island.

The inhabitants fled in every direction.

    Some leaped into the water.

      Some ran down the beach.

    Some ran up the beach.

    Some disappeared.

Into the thick vegetation bordering the white yellow sand beach.

Duff stared at the rapidly disappearing population. "What did you do, Dear?"

"Nothing."

"Where are they?"

$1.98 threw his hood over his head.

"Dear?"

"I do not know," came the muffled reply.

"WHAT?"

He sat down. On the warm, dry white-yellow sand. "I followed whatever her name is, was. This is where she came. But I do not known where we are."

"This is not good, Dear."

"I know."

She sat next to him and held one of his hands. "Don't worry. We will just have to talk with some of the local folk." She nudged him with her elbow. "Even if we have to trap one."

Ten Used.

It was a surprisingly neat room. It was a surprise because the outside of the building was mostly decay and disorder, one step from apparent collapse.

Renmel the Doorta watched this strange pair very carefully. He, Renmel, was a he and had never seen anything like them before, especially Iztar.

Hand'l sat at the table. Iztar stood.

"Ziptik told us," explained Hand'l.

Renmel nodded.

"We seek a person with an ever shifting name." Hand'l waved one hand loosely. "Not to harm, never to harm. We merely wish to find."

Renmel nodded. "What?"

"Here called Arnal and Daral and Mornal."

"A female," stated Renmel.

Hand'l nodded.

Renmel stared at him. "The next several will not speak with fierce appearing seekers."

Hand'l shrugged. Iztar shifted from appendage to appendage.

"The end point is known."

"You are a find." Hand'l set a large sack on the tabletop. "It will be good to skip over many twists and turns."

Renmel nodded. And began to describe exactly how to get there.

Grandeville. Tinker's Place. Late Afternoon.

"I called The Chief and told him that she had the flu."

Chantal dropped into a chair and looked over at one of the couches. Smoke had laid Braidna there. Messenger and Chicken had pulled an Afghan around her and had slipped a pillow under her head. Smoke had insisted that she didn't need medical help. It was something else.

"Guarded deep," stated Smoke. "There is much hidden. I do not think that she even knows what it is."

"How could she not?" Tinker frowned at nothing in particular. They all felt his worry gathering and growing.

Smoke shrugged.

"Cool it," hissed Chantal at him.

"But what is wrong with her?" Messenger blinked back her tears.

Smoke shrugged yet again.

Tinker sighed. "Not good."

Fair Morn returned. From her room. Cradling her cannon in her arms. It looked like a very strange machine gun.

"Now what?" he mumbled.

"Felt the need," she replied, leaning against a wall next to the archway to the dining room.

He reached out. They all felt nervous.

"Me too." Chantal jumped up and hurried into the hall. And returned shortly, strapping the wide leather belt around her waist, pushing the holster into just the correct position for her right-hand cross draw. She tossed the other holster to Smoke.

"Merde," he grumbled as he watched Smoke slip on the shoulder holster holding the very large pistol, both given to her by Master Chen. She winked at him.

And then they were there. The pair of them. Smiling at him, black shark teeth gleaming, eyes pulsating with soft red glow.

"It's them," gasped Chantal. "The Tark babes."

"Ah ha," said Amamaedur.

"Ah ha," echoed Ahamaezur.

The greeting had nothing to do with their names. It was one of the first things that Tinker had said to them when they had met each other in the Tark elseplace and they assumed that it was a special greeting. Their eyes glanced at his hands and noted that he still wore the ring that they had given him. They stepped close to him as he jumped to his feet. They smiled and made low huffing sounds deep in their throats.

"Ummmmm, ladies?" He reached out. They were both where they appeared to be.

The Core Pair looked around the room. So Tinker introduced everyone to everyone. "And that is Braidna. A friend."

They tugged him to one of the couches. And sat, on either side of him. He could feel the heat radiating from them.

"Ummmmm. How come you came for a visit?"

Amamaedur looked past him at Ahamaezur, worked her throat muscles, and cleared her throat. His language was so hard to speak. "Krazkarlar," she coughed. "Were pan atch." Her eyes bored into his. Amamaedur growled.

"Hold it," he snapped. "Ummmmmm, let's try this another way." He looked over at Szart. "Ask Kartz to come, please. She seems to understand their language." Szart nodded. "Soon," she said. She knew that Kartz, the Nagar, another type of witch could do this.

He looked at Fair Morn. "How about you make them a sandwich, a thick roast beef one? Or two?"

She stood. "Right away, One. I'll have some also."

Tinker sighed. Two very warm bodies leaned against him. Just a little.

So they sat.

Amamaedur and Ahamaezur ate the sandwiches, heavy on the roast beef, although they did seem to enjoy the dill pickles as well. And the rest of them decided to have a snack with them, joining Fair Morn.

They were mostiy sitting at the dining room table. Messenger remained in the living room with Braidna.

Then they heard it.

The small sports car pulled into their parking area. And two doors slammed.

Chantal jumped up And went out to greet them, Raj and Kartz. And shortly returned with Kartz. "Raj is checking on Braidna." Raj was a very skilled Doctor who practiced at the hospital in Grandeville. He had married Kartz who had agreed to live in Grandeville.

Kartz pulled over a chair and sat next to Tinker and nodded at everyone around the table.

"Thanks for coming," he said. "We need a translator." He indicated the Core Pair. "Will you do that?"

"Yeel." Kartz began to speak with them

And, after awhile, the air crackling around her, she looked at Tinker.

"What?"

"Bad bad."

"What?"

"Krazkarlar, the winged demons. All gone. Elseplace emptied." She gurgled deep in her throat. "Tark killed everything. Tark sets realigned."

Amamaedur and Ahamaezur eyed the platter. Fair Morn shoved it towards them. They each took another sandwich and more pickles.

"So why did they come here?"

Kartz gently touched the appropriate ring on his finger. "You, The Prime Male. Krazkarlar attacked here. Flying wrong wrong. Called out by The Evil One."

"My Lord!" gasped Chicken, grabbing his forearm.

"Merde," he suggested.

Szart looked at Sha'gar and Sgenn.

"The ward killed them," stated Fair Morn.

"Most true," agreed Chicken, releasing his arm.

"Ummmmm." Tinker looked back at Kartz. "I don't understand. Why kill an entire, ahh, race, when we are protected from them? Seems like an over-reaction to me."

Kartz shook her head. "Winged ones searching for powerful things, disrupting the order. Bad bad." She indicated the Core Pair. "Order restored. Tark say big terror danger you."

Somewhere down deep, things grumbled. The house shuddered.

"Stop that!" he snapped at Sgenn.

Amamaedur and Ahamaezur bounced from their chairs, taking defensive positions, eyes flaring bright red. Four Prime Males leaped through the opening, chain mail glittering, blades flashing

"I'm safe, I'm safe," he growled at them all. "And how did those guys get in here?"

"By George," gasped Raj as he stepped into the dining room from the living room.

"Nowp." Kartz shook her head. "Tark! Prime Males."

Kartz gently touched Tinker's arm. "Witch Master?"

Tinker twitched. "What?"

"Your ward allows them to come in."

Sighing heavily, he slumped in his chair and watched the Prime Males relax and go into the living room. Amamaedur and Ahamaezur had grumbled something at them and then sat back, their eyes watching Tinker carefully. But they ate their sandwiches while they did so.

"Ummmmm," said Tinker. "Do they have any idea what this powerful thing is, ahh, that the winged demons were seeking?"

"Nowp."

He looked at Amamaedur who nodded, and swallowed. Ahamaezur stood, took a small sack from her belt, walked around the table, and stood behind him. Bending over, she nuzzled his neck, taking careful small nips with her razor sharp teeth, gurgling deep in her throat.

Then she set the sack on the table in front of him and returned to her seat, grumbling deep in her throat to Amamaedur who grinned broadly, black teeth glittering in the room light.

Tinker carefully emptied the sack on the table top. A round object rolled out, glowing soft blue. He carefully touched it with one fingertip and picked it up. "What is it?"

After some discussion, the Core Pair stopped.

Kartz said, "They do not know. But it was heavily guarded. They feel that it is very important." She stared at his arm. Soft blue was slowly covering it, crawling up toward his elbow.

He dropped the sphere onto the table top. The cloud instantly disappeared.

Kartz grabbed his arm and carefully inspected it. "Fine fine."

"Certainly wish we knew what was going on, this time?" He looked around the table.

Blank faces looked back.

"Ahem," said Raj, laying both hands on Kartz' shoulders.

"Yes?" asked Tinker.

"That young woman is quite all right. Far as I can tell, it is just a very deep sleep. Call me if she doesn't wake in, let's say, ummm, twelve to fourteen hours." Raj cleared his throat. "Ahem. Any idea what caused that?"

"Not really."

"Quite strange, you know."

Tinker looked at Smoke.

It does seem like a deep sleep. But her mind is completely closed off.

"Rather strange tattoo, ahem, as tatoos go, ahh, that is." Raj fiddled with his tie. "Something that the folk in this area do, I suppose?"

Tinker looked at him. "Tattoo?"

"Oh." Raj flushed. "Sorry. Don't say anything to, ahhh, Braidna, will you. Rather private, I suppose."

Tell you later, said Smoke. She winked at him. *Unless you want to do your own inspection.*

Don't start, he growled, hoping against hope that this conversation was over.

So, Now What?

Medi Rope Stud.

It banged in and out.

Nar Danda.

It banged in and out.

Abner's Hole.

It banged in and out.

Ten Used.

It banged in and stopped. It was following the one it sought but the path was very crooked and bent.

It had to think.

And rest.

And worry.

It had crossed over several other paths too frequently for coincidence. Others were after the one that it sought. It quivered and shook, fighting the urge to change. It had to wait for the correct moment.

Bahn Duhr Tohr. The Royal City.

"OI, GAVALT!"

Mirf crashed back in her chair, emptied her mug and held it out in the general direction of Hanred who hastily refilled it. "A mess," sighed Mirf. "A big mess. A large mess. A gigantic mess. A super colossal mess." Her eyes glittered wildly. "Why me?"

Ripple snapped protection over Hanred. She recognized a crazed hob-goblin look when she saw one. Especially from her earlier association with Mirf when Mirf had been one, both as a hob-goblin and as a rather crazed individual.

Sitting straighter, Mirf looked at Ripple. "Any idea of which way to look? Can't have those meshugge magicians altering the universes."

Ripple stared at her.

"So?" demanded Mirf.

"I do," stated Ripple, in that firm no nonsense tone of voice that told all that this witch meant what she was saying.

"Tell me."

"No."

"Vat?"

"I will take you." Hanred jerked. Ripple patted his thigh.

Mirf's eyes squinted into the thinnest of slits, small wrinkles forming at the corners of her eyes. "You are going with me? With us?"

"Yessssssssss."

"And you, Ripple the Witch, the Bad Nasty from a long line of bad nasty Faan, are going to protect me, ahhhhh, all of us?"

"Yessssssss."

Mirf sprang to her feet, arms flying wide, laughing loudly. "Vunderbar! I though we were all dead ducks already. I owe you. M.C. owes you. The universes owe you." She shrugged one shoulder. "So OK., maybe that is a little overblown, but not by much. So I'll get you whatever you want. Within limits." Dropping back into her chair, she grabbed the jug. "When do we leave?"

A Small Island.

They strolled down the beach, walking near the water, where the sand was hard packed, enjoying the warm and sunny but not too hot climate. And around a sharp curve, around a small hillock, to stop and to stare.

The cluster of buildings, scattered along that edge of the dense growth edging the wide beach, were constructed from local vegetation and tended to blend in, color by color. The inhabitants that had run this way had obviously told everyone about their visitors as the population stood, some in a small cluster in front of the buildings, some in doorways, all looking in one direction. At their visitors.

"Calm, Dear." Duff released his hand. "They appear more curious than agitated."

"None of them resemble the one we are trying to find."

"Most true, Dear." Duff headed them toward the largest cluster, the one that had opened and discharged a very elderly woman. She stood, waiting, with one hand resting on a young woman's shoulder, and watched this strange pair approach.

"Greetings," said Duff when they were close enough for normal conversation. "We mean you no harm."

"Not a child," stated the old woman. "A small woman." The others nodded, eyes darting to still others.

"May we talk with you?"

The old woman slowly settled to the sand, the rest doing the same thing, forming a wide crescent facing Duff and $1.98. Duff tugged him to a seating position.

"We seek a person that we think came here," she explained.

"She is not here," replied the old woman.

"You know who we mean?"

The old woman smiled. "She caused some excitement when she arrived the same way as you did. People thought that she was a god. At first. Same as you." Her eyes darted here and there. "Short memories."

Duff felt $1.98 jerk. "Short?"

The old woman nodded and looked at Duff. "Long ago. When I was a young woman, and as beautiful as you, a woman with golden skin appeared, very frightened. I knew that she was not a god. Gods do not frighten." The old woman nodded and stared at Duff and $1.98. "You are not frightened. Perhaps you are gods?"

"No. Travelers."

"She lived with my family as one of my several sisters."

"Is she here?"

The old woman smiled broadly. "She married a sailor and went away."

$1.98 sighed. "Where?"

The old woman shrugged. "Sailors go everywhere."

It hit the soft sand, stumbled forward, and stopped, swaying slightly. And grunted to itself.

It had bumped into one of the paths that it had been criss-crossing during its search. The beings responsible were not far ahead. Quickly scanning the immediate area, it hurried up slope and faded into the thick vegetation bordering the wide beach. And headed in the same direction as these others, hoping that what it sought was not far ahead. It could feel the pull.

Iztak One Over.

E'Nilt stomped from the town and across the open field and kicked M'Ban on the snout.

The dragon had been sleeping. One gigantic eye popped open and peered at the glowering Hephira.

E'Nilt waggled her hand in front of that eye. "Is this what you wanted? They had it hidden inside a box inside the wall."

"Yesssssssssssssssssssss," hissed the dragon. "You are very clever and resourceful." She lifted her head from the ground and stood. "Hang on to it."

"Take me to an elseplace," demanded E'Nilt, "where I can obtain appropriate clothes!"

"I know just the elseplace." The great dragon gently enclosed the tiny woman inside the claws of one forefoot, lifted into the sky, wings beating lazily. "Griz, griz, griz."

"Peculiar sense of humor," grumbled the Hephira, looking at the multi-pointed star she held and the blue mist that enveloped it and her hand, wondering what this thing was good for.

Grandeville. Tinker's Place.

Gentle as fog they faded in, a soft black mist.

It was a new spell, found by Ripple in one of Hanred's ancient tomes. This particular volume had hardly ever been opened. It had been used to stabilize one leg of the storage table most of the time.

The Core Pair leaped to their feet, barking commands to

the Prime Males.

"YOWP!" Mirf jumped backwards as Quan and Fred lunged in front of her, weapons flashing into their hands.

The air crackled around Ripple as she banged protection over Hanred, a blazing green wand snapping into her hand. "DEMONS!"

"Merde," grumbled Tinker as he looked out from the rear deck where they had all been sitting and relaxing. "STOP!" he bellowed into the confusion. "EVERYONE!"

He stood and gently reached out, his arms bumping into the Core Pair. They were not where they appeared to me. They eased closer to him, their images stepping away.

"Those are friends," he explained. And called introductions. And sat back down.

When all had come up onto the deck, he looked at them. "Why are you here? Ripple, sit somewhere."

Mirf stepped around Fred and Quan and leaned forward, peering at Tinker. "Ho boy! Now you are collecting exotica. A matched pair. My, my, my, my, my, my, my." Then she dragged over a chair. "How about a cup of coffee?"

He stood and led them all inside, to the living room, and glared at Mirf. "Why are you here?"

Mirf shrugged. "Beat's me. Ripple dragged us here."

Everyone chose their choice of chair or couch. Ripple called over a chair over and waited for Hanred to sit in it. Then she made herself comfortable in his lap, and looked at Tinker. "She," a brief nod in Mirf's direction, "told us that The Wizards of Trefil from The Guarded Lands are astir."

Amamaedur barked short commands and two of the Prime Males leaped up and disappeared.

Tinker could feel the sudden rise in the Tark's body temperature.

I don't like this.

Steady on, My Lord.

Cool it, Cowboy.

"And," continued Ripple, deliberately ignoring everything, "I felt that you were somehow involved."

Sha'gar's eyes jumped from Sgenn's to Szart's. They nodded.

"Hold it!" snapped Tinker.

Szart frowned at him.

Sha'gar looked unhappy in his direction.

Sgenn just looked.

Smoke stood and headed back toward the rear deck. "Back in a minute."

And ran into a small figure who had just stomped angrily into the living room. "Paaz namble that dragon and all her eggs! OOOOOOOF!"

Tinker looked over and wasn't sure at who to glare at first. "What are you doing here?" He looked over at Ripple.

"Not me!" she snapped. "Who is that foul-mouthed child?"

Smoke slipped into the hall as Chicken leaped up and hurried over. "Princess E'Nilt, how come you here?"

E'Nilt glared past her. "Watch your mouth, witch!" And looked up at Chicken. "M'Ban brought me, Royal Queen." And smiled at Tinker. "Hail, Mighty King." She looked around the room. "As strange a court as has ever been seen."

Szart stepped over to Ripple and Hanred and said, ever so low. "Do not, Mother." She had recognized the look in

Ripple's eyes. It was the calculating look a witch got when she was trying to decide which ever so nasty spell to release. Ripple was eyeing E'Nilt.

E'Nilt walked over and stood in front of Tinker. "What power allows the keeping of two demon pets?"

Amamaedur looked past him at Ahamaezur who licked her lips. He could feel their muscles tensing.

"They are not pets, they are friends." He quickly slipped his arms around their waists and looked from one to the other. "Princess E'Nilt is a friend also." And felt them begin to relax.

A Prime Male bounced in from somewhere. And gurgled growled at the Core Pair.

Tinker felt them relax even more.

Better come out and take a look, MindMate.

What?

Come look.

Sighing heavily, he slid his arms free, and headed for the rear deck, down the hall, wondering why E'Nilt was wearing such a strange costume.

Outside, he stepped up beside Smoke and stared, "Now what's going on?"

They were swarming toward the house, flowing in two directions, weapons glittering.

He pointed. "Is that what I think that it is?"

"Oi gavalt," whispered Mirf, slipping up to his free side. "Hundreds of them."

Smoke pointed past the hordes. "That is M'Ban."

Je'leel joined them. "E'Nilt Princess told me. I asked Mother Szart to send a call to Eulin."

Tinker sat, heavily he sat, on one of the wooden

benches. "If anyone sees them, we will have every branch of the armed forces hard-charging up here. And how do we explain a gigantic new hill?" He looked at Smoke."Where's E'Nilt?"

"Upstairs."

"Huh?"

"Szart is getting her some better clothes."

"Any idea why she is here? Or the dragon?"

"Nope."

Kartz hurried from the house, joined them, and pointed at the demons. "The Core Pair had them come. They said that the Wizards of Trefil are ugly bad martark'na."

"And that?" He pointed at the great black hill covering a good portion of their first pasture.

"Nowp. They have no eberlan . . . ah, business with dragons." She nudged him. "Dragons are not good to eat."

The air shimmered and she swirled in with a puff of violet. And kissed him. "First Greetings Vander Lord Father. Szart said to hurry come." She slipped to his side as Smoke made room. "What are you doing with all those demons?"

He sighed. "I am not doing anything with them. It is an infestation."

"Oh." Eulin kissed his cheek again. "Shall I get rid of them for you?"

Amamaedur and Ahamaezur bounced out of the house, making deep throated huffing sounds.

Eulin spun and stepped between them and her father. "HALT!"

Tinker grabbed his daughter by the shoulders. "They are friends." He smiled at the Core Pair past his daughter's shoulder. "This is my daughter, Eulin."

Amamaedur and Ahamaezur stepped close, leaned in and nuzzled either side of Eulin's neck. And stepped back.

"Father?"

"What?"

"Two? Female demons?"

"It is a long story," he mumbled.

Eulin laughed. "They are lovely." And turned and whispered to him, "In an athletic sort of a way."

"Never mind."

"Most Vander, Lord."

"How about," he suggested, "going out there and asking M'Ban what she is doing here and how she got here?"

"Father, dragons can go anywhere that they wish to go. But I will ask her why?" Eulin spun away, jumped down to the path, and hurried out into the first pasture, slipping seemingly unconcerned through the ever-shifting demon ranks.

He looked at the Core Pair and waved one hand at the great arc of Tark. "What are they doing here?"

Amamaedur grunted something.

"Guarding you," explained Kartz. "From those wizards."

"We don't know any wizards. Nor have we ever met any."

"Faan witch Ripple said that they were a threat!"

He frowned at the Core Pair. "Send them home. Please?"

A Small Island.

It peered out at the large numbers of beings sitting on the warm sand. All but two were facing one way. Carefully reaching out toward the strange pair, it checked them, it inspected them, and it knew. They were also searching. It sat. And watched. And thought about this.

Space. 01.10.45.36. In Ship's Notation.

He took another doughnut from the basket, admired the chocolate frosting, and took a bite. And glanced over at the wall, at the image on the wall. It was a small planet, one of two, circling a moderately-sized sun.

"Sensor's report a culture of low-level technology." Gyre dabbed away a bit of chocolate on his chin.

"That is Chimera Icide?"

"Yes. Ship portal jumped."

He slipped his thick arm around her waist. "Was there a reason to hurry?" And finished the doughnut. "Some threat?" He smiled at that thought.

Gyre handed him the last doughnut. "No threat."

Macabre delicately tasted the green and red swirled frosting. "Ummmmmmm, too bad."

"I thought unknown artifacts are best delivered as fast as possible."

He nodded. "Probably correct in that." And stood. "Let us go and deliver it."

She stood as he did. "Carefully."

"HO! Ho, ho, ho, ho, ho. Better than that. Ready that small cannon." He smiled, a great wide smile, of no humor at all.

Grandeville. Tinker's Place.

Tinker smiled and hugged them, in turn. "Thanks." He turned back to look out over and across their flower gardens and first pasture, now empty of the demon set. And at his daughter hurrying toward them. The great black hill sitting in the first pasture shifted a little and was still.

Eulin walked up and onto the rear deck, frowning. "Father, what are you doing? This time?"

"Huh? Nothing. Staying home. Being overrun with visitors. That's it." He frowned back at her. "Why?"

"Certainly your daughter," laughed Chantal, walking from the side door. "Ugly frown, a matched pair." Two frowns turned in her direction. So she kissed them, Eulin and Tinker. "And you relax, John."

He nodded, sucked in a deep breath, and did. "What?" he asked Eulin.

She nodded toward the black hill. "She says that you are in danger."

"What?"

"And that she brought the Princess E'Nilt here."

Tinker sat on one of the wooden benches. "There has to be more story to it than that."

Eulin nodded and sat next to him. And explained.

"Pretty strange," mumbled Chantal.

"Once in every great while," added Eulin. "Dragons can be very sly."

"That one is draakl meat," snarled E'Nilt as she stomped from the house and over to them, wearing clothes that almost fit. Je'leel followed, walking out much more casually, closing the side door. She smiled at her half-sister Eulin.

Eulin looked at E'Nilt. "The Wizards of Trefil are coming here. M'Ban said that you may thank them after they arrive."

"What?" gasped E'Nilt.

"Gonna get their butts shot off if they try anything," grumbled Chantal, glaring over at Smoke, who nodded, one very slight nod.

"Merde," mumbled Tinker, wondering whether their house and home would survive. "How does M'Ban know that?"

"Dragon sense," replied Eulin. She smiled at him. "The object that E'Nilt, Princess E'Nilt, brought is a special gift of special power. They will be very grateful for that gift."

"Well," he sighed, "does M'Ban know why those wizards are coming here? And how they are planning on slipping past the ward?"

"She laughed."

"Laughed?"

Eulin nodded and slipped an arm under his. "Dragons have a strange sense of humor."

Ripple joined them. "They seek something lost."

He glanced sideways at her. "Here?"

"Yessssssssssssss."

He stood, looked at the ever gathering group out here on the rear deck, and laughed. "Well, those wizards are going to be a very disappointed bunch because we do not have anything that could be their's other than those strange blue things. And they just arrived."

"Hum hum." Ripple looked down at E'Nilt.

"Pag taffle!" The Hephira, crossed her arms over her chest. "I shall talk with them when they arrive. You are safe."

Ripple smiled at her. Hanred, just joining the group, hastily stepped to the witch's side. "Let us go visit that dragon,

Dark Love. It is a rare opportunity." Smiling witches were one step from doing something vile.

"Hum." Ripple allowed herself to be led away, grumbling softly about short folk.

Watching the pair walk out through the flower beds, Tinker crooked a finger at E'Nilt. "Look, shorty, let's have no more Royal smart mouth for awhile. I really getting tired of it."

E'Nilt jammed her fists on her hips, foot starting to tap. "Great King!"

"Damn right," snarled Chantal. "And don't you forget it!"

They carefully edged up to the enormous head, the air crackling around Ripple as she cast every protection she knew over herself and her mate for life. One gigantic eye popped open and stared at them.

"A witch," mumbled the great dragon. "At least you smell like one, all dusky magic."

Ripple cleared her throat. "I am Faan witch Ripple and this is mine, Hanred."

"The one called Old Hanred?"

Hanred bowed. "The very same" He smiled. "I did not realize that dragons paid attention to matters as trivial as that."

"Griz, griz, griz," she laughed. "I was told all about you by a small grey who enjoyed such matters."

Then, while Hanred and the great black talked, Ripple relaxed, as much as a witch ever relaxed. And as she did, she marveled, once again, at her mate's ability to interact in such a casual manner with whatever it might be. So, she watched and waited and then, at the appropriate time, asked, "Why did you bring that short, unpleasant person here?"

"She wished to visit The Wizards of Trefil and thank them, for all they did for her."

"When?"

"Many ages ago during The Great Battle at Carcan when the Ch'Karakzen were eliminated."

Ripple looked at Hanred who was staring at the dragon. "Husband?"

His eyes jumped to her's. "She means that the Princess E'Nilt is the same one as told in the tales."

Ripple stepped closer to the dragon. "Explain."

So M'Ban did.

Late Night.

The great beast drifted shadow soft down the hall and into his room, her back brushing against the top of the door jamb.

Wake up, MindMate.

Messenger's eyes popped open. She stared. And screamed, "MOM!"

In a single, violent thrashing heave, he rolled from the bed and onto his feet. "What?"

"What's happened?" asked Messenger.

Sliding sideways on bare feet, he banged on the room lights. "Now what's going on?" And stared at her

I don't know, MindMate. But Braidna is gone.

Messenger's shout had waken them all, the rest of himself. He could feel them hurrying toward his room.

Chicken burst in first, long knife clenched in her right hand. "ODDS BLOOD! What be this?"

Fair Morn jumped in followed by Chantal.

"Smoke!" gasped Chantal.

Fair Morn stared at the great beast. "How did you get into that shape?"

Is that a pun?

Szart ran in, banged into Fair Morn, and whipped out a long red wand.

Sha'gar raced in, grabbed her now sister's hand. "Stop! That is Smoke."

"Magic'd foul," snarled Szart.

Sgenn stepped quietly into the room. "No. That is her first form." She looked at the gigantic cat-like creature occupying a large portion of the bedroom. "How did you do that?"

I didn't. I woke when Braidna disappeared and was this way.

"Hum." Szart turned and ran into the hall. Sha'gar hurried after her.

"Certainly big." He reached down, grabbed his pajama top and yanked it on.

Smoke lowered her head and licked his cheek. *Fully grown.*

Jerking away from that rasping tongue, he batted at her with one hand. "Stop that!" He looked at the rest of them. "Any ideas?"

"Nary a'one, Me'Lord." Chicken ran her hand over the dense, black fur. "Most plush."

Thank you. Smoke sat, folding her long rabbit ears back to keep them from banging into the ceiling. *Whatever took Braidna must have done it. Somehow.*

Szart snarled back into the room. "Kar ptar tak tak."

"Witch coarse," hissed Sgenn.

Sha'gar returned, the air crackling around her, eyes pulsating deep fire. "The Evil One. He left a strong trace."

"Merde," grumbled Tinker, sitting on his bed set flush to the floor. "Sit, sit. Let's decide what we're going to do about it, this time."

They all sat.

And began to talk.

While they talked, something bubbled up from the deep down and followed that trace. No-one saw it or felt it go. Sgenn had been very careful.

Je'leel hurtled into the room. "Daaaaaaad!" Followed by Eulin hastily yanking on her pajama top.

"Sssssssssh, ssssssh. It is alright." He slipped an arm around Je'leel as she thumped down next to him.

Eulin stared at the great black beast. "Mom? That really you?"

So he told her and Je'leel all that they knew and had begun to discuss.

Eulin leaped back to her feet and ran from the room. And out into the pasture. To stop and to stare. The great black dragon wasn't there.

"Go find her," she told a tiny blue-green that had appeared at her call. "I want to know what she is up to." The sparrow-sized dragon squeaked and disappeared. Of all the dragon races, the tiny blue-green were the most adept at finding. Eulin headed back toward the house, wondering what her father and her mothers had gotten tangled into this time.

"But, Our Prince, why would most foul Dram steal Fair Braidna and change our Dark Sister Self so?"

He shrugged. "Who knows. Probably just felt like

making trouble, I suppose."

"More to it than that, John. I doubt that creepo ever just does things unless he has, for him, good reasons." Chantal glowered at the floor.

He sighed. "Let's pack. And get ready."

Eulin walked in. "M'Ban is gone."

"Worse and worse," he grumbled.

"I sent a tiny blue-green to find her."

"And I," said Sgenn, ever so softly, "sent a seeker to find The Evil One." She smiled, that gentle half-smile. "He will die."

Grey Ghost. Once A Fairly Pleasant Place.

"You," she said, "may not harm her."

He looked at her and smiled. "Heh. Who are you to tell me what I may or may not do? I took her, fair and square. I may do whatever I want to do. I felt like having pleasant company. And it is fun to irritate John."

"No. In this instance you may not do that, harm her."

He pointed. Lightening flashed out. And bounced back, high into the sky. "What?"

"You can not harm me."

"You working for that meddling red pest?" He glared at her.

"I work for no one."

"In that case, move your foot. I would admire my prize."

The great claws retracted. He stepped closer and looked down at the sleeping form. "Lovely." And knelt by her side. "Why does she sleep so deep?"

"I do not know."

"Heh. Why do you interfere?"

There was a bright blue-green flash as something popped in and out.

He looked up. "What was that?"

"A tiny one. I do not interfere."

He stood and glared up at her. "You most certainly do. Heh. And why, pray tell, can't I harm you?"

"Wild forces primordial there are, in the universe of universes."

He folded his arms over his chest. "So?"

"There are four of these forces in all the universe of universes."

"Heh." He smiled. "There are only two. Good and evil."

"Griz, griz, griz." She lowered her head a little. "You met Ancient Magic once, I heard."

He recoiled and rubbed one arm. "Ugly stuff."

"It is one of the primordial forces."

He beckoned over a chair and sat. "Heh. So that is three!"

"Three?"

"Ancient Magic, that red meddler, and myself."

"Griz, griz, griz."

"Heh. Explain."

"Ancient Magic isn't all. Just one of the several in that category. And you miscounted."

"So tell me. What is the fourth force? Heh."

"We are."

He carefully scanned the area. It was empty. Not counting the sleeping woman and the immense black dragon.

"We?"

"The dragon race. We are the fourth force." She stared

down her snout at him. "You are the first to know this, Dram, The Evil One." Green fumes leaked from the corners of her mouth. "But this piece of knowledge will help you not. It will give you no aid. Griz, griz, griz."

From deep below something mumbled.

Dram leaped to his feet. "What was that? I am having all together too many unwanted visitors." He glared at the dragon as the noise faded away. He stepped to the edge of the platform and stared at the ground. A patch of green was crumbling into brown. "Those things were locked many layers deep. Beyond below in the deep dark."

"Griz, griz, griz."

Dram glowered up at her. "Very strange sense of humor."

She snorted, squirting dark grey smoke over him and the platform.

He jumped back, gesturing angrily, ordering the cloud away. "So, what about those things?" Stepping back, he pointed at the brown patch on the ground.

M'Ban lowered her head until it was level with his. "There are a rare few who can call those, those things, those things of another Ancient magic that were made, and once made, are forever there. Those dwellers of the deep below will obey totally one of those few who can call them. I would leave them alone, if I were you, Evil One. Griz, griz, griz." Turning her head, she carefully inspected the sleeping body

Grandeville. Tinker's Place.

The tiny blue-green flashed in and perched on her shoulder and chirped softly into her ear, and disappeared. She looked over at the couch where her father sat slumped, trying to ignore the fingers poking at him from either side. Messenger and Chicken had decided that he required distraction.

"Dad. M'Ban is visiting with Dram."

His eyes popped wide. "What?"

"The tiny one saw her there."

"What is she doing there?"

Eulin shrugged.

Sgenn walked into the room, pulled a chair over and sat in front of him. "She guards Braidna. The Evil One took her."

Tinker sighed. His eyes wandered from face to face. "Any ideas about what we should, or can, do?" Mostly blank faces looked back. The Core Pair grunted and gurgled to each other.

Outside, on the front lawn, something popped. Loudly.

"Careful, Dear," cautioned a soft voice.

The front door opened.

They walked in.

"Now what?" he grumbled, staring at them.

"This is strange," stated Duff.

"This is very bad," agreed $1.98.

"This is getting worse and worse," mumbled Tinker.

Suddenly $1.98 grabbed Duff, wrapping her in many layers of protection and snatched a long thin black wand from his left sleeve, the air snapping and crackling wildly around them. He had just seen the Core Pair.

"KNOCK IT OFF!" Tinker surged to his feet and quickly stepped over to where the Core Pair appeared to be. They weren't there. "They are friends of ours," he said to $1.98 and Duff. "Friends!"

"Dear!" snapped Duff, squirming and trying not to

twitch. "Get this goo gark off. It itches. And put that thing back in your sleeve."

$1.98 stuffed the wand up his sleeve and said something. The air settled down. Duff smiled. And Tinker felt body heat radiating from either side of himself. So he slipped an arm around either waist and looked at his new visitors. "What are you doing here?"

Duff smiled and explained. All about their search and how it had led them here.

"Me'Lord," gasped Chicken, lurching to her feet, stepping close. "Think thee that they do a'seek after Fair Braidna?"

"Can't be." He shook his head. "She was born here." And waved one hand. "Can't be. She is not from out there."

"Most strange."

The Cole Pair gurgled deep in their throats.

"House is certainty getting cluttered," he grumbled.

"Who is Braidna?" asked Duff.

Chantal joined them. "A young woman staying with us."

"Does she have a mate?"

"Nope."

"The villagers told us," said $1.98, "that the one we seek married a sailor person and that it was a long time past."

"Braidna is only twenty-eight," stated Chantal. She looked at Tinker. "Those babes certainly radiate heat."

Amamaedur smiled at her, black teeth glittering.

"How about we all sit down," suggested Tinker. "You staying long?" he asked Duff.

"MAR NUG NA!" Duff had just seen Smoke sitting far

to one side, partially blending into the shadows.

"It's Smoke," explained Tinker, spinning, heading back for his place.

Chantal beckoned to Messenger and Fair Morn. "Let's make something to eat before he starts grumbling about that, also."

"Piffle," suggested Tinker.

The Core Pair dropped on either side of him, still watching Duff and $1.98 who had found some space on another of the couches.

"Ahem," said Tinker. "How about everyone who doesn't already know someone introduce themselves. I am losing track."

So, they did.

Off To See The Bad Guy

Grandeville. Tinker's Place.

"Well?"

He looked at his rather crowded living room, slumped deeper into his couch, and sighed. "Who's going and who's staying home, here, or whatever?"

Amamaedur and Ahamaezur leaned close, lips brushing lightly on either side of his neck, shark teeth gently touching, grumbling deep in their throats.

"Careful," he whispered.

"I am," stated Eulin firmly. "Vander Lord. Going with you."

Dat, having woken up from one of her indjinn naps, was now sitting on Chantal's shoulder, her hand buried deep in Chantal's hair, waved her free hand at him. "I wish to come, Great Master."

Je'leel sat straighter and looked at him. "Father?"

"What?"

"I think that is enough people."

He nodded, eyes jumping from face to face. "I think that you are right. Dram is a certifiable nasty. No sense in anyone else sticking their head into whatever he is playing at this time." He pushed himself more upright. "Right! Everyone else stays here."

Chicken jumped up. "We will Ourselves ready, My

Lord."

"Just weapons, Princess. We are not going to be wandering around. Just get in, snatch Braidna, and get home again."

Chicken grinned. "Oh aye, weapons only it do be." She hurried away, trailed by Fair Morn.

Smoke flowed after them. *I will wait on the rear deck.*

Tinker stood. "O.K., let's get dressed and do it!" He headed for his bedroom.

They followed him into his room.

"Ladies, I do not need company, or protection, while I change my clothes." He pointed at the door. "Out."

Gurgling softly, the Core Pair stepped outside. He slammed the door, quickly changed his clothes before they decided to pop back in. Then he looked in the mirror over his dresser, and said to his reflection, "Boy, am I ever gonna be glad when this is over and done with."

As he stepped into the living room, trailed by the Core Pair, he stopped and stared at Eulin. She wore trousers, blouse, and jacket of billowing fogsoft lavender. "Shouldn't you wear something, ummmmm, more sturdy, ahhh, like armor, or something?"

"Father, this is proper Vander wear. I am well protected."

He nodded.

"It is true, Vander Lord."

"O.K."

Chantal walked in. "Let's go, Stud. Looks damn flimsy to me, Daughter."

"Vander weave, Mother."

"Where's Dat?" he asked.

A small arm poked out from between two buttons on Chantal's shirt and waved at him.

Eulin laughed.

They headed for the rear deck.

Grey Ghost. Once A Fairly Pleasant Place.

They swirled in, in a twisting cloud of black that went somewhere.

The slight figure dressed in off-white, near grey, peered at them and waggled one hand in their direction. "So, it is John and his collection come to visit. Heh."

Dram smiled. "Nice fur, Smoke. Certainly large. Heh. How did you do that? Heh?" He laughed and winked at Tinker. "Are you getting, as they say in your elseplace, kinky?"

"Not funny," grumbled Tinker.

"Damn dumb joke," snarled Chantal, glaring at Dram.

He nodded at her. "I remember you." And rubbed the side of his jaw. "You are the one with the bad temper." He pointed. "I suppose you want that sleeping one back? Heh?"

They all looked. Braidna lay along one edge of the platform, sound asleep. M'Ban was lying on the grass, stretching her vast bulk far to one side. She lifted her head and peered at them.

"Right," agreed Tinker. "We came to get her and to get Smoke changed back."

"Well John, you can't blame everything on me this time. Heh. Not everything." He pointed at Smoke. "I didn't do that. I truly prefer her in her human female shape form, not that big monstrosity."

"Merde," suggested Tinker.

Dram shook his head slowly. "Didn't that meddling red fowl tell you anything? There are always limits to magic, even for me. If I had changed her, I could change her back. So, if I did, I could. But I didn't, so I can't. Heh." He shrugged.

"Damnation."

"But it is true. Heh." Dram laughed. "Hard to believe? Heh? But true."

I am not a monstrosity, grumbled Smoke.

Dram jerked upright and stared past Tinker. "What are they doing here?" The Core Pair were staring fixedly at The Evil One.

"Nothing," replied Tinker. "They are just very unhappy about some sort of winged things you were sending here and there. They were worried."

Chantal snorted. "Worried! They ought to have indigestion. They ate them all."

Amamaedur looked at Ahamaezur. They slipped sideways, no longer appearing to be where they were.

Dram leaped to his feet. "You make them behave, John."

"Do what?"

Dram tromped to the edge of the platform and glared down at him and stomped one foot. "Make those things behave."

Tinker folded his arms over his chest. "Just how am I supposed to do that? Far as I can tell, no one pays any attention to anything that I say, most of the time."

"Heh." Dram pointed a rigid, quivering finger at him. "That ring you wear says you can do that, Prime Male of The Tark."

Unfolding his arms, Tinker looked at the ring, "Really?"

"Don't you play clever with me." Dram whirled about and yelled, "And what do you think you are doing?" Eulin had walked over and was talking quietly with M'Ban. She looked up at him.

"Holding a conversation."

The air glowed around Dram. "Do not be insolent with me, young lady!"

"You do not frighten me."

"Heh." Dram stalked over and leaned toward her. "Are you feeble-minded?"

"I am Eulin."

"Heh. Any last words, Eulin?"

"Do you threaten me?"

Dram smiled. "Heh. Of course."

M'Ban stood, green fumes oozing from the corners of her mouth, a gigantic black hill, and peered down at him. "It is not good to threaten her." Smoke and soft puffs of flame punctuated her words.

Dram bent further over and stared at Eulin, nose almost touching nose. "What exactly is going on here?"

She reached up and patted the side of his face with one hand. "I am a Dragon Master." She smiled and winked at him.

Leaping away, Dram spun and fell back into his chair. And crooked a finger at Tinker. "John, what exactly have you been doing since last we, heh, visited? This is very upsetting you know." He waggled one hand at them.

"We came to get Braidna."

"Who?"

Tinker pointed. "Her."

"You can't have her. She is mine. I stole her, fair and

square."

Sgenn slipped up to Tinker's side.

Dram smiled warmly. "She is new. Don't you ever stop, John? Every time we meet you have somehow acquired some new female or other." He leaned back, resting his head against the high back of the chair. "How can you of all people begrudge me just one? Even if all she does is sleep. Still, she is more pleasant company than most of the stuff I have to associate with."

Sgenn walked over to where Braidna lay.

"She has a funny smile, John."

Tinker shrugged.

"Swap?"

"Huh?"

Dram nodded at Sgenn. "I take the grey haired one in exchange."

"No deal."

Dram sat up. "This is really getting tiring. Heh." He pointed at Braidna. A blue ravager faded in. "You may consume her."

It lurched toward the sleeping form, eyes fastened on its victim.

Eulin said something to M'Ban. The dragon reared up and up, lips curling back from gigantic teeth.

Something black reached up.

And grabbed the blue thing by the neck.

And yanked it flat against the stone platform.

The head snapped off.

And rolled over the edge.

Dram jumped up. "Where did that come from?" He

looked around. "Heh. I think that I require another elseplace. This place is becoming infested."

Sgenn hoisted herself onto the platform and stepped between Dram and Braidna. "I called." She smiled a soft half-smile at him. Deep below something grumbled. The platform vibrated.

Dram looked past Sgenn at M'Ban.

"I told you," said the great black as she grabbed Braidna in one great front foot, Eulin in the other, and surged into the sky, wings lazily beating. "Griz, griz, griz."

"My Lord," screamed Chicken.

"They're safe," shouted Chantal, grabbing her revolver, running up to the platform with Chicken.

Dram ignored them, watching Sgenn carefully. "You? Called it?"

"Yes." She slipped closer to him.

"Any closer and you die."

She stepped closer.

Dram jerked.

And disappeared.

"He is gone," said Sgenn.

"Dead?"

"Fled." She jumped to the ground.

Grandeville. Tinker's Place.

They thumped down onto the rear deck.

Where they were greeted by Eulin. "Hello Father, Mothers." She indicated the house. "Braidna is inside, on one of the couches. Aunt Ripple thinks that she can wake her up."

As they walked into the living room from the hallway they saw Ripple lean over and rap Braidna on the forehead with a gleaming silver wand.

Braidna's eyes popped open. "Who are you?"

"Ripple," stated the witch, yanking Braidna's garment open and plunging the wand into the center of her chest. With a loud gasp, Braidna sagged and went totally limp.

Szart pushed past the startled Tinker. "What did you do, Mother?"

"This one is protected strange. Stand back, Daughter." Shoving Szart away, Ripple snatched the wand free and watched the small wound disappear. The color flowed back into Braidna's skin, shifting from pale yellow to soft gold.

Braidna's eyes opened and danced, seeking a familiar face. "John! What is happening? Who is she?" Then she screamed and jerked and stared. "Must be hallucinating."

She sees me as I was, not as I am, Smoke told the rest of herself. *And as I am. Now. At the same time.*

Ripple leaned over and poked. With one finger. "Strange design. Strange place."

Braidna yanked her garment closed. "Stop that!" And heaved herself up and around.

"Who are all these people?" She indicated the Core Pair. "And why are they made up that way?"

Sighing heavily, Tinker dropped into a couch. "House guests." He looked around the room. "Who are probably getting ready to go home. Right?"

Ripple sat in a chair. Already occupied. By Hanred. Who made sure that his lap was ready. "Wrong," she stated as witch firm as a witch could ever be.

"Ho boy, Sleeping Beauty is awake." Mirf stood there, large sandwich held in one hand, having just come from the kitchen. She held a bottle in the other hand. "Nice skin color." And dropped into the couch next to Amamaedur who sat on the other side of her with Ahamaezur. She nodded at Braidna. "So, bubeleh, what kind of kiss did that?" She took a large bite from her sandwich and mumbled to Amamaedur, "You want some, go make your own."

Amamaedur snorted.

"Braidna," said Tinker. "This is Mirf, Special Investigator, Monetary Control." Then he introduced all the others, leaving out who or what they were. He figured names were more than good enough. For now. He explained. Just a little.

"For how many days?" she asked.

"Just a couple."

Braidna lurched further upright. "I need a shower." She stood and headed down the hallway.

Ripple watched her go and then looked over at Tinker. "Chosen one, she wears the mark of The Im'a'Zhan."

"The what?"

"HER?" E'Nilt bounced to her feet and stared at Ripple.

"It means," continued Ripple, ignoring the interruption, and E'Nilt. "The Enchanter."

"Ho boy," gurgled Mirf, licking her fingers and leering at Tinker. "You can certainly pick them. That is really a unique talent you have there, believe me. Such a talent like I never heard of before."

Szart yanked in a green wand as Sha'gar pulled in a blue. Then both dumped protection over Tinker.

He looked from them to Ripple. "What's going on?"

"Nothing. They just worry about you."

He sighed. "Enchanter? What sort of thing is that. So far we have only met witches and magicians."

"Not a enchanter," snapped Ripple. "The Enchanter. There is only one. At a time."

He glared at her.

She blinked.

"Mother," hissed Szart, watching the dark gather around Ripple, who like all witches, didn't like having looks like that directed at them. "Explain to him!" The air crackled around her.

"Calm, daughter, calm." Ripple nodded, knowing that any member of her Faan witch clan would automatically protect their mates for life, indicated the hallway with her chin. "That person is The Enchanter. I saw the mark, the special engrat etched into her skin. It takes special powers to do that, a mother to daughter transfer."

E'Nilt stalked over to stand in front of Tinker and stared into his eyes. "What is she doing here?"

Duff clenched $1.98 arms. His hand had been sliding up his left sleeve. "Steady, Dear."

"Living here," replied Tinker. "For awhile."

"Did she mate with you?" demanded E'Nilt.

"What?" He jerked.

Chantal jumped to her feet. "Cool it, shorty!"

E'Nilt whirled around. "I am The Princess E'Nilt!"

"You are gonna be the punched in the mouth in a minute Princess E'Nilt, if you don't watch your mouth and that Princess demanding attitude!" growled Chantal. She waved her arms wildly. "Everyone out of this room except us and Ripple. NOW!"

"Ho boy." Mirf stood and headed for the kitchen beckoning her assistants and clerks to come along. "Time to find a safer room."

Duff and $1.98 followed them.

E'Nilt stomped into the hallway, glaring at Chantal as she slipped past her.

The Core Pair walked on careful silent feet toward the kitchen. They smelled the ham being sliced by Mirf.

"O.K." Chantal dropped onto the couch next to Tinker and looked at Ripple. "Tell us all about this Enchanter babe."

So Ripple did.

The Enchanter was the first daughter of The First High. The power-talent passed from mother, The Enchanter, to daughter, sometimes skipping over a generation. Enchanters had skills similar to magicians and witches with other arcana added in.

Ripple paused and looked across the room at Smoke. "They, unlike most witches or magicians, can shape change others at will."

Chicken gasped. "My Lord! Fair Braidna do alter Smoke?"

"Beats me."

"She could," added Ripple.

Chantal snorted and looked at Fair Morn. "Well, golden babe just better put Smoke back the way she was or I am gonna blow her butt away."

"She was asleep," grumbled Tinker.

Braidna walked in wearing one of the large white robes, towel wound around her head. "Why are all the house guests hanging around in the kitchen? They could eat in the dining room." She sat in a chair and tugged her robe closed.

"We are holding a private meeting," stated Ripple.

"Oh." Braidna stood. "I will be in my room."

"Sit down," ordered Chantal. "You are the subject of the meeting."

Tinker nodded. "Please? Sit?"

Slowly she sat, running her fingers across her neck. "It's gone!" She looked at Tinker, face flushing. "I lost her!"

Lady Chen stepped into the room. From somewhere. "No. I was just elsewhere." She bowed to Tinker and then to Braidna.

"Elsewhere?" Braidna looked from her to Tinker.

"Humble apologies." Chen bowed again to Braidna. "But you were safe. So I decided it was no longer necessary."

"I think that I am missing something." Braidna frowned at the floor.

Ripple stood, walked behind the chair and looked over Hanred's head at Braidna, carefully wrapping multi-layers of protection over him. "Yessssssssss."

"Umm," said Tinker. "This is going to be hard to explain cause we don't have a really good idea either."

He told Braidna all that had occurred and all that Ripple had told them.

Braidna stared into the silence of the room. "No." And shook her head. "Not possible. It is just not possible!"

Duff and $1.98 walked back into the room. And took chairs. Then Duff began to explain all that they had done.

"And the trail led us to here," added $1.98. "It was your mother whose trail we were following."

Sgenn stood and slipped around the couch where

Tinker sat, to stand directly behind him, eyes watching Braidna.

"You wear the engrat," stated Ripple. "Mother passed, Mother etched."

Braidna frowned at her. "The what?"

"Tattoo," said Tinker. "On your, ummmm, anatomy."

"And this is supposed to do what?"

"ZAR TIK!" snapped Ripple. "Not supposed to do, dit dat! You are The Enchanter!" The air snarled and growled around her.

Szart leaped up, yanking in a golden wand with a glowing orange tip. "Mother! Be calm!" And stepped carefully over to Ripple. "Please?"

The front door banged open.

And it lurched in.

Quite A Change

"What is that thing?"

Tinker stared, ready to attack it or to run the other way.

The thing's yellow eyes fastened on Braidna, ignoring all else. It spoke. "B'har nam kzar upsta."

Braidna gasped, jerked, and replied. "B'har upnam upsta a'haz." Then she looked at Tinker. "This is hard to believe, really hard to believe. I understand that language. I can speak that language. And . . . and, ah, . . . and." She sighed. "And . . . I seem to be some sort of a princess, according to what it just said." She indicated the creature. "That is a Messenger Daiz. It also protects."

"Damn ugly," grumbled Chantal.

"It has had a hard journey."

The Daiz began speaking, more and more rapidly, until the words seemed to run together into a single stream of sound. Then it stopped.

"Ha'ap ca'ata!" snapped Braidna as she dropped heavily into her chair. Her eyes jumped from face to face and finally fastened on Tinker's.

"Oh, oh?" he mumbled.

"Help. I need your help, John. All of your help."

Chantal stomped over and sat on one arm of Tinker's couch. Chicken settled nearby.

"What kind of help?" It was a very cautious question, a very cautious Tinker question.

"My Grandparents are coming. Ummmmm, that is, my mother's parents." Her face flushed.

"I don't think that I like the looks of that flush," snarled Chantal in a low tone.

Tinker slumped even deeper and frowned. "What?"

"I am supposed to have a consort."

"No dice!" snapped Chantal. "He has got all the babes that he needs."

"Merde," he grumbled.

Braidna leaned toward him. "You don't have to, ummm, do anything." Then she frowned. "The term actually translates into something like fondle pet, more or less." She crashed back into her chair. "My father and Grandfather Chen really have a lot of explaining to do!"

Chicken laughed and leered at him. "Fondle pet, My Lord? Tis most interesting a'term."

"Boozle," he mumbled.

Chantal leaned in his direction. "Babe magnet, you are not fondling or petting any Chinese Princess, regardless of the reason."

Messenger giggled and grinned at Tinker. "She is pretty. And brave. And a nice person. Really really."

"Forget it," he snarled, not liking the drift of Messenger's comments.

"And," stated Messenger, grinning even more broadly, "'you already ripped her gi off."

"Kitten," snapped Chicken, winking at her.

"Well, he did." Messenger ducked her head. "And she

didn't get upset either."

"Out of control," he grumbled.

"Certainly are," agreed Braidna, wondering what was going on inside this rather strange conversation. "And it was just an accident. Just a training accident. And he didn't rip it off either."

"Heh heh heh," stated Fair Morn.

"Quiet!" snapped Tinker.

Very healthy, purred Smoke.

"Goes for you also," he sighed, looking at Smoke. Then at Braidna. "How about putting that whatever . . . messenger thing somewhere?" Tinker straightened up, grumbling at the Core Pair, now returning to the living room holding thick ham sandwiches in their hands "All right, all right, I don't need guards." And then he pinched the occupant of the couch arm.

"Me'Lord?"

"Cause you're there, Princess."

Braidna rose and headed for the hall. "The Daiz will wait in my room." She led the strange creature away. "Pa'arzaa," she commanded.

"Na'at!" it replied.

"Pretty strange, all right," he said to no one in particular.

"Well," said Messenger, "she is nice."

Tinker sighed.

Chantal glared at her. "He's got all the royalty that he needs."

"A Queen here." chanted Fair Morn, "a Queen there! Here a Queen, there a Queen, everywhere a Queen Queen."

"Go outside and run around," he told her, heading for

the kitchen. "You are getting goofy." After filling a cup from one of the coffee pots, he leaned against a counter top, took a cautious sip, and wondered why Chen hadn't said anything about Braidna being some sort of a Princess. So, he walked over, took down the phone, and dialed. He would just ask him.

As they entered her bedroom, the Daiz shuddered and began to change. It folded around her, enveloping her, dragging her into its embrace.

Her skin tingled as the thing slid caressing napods over her. "Let me goooooo . . ."

It did. Dropping the limp body puddle soft sprawling onto the floor. The Daiz wobbled, faded, and was gone. Its job was finally done.

The body twitched. Jerked. And slowly straightened out its limbs.

Then strange green eyes peered down into dark brown eyes just wobbling open. Lady Chen gently lifted Braidna from the floor and laid her on the bed. Tugging a blanket over the mostly limp body, Chen nodded, and smiled at her. "Rest, Lady Princess. The thing has given you your heritage. My Mighty Master will be surprised." Chen stroked the jet black hair back from Braidna's forehead and slipped from the room, gently closing the door behind herself.

Slowly Braidna pulled her arm free so she could hold one hand in front of her face. . It looked the same as it always had. Then she looked up at the ceiling and wondered what had happened to her clothes and to herself. And fell asleep.

Szart looked at Sgenn and Sha'gar and hissed. "That

was a magic pulse. Very strong strange magic pulsing inside our house."

Sgenn shrugged. She had already put a watcher in Braidna's room. Her eyes glanced over at Smoke, who sat relaxed and calm.

No threat, said Smoke, *from Braidna.*

Sgenn nodded and poked Szart in the ribs. "Don't be so witch."

"Tar tar," suggested Szart.

Tinker glanced in her direction.

"Nothing," snapped Szart.

Tinker nudged the arm dwellers of the couch he sat on. "Let's go sit on the rear deck." He stood and headed that way, trailed by Chicken and Chantal.

On the rear deck, he dropped onto one of the benches and leaned back against the deck railing. "Now what's going on?"

Chicken sat next to him and patted his thigh. "Nary a'fair idea do We have, My Lord."

Chantal dropped on his other side. "Beat's me, G.I." And nudged him with her shoulder. "But!"

"What?"

"No more additions. Even if she is nice, beautiful, a real babe, or whatever. Right?"

"Uh huh." He wondered why Master Chen was so closed on the subject of Braidna.

"Good."

"Fair Prince, surely Fair Braidna implied that not?"

"Don't give a damn," grumbled Chantal, "whether she did or didn't."

"It seems," suggested he, "that we are getting a wee bit prematurely agitated."

Chantal grunted. "Right. And exactly how many of us were acquired that way?"

"Acquired? What way?"

She nodded. "Right . . . acquired . . . little indirect statements, like consort."

"Oh."

"Uh huh."

He sighed. "You are over-reacting."

"Harem jealousy. Bad enough as it is."

Chicken waggled one hand. "Naught but mere Princess."

"Merde," he mumbled. "So what?"

"We do be Queen as do be Most Royal Lurin. Thus and thus, thee hast nay need for mere lessor ranks, Our Lord."

"Erg."

"Tis true," she added, nodding at him.

"Sure."

Chantal twisted around and thumped him on the shoulder. "Don't be so damn noncommittal."

"I am not being noncommittal."

"Ha!"

"Just cautious."

Chantal growled.

"And that is why."

"What?"

"Growling, snarling, grumbling, and beating on my body tends to make me cautious."

Then she slipped soft golden silent from the house and

walked over to stand in front of them.

"Humble apologies, Tinker Lord, for all the bother my presence has brought to your noble house." Braidna bowed, straightened up, and smiled at them. "I am who I have always been. It is just that now I know all that I must know. I am really sorry for all the problem my presence has caused. But then, no one had any way of knowing, not even my Father. Mother fled her role in my families affairs. But events have caught up to her daughter. May I join you?"

Tinker nodded. "Sure."

Braidna pointed. The heavy table slid to one side, shoving the other tables as well. A chair skidded over. And she sat, facing him, knees almost touching knees. She laughed. "I am about as surprised as you look. Not long ago I was just a lady cop with the G.P.D. Now what am I? I am what I am?"

"Which is?" he asked.

Braidna looked from face to face. "Well, I seem to be a Princess of some sort or other in a family of magic users of some sort or other. Which is not very precise, I know." She grinned at them. "And not long ago I was having trouble accepting anything like that at all."

Quiet as ghosts, Szart, Sha'gar, and Sgenn slipped from the side door of the house behind her.

"No harm," stated Braidna loudly, without looking at them. She blinked. "John?" she asked gently. "How does one not let this kind of, umm, power get out of hand?"

"By understanding their obligations," stated Chicken. "And remembering your own past."

He smiled. "Don't ask me. Talk to those guys." He indicated the trio standing there, carefully watching Braidna.

"They know all about things like that, not me."

Messenger came from the house and giggled. "She is glowing golden, soft golden bronze." She stepped past the trio and Braidna and sat on the bench next to Chantal. "Really really pretty." And grinned. "How did that happen?"

So Braidna told them.

"I looked up consort in that big dictionary," announced Messenger. "It means united in affection or company or harmony or marriage. And other things." She nudged Chantal. "Soooooo, he could do that." She giggled. "He is pretty good at affection and company."

The loud sigh came from Tinker.

Fair Morn and Smoke joined them. "Certainly is," agreed Fair Morn.

"Just company, John?" asked Braidna. She chewed on her upper lip. "While my grandparents are here?" She nodded at Smoke. Smoke blurred and became what she had been, a pretty woman with thick black hair and bronze skin and great seeming to glow orange gold eyes.

"Ummmmmmmm."

"He'll do it." Chantal slipped an arm over his shoulders.

"Booga," he mumbled.

"Many thanks," said Smoke to Braidna.

"Most Royal a'consort," stated Chicken. "Most proper a'consort."

He nodded. "It seems that I have been, once again, volunteered." He smiled at her. "So, what do I have to do?"

Braidna shrugged.

"What?"

"I really have no idea. Just stand near and look

attentive, I suppose." She leaned back in her chair. "I don't know. All I know is the vague idea that I ought to have one. Have to play it by ear."

"Merde!" He frowned at Chantal and then at Chicken. "We always seem to get into big trouble doing things like that."

Chicken shook her head. "Nay, Fair Prince, for Courtly Consort be most proper and quiet. Mere decoration."

"Humpf."

Messenger giggled and grinned widely at him. "She also said fondle pet. He is good at that tooooo."

"Knock it off," he snarled.

"Ooops," said Messenger.

Braidna's face flushed red gold as Messenger ducked her head and mumbled, "Sorry."

"Nik tik do," snarled Szart.

"Ssssssh," hissed Sha'gar at her. "He will behave."

"I do not worry about him."

Braidna looked at Messenger. "All he has to do is be proper and quiet. I think. Certainly does not have to take that label literally." She tugged the neck of her robe closed, again.

Tinker cleared his throat. "Ahhhhhh, any idea about when your grandparents will arrive?"

"No. Just soon."

"Well, then." He looked around at the group cluttering up the deck. "I suggest that we worry about other things, like various and sundry chores that always need doing."

As they scattered, Braidna stopped Chicken, leaned close, and whispered to her, "May I borrow some clothes? Mine seem to have disappeared."

"Most certainly, Fair Princess." Chicken frowned, just a little. "Most strange, that."

Braidna nodded. "Certainly is."

In the kitchen their visitors began to leave, each in their own fashion, back out into the universe of universes.

As they stepped off the deck and into one of the sections of flower beds, Smoke hooked an arm around Messenger's neck. "Kitten, he does not need another."

"It was just a tease."

"He does not need a tease. Either."

"Well, she is pretty. Really really."

"He does not need a pretty."

Messenger ducked and slipped under Smoke's arm. "She just glows magic. I have never seen anyone do that before."

"Glows?"

Messenger nodded. "Her skin glows. Soft golden."

Smoke blinked. "Her skin tone has changed. That must be why."

"It is a very powerful magic. I don't think that she really knows how powerful." Messenger looked around to make sure that they were alone. "Szart and Sha'gar were really upset."

"And Sgenn?"

Messenger giggled. "She never seems to get upset about anything."

Smoke smiled. "True."

Braidna wandered into Chicken's bedroom and began to slowly browse through Chicken's closet wondering what she should wear. They were about the same size so any of the clothes ought to fit. Finally, without thinking, she began to select. She could feel her grandparents approaching. Soon they would arrive.

Becoming All You Can Be

Grandeville. Tinker's Place.

Their house guests were gone. E'Nilt had given him the gift she was carrying and ordered him, in a very gentle way, to give it to their soon to be visitors. She said that she would visit those Wizards when affairs were more settled. Then M'Ban had lifted up and disappeared, taking the Hephira with her.

They walked into the here from out there. Soft pastel emerald, loose fitting clothes moved gentle sigh as they walked. The soft golden hue of their skin seemed to have an internal luminesce. Gliding up onto the rear deck, they stopped and looked around, totally confident, totally unconcerned.

"We have come for our daughter's daughter," said the man.

"Who keeps her from us?" asked the woman.

"No one does." Tinker rose to his feet. "Braidna is inside. I will tell her that you are here."

"No need. She knows that we are here."

The pair turned toward the side door. It opened and Braidna stepped out. And stood, inspecting the couple. They nodded at her.

"It is good," said the man.

"To find you," finished the woman.

"I am Braidna. This is a friend, John Tinker."

"Ahhhh," said the man.

"Your consort," added the woman.

"No," corrected Braidna. "He is a friend. Not a toy!"

They stared at her.

"A friend?" The woman looked over Tinker very carefully.

"Yep." Tinker waved one hand. "So are the rest."

"Introduce yourselves." Braidna nodded at her Grandparents. "It is proper here to do that."

Frowning at her, he said, "Ragnok."

She smiled. "Bizl." And stepped over and gently touched Braidna's arm. And blinked back a tear. "How like our daughter you are. We have searched for a long time. For a far and a many distance."

Messenger came bustling down the deck from the other end carrying a large tray. "I made iced tea." As she walked past them she said, "Hi."

Ragnok stared, Bizl clenched Braidna's arm tighter. "Not possible."

"Grandmother? What is it?"

Bizl indicated Messenger who was singing softly as she filled the glasses. "Her."

"I don't understand."

"She is a magic weaver. I can feel it."

Ragnok stepped close. "How is that possible?"

"She is unique," said Tinker.

"And a friend," added Braidna.

"She is your friend?" Ragnok looked at Tinker.

"Ummmm, yes." Tinker decided not to try and explain. "Kitten?"

Messenger bubbled over carrying two glasses. She handed them to Bizl and Ragnok. "Sugar and lemon are on the table."

"These are Braidna's Grandparents," said Tinker. "Ragnok and Bizl."

"Hi," beamed Messenger. "I am Messenger." She smiled at them. "Staying for dinner? Smoke is cooking. Steak and potatoes."

Ragnok took a careful sip from his glass. And looked at Braidna.

"Steeped leaves," she said.

He nodded. "Interesting."

"You have control of . . . her?" Bizl indicated Messenger and looked at Tinker.

"Sure." He threw an arm around Messenger's shoulders. *Tell you later, kitten.*

Bizl stepped close and laid a gentle hand on Braidna's shoulder and looked deep into her eyes. "He is your friend consort?"

Braidna relaxed, exhaled, and whispered, "Yes."

"Has he taken you yet?"

Braidna's face flushed.

Tinker jerked.

Messenger gasped.

What? said all the rest in his mind.

Chantal lurched to her feet glaring at Bizl.

"Oh oh," whispered Messenger.

"No," stated Braidna. "He is not a fondle pet. He is a friend."

Bizl smiled. "It is a friendly thing to do."

Ragnok took one step closer. "It is a must!"

"NO!" snapped Braidna.

"Oh, my," gasped Messenger, staring at Braidna. "It is forming a cloud around her."

"What?" Tinker stepped back.

"Her magic," whispered Messenger. "It is just pouring out, all fuzzy cloud."

Bizl stared at Messenger and yanked her hand away from Braidna. Everyone could hear the soft crackling noise.

Sha'gar and Szart cast protection on the rest of themselves. And something black oozed up, large eyes gleaming green fire. It stared down at the grandparents and licked its lips.

Ragnok jerked, staring at it. "Who dares call the down deep? That is an abomination."

Sgenn slipped up beside Tinker, grey robes floating gently around her, grey eyes watching Ragnok. "I did," she stated, all quiet calm. "We are not pleased that you come here and think to tell us how your daughter should use us. It is not nice."

"Please," said Braidna. "You must understand that some of the old ways are not appropriate." She shook her head. "I will not use anyone like that." Her eyes flashed golden fire. "NEVER!" Something not seen pushed Ragnok and Bizl backward, and backward, until their backs bumped into the deck railing. Bright light flared as they fought back.

Sha'gar snatched in a flaming red wand and stepped in front of Tinker, hissing loudly. Red billowed around her.

Messenger reached through it and poked her in the side. "Stop that! Braidna is telling them."

The light blinked out. Ragnok and Bizl stared at them all.

"Who," croaked Ragnok, staring at them, "are you? What are you?" He pointed a quivering finger at Sgenn.

"My friends," stated Braidna firmly.

"How about we all sit down and have a nice quiet talk?" asked Tinker, gently pushing Sha'gar to one side.

Sgenn slid her hands from her deep, baggy sleeves, and smiled a gentle, soft half-smile at the Grandparents. "I am Faan theurgist Sgenn. He does not require additional females." She looked sideways at Braidna. "Regardless of their beauty."

Grumbling loudly, Sha'gar sent her wand away and allowed the red to fade.

Messenger peered past her at Braidna. "You are still crackling."

"Oh!" Braidna blushed. The air went still. She sagged.

Tinker grabbed her. "Better sit down." He eased her over and into a deck chair. She was wringing wet.

Ragnok walked over and sat. So did Bizl.

The black around Szart disappeared. Sgenn nodded. The thing merged back into the earth.

Tinker looked at the Grandparents. "You wanna start over? Without the demands?"

Ragnok cleared his throat. "Yes. Perhaps we were too brusk."

Smoke walked down the deck from the kitchen accompanied by Fair Morn. They were carrying trays of cups and steaming pots. "Coffee and cocoa," Smoke announced.

Fair Morn set her tray on the table and took a seat. A great ugly black thing was in its holster strapped on the outside of her right thigh. "Taking no chances," she announced.

Tinker sighed and starting filling cups and handing them around.

Ragnok began to explain. How their daughter, refusing to do they wanted, refusing to do her duty as The Princess, had fled the lands out into the elseplaces. Turning and twisting so cleverly that they had only recently found her trail. It was obvious, he stated, that she had mated. She knew the necessity of that, having a daughter. And it was obvious that their daughter had passed the magic to her daughter. Now the problem was, he cleared his throat and looked at Braidna and all the others watching, was that she needed to mate as well. Otherwise her magic would continue to grow out of control. He blinked and stared off into the distance. Unchecked, it would eat her alive.

He looked around again. And explained that their knowledge of the elseplaces was poor and that they hadn't intended to, he cleared his throat again, to trod so heavily on the local cultural values. They had closed their lands to the outside long long ago, after the great war.

Bizl smiled and nodded and explained more about their lives and customs. And the need for their Granddaughter to take that which she was. If she didn't or failed in gaining control of her powers, then she would certainly die. And so would their line of magic. She lifted one of Braidna's hands and kissed it.

"We are so sorry, daughter of our daughter, to suddenly impose such burden upon you. But other forces wish you to fail. We would not be surprised if you hadn't already been attacked."

"I was," whispered Braidna. "They saved me."

Ragnok coughed. "Accept our thanks, friends of our daughter's daughter, for all that you have done. We are debt-tied to you. Many times over."

Tinker shrugged. "We really don't need anything."

"Nothing?"

"Just peace and quiet."

Ragnok smiled. "Just so." And took another sip from his cup. "Interesting beverage." And cleared his throat. "May I ask?"

"What?"

"Why is that . . . theurgist so very concerned about . . . ah, things?"

Sgenn looked at Ragnok, expressionless grey eyes. "I am his."

"Oh," gasped Bizl. "He is already mated!" Her eyes jumped to Braidna. She smiled. "Not really a consort after all."

"No," stated Braidna. "Not at all."

"Shisa nbla," mumbled Ragnok.

"Manr n'zle," snapped Braidna, face flushing, again.

"Int am t'pr," replied Ragnok.

Chicken stepped up behind Tinker, settling her hands on his shoulders. "Mighty Lord, shall we an early dinner have?"

"Sure." It seemed like a safe thing to do to him. No one should get excited about that.

But they did.

For just a moment.

Braidna had walked off with Chicken and Chantal to

help prepare dinner. Her Grandparents started to interfere. Then jerked. Then didn't. Braidna had done something. And explained.

"I need to think," she whispered to Chicken and Chantal as they headed down the deck toward the kitchen

"Most vexing a'problem this," agreed Chicken.

By the time the meal was ready to be set on the table, Braidna nodded to herself and said, "Fred Frinkle."

"Who is that?" asked Chantal.

"GPD policeman. I'll go see him right after dinner."

"Sure you want to do that?"

"With his macho ego he won't mind." She smiled a quick smile. "He is as close to a fondle pet as anything you could ever find."

Chantal wrapped her arms around Braidna and hugged her. "I don't like that idea at all."

"I know," mumbled Braidna. "Me neither."

It was a very quiet dinner as all knew what she was going to do. Except her grandparents.

After dinner, Braidna made a quick phone call, came back, and said, "Big Darlene's," as she headed outside and to her car.

"Merde," grumbled Tinker.

Chantal left the room and made a phone call. And came back and winked at Tinker. "Red said that he and Green would look in, once in awhile. Just in case.

"She doesn't need a chaperone," he grumbled.

Then, most of them settled down in the living room, reading. Chicken took the Grandparents on a tour of the place. And while they walked through the house, she explained who and what they were. Ragnok nodded. They had heard tales, even in their closed off and isolated region. Then she took them outside to wander the area immediately adjacent to the buildings.

In the living room, Tinker was deeply slumped, merging into the couch and the novel that he was reading.

Smoke was lying on the same couch, stretched out, head in his lap, staring at the ceiling, a low rumble purr coming from her throat. She was listening inside his mind to his novel.

He was holding the book with one hand. Somehow his other hand had slipped inside her shirt. She popped another button loose.

Messenger was brushing Szart's hair into a soft shine while Sha'gar and Sgenn were talking in low tones about something.

Fair Morn had decided to make popcorn.

In the dining room, Chantal had disassembled her revolver and was carefully cleaning and oiling all the parts.

All in all, it was a fairly quiet evening for them.

Then the outside kitchen door banged open and slammed against the wall and Braidna stomped into the room.

"Short date, huh?" Fair Morn smiled at her and sampled the popcorn. "Have some. Fresh made."

"It wouldn't allow him," growled Braidna, snatching a handful.

"What's it?" Fair Morn refilled the popcorn popper and started the next batch. And held the bowl out. "Have some more. Do what? What did the it do?"

Braidna did.

Took another handful.

"The magic! Anything. After he thumped off the floor twice, he decided that I was somehow responsible and pointed at the door, all injured male pride and indignation."

"Wow."

"And all he did was to try to slide his arm around me. We never got to Big Darlene's."

"Double wow!" Fair Morn emptied the popper into another bowl.

"Take that one to the living room. They're gonna be surprised that you are back so soon." She refilled the popper and started yet another batch.

They were.

And more so after she explained.

"Well," said Smoke, now sitting next to Tinker on the couch, holding one of the bowls, munching away. "That is interesting. Maybe we ought to run a small experiment?"

Everyone stared at her.

"Like what?" Braidna frowned at her.

Smoke stood and pointed. "Sit there, right next to Mr. Daring."

Tinker glared at Smoke. He remembered the last experiment she had suggested. It had been a disaster.

"Go ahead," urged Smoke to Braidna. "He won't bite." She handed the bowl to Messenger.

Braidna sat.

Carefully she sat.

Next to him.

Smoke moved everyone away and yanked the furniture here and there, clearing a wide space in front of them. "Ready?"

"For what?" Braidna was watching Smoke very carefully.

"Just relax. MindMate, slide an arm around her." She laughed. "You shouldn't hit any of the furniture now."

Tinker sucked in a deep breath, sat upright, planted his feet, and exhaled slowly. Then he carefully, gently, reached up and ever so slowly inched his arm up and around her shoulders.

"Bingo!" announced Chantal, from the doorway to the dining room.

"No!" snapped Tinker, staring at his arm, still over her shoulders.

"I do not understand," said Braidna. "Fred didn't get that far before he bounced off the floor."

"Wait awhile," suggested Smoke, as he started to pull his arm away. "Maybe it works at different speeds for different people."

Tinker sighed.

"Sorry," said Braidna.

"Try her waist," ordered Smoke after they had waited for some time, after she had yanked a couch further away.

He pulled his arm free, slumped a little, and slid the arm between the couch and the small of her back.

"Bingo again," stated Chantal. "One more time and you win the kewpie doll."

"Knock it off," he snarled.

"Relax," she snapped back. "You are making us all nervous." She leaned against the entry edge, folding her arms over her chest.

Smoke looked at them. "Kitten, what do you see?"

Messenger looked. "Nothing." She giggled. "Other than the normal soft glow."

Smoke sat in a chair and leaned forward, hands on knees. "Next test. Ready?"

Tinker frowned.

Braidna nodded.

Smoke winked at them. "MindMate, sneak your hand up her rib cage and give her a friendly squeeze on that soft swelling."

His eyebrows flew up. "What?"

Braidna blushed.

"It's for the good of science." Smoke laughed.

He sighed.

Braidna nodded, and slumped a little. "Go ahead." So he did.

"He wins." Chantal went back to finish her chore.

"You can let go," said Braidna.

His hand jerked away, arm yanking free.

"Very interesting," observed Smoke.

"Certainly is," agreed Messenger. "Really really."

"Hum," said Szart.

"Hum," agreed Sha'gar.

Sgenn frowned.

"I don't like this." He glowered past his boots at the rug.

MindMate, said Smoke, in just his mind.

What?

I think that some aspect of her magic is under her control but that she doesn't realize that yet.

And?

She didn't want that Fred person.

And?

As Chicken would say, you, we, have a dilemma.

Which is?

Fondle pet.

Merde! His eyes bored into Smoke's. *We are done adding. Absolutely.*

Including outliers, satellites, shadows, other Queens and Princesses, or any other thing.

All those are something else. Not us. She winked into his glower. *Just associates, so to speak.*

He struggled upright. *You telling me that she wants to be an . . . associate?*

Somewhat like Sa'ar is. I don't think that she realizes it.

Well, you guys get to talk her out of it. He lurched to his feet. "Gonna get a cup of coffee." *And I don't like it!*

Smoke stood and beckoned to Braidna. "Let' s go sit on the rear deck and talk."

He poured a cup of coffee and growled at Smoke. *Why is it always me? There are universes of guys out there!* He stomped back into the living room and dropped into his chair.

Every eye watched him. He clamped his mind shut and watched them relax, Then he picked up the novel that he had been reading and started where he had left off.

They were leaning against the railing, looking out over the flower beds, the first pasture, and into the trees covering the slope reaching up into the forest beyond.

Smoke had carefully explained to her what she felt, what she thought, was the problem.

"Oh." The red flared up over the high cheekbones as

Braidna's fingers dug into the wooden top rail. She turned and looked into those great orange-gold eyes watching her ever so carefully. "I didn't . . . I don't . . . " She wrapped her arms around Smoke and mumbled, "How did my life get so complicated, so fast?"

Smoke gently patted her back. "That is what he keeps asking."

Braidna released her and turned back to stare across the flower beds and the open fields. "Who?"

"Him."

"Don't you ever use his name?"

Smoke smiled. "Not much. There is no need. We always know who we are referring to, and he is my MindMate, a special term among my folk."

Braidna leaned on her forearms. "Everyone calls him that?"

"No. Each one uses terms that are comfortable to them. The Princess tends to be rather royal in terminology. Messenger calls him MyTinker. And so forth."

"But what am I to do?"

Smoke leaned on the railing, arm brushing against arm. "That is for you to decide."

"What does he . . . John, want to do?"

Smoke laughed.

"Not funny."

"Perhaps. Among my folk this is just not a problem. But among his folk it is. Apparently."

"So, same question."

Smoke nudged her with an elbow. "Let's talk about that."

In the living room, Messenger sat straighter and stopped tickling the large white male cat's belly. "Gosh!" The cat looked insulted at her.

"Whish," hissed Chicken, gently nudging her with one boot tip. She and the Grandparents had just returned from their tour.

"Damn babe magnet!" Chantal glared at the clock. "Long day tomorrow. Lots of live stock to visit." She headed down the hall.

And shortly afterward, they headed to their bedrooms. Chicken guided the Grandparents to their room and bid them goodnight.

And night wrapped everything in the dark of a moonless sky.

Far across the valley the sun crept up from behind the mountain ridges and shot bright shafts onto the green fields and the meandering river in the valley bottom. Little moved other than a random cow or two as day greeted everything.

He lay flat on his back, staring up in the general direction of the ceiling.

She lay on top of him, forearms resting on his chest, back arched, staring down into his eyes. "They are really a nice blue."

"Morpt."

"Rest is pretty nice. Also."

"Braidna?"

"What?"

"What are we doing?"

Her face flushed. "Not much."

He sighed. "Merde."

"What?"

"You already sound like them."

"Who?"

"Me. The rest of me."

She lowered herself until she could brush his lips lightly with hers. "Didn't mean to. It was just that your question begged for that answer."

"Uh huh."

She sat up, blanket spilling down around her hips, skin a soft gold in the dawn becoming day. "Shall I slip back to my room before they wake up?"

"Won't matter. They know."

The flush crept over her face. "They do?"

"Yep. I imagine Smoke let them know."

"Everything?" she whispered.

"Nope. Only that you are here, in my bedroom. They'll assume that we weren't, or aren't, playing cards."

She frowned. And twitched. "Certainly aren't doing that."

They were gathered around the dining table in various stages of breakfast as each had wandered in and sat in their usual disorderly way.

Messenger was explaining the various foods to Braidna's Grandparents when Chantal walked in, dropped into her chair, and pulled her coffee cup over, eyes mere silts, and took a sip.

"She wakes up really slow," whispered Messenger to Bizl. Bizl nodded and smiled knowmgly at Ragnok.

By the time Chantal's eyes were open fully and she was sitting up and eating breakfast, Tinker and Braidna walked in, each wearing one of the thick white robes, hair wet from the shower.

Tinker dropped into his chair. Chicken filled a cup and shoved it over to him. "Fair Morn, Me'Lord."

Ragnok stared from Tinker to Braidna and gasped.

Bizl smiled.

Messenger looked from him to her. "Oh my gosh!"

Braidna sat next to Bizl. "Pass the egg puff, please." She pointed at the appropriate pan.

Tinker peered over the top of his cup at Messenger who was staring all round-eyed at him. "Now what?" And took another sip.

Messenger giggled. "You have a kinna little gold star just above your left eyebrow. So does Braidna."

"What be this?" Chicken leaned forward and stared at him. "We do Ourself see naught, Fair Prince."

Ragnok stared at Messenger. "How can this be?"

Bizl smiled at Tinker. "We are double-debt, now marked Avival."

Messenger slipped lower in her chair and whispered loudly, "I didn't do anything."

Tinker scanned the faces around the table.

Chantal nodded and tapped the table top with the handle of her knife. "Cool it, Stud Butt. You are making us all nervous."

He clamped his mind shut. "What's going on? Now?"

Bizl laid her hand on her husband's forearm and spoke softly to Tinker. "Members of our line can see the Avival mark." She turned her head. "Is this not so, Messenger?"

Messenger shook her head. "I don't know. But you and him have small vertical bars."

Bizl looked back at Tinker. "Our grand-daughter chose stars. The mated-ones are so marked."

Tinker looked at Braidna. "Mated ones?" He eased his mind open.

Her face flushed.

Messenger giggled.

"Shhhhh," whispered Smoke.

"I am losing count," mumbled Chantal.

Szart nudged Sha'gar and watched the red flicker in her eyes fade.

"Hum," said Sgenn.

Merde, grumbled Tinker.

Not us, said Smoke into their collective being.

Damn grump! mumbled Chantal.

She is very pretty. And very nice, suggested Messenger. *Really really.*

That does not matter, he snapped.

Ho, ho, ho, snorted Chantal. *Or are you loosing your highly refined tastes?*

You know that is not what I meant.

Yum, yum, yum, laughed Fair Morn.

Smoke?

MindMate?

I want you to probe deep. And see whether Big Red didn't do something to us at some time.

To?

Me. Us.

She slipped in and floated deeper and deeper.

He better not have, growled Chantal.

I could put a close ward on you, suggested Szart. *Keyed to those you wish.*

Nothing there, reported Smoke.

"John," said Braidna. "We will be leaving soon. I have to retrieve another object before I go home." She shook her head. "This is really going to be hard to explain to Father."

"Don't." He frowned. "Umm, just tell him that you have taken a new job, out of the country."

"I suppose." She stood. "I will get dressed. And go now." She strode from the room.

"Now," growled Ragnok, pointing at Messenger, "Explain that!"

"Not polite," said Bizl, patting his forearm.

He jerked. "Apologies."

Messenger hitched herself back in her chair. She had slumped almost out of sight. And looked at Tinker.

"She can see magic," explained Tinker. And grabbed his coffee cup, just filled by Chicken and took a sip. "It is the way that she is."

"Unheard of," snapped Ragnok.

Messenger blinked.

"Well," grumbled Tinker. "Now you have heard!"

Bizl patted her husbands arm. "Perhaps we have been isolated too long, our lands?"

Ragnok leaned back and grumbled. "Perhaps."

"There is no threat," continued Bizl. "Messenger is his, and he is Barna a'um'na."

That is you all right, snarled Chantal. *Barna a'um'na. Must mean babe magnet.*

Poogle, he suggested as he stood. "I believe that we have a number of things to do." He headed towards his bedroom to change clothes.

Everyone scattered.

Chicken remained with the Grandparents to be hostess.

Chantal stomped into his bedroom just as he yanked on his jeans and wrapped her arms around him. "Sorry, John. I keep forgetting how easily we get sucked into the strangeness of the other elseplace's cultural values."

He kissed the tip of her nose. "Me too." And sighed. "I keep forgetting that as well." Then he freed his arms from her clutches and ran tickle fingers over her ribs. "Know what I think?"

"Damn fast recovery, Stud."

"I think that we should pay a visit to Big Red. This sort of complicated twisting seems to be his type of plotting and planning and it happens too frequently to us."

Chantal frowned. "Is he responsible for this?"

"It's a thought."

She leaned back, his hands locked in the small of her back and scowled. "That is disgusting."

"Huh?"

"Using you as the stud to the universes."

One corner of his mouth pulled sideways. "It was just a thought."

"I think that you are right."

"Why?"

"Well, Simba Leader, think of all the relations that you have already, all of the folk that you can call on for aid and assistance if some really bad guy shows up that B.R. thinks ought to be gotten rid of, for the good of the universes."

"And?"

"I think that meddler has made you into his equivalent of a mafia lord."

He tugged her close and slid one hand up to tickle the back of her neck. "And now there is one more group to call upon, huh?"

"Yep." She reached up and tapped his forehead, over one eye. "One more. And the network spreads in new directions. And a new magic using group is involved."

"Merde!" His eyes popped wide.

"What?"

"We had R-Bar and the others built a ward to keep out everything that we didn't want in. Stray witches. Stray magicians. And every kind of demon, having the a'demons do that, out there except the Tark. And he found a way to sneak her in." He dropped his arms. "Let's take a hike. I need to think." He had no idea how the Divineal did what they wished to do, come and go as they pleased.

"I'll get dressed and meet you on the rear deck." She spun away and hurried to her room, pausing to phone her clinic and to tell her partner that she would be gone for a short while.

They stepped into the cool shadows at the west edge of the second pasture just to escape the warming day.

He sighed.

She stepped around and faced him, giving him a gentle poke in the stomach with one finger. "What's a matta, Simba

Leader? Getting out of shape?"

He looked into her grey-green eyes, worry wrinkles forming in their corners. "Piffle."

"I am not."

"What?"

She inhaled and peered down at the swelling of her shirt. "Insignificant."

He laughed. "Certainly not. It is a toss-up between you and Fair Morn for significance if we twist that word's meaning all out of shape."

She exhaled loudly. "She has an advantage."

"Oh?"

"Sure. She was a magical jest. Handcrafted, so to speak, by Big Red. I just inherited my mother's development with some alteration by my father's genetic input."

His face fell into blankness.

"John!"

"What?"

"What's wrong?"

"Everything. Nothing. I don't know."

She laid a cool palm against his forehead.

"I am not sick," he grumbled.

Her hand slid gently over his cheek and away. "Oh?"

"It's Braidna. And all that."

"Ah, ha."

"Don't start."

"Not me lusting after that China Babe."

He glared at her. "I am not lusting after some China Babe! And that is the problem."

She stepped closer. "It happens to guys all the time."

"Merde."

Yanking his shirt loose, she slid her hand over his stomach and down behind his belt. "Just let the kindly doctor give things a look."

He jerked. "Stop that!"

Sliding her hand free, she stepped up against him and bumped gently against him. "Certainly not your problem. Stud. Things seem to be all right. Just a healthy growing boy." She grinned.

"Not going to be anything of me left."

"Old wive's tale."

"'Huh?"

"Female vampires sucking away male essences."

He grabbed her by the upper arms. "You are deliberately not paying attention, right?"

"Nope. You are just not making any sense at all."

"I do not liked being used like that."

"Bad timing, Cowboy. You can take a vow of celibacy after we wear that damn thing out." She fumbled with his belt buckle. "Time to strike while the iron is hot, in a manner of speaking."

He yanked her arms behind her back. "Chantal!"

"Lover?"

He released her and stepped back. "Button your pants." She did. "Let's go sit over there in that deep grass. And talk." He pointed.

She sighed dramatically and looked as pitiful as she could.

He walked out into the grass and waited.

"Sit down," she commanded. "Cross your legs." And

watched him until he did. Then she stepped around, over his legs, and sat down in his lap, and hooked her legs around him, ankles crossed, arms encircling his waist. "Now. What is this all about? What is there about this Braidna babe that has put you into such a funk, such a blue mood?" She brushed her lips across his forehead. "You know that we will agree to add her if it matters that much."

"Not that," he grumbled. "It is the fact of being dragged into something that we had no idea about, that we didn't know was coming, or had any idea of what we were being mired in. I am so tired of being manipulated by the damn elseplaces and all of their problems." His hands slid around her waist. "She got manipulated as well. Now she is the leader of something, of her Grandparent's clan, or whatever it is."

She kissed him, tugging the back of his shirt free. "And you are worried."

"Uh huh."

"She is very pretty." She leaned back in his arms and began to unbutton his shirt.

"Yep." He smiled. "So are you. And all the rest. Very pretty."

"And all this blue mood is worry about us? Again?"

He slowly leaned forward until she lay on the grass. "Yes. Braidna was manipulated. I was certainly manipulated. Which means that you and the rest were manipulated. And I do not like that because someone might be injured." Sitting back he began to undo the rest of the buttons on her shirt.

"Or die," she added.

He sat back and stared at her, past her, and whispered harshly, "Yes. Or die." And blinked back tears.

Lurching up, she wrapped her arms around him and toppled him over.

Chicken nudged Smoke. "Me'thinks tis time we do pack for a'traveling to go."

Smoke nodded. "Let's. It has been some time since we visited Paradise."

They hurried away to collect their gear.

Braidna stepped from the door out onto the rear deck. "Where is everyone?"

Messenger giggled. "He and Chantal are, ummmm, taking a hike. The Princess and Smoke are packing."

"Packing?"

Messenger nodded. Violently. "Yes. We are going to visit Big Red and tell him to stop doing things. It is really really not nice."

Braidna nodded, not sure what Messenger was talking about. "Will you tell them all goodbye for me, we are leaving now." She handed a gold ring to Messenger. "Give this to John, please. And tell him to wear it when he travels out there. Please?"

Messenger took the ring and tickled it. "It is very nice. Thank you."

Braidna's Grandparents walked from the house and looked around the empty deck. Then Braidna bent over and kissed Messenger. "Bye. I will miss you all." Straightening up, she took one step back. They disappeared in a golden glow.

"Gosh."

Chantal rolled onto her side and tickled his ear, with

one fingertip. "Maybe we ought to cure your worrying this way all the time."

"Wonder what that ring does?"

"Oh, good," laughed Chantal.

"Huh?"

"Something else to worry about." She sat up and flopped on top of him.

"OOOOOF!"

She cackled a deep evil cackle.

"What?"

"Time to steal away your male essences again."

"Gonna have to wait, Draculetta."

She rolled off and sprawled. "Guess you are gonna have to just mess around then."

"O.K."

Smoke dumped the last of the packs next to the wall and winked at Chicken. "We'll leave tomorrow. They will be napping all afternoon."

Do We Really Need This?

Paradise. The Usual Warm and Balmy Day.

In roiling swirl of black they thumped down into the open cobblestone paved area in front of the Tudor-style structure.

On all sides, the grass was green, thick, and neatly mown. In the distance, past the house, they could see rank after rank of forest covered ridges, fading green haze into the deep blue cloudless sky. The air temperature was just right, as always.

The main door banged open and a large man dressed in clothing of various shades and tones of red bounced out, beaming happily at them.

"John! Ladies! What a pleasant surprise. It has been so long since your last visit. Come in, come in. Drop your things and make yourselves at home. I will just send your gear to your rooms." He smiled, waggled a finger and watched as their belongings disappeared. "Refreshments?"

"Sure," said Tinker as he followed Big Red into the house. The rest trailed after them.

They settled in a comfortable living room and waited while their host hustled around seeing to it that each had whatever beverage they wished. Then he thumped down heavily into an overstuffed chair, upholstered with a deep burgundy colored material.

"So John, how have you been?"

"Fine."

"Good."

"Other than that b.s. you pulled with Braidna."

"Oh! Ahhhh, I see. You figured that out." Big Red tried to look embarrassed Then he tried to look surprised. Then he gave up. "It had to be done. After all, she is the rightful, and only, heir, ahhhhh, heiress, to that line of magic." He looked at the rest of them. "Ahhhhh, I see. Everyone is unhappy because John, ahhhh, ummmmm, well, you know, did, ermmm, what had to be done. It was necessary, you see."

"Nooooo," hissed Szart.

"Nooooooo," echoed Sha'gar, eyes flickering red.

Big Red sat up. "Careful, careful. We will have none of that in my home."

Sgenn looked at him. And tilted her head slightly to one side.

Big Red looked back to Tinker. "They are really quite fierce, aren't they?"

Messenger sat straight and glared at him. "What you did was really really not nice."

Chicken nodded. "Most true."

"Perhaps if I explained!"

"Do!" stated Chicken, using her most Royal tone of voice.

"Of course." Big Red leaned back in his chair and nodded. And then began to tell them all about the Wizards of Trefil and that far isolated corner of the universes where they dwelled and why what had happened had to happen.

When he finished, Chantal cleared her throat into the

silence. "B.G., John doesn't need to be manipulated by you. We don't need to be manipulated by you. Find some other stud to stick it to whatever fairy tale Princess you feel like rescuing."

"Urr," replied Big Red. He glanced at the faces staring at him. The door from the hall opened and Dancing-All-The-Day, his wife, walked in, took one look at her husband and stated, "What have you been doing to him, to them, this time?"

Big Red ducked his head and really looked apologetic. "Cementing certain political alliances."

"How?"

"Urrrrr." He ordered his glass to refill. With red wine. "It wasn't unpleasant." And took a sip.

"Who was it?"

"Braidna. Lyral Princess of the Wizards of Trefil."

"Dear?"

He reached up and gently tugged her head down and whispered in her ear.

She straightened up and looked around and nodded. "Yes. Not unpleasant." And looked at her husband. "I really do think he has no need for that, ahhhhh, kind of political cement work. And certainly not without any warning at all. That was truly an imposition of the worse kind!"

"It had to be done." He cleared his throat. "She really would have died otherwise. And she, ahem, had already selected him, ahh, John." He smiled. "So it wasn't entirely my fault."

"Other than seeing to it that she lived in the same town with us," interjected Chantal.

"Mea culpa," said Big Red.

"Not good enough," snapped Chantal.

"What?"

"Leave us alone," she growled.

"Really really alone," added Messenger.

Big Red slumped in his chair, looking honestly sad. This time. "I can't. John is needed. He really is, often, the key to events." He shot both hands out, palms out. "And I didn't do that! And I do not know how come! I just know that it is true, that's all. Just like I knew that when Braidna's mother fled her duty that she had to have a daughter to carry on her line. All I did is see to it that she had a daughter and that the daughter would, ahhh, meet John and etc., etc., etc."

He looked at Tinker. "I know, John. I really do. But, as you know, there are things even I cannot interfere with. And this is, was, one of them."

"Dear?" Dancing-All-The-Day gently set her hand on one massive shoulder.

"Almost anything that he wishes, or wants," stated Big Red. "Almost."

"I do not need anything," grumbled Tinker. "Nothing," he growled.

Eyes jumped every which way as they reacted to his agitation.

"Yes you do, John, oh yes you do." Big Red smiled at him. "All of you do."

"NOT FROM YOU!" shouted Tinker, leaping to his feet.

Szart bolted for the door, witch flight reaction.

"HA!" stated Big Red, popping his hands together. One sharp loud sound.

Szart halted and spun around, eyes flying wide, staring from Tinker to Big Red. "Arpt naptar nar," she gasped.

Sha'gar sagged a little. And Smoke smiled.

"Most gracious a'gift." Chicken bowed her head

"Glad to help." He beamed. "You should have come a long time ago."

"What did you do?" asked Tinker. "This time?"

"Small thing," replied the red magician.

"It is gone, John, gone." Chantal brushed a tear from her eye. "All that fear and agitation we got from the Faan. It is gone."

"Forever," added Big Red. He beamed. "Smoke saw what I did." And laughed. "So, if you ever need a special favor from any witch clan with that problem, I think that you will always be able to strike quite a bargain."

Tinker sighed. "Thanks. I really mean that."

"Least I could do for my, ahh, imposing on your, ummmm, hospitality."

"That's a new word for it," mumbled Chantal.

"Hospitable," stated Fair Morn. "Entertaining guests in a friendly, generous manner."

Messenger giggled. "He was certainly friendly with Braidna."

"And me'thinks most generous," added Chicken.

They all laughed, except for Tinker.

Dancing-All-The-Day excused herself and left them to do other things. Big Red stood. "Shall we go outside and stretch our legs?" He headed out.

As they followed him, Messenger slipped her arm under one of Tinker's. "MyTinker, you haven't been very hospitable for some time." And giggled.

He sighed.

The rest carefully suppressed their laughter.

Once outside, everyone scattered in all directions, just to stroll about and to enjoy the pleasantness that was Paradise, the home created by Big Red.

Smoke strolled off with Big Red, deep in a discussion of what he had done to take away the female witch panic reaction to their mate's agitation.

Fair Morn lifted into the air, great butterfly wings glittering multi-colors, and sailed down the slope into a broad valley.

Tinker and Messenger headed down a wide path, down into a wide, bowl shaped depression.

"Recognize that lake, kitten?"

Messenger giggled happily. "Yep. That is where you skinny dipped me."

"Huh?"

"You were being very hospitable." She swung his arm happily, back and forth.

"And where Fair Morn brought us lunch."

"Yep. Yep. Yep." She released his arm and began to unbutton her shirt.

"Kitten?"

"Skinny dipping."

"Oh." He began to unbutton his shirt. The air felt like it was exactly the right temperature. And as this was Paradise, of course it was.

Then they walked out onto the wide sandy beach and around one edge of the water and dropped their clothes and boots in a big heap. They waded into the mild ever so pleasant lake.

Messenger bobbled up and down in front of him. "This is much better than our swimming pool."

He laughed. "Certainly is." And kissed her.

And after awhile, she said, "He is really a very nice person. He just doesn't always seem to understand."

"Who?"

"Big Red."

He laughed again. "Certainly doesn't." And kissed her. Again.

They surged toward and up onto the beach. A shadow passed over them, And then settled to the beach, great wings fluttering. "I brought you some large beach towels." She winked and lifted back into the air. They watched as she soared higher and higher and finally out and over a ridge line.

He unfolded a towel. And unfolded it. It was as large as a queen-sized bed. It was also thick and soft as a feather comforter. "Some beach towel." He flapped it out and watched it settle to the sand.

"Really nice." Messenger crawled into the middle and watched as he joined her.

"Certainly is." He kissed her again.

Much later, she rolled onto her side and tickled his ribs until his eyes popped open.

"Huh?"

She giggled. "Very hospitable. Really really." And laughed happily.

"What?"

She pointed past his chest down the beach. "Here comes lunch."

He looked. And saw her, sailing at a steep angle down toward them, a large wicker basket held in one arm. With a soft thump, she dropped next to them.

"He figured that you would wake up with an appetite." And set the basket on his stomach.

He set the basket aside and yanked a blanket up and over himself and stared at her. "Who are you?"

"Early Dawn, Honored One." Her great dark leather bat wings popped closed as she sat and opened the top of the basket and began to set things out. Finally, she set the basket to one side and smiled at him.

"Do you do that to her often?"

"What?"

Messenger giggled and sat up, leaned over him, and grabbed her. "OH! She is real!"

Early Dawn smiled at her, pointed teeth glittering white. "I am newly created."

Messenger let go.

Early Dawn began to unfasten her upper garment, a soft leather vest.

"What are you doing?" he hissed.

"Removing my garment so she may better feel me."

"Stop!"

"Why?"

"Just go back and tell Big Red that it is not funny." He sat up. "Oh, and tell him thanks for everything."

Early Dawn sat back and looked unhappy at him. "I could always glide into your room on the wings of night?" Her wings popped out to full extension and fluttered gently. "When she is asleep?"

"No! Not necessary." He smiled. "Nice offer. But no."

She set one hand on his chest, leaned over and kissed Messenger. "I will return and take everything away later." Standing, she gave a slight hop and soared out over the lake and upward.

"Another Big Red jest," he grumbled.

"She is very pretty."

"Of course. He did it."

Messenger hobbled around him on her knees and began to fill her plate. "She is not as tall as Fair Morn nor as, ummm, so large."

"Pass the radishes, please."

"Her skin is soft dusky brown color that goes well with her wings. Potato salad, please."

"Here."

"Well, I think that she is pretty, isn't she?"

He nodded. And swallowed. "O.K., pretty. But did you notice her smile? He gave her vampire teeth." And took another sandwich. "Probably bites."

Eventually they went for another swim and a splash in the lake. And eventually they wound up back on the beach blanket. And eventually they fell asleep.

His eyes popped open. Soft lips were brushing lightly over his chest at the base of his neck

"Knock it off!"

She sat back and blinked down at him. "I was just curious."

He quickly ran his hand over his chest and the base of

his neck, checking his fingers for blood stains.

"I didn't bite you." She smiled.

Messenger sat up and waggled her fingers at Early Dawn. "Hi!"

Tinker sat up and tossed her shirt to Messenger. "Get dressed." She shrugged on the garment and tucked the blanket around her waist.

"What do you want?" he asked.

"I came to take things away. But it doesn't look like you are ready for that, yet." Her eyes shifted to Messenger. "Will he be wanting you again?"

"Certainly hope so." Messenger giggled.

Early Dawn sat back on her legs and crossed her arms over her chest and nodded at her. "I will wait."

"No, you will not," he snapped. And sighed. "He just doesn't seem to equip his jests with much knowledge, does he?" It was a more or less rhetorical question.

Early Dawn sighed back. "I am only a few hours old." She smiled at him. "You taste good." She licked her lips and looked at Messenger. "Is that why she allows you to do that?"

"Go away," he grumbled. He wasn't ready for one of those conversations. It was bad enough with the rest of them.

"Sorta," replied Messenger.

"Merde," he mumbled.

"Bat guano," suggested Early Dawn.

"Doggy doo doo," giggled Messenger.

"I don't need this," he grumbled softly.

Early Dawn looked at Messenger. "You are the controller called Messenger?"

"Yep."

"Would you please release him so that he could play with me as he was playing with you?"

"Gosh!" Messenger stared at her.

"No!" snarled Tinker, violently waving his hands at her. "Flit away."

Early Dawn frowned at him. "My existence is short. I want to know what a real female is like, not just a female jest of little knowledge or little time."

"Oh, my." Messenger blinked back a tear.

"I will not be sucked into this game," he growled at them both. "Go away! Go tell Big Red that this is not funny and that I do not like private jokes and jests like this."

His arms waved more wildly. "We just had that conversation with him and here you are, here you still are. That damn magician doesn't ever pay any attention at all." He fumbled under the blanket, found, and yanked on his jeans.

"Kitten, get the rest of your clothes on. Early Dawn, get out of the way." He tossed the blanket at and over her and looked around for his boots and socks. "Damn dumb joke."

Early Dawn threw the blanket aside, scooted back, leaped to her feet, and grabbed him by the upper arms, lifted him into the air, and shook him back and forth. "I not a damn dumb joke!" Releasing him to thump to the ground, she covered her face with both hands and began to sob.

Tinker reached out and gently touched her arm. "I didn't mean you."

Her hands dropped. She blinked and wiped her eyes with the backs of her hands. "Get off those things so I can take them away."

He stepped to one side and watched as Messenger

helped gather everything together.

Then, arms laden with blankets, wicker basket hooked over one, Early Dawn gave two quick pumps of her wings and sailed up and out over the lake and up the far slope, an ever dwindling speck merging into the blur of the forest background.

After tying his bootlaces he straightened up and tossed an arm around Messenger's shoulders. "I wish that Big Red would stop doing things like that."

She nodded. "She seemed like a nice person."

He sighed. "For a magical jest."

She nodded. And whispered, "Don't be angry with her."

He smiled. "It's not her fault. Let's head back and see what other kinds of mischief he has been up to."

She spun, grabbed his arm, and tugged him into motion.

As they walked up and over the last final ridge and into the open meadows close to the house, he decided that it must be close to dinner time, at least as judging by the shadows.

"LOOK OUT BELOW!"

Fair Morn soared past their heads, laughing happily. She swirled into a tight spin, settled to the grass, folding and folding and folding her great butterfly wings.

Another whipped in from their side and dropped lightly to the grass next to her side, her wings snapping closed. She stepped closer to Fair Morn's side. Fair Morn threw a comradely arm over the shorter woman's shoulders, grinned at him and Messenger, and announced, "This is Early Dawn. We have been flying together."

"We've met," he grumbled.

"I brought them lunch," stated Early Dawn.

"Let's go eat." Fair Morn dragged her arm away and headed for the house. "I am famished."

Early Dawn hurried to her side. "Me too."

As they hurried inside they heard Fair Morn ask, "Have you ever tried a loop?"

After dinner they all settled in the living room. Chantal held her glass high and said, "Many thanks, B. G."

He looked startled. "For what?"

She took a sip. "For ridding us of that witch fear thing."

"Least that I could do." He beamed at them. "Can't have my favorite people being bothered, ahem, that way." Then Big Red entertained them with various magical games, explaining various small points to Szart and Sha'gar about whatever spell he was using at that moment.

After quite some time into the performance, Fair Morn dropped into the couch next to Tinker, leaned close and said in his ear, "Heh, heh, heh, heh, heh."

"What?"

"I won. Short straw."

"What?"

"You."

"Oh?"

"Heh, heh, heh, heh."

Then the show was over and all trailed up to their bedrooms.

As they walked into his assigned room, he stared and pointed. "What is that?"

They stood just inside the door. It appeared to be a

cloud, sitting in the middle of the floor.

She walked over, spun, and fell backward. And floated gently on top of it. "The bed."

He walked over and laid a palm on it. It was slightly warm and felt more like a water bed than a cloud.

She rolled over and crawled out into the middle of it, sprawled on her back, and grinned up at him. "Pretty nice, huh?"

"Interesting bed."

"Me."

He sighed and crawled over to her. "Now what?"

She laughed. "Oh, the usual thing. You take advantage of my lovely self, The Winged Warrior, Beauty of The Skies, in your usual beastly way, overwhelming my defenses, pinioning my helpless self to this cloud, ravishing me until I swoon from delight and sensory overload."

He sat up and plucked a button loose on her shirt. "Now what have you been reading?"

"The recycled bodice rippers at the used book store."

He tugged her shirt free. "Though so."

She grinned up at him. "You going to work your wicked ways upon me?"

"Did cross my mind. But I do think that you ought to widen your literary interests."

"Wonder if we can get one of these clouds for my bedroom at home?" Fair Morn smiled.

He woke in the dark of night. Moonlight streamed bright patch across the floor and onto one wall. A warm body sprawled on top of him, arms and legs wrapped, soft lips brushing the junction of neck and shoulder.

"Fair Morn?"

"One?" Her voice came from his left side.

"You wanna tell me what's going on?" he asked whoever it was.

She sat up, bounced to her feet, and yanked the intruder away, and punched.

"Ooooops," said Fair Morn.

"What is she doing in here?"

Fair Morn sat and patted Early Dawn on the side of the face. "I think that she wanted your body. Hope that I didn't hurt her."

"You can't. She is a magical jest." He sat up and looked at the large welt forming in the center of Early Dawn's forehead.

Her eyes wobbled open. "That is not at all what I thought that it would be like." She looked at Fair Morn. "How can you allow him to do that to you? My head is throbbing."

"I punched you. I thought that he was being attacked."

"I wouldn't do something like that."

"Creeping around in the middle of the night is not a very clever idea." Tinker found and yanked on his pajama bottoms. And looked around. "Where are your clothes?"

She sat up and pointed. "There."

He jumped to the floor, walked over, snatched them up, stomped back, and shoved the pile at her. "Get dressed and go away," He sighed. "Go ask Big Red to make a male jest. Then the two of you can do whatever you want to do to each other."

Early Dawn tugged on her leather trousers. And looked at Fair Morn. "Why does he do that to you and that young girl, but not me?"

"She is not a young girl and it is too hard to explain," hissed Tinker. He sat on the edge of the cloud. "Put your vest on. This is some sly trick of Big Red's, isn't it?"

Early Dawn shook her head. "When I came into existence he said that I was beautiful and should be friendly and helpful. Am I not?"

"Right." He pointed at the door. "See you in the morning."

Her shoulders sagged as she walked slowly toward the door, then she spun and ran at the large open window and leaped out, head first.

"Merde!" He raced to the window and leaned out. There was nothing down below. No large splatter of crushed body on the cobbled pavement.

"There she goes." Fair Morn pointed at a dark speck circling higher and higher into night sky.

He nodded, walked back, and crawled out into the middle of the cloud. She joined him.

He sighed. "I still think that it is some kind of sneaky Big Red ploy. First Braidna, now that damn vampire bat."

She kissed the corner of his shoulder. "I remember when I was brand new and saw you and kitten on the beach. I had the same curiosity."

"Ah ha!"

"You want her back?"

"No. It is Messenger. That sneak knows how empathetic she is."

"She is very pretty."

"Of course. He created her."

"Her wings are very nice."

"If you go for leather."

"Very acute hearing."

"Figures. Probably like a bat."

"Can't get pregnant."

"I do not care."

"Her ears are sorta pointed."

"Didn't notice."

"So are . . . "

"Forget it!" He lurched upright. "What did you say?"

"Sorta pointed, rather nicely shaped."

"No, no. About her hearing."

"Oh. She has very acute hearing."

"Damn!" He leaped from the cloud and dashed into the hall. Then back into the bedroom. "Which one is kitten in? Come on, come on, don't just lie there."

She jumped down and hurried into the hall. And pointed. "Third door."

He ran, slid to a halt, threw the door open and charged inside. This side of the building was in total darkness.

Messenger sat up, eyes glowing faint green. "MyTinker?"

"That damn bat in here?"

"Ummm."

"You didn't?"

"Ummmmm."

"You did!" He sagged, and leaned against a wall.

Messenger began to sob. "She was so sad."

"That fink! The sneaky, rotten bastard!" He spun in the direction of the faint rustling sound. "Who's there?"

"I am not a fink," said a quivering voice. "Nor sneaky, nor rotten, nor a bastard. I am a female."

He fumbled around until he found the light switch. She sat in a corner, wings wrapped around herself, just her eyes showing. The small claws at the wing wrists held the folds in place. He hadn't noticed them before.

"She did it, didn't she?"

Messenger hiccuped and wiped her eyes with the sleeve of her pajama top.

"Yes. I am real now, no longer a jest."

He dropped, sitting in a rather crumpled heap on the floor against the wall. "Now what are we going to do?"

Fair Morn walked over, sat on the bed and hugged Messenger. "Maybe she sleeps all day?"

"I am not a bat," grumbled Early Dawn.

"There just has to be some way to stop this from happening to us all the time," he mumbled. "There just has to be some way."

Fair Morn patted the bed. "Come sit here."

Early Dawn unwrapped her wings, stood, and snapped them closed. "I will not allow you to hit me again."

Fair Morn nodded. "I am really sorry about that."

She walked over and cautiously sat near them, her body tense, ready to defend herself.

"You are safe with us," said Fair Morn.

Early Dawn pointed at Tinker with her chin. "What about him? He sounds very unhappy. Very, very unhappy!"

Fair Morn winked at her. "He'll get over it."

"You sure?" She frowned. "It would be hard, I think, living with someone like that, with someone that doesn't like you." She stared at the floor. "I know so little about being real."

Fair Morn threw an arm around her and hugged her and whispered, "We will all help you. It will be all right, you'll see." And kissed her.

He sighed.

A long, loud, slow sigh.

And stood.

And stared at them.

He snorted. "Welcome to the real world." He turned and wandered out the door and down the hall, staring at the floor.

Fair Morn whispered something to Early Dawn. Messenger giggled.

And sometime later she slipped silently into the room and crawled over and lay by his side. "Fair Morn said that I should. You feel very comforting."

"O.K."

"She said that if I asked you to, that you would hold me."

"O.K."

"Hold me, please?"

"Sure."

She rolled toward him.

He slipped his arms around her, and sighed. "Somehow things will work out."

"That is what Fair Morn said," she whispered, snuggling closer. "And she was right. You are nice and warm." She carefully kissed his cheek.

"How about we just try sleeping? Quietly sleeping."

She closed her eyes, took a deep breath, exhaled, and fell asleep.

He sighed. "Wish that I could do that."

Grandeville. Tinker's Place.

The sunlight woke him.

He stared up at the ceiling and jerked violently awake. "Damnation."

And reached out.

To the rest of himself.

They were all at home.

Sitting up, he flapped the blankets away. She lay on her back, sound asleep. It was Early Dawn.

Smoke slipped into the bedroom on silent feet. "MindMate?"

"Beat's me. But we are getting sucked deeper and deeper into some kind of crap again." He slid from the bed and stood. "What are we going to do about her?"

Smoke shrugged. "Let's make breakfast."

He sighed. "Might as well. Hope we don't have any visitors for awhile."

Not A Bat In The Belfry?

Grandeville. Tinker's Place.

They were standing in the kitchen just loading the last bunch of pancakes on a large platter when Early Dawn ran into the room, eyes wide. "Where are we? What did you do?"

"Really need some pajamas," observed Smoke. "Can't sleep in leathers all the time."

"Home," replied Tinker. "Big Red sent us while we were sleeping."

"Oh." She stared at the platter. "Funny looking food." She looked at Smoke. "Why not?"

"Pancakes." Smoke took the platter into the dining room, grabbing the syrup pitcher as she passed by. "It is breakfast time. Tell you later."

Early Dawn stared at the room, at the appliances, at the kitchen cabinets. "This is really your home?"

"Yep." He grabbed a coffee pot. "Come on. Time to eat."

As they sat, eating, just starting actually, Chicken wandered in, dragged her fingers over his shoulder and sat in her chair. "Fair Morn, Winged Ones." And poured her cup full.

Fair Morn shoved over the platter and the syrup pitcher, taking a few pancakes first.

Early Dawn held a pancake in two fingers and took a tentative bite from one edge.

"Use thy utensils, wench," ordered Chicken.

She dropped the pancake, watched Fair Morn and then copied her actions. And mumbled, "Fingers are easier."

"Piffie," snorted Chicken.

Tinker sighed.

Chicken filled his cup. "Fret thee not, Sweet Prince. Things do themselves work out."

He reached for the pancake platter. "Sure." He wasn't convinced that they would this time. Not at all.

"Morning, morning, morning," said Messenger as she bubbled into the room. "Oooooopsie!" She stared at Early Dawn and dropped into her chair. And whispered to Smoke, "How'd she get here?"

Smoke shrugged. "Have a pancake." And snatched the platter from in front of Chicken and passed it to Messenger.

Chantal walked in, coffee cup in hand, awake for once, and dropped into her chair and mumbled, "Guess we will have to take Biker Babe to town and buy her some new duds." She dragged the platter from in front of Messenger. "Or some tattoos."

"Oh boy!" Messenger beamed at Early Dawn. "Shopping is fun. Really really."

Early Dawn looked around the table. "Bye Keer Babe?"

"Yep," mumbled Tinker. "Chantal thinks you need more than leather trousers and a vest to wear."

"Oh. I do? Why?"

"Because." And wondered, once again, why it was always happening to him. "That's why!"

"Visitors, " said Smoke, pouring syrup on a large stack of pancakes on her plate.

He jerked. "WHAT?"

"No doughnuts?" asked a rotund man as he walked into the dining room from the kitchen, a tall slender, silver woman at his side. "Ship said you were up and eating so we just let ourselves in."

"Didn't know that you were coming," grumbled Tinker.

Macabre sat, Gyre by his side. "What are those things?"

"Pan Cakes," stated Early Dawn, taking a bite from a large chunk she had speared on her fork.

"Interesting," said Macabre, meaning both the food and her teeth. He watched Fair Morn demolish another stack and then served Gyre and himself. And chewed carefully. "Another tasty food item."

He smiled, a genuine smile. "But not as good as doughnuts."

Early Dawn frowned and started to ask. Fair Morn quickly stood and announced, "Shopping time! Messenger and I are taking Early Dawn to town." She winked at Tinker. "She won't smile at anyone."

"Why not?" Early Dawn frowned at her.

"Oh boy." Messenger bounced up and hurried into the kitchen after them, calling, "I'll drive."

"Tell you on the way into town," said Fair Morn.

The trio hurried from the room.

Macabre looked at Tinker.

"Long story," he mumbled.

"Ah." Digging into a pocket, Macabre extracted something and set it in front of Tinker.

"Here. Brought you this." He frowned. "I do not know. Just that you were supposed to get it." Then he set a rod of the same color next to the object. "This goes along with it." And smiled. "Long story."

Tinker sighed as he looked at the things. "Looks like our long stories are all part of the same story."

"I'll tell you mine, if you'll tell me your's." Macabre took a few of the surviving pancakes.

Smoke winked at him.

And so, they shared their information.

Macabre sat back and stared at Tinker. "You do lead an interesting life." Then he stood. "Time for us to go. Places to visit. Things to kill." He started for the kitchen and the back door. "Call if you need help. But I don't see how you could."

Gyre hurried to his side. And then they walked out and away from the house.

Tinker sat and stared at the objects. "Bet that all this stuff belongs to Braidna."

"Indeed," agreed Chicken.

The rest came in and settled in their chairs.

"I will ask Eulin to find her." Szart, leaned back and sent a brief call.

And after more discussion they scattered around the house to do things that needed doing.

It was in the middle of the afternoon when their pickup banged up the road and into the parking area and splashed through the puddles.

Tinker, Chantal, and Smoke had been washing Chantal's sports car. Somehow, in the washing process, the washers had become drenched and the washee merely wet. Chantal had accused him of doing it deliberately just so he could stare at their bodies.

He suggested that a certain Cowgirl had first dumped a bucket of water on Smoke, which had somehow caused everything within a twenty foot radius to get good and wet.

The driver's door of the pickup popped open and Early Dawn thumped down. "That was easy."

He stared at her. "You drove?" Then at Messenger. "You let her drive?"

Messenger jumped out. "She is a fast learner. Really really."

Fair Morn walked from the passenger side and began to gather up the packages strewn around in the bed of the truck. "We stopped for a little snack. Also."

"Little snack?"

"Three, four."

"Me too." Early Dawn smiled. "They were pretty good."

"I only had one, hamburger." Messenger took a few of packages from Fair Morn and nudged Early Dawn. "Let's go inside and get you dressed, show him all the neato clothing we got you."

The pair headed inside. Fair Morn rolled her eyes at Chantal. "Pretty thin shirt material. Show off."

"Smoke did it."

"Merde," suggested Tinker as he turned the hose on Chantal and then Smoke. "Trouble cat!"

Fair Morn ran for the house clutching her packages.

Chantal leaped back and away. "I'd say that the car is clean, very clean. I'm gonna go get dry and have a cup of coffee before the style show."

Smoke raced for the front deck and door and yelled back at him, "Time for you to ogle someone else's bod."

He shut off the water and coiled up the hose. And nodded to himself. Chantal's car was certainly clean, spotless in fact.

Chicken met him at the back door and handed him a large white towel. "Here, Me'Lord."

"Thanks, Princess."

She smiled. "Most clean a'automobile."

"Yep." Vigorously rubbing his hair with the towel, he headed for his bedroom, leaving a trail of wet footprints down the hall, across the Chamber, and into his bedroom, where he shed his t-shirt and trousers, finished drying off, grabbed a dry shirt and other clothes. Leaving everything in the laundry room, he walked into the kitchen, grabbed a cup of coffee and a handful of cookies, and wandered into the large living room, crunching loudly.

After dropping into his chair, he looked at the rest, and grumbled, "We ready?"

"Yep," replied Fair Morn.

"Yep, yep, yep, yep, yep," bubbled Messenger.

Slumping comfortably, he finished the last cookie, stretched out his legs, and waited.

"It's . . . show time!" called Fair Morn.

Early Dawn stepped from the hallway. She was wearing a long-sleeve, loose fitting shirt, trousers draped over Wellington boots. Everything she wore was in various shades of brown. "They said these were nice things."

"Most true," agreed Chicken.

"Right," he said. "Nice."

Chantal snorted. "At least Big Red has moved out of his centerfold mode." She rubbed her hair dry with a large towel.

"Nothing wrong with that," grumbled Fair Morn.

"Hum," said Szart.

"Hum hum," agreed Sha'gar.

Sgenn nodded.

"Yum yum," observed Smoke, standing behind his chair, gently fluffing up his hair. She wore a thick white robe.

Early Dawn's eyes jumped from face to face, worry wrinkles forming at the corners of her eyes.

"You are beau . . . ti . . . ful," gurgled Messenger. "Really really." She grinned at Tinker. "Isn't she?"

He nodded. "Not bad for a large bat." He laughed, stood, walked over, and gently wrapped her in his arms. "It is all true. You are lovely. And none of them would lie to you. Nice clothes. Did you also get some work clothes?"

"Oh yes. They insisted on that! And pajamas, a soft tan color. Fair Morn said that you enjoyed divesting us of our pajamas. Shall I put them on now?"

"NO!" He stepped back and frowned at Fair Morn. "Sometimes they get out of line. Maybe most of the time." He turned and glared at the rest of them. "O.K., we have things to do around here. Winter is not all that far off and will be here before we know it. Gear needs cleaning and packing."

Everyone hurried away. Fair Morn went with Early Dawn.

And so.

They scattered.

He went upstairs to work in his office. There were many pages to edit and reedit. He sighed. His publishers never seemed to be happy.

Fair Morn led Early Dawn out to the immense pile of

cord wood, after they had changed into appropriate clothes: jeans, flannel shirts, and sturdy boots. And handed her a splitting maul.

"Just watch what I do. Then you can help." She grinned. "But there is something you have to keep in mind, always" The maul arched down, the wood split into two pieces, bouncing in different directions. She tugged the maul from the dirt. "When Big Red created us, he made us much stronger than most creatures we will ever meet." Another swing, another loud crack as wood split and jumped.

"But we do not look like we are." She grinned wider. "So you have to be careful. No one expects females to be that way. And you do not want to hurt anyone by accident either. Especially him."

"Is he delicate?"

"Nope. But you don't want to crack his ribs by overdoing a hug."

"Oh!" Early Dawn smiled. "I will be very careful." And swung her maul. And watched the two pieces of wood bounce away. "This is easy."

"Yep."

"Do you always feel slightly hungry?"

"Yep. I think it is the metabolism he gave us, us being fliers and all."

Early Dawn frowned. "Being real is much more complicated than I thought it would be."

Fair Morn laughed and wrapped her in a hug. "But it is better than just being a short time magical jest."

"Ooooof!"

"Ooops. I forget sometimes." She released Early Dawn.

"See what I mean?"

"Yes."

They set to work.

And eventually stacked the split wood inside the large storage shed.

The gentle knock at the door took his eyes away from the computer screen to the clock on the wall. That late already? "Come in. I didn't realize that it was that time of day."

She walked in carrying a tray which held two cups, a coffee pot, and a plate of cookies.

"Fair Morn said that it was my turn."

He smiled at her. "Come in. Have a cup and some cookies." He shoved a shapeless stack of paper to one side making room for the tray. "Here."

She set the tray in the clean spot. "May I hug you?"

"Huh?"

"Hug you."

"Oh. Sure." He stood.

She did. "I just wanted to see something."

"Ummm." He sat and grabbed a cookie. "Thanks."

"You are welcome."

"OOOOOF!"

"Am I too heavy?"

"Nope. Surprised."

"Fair Morn said that I was to sit in your lap."

"Ummm. It seems that she is just full of advice and ideas."

She nodded. "She has been telling me everything that I need to know to be a real person living here."

He took his cup from the desk and took a sip and looked at her serious expression. "So how do you like it, being a real person living here, for almost a whole day?"

She smiled. "I like it!"

"Sure?"

She nodded. "As a magical jest I was just sort of vague and, ahhhh, temporary." She sighed. "It is hard to express." She stared into his eyes. "I do not think that the Red Magician understands how it feels,"

"You can tell him the next time you see him."

"I will. Yes!" She nodded.

He thought that would be an interesting conversation to listen to.

"J.T.?"

"J.T. ?"

"Fair Morn said that I should have my own name for you."

"Oh."

"Are you going to sneak your hand up under my shirt and fondle me?"

He managed to not choke on the mouthful of coffee and cookie crumbs, just. "What?"

"Fair Morn said that I should expect you to do that. And that I shouldn't hurt you when you did that."

"Do what?"

"Fondle me."

"I think that I will kick her butt," he grumbled. "Hurt me?"

She nodded. "She made me realize how strong I am when we were splitting the wood and that I should be careful."

"Ummmm, how about you talk with Chicken and Smoke and let them tell you about being real and all that?"

"I will do that. May I escape now?"

"Sure. Smoke and Chicken. I will have a little talk with Fair Morn." After she stood, he put everything on the tray and followed her out and down to the kitchen. He was met there by Chicken and Smoke.

"Princess, you really need to talk to her." He glowered at nothing in particular. "Where is that oversized moth?"

"Living room," said Smoke,.

"Most contritely a'waiting," added Chicken.

Sliding the tray onto a counter top he headed that way, and was yanked to a halt by Early Dawn.

"HEY!" Her fingers dug into his upper arms, holding him in place. "OUCH! And leggo!"

"You may not hurt her," snapped Early Dawn.

He sighed. "Talk to her. Please?" He looked as far over one shoulder as he could. "No one is going to hurt anyone. Now let go!"

She did. But watched him carefully as he headed toward the living room, rubbing his upper arms. All heard him mumble, "My life just gets weirder and weirder and weirder. There just has to be a way to stop it. Merde."

"Mine Own bedroom be most comfortable for to talk," suggested Chicken.

Smoke nodded. "Come on, we have a lot to talk about."

Fair Morn watched him as he dropped into his chair. "Don't be angry, One. Please? I forgot how new she is." She tried a small smile. "Smoke and The Princess will fill her in on everything." She stood, walked over, and sat on the floor in front of him. "Please?" She wiped away a tear. "Don't send her away. I like her. It is like having a real sister, someone just like me. Wings and all."

He stared down, at her sagging posture, slumped shoulders, poking at the floor with one finger nail. And sighed. "But we can stop all that romance novel nonsense, can't we?"

Her head snapped up, a big grin flooding across her face. Then she bounced to her feet, lifted him from his chair, and hugged him.

"OOOOF!"

"Ooops." She set him down. "Forgot." And looked sheepish. "I warned her about that."

"And other things, I suppose?"

"Yep." This time it was a very controlled grin. And a kiss. And after awhile, she said, "We split two cords of wood. And stacked it in the shed."

"That's impressive."

She smiled wider. "That's me." And laughed as he frowned. "And Early Dawn." She lightly rubbed a large ornate ring against the side of his face. "I gotcha!"

"Oh, boy."

"Heh, heh, heh, heh, heh, heh."

"So whatcha wanna do?"

"Make a roast beef sandwich." She spun from his arms and tugged him toward the kitchen. "Just a little snack before dinner."

Chantal leaned over Messenger who was sprawling in the hammock on the rear deck. "That was nicely done."

Messenger giggled. "I think that she learned that from you."

Chantal shrugged. "Comes from being a multi-bodied organism with a group mind, I guess."

Sha'gar walked from the house and joined them. "Who is making dinner?"

"Him. And Fair Morn."

Sha'gar's eyes flew wide. "He cooks?"

"Not very often," grumbled Chantal.

"Wonder what we will get?"

"Fried bat," suggested Chantal.

Inside Chicken's room Early Dawn jerked and frowned. "That was not very nice!" Her keen hearing had overheard the conversation on the rear deck.

"She was joking." Smoke was lying on the floor, fingers laced over her stomach, staring up at the ceiling. "And he is really bad at that. Just have to ignore it."

Chicken was brushing out the tangle that was Early Dawn's hair. "Most messy."

"I did it."

"Indeed? Then thee do have much to learn, it do seem a'Us."

"Yes, I do. I didn't realize how hard being real was going to be."

"We understand, We do."

"What are we making." Fair Morn handed him the next item he requested.

"Thai. I thought that we would cook something that no-one has done before." He set the three cookbooks on the table. "But I think that we could use some additional help."

Chantal walked in. "I volunteer. You need some talent

in here."

He winked at her.

"I meant cooking."

He laughed, opened one of the cookbooks. "This recipe. I will make a different one. So will Mothra." He handed the other book to Fair Morn and indicated the correct recipe. "It makes a lots of rice."

"Yum, yum, yum," said Fair Morn. She liked the idea of lots. And hot and spicy as well.

And then.

A little more than a hour later.

Dinner was ready.

And served to one and all.

"Gosh!" Messenger looked at the artfully arranged serving platters.

"Indeed," agreed Chicken. "Most impressive, Our Lord."

He laughed. "I had a little help."

"Right," said Chantal. "Pass the rice."

Sgenn held up something and waggled it back and forth. "What is this thing?"

"Shrimp," stated Chantal. "Don't eat the tail. That is the part you are holding in your fingers."

He looked around the table. "Haven't we had shrimp since she arrived?"

"Guess not, G.I.," mumbled Chantal. "Most of the cooks have a rather limited repertoire."

Chicken set down her fork, unbuttoned the top three

buttons on her shirt, and peered inside. And sighed dramatically. "Most limited." She winked at him.

Him sighed equally dramatically, and grumbled, "And conversations."

All in all, the dinner passed rather quietly, for them. It was the three new dishes that held their attention. He made a mental note of that. Perhaps he ought to cook more often.

Long after dinner, he was slumped deep in one of the couches, even deeper inside the book he was reading. He had passed through several chapters before he became aware of the slight pressure from either side. Two chapters later, he put the book mark in place and looked.

Fair Morn sat against his left side. Early Dawn was on his right.

"Ummmm?"

"One?"

"J.T.?

"What's going on? This time?"

"Just sitting and reading," said Fair Morn, holding up the paperback. "Bodice ripper."

"Me too," said Early Dawn, holding up her thin book. "Dick and Jane."

He struggled upright. "What?"

"Chocolate lust," breathed Fair Morn, deep in her throat.

"Dick and Jane. Two young children," explained Early Dawn.

"Oversight on Big Red's part," stated Fair Morn. "We're teaching her how to read."

"Oh. Really?"

Early Dawn nodded. "It's not that hard."

"Most fast a'learner, Me'Lord." Chicken leaned on the back of the couch and tostled his hair.

"Shouldn't take too long," added Smoke, joining Chicken, tickling his ear.

"Stop it!" he hissed, waving one arm wildly over his head.

"POUNCE!" cried Messenger.

He tried to slide from the couch, seeing motion on all sides.

"OOOOOOOF! Damn!"

"Fair Morn?"

"Early Dawn?"

"Whose hand is that?"

"Beat's me."

"OFF!" demanded someone from the bottom, shoving at an arm and a leg.

"Unhand me, cur!" snarled Chicken.

"Ooopsie," giggled Messenger.

"Will you guys get off?"

Smoke sat up. "Sounds pretty grumpy."

"Hum, hum, hum, hum." Szart slipped free and tapped Sgenn on a shoulder who shoved Chantal to one side.

"Careful what you push," grumped Chantal.

Then, they all sat in a loose circle and looked at him.

"Bug nuts," he grumbled. "I am gonna get the water tested."

Early Dawn looked at Fair Morn who said," He does grumble a lot."

"I think," said Sha'gar, poking him in the side, "that I

would like some ice cream."

"Fetch!" he hissed. "General," he said to the ceiling, "I think that we are surrounded. Anyone know where all these Indians came from?"

"I'll get it." Messenger bounced to her feet and hurried toward the kitchen.

Chicken stood. "We will Ourself fair bowls and spoons be a'getting." She hurried into the dining room.

Early Dawn leaned close to Fair Morn and whispered, "Is he all right? He isn't making any sense."

"Yep. Nothing a little ice cream won't fix."

They decided to have an ice cream picnic on the floor in the living room. And everyone decided that everyone had to sample whatever flavor anyone else was having.

Everyone agreed that it was a wonderful idea, a great idea, and beamed and smiled at Sha'gar. Even Tinker smiled, who sat by Sha'gar's side, leaning back against one of the couches, watching Fair Morn and Early Dawn finish off a gallon of vanilla ice cream. Each.

Fair Morn stood and stretched. And winked at him when she saw him looking at her. "Pretty nice, huh?" And laughed as he sighed. "I think that I will go outside and flit about for a while." She leaned over and touched Early Dawn in the center of her forehead with one fingertip. "Tag! You're it!" She spun and ran for and out the front door.

Early Dawn leaped to her feet and raced after her.

"This ought to be interesting." He stood and headed for the rear deck.

The moon was full, flooding everything with soft silver light. He stood by the railing and looked up and around. Then he saw them. Fair Morn was in a steep glide, aimed toward the house, hurtling down from the general direction of their barn. Somewhat higher and coming faster was Early Dawn.

Fair Morn looked back, hovered, floated soft as a cloud. Then she suddenly tilted sharply to one side.

Early Dawn shot past her, snapping sideways, and upward, searching.

"Heh, heh, heh," cackled Fair Morn as she coasted owl silent over his head and just up and over the edge of the house roof.

"Heard you!" shouted Early Dawn as she rocketed down, wings making soft popping sounds. She zipped along the long axis of the rear deck. Her passage ruffled his hair.

"WATCH IT!" He saw her circle out around the far end of the building.

Fair Morn coasted around the large tree that stood at the far end of their swimming pool and hovered, looking around for her pursuer.

Early Dawn shot from the end of the building, diagonally across the flower beds, low and then upward, and flashed past Fair Morn. "TAG!"

He heard cloth rip.

"Evil Bat!" gnarled Fair Morn, twisting and heading toward the far slope and into dense forest shadow.

Some time passed, and then he saw Early Dawn circle over the first pasture and head for the house. As she drifted along, carefully searching, he saw a small dot rise near the ridge above the forested slope. It seemed to tilt and plunge at a very sharp angle.

Suddenly Early Dawn twisted as Fair Morn reached for

her, butterfly wings snapping full open from their half-closed position.

"Vengeance of The Winged Warrior," laughed Fair Morn. "LOOK OUT!"

Water splashed high into the air and drenched him. He turned and ran to the edge and stared into the black water. Fair Morn waved at him. "I need some help, One."

He waded into the shallow end, grabbed her under the armpits, and hauled her out. "You hurt?"

"Wet wings." She lurched out into the open grass and flopped onto her back, great wings spread wide.

Early Dawn heaved herself from the swimming pool, wings flapping wildly. "That's the advantage of waterproof leather. Big Red was smart that way."

He headed for the house. "I'll get towels and robes." When he returned, he handed one of the thick white robes to Early Dawn. "Here, put this on. What happened?"

Early Dawn looked down. Half her shirt was ripped away, the remnants hanging loose down to her left knee. "She did it." She shrugged on the robe.

He walked over to Fair Morn. "You too?"

She grinned up at him. "She started it." She had lost all the buttons on her shirt and that portion where the pocket had been.

He knelt and began to wipe down her left wings with a large towel and tossed another towel to Early Dawn so she could begin on the other side. "You two should be more careful," he grumbled.

Fair Morn stood, spun, and flopped onto her front so they could dry the back. When they were done wiping away the water, she stood and folded and folded and folded the great butterfly wings and shrugged on the offered robe. Grinning broadly, she threw an arm over Early Dawn's shoulders. "She is a lot faster but not so maneuverable."

"And not as sneaky," added Early Dawn. She shivered. "I am cold."

"This way." Fair Morn led her into the house and into the tub room.

He waved at the heads bobbling just above the steaming water. "Night." And hung the towels in the laundry room and headed for his bed,

A warm body nudged him and yanked around the blanket. His eyes flew open and registered from the light shaft on the floor that the moon was close to sliding down behind the far ridge. "You done thrashing around?" he grumbled, thumping his pillow into order.

"Yes."

He lurched upright. "What are you doing in here?"

She yanked the blanket up to her chin and waggled the fingers of one hand at him. She was wearing the large ornate ring. The jewels glittered in the moonlight.

"Oh." He toppled back. And sighed. *Early Dawn?* She didn't react and he couldn't feel her presence the way he could feel the rest of himself.

"Is this a magic ring?"

"No. It is just a sort of an agreement ring."

She rolled onto her side and slipped an arm over his chest. "I am real, not a magical jest."

"I know."

"Fair Morn said that you were very nice."

"She is biased."

"You are nice and warm."

"You said that before. You too."

"Kiss me."

"You're not gonna bite, are you?" He laughed and rolled in her direction.

"No. Of course not."

In the morning he flopped into his chair at the dining room table and stared into nothing at all.

Chicken filled his cup and shoved it into his hand. "Fair Morn, Me'Lord."

"Ump."

Early Dawn smiled at her as she walked into the room, wearing one of the thick white robes, water dripping from her hair.

"Get thee hence and dry thy hair," snapped Chicken pointing toward the kitchen.

Early Dawn jerked and hurried away, passed Fair Morn coming the other way, dragging on her pajama top.

"Weirder and weirder," he mumbled, taking a sip from his cup.

Chantal walked in and crashed into her chair. Fair Morn handed her a steaming cup.

They all settled around the table, speaking very softly, watching him and Chantal, both notorious slow wakers. Early Dawn smiled at Fair Morn who nodded and slid a platter over, first hooking a large serving of sausage and eggs onto her plate.

Tinker peered around the table, his eyes mostly open. Chicken nudged his arm with the newly filled cup. "We need to talk," he grumbled.

"Pon?" She served him and herself.

"Bats."

"Fair Prince?"

"One. Bat. One very large bat."

"I am not a bat," mumbled Early Dawn.

"Grumble, grumble, grumble," grumbled Chantal, now fully awake. She glowered at Smoke.

"I don't know," replied Smoke.

"I'm sorry," whispered Messenger, sinking in her chair.

"Not your fault, Kitten." He spread jelly on his toast. "I think that we were manipulated by that ultimate manipulator, Big Red."

"Damn red fink," growled Chantal. "Pass the toast, please."

Szart nudged Sha'gar and indicated Early Dawn with her chin. "Hum."

"Hum hum," replied Sha'gar.

Dat wandered in from the living room, stopped behind Early Dawn, and peered over the top of her head, and inside her robe. Then she walked to her chair and said to Chantal. "A possible yum or two. Perhaps I should fix her."

"She doesn't require fixing. Have some cocoa."

Dat filled her cup. "Just thinking of my Great Master."

"He is overstocked as it is." Chantal looked at Szart and Sha'gar. "There must be some sneaky magic to prevent this from happening all the time."

Szart shook her head. "The Red Magician is one of the

absolute forces in the universes."

"My Great Master likes yums," stated Dat.

"We are all yums," growled Chantal. "Forget it."

"Gimble, gimble, gimble," grumbled the indjinn back at her.

"Everyone does not need their anatomy enhanced," hissed Chantal.

Early Dawn looked worry at him, wrinkles creasing her forehead.

"You are fine," he said. "Just fine. Everything is fine." He looked around the table. "Everyone is fine, just fine. All the parts of everyone are wonderful. And you," he pointed at Dat, "will stop worrying about everyone's anatomy. No one here requires fixing up, altering, enhancing, or any other messing around with." He stood and stalked into the kitchen.

"Bad bothered," hissed Szart.

Sha'gar nodded and leaned close to her. "You could be taller."

"Bak bak ntap tik," suggest Szart, who was the shortest of all of them.

"Witch coarse," observed Sgenn.

"Zig tik Dah'ga ptar rak" hissed Szart.

Sha'gar stared at her, red flaring deep in her eyes. "Most sorry sorry Faan witch Szart sister self."

Szart blinked, black fading from around her. She leaned over and kissed Sha'gar on the side of her face. "Witch sorry."

She looked down at him and stated firmly. "I am not a bat."

He was lying in the thick grass, out beyond the flower

beds, out beyond the rear deck. Watching the few clouds turn into interesting forms. "I know. I was feeling grumpy."

She knelt next to him. "They are being unpleasant."

"I know. It is because of that damn red pest and the stuff he has dropped us into again. They are getting worried."

She knelt, grabbed his hand and held it in both of her's. "I will not let that Dat do things to my body."

He smiled up a her. "She won't. Indjinns just have a sorta one track mind when it comes to what they consider female beauty. You have to learn to ignore Dat."

"I will." She looked at the grass, at the open space, open yet secluded. "What are you doing?"

He smiled. "I was just enjoying one of the rare pleasures in life."

"What?"

"Laying on my back and watching the clouds."

"May I do that?"

"Sure." He laughed. "Lots of room. It is a big pasture."

She released his hands, stretched out in the thick and tall grass. Next to him. "Just watch the clouds?"

"Yep. And imagine what they look like."

Chantal cornered Smoke and Chicken in the large living room. "O.K., you two, what are we going to do about her?"

"Tis conundrum."

"We are a large group," said Smoke.

"Damn right we are. There are eight of us babes in this pride already." Chantal propped one foot on the lower shelf under one of the large picture windows and stared out.

"Give her back?" Smoke's minds reached out.

"Although I do not think that she would do that."

Chantal nudged her. "Do you see anything in her mind that would tell us what Big Red is up to this time?"

"Nope. Her memories are very shallow. She is only a few days old and I doubt that B.G. would tell anyone what he is about."

Chantal snorted. "Hard to remember her actual age when she looks like she ought to be about twenty-seven or so."

"Most pleasant a'person," suggested Chicken.

"Dodging the issue," grumbled Chantal.

"Such as?"

"Whether she becomes us or not," growled Chantal. "Number nine in what feels like an ever-expanding menagerie."

Fair Morn entered the room and joined them at the window. "A collection of wild or strange animals kept in an enclosure for exhibition?"

Chantal laughed. "I'd say that is a fairly accurate description of this place. Except he works hard at keeping us from being exhibited en masse."

"Indeed," agreed Chicken.

"Back to the question," grumbled Chantal.

"Does he want to?" asked Fair Morn.

"No," replied Smoke. "He has been puzzling over the problem ever since Messenger set her free. Unlike all the other times, there is no pressure to bind in." She nudged Chantal. "Except for you, of coarse. You were Ripple's mistake. We were mutually trapped, so to speak."

"Yeah, I know." She slid an arm around Smoke. "Can't say that it hasn't been interesting. Should we ask all the others?"

"I think that we should wait and see. I do not think that we are in any rush, are we, Cowgirl?"

"Nope. Just thought that we ought to talk about it."

Smoke patted Chantal's thigh. "He is very calm, so far, and seems to just accept her just as she is."

"Wings and all."

"Nothing wrong with wings," said Fair Morn. "And all."

"Especially the all," stated Chantal.

"Our all do be most pleasing a'him," observed Chicken.

"Her's are all right." Fair Morn smiled. "For a magical jest that is not so centerfold, ahhhhh, enhanced."

"Guess that is settled then," said Chantal.

Smoke nudged her. "You worry almost as much as he does."

"We are out of rooms. You better start thinking about that little problem." Chantal laughed. "Unless you want to stick a coffin in the attic."

"She is not a bat or a vampire just like I am not a butterfly," stated Fair Morn. "Mostly."

"A joke," replied Chantal. "Good thing that her skin isn't pale white cause with those wings and teeth she'd look like an escapee from a B-grade horror movie."

Fair Morn nodded. "Maybe we could get Big Red to change things?"

"With his sense of humor? She might wind up with a tail."

Smoke smiled. "Tails are very nice. Mine was very nice." She poked Chantal on her shirt pocket. "But I think this form is very nice, also."

"Watch what you are poking."

"Lots to poke, globular one."

"Meeting is adjourned!" Chantal stood and headed for the front door. "Think that I'll go into town and grocery shop."

"Let's go." Fair Morn hurried after her. "We can get some doughnuts. Too."

Just A Little Excitement

Grandeville. Tinker's Place.

After some time, after a number of clouds had passed, she rolled onto her side, cradled her head on her arm and stared at him. "This is nice."

"Uh huh."

"Sun feels so good."

"Yep."

"Makes my skin tingle."

He rolled his head to her direction. "Put your robe back on."

"I like it off." She smiled. "The air is warm."

He sighed. And went back to staring at the clouds. Then he jerked. And sat up. He had just heard the soft pop as she deployed her wings. "Oh no you don't!"

"What?"

She was sitting up and scratching behind one ear with the small wing claws on that side. She curled the other around to cast shadow on his face. "Ermmmmm," she hummed. "It feels so good." The wing quivered.

"No flying around like that."

She gaped at him. "Without my clothes?" And grinned slyly. "Does Fair Morn do that?"

"No!" One corner of his mouth pulled down. "Sorry. My mistake. I misunderstood."

"Oh, J. T." She grabbed and hugged him.

"OOOOF!"

Her arms flew wide. "Forgot."

"S'O.K.," he wheezed. "Happens all the time."

She stared at him. "Did I hurt you? Fair Morn told me to be very careful, very firmly she told me that. And now I have failed."

He smiled and shook his head. "No, really, I'm fine. Just had the air squeezed out, that's all." And cleared his throat. "Ahhhhh, how about putting your robe back on?"

She nodded, her wings popped closed. She shrugged on the heavy white robe, tugging it shut. "There."

"Much better."

"Then I deserve a reward."

"Huh?"

She knocked him flat and sprawled on top of him, grinning wildly, peering into his eyes. "Kiss meeeeeeee."

"Bug nuts," he mumbled. And did.

Smoke nudged Chicken. "A strong pouncer."

"Indeed." She scattered the wood chips around the base of the bushes. She and Smoke were helping Messenger work on one of the many flower and shrub beds just beyond the edge of the rear deck.

She faded onto the rear deck in a gentle violet mist which became a young woman dressed in billowing lavender garb. She gasped. "Mothers!" And tried to look dismayed, shocked, and then stared at them. She failed with dismay and shock so she just laughed as they stood and stared at her as she asked, "Does Father encourage you in this? In this informal style." None of them were wearing their shirts. Then she looked around. "Where is he?"

Chicken pointed. "Pon fair First Pasture."

She looked over the tops of the low shrubs. "Where?"

"Checking the wildlife." Smoke smiled.

Messenger giggled. "Bat watching."

"Mothers?" She carefully looked at them. They appeared quite healthy, just rather dirty.

"Let us away for to shower ourselves," suggested Chicken. "Fair daughter couldst make lemonade!"

"Sure." Eulin started for the kitchen while the others headed toward the shower room.

Eulin is here. Smoke winked at him. In his mind he saw a great cat-like face with a grin and a very lewd wink.

"Ummm," he said, staring up at a passing cloud. She gave him a little nip on the side of the neck.

"We ought to go inside and take a shower."

"Why?"

"We have company. My daughter just arrived."

She sat up and grinned. "I like being real. You have a daughter?"

He nodded.

"Fair Morn said that I shouldn't ask this, but I want to know, please?"

"What?" It was a very cautious question.

"Am I really beautiful?"

He smiled. "Yes. You are. Big Red has good, ahhhhh, taste." And laughed. "Just bad taste, ahhh, so to speak, in what he thinks is funny."

She frowned. "You are not just being nice?"

"Nope." He grinned. "A real babe."

She laughed happily. "A real babe." And curled one wing around and pinched his cheek with her wing claws.

"With bat wings," he added.

So, she tickled him.

"How about we get dressed, go take a shower, and see what my daughter is up to."

She stood, snapped her wings away, grabbed her robe and tugged it back on. And watched as he pulled his clothes on.

They strolled up and onto the rear deck, admiring the new work that had been done in the flower beds, and into the house and the shower and tub room. Just in time. To hear Chicken cursing wildly.

"Foul Feline Wench, unhand Us!"

"Heh heh heh," cackled Smoke.

Messenger hurtled from the shower room opening, grinning wildly, and leaped into the gigantic hot tub, water splashing and surging in every direction.

He guided Early Dawn around to the other side of the shower room and dumped his clothes into the laundry hamper and stepped into the steam filled shower room.

Smoke had Chicken's arms clamped behind her back with one hand while with the other she was vigorously washing Chicken's hair. Great gobs of lather were running down over her face and body.

"Don't ask," said Tinker, handing Early Dawn a bar of soap. "There are times when one does not want to get involved. And this is one of those times."

Suddenly Smoke released Chicken, ran to the door, and

dove.

"EEEEEK!" screeched Messenger, just before the loud splash.

Chicken fumbled around, located a shower head and rinsed off the thick layer of soap suds. Wiping her face with her hand, she glared at him. "Most cowardly, Our Lord, for to not rescue this, Thy Verra Own Queen, from most vile abuse."

"Looked pretty clean to me." He laughed. "Besides, you probably started it."

"Right!" yelled Smoke from the hot tub. "Skinny started it."

"Vile wench!" howled Chicken, hurtling out the door and into the tub.

"EEEEEEEK!" screeched Messenger, just before the loud splash.

"Wash my hair?"

"Sure, turn around."

Early Dawn did. And he began to work up a thick lather. She arched her back as the lather flowed and as he worked lower. "That is very nice," she rumbled low in her throat, peering down at his hands.

"Couldn't resist."

Eulin poked her head in through the outside door. "Lemonade's ready."

The hot tub crowd boiled out, grabbing up robes. As they settled around one of the large wooden tables, the rest filtered in from various directions.

"I made lots," explained Eulin. "Hello, Mothers. Where's Father?"

"Getting clean," said Chantal.

"Toweling off," added Je'leel, joining them. "Hi, Sister."

As they strolled from the house also wearing thick white robes, Early Dawn said, "She is beautiful."

"Eulin, Early Dawn. Early Dawn, Eulin." He took a glass of lemonade handed to him by Chantal. "Thanks."

"Father?"

He sighed. "Big Red."

Eulin smiled. "Again?"

"What's up?"

She sat. "I thought I'd tell you where everyone went when those Wizards came."

He nodded and sat next to her. "Wondered about that."

So, Eulin told him, and them.

"They are still out there?"

"Kartz told me that you are The Prime Male ring wearer and for them that means they have a moral responsibility to guard you from most other things."

Eulin looked around and smiled at her father. "They only ate a few deer and a couple of Doc's cattle."

Then it dawned on him that no-one had known that they were there. It was a very spooky thought imagining the forest crawling with carnivorous demons slipping silently along, a hazard to all living things. He smiled to himself and thought that it was a good thing that it wasn't hunting season.

He cupped his hands around his mouth and shouted, "COME OUT, COME OUT, WHERE EVER YOU ARE!"

They flowed out and across the first pasture, toward the rear deck. A partial set.

"Holy COW!" He stared at them.

"Most impressive," said Chicken.

The Core Pair leaped onto the deck and walked over to stand next to him, gurgling deep in their throats.

"Hi," he said. And sighed. "Thanks. But I don't think that it was necessary."

They leaned close and nuzzled the side of his neck.

"Careful."

They stepped away, a little, huffing soft puffs of breath. It was laughter. Tark demon laughter.

He could feel the heal radiating from them. "Um," he waved one hand, indicating the ever shifting numbers, standing, watching. "Do we really need them? The wizards are gone?"

Amamaedur looked past him at Ahamaezur. Ahamaezur barked. The partial set whirled and poured into some small opening, back to their home.

"But you are staying, right?"

They gurgled and stepped closer to him.

"Ummm, O.K." He looked from side to side. "Shall we just relax and take it easy?" He turned and walked back to the table and dropped onto one of the wooden benches and snatched up his coffee cup. And nodded. "Yep. Certainly relaxing, all right." Then he realized that the core pair were eyeing Early Dawn.

Amamaedur reached out and poked her with one finger.

"She is a friend."

Early Dawn poked Amamaedur back and looked at him. "Are they jests?"

"No. They are carnivorous demons called Tark.

Ummmm, they are friends."

Ahamaezur huffed deep in her throat and licked her lips.

Early Dawn nodded and smiled at them.

Both Tark snorted and stared at her. And instantly moved sideways, no longer standing where they seemed to be. And grabbed her from either side.

"J.T.!" yelped Early Dawn.

"Merde!" He leaped to his feet.

Amamaedur was hurtled over the railing into a flower bed. Ahamaezur crashed into the house wall. With a loud pop, Early Dawn's wings flared wide and she shot straight up.

"HOLD IT!" He ran over to Ahamaezur, who shoved herself to her feet, and shook her head. Then stared at Early Dawn as she hovered over the swimming pool.

Snapping and hissing Amamaedur swarmed back onto the rear deck, and snarled.

He stepped between the Core Pair. "STOP IT! What's wrong with you two?"

They carefully checked each other for damage, then looked at him. Amamaedur bared her teeth and pointed at Early Dawn. Ahamaezur grabbed his hand and clamped her teeth around it.

"Ah ha," he said.

Ahamaezur released his hand. Amamaedur nodded, and said, "Ah ha."

He beckoned Early Dawn over and threw his arms around the Core Pair as they moved to stand by his side. "She is not a demon. She is like Fair Morn only she has different kinds of wings and teeth." He tugged them against himself.

"She is a friend. Nothing to worry about."

Early Dawn settled in front of him and snapped her wings closed. She looked from Amamaedur to Ahamaezur. "Did I hurt you?"

Amamaedur huffed laughter and stepped forward and gently clasped Early Dawn's upper arm and looked at Ahamaezur. And gurgled something. Ahamaezur snorted.

"What?" asked Early Dawn.

Amamaedur smiled at her and clacked her teeth together. Ahamaezur stepped forward, took a small sack from somewhere and fished out something and handed it to Early Dawn.

She took it and looked at them, and then at him. "It is a blue stone."

He smiled. "It is a great gift. That stone is held in the highest regard among The Tark."

"Oh." Early Dawn smiled at them. "Thank you."

The Core Pair stepped close and nuzzled her neck.

"That tickles." She laughed as four hands ran over her body. "Certainly friendly."

The Core Pair stepped back and huffed deep in their throats.

"I think," he said, "that you are now considered one of them."

Amamaedur leaned against his side. So did Ahamaezur.

"They've never met anyone with teeth like that other than their own race." He cleared his throat. "So, I think that they thought that you were some new variety of carnivorous demon that they hadn't seen."

She nodded. "Big Red told me."

He stared at her. "Told you what?"

"He said, never be surprised at anything that happens around John. And it is true." She leaned forward and kissed him. "Things do happen around you."

"You want some more lemonade, Cowboy?" asked Chantal. Loudly. "Or are you just gonna stand around fondling things?"

Glowering at her, he stepped away, took a full glass and sipped. "Pretty good." He noticed Eulin looking at Early Dawn as she smiled at Fair Morn.

Something flashed in. The tiny blue-green dragon perched on Eulin's shoulder and chirped in her ear. And disappeared.

"Found her," said Eulin.

He stood. "O.K., let's change into travel clothes and take those artifacts to Braidna." He was anxious to get them out of their house and out of their possession. He hurried into the house to get ready.

Fair Morn took Early Dawn with her.

The Core Pair drank some more lemonade.

A Real Disaster

The Guarded Lands.

They swirled in, a whirling cloud of black. It was an effect that Szart particularly liked.

They were standing on a gentle slope not far from the top of the low hill. Braidna was standing on the brow of the hill, facing away from them looking down the back slope, in a very animated conversation with someone not visible from where they stood.

Tinker looked around. It seemed to be the middle of summer here. All gentle, warm breeze and clear sky. The grass was green and lush. In the distance could be seen scattered clumps of trees.

"O.K.?" He received various nods and smiles.

As they crested the hill and saw the others, the Core Pair snorted, snatched long, serrated blades from somewhere, and slipped out to either side, no longer where they appeared to be.

"What is that thing?" He yanked down the great black sword. It danced lightly in his hand. On all sides he knew they were holding weapons.

Chicken's blade whistled through the air as she whipped it from her scabbard. "Most ugly a'thing, My Lord."

Braidna was talking with a large man and a much larger something that appeared to be mostly tentacles. Without turning, she said, "Welcome, John. This is Hand'l and Iztar. Hand'l is the man."

Hand'l watched them carefully as they walked up, spreading sideways. "Whoever you are," he stated loudly. "I have no quarrel."

Stepping up to Braidna's right side, Tinker nodded. "What's going on?"

Fair Morn nudged Early Dawn. "Stay back. I need a clear field of fire." She stroked a lever on her weapon into a new setting and held the space cannon cradled in her arms. "Tight focus."

Early Dawn stepped back and whispered, "What is that ugly thing standing there?"

Fair Morn shrugged. "No idea. We have never seen anything like that before."

"Just a little discussion," answered Braidna. "This pair seems to think that I should care about an errand they were sent upon."

"Oh."

"Your Mother had it," stated Hand'l.

"We have already gone over that," snapped Braidna.

"What?" asked Tinker.

"The Tered of Gth," she said.

"Oh." He looked at Hand'l. "Why not just go away if she says that she doesn't have it?"

Hand'l stared at Tinker, then he smiled.

Tinker sighed. "Don't do anything, ummmm, Hand'l. Please?" He could feel the urge from his weaponkin, eager to kill.

Sgenn stepped over, stood by Braidna's other side, and stuffed her arms into the wide sleeves of her grey robe. Deep below something moved. She smiled at Hand'l, a soft half-smile.

Hand'l nodded. "Princess, this hill will be littered with dead friends soon. We came for the Tered."

"Merde," mumbled Tinker.

Hand'l slipped past the sword point and grabbed Braidna by the throat. "Your magic and these archaic soldiers will do you no good."

"STOP!" shouted Fair Morn as Early Dawn leaped past Sgenn and clamped one hand on Hand'l's extended arm

"NARRRR!" he howled, releasing Braidna and thrusting a short blade at Early Dawn. She leaped sideways as the blade flickered past..

In one smooth motion, Iztar flowed forward and sucked Early Dawn inside.

The great sword flicked and Hand'l's weapon tumbled in two pieces.

Braidna gasped. "They are Darnar Mage! Be carefull!"

"Ptar nak," hissed Szart, dumping protection over everyone.

Chantal charged up, jammed the tip of her revolver under the chin of Hand'l, cocking the lever back as she did. "Tell that pile of ugly to release our friend or your brains are going everywhere."

Another short blade plunged into her lower abdomen.

"Damn!" gasped Chantal, firing.

The shock threw Hand'l back as a red fog blew upward.

Chantal staggered backward, holding her mid-section and waggling the long-barreled revolver at the other thing.

Smoke reached, pushing Chantal's pain deep and helped her drop her pack so Chantal could tell Smoke which medical supply to use.

"Me'Lord!" Chicken was slashing wildly at Iztar, dancing here and there as tentacles failed in her direction.

"ONE," yelled Fair Morn. "I DON'T KNOW WHERE TO SHOOT."

Sgenn slipped her hands back inside her sleeves and calmed walked over to the monster. "Let her go."

"Get away from that thing," snapped Tinker, running toward the far side of Iztar. He figured he could just cut bits and pieces away until Early Dawn was freed.

Sgenn was dragged inside.

"Medre." He stared, now afraid to do anything at all.

Off to one side, Smoke ripped Chantal's shirt open and began to work on her wound

Iztar shook, grunted and began to leak green fluid from a number of spots. Then ripped open. From the inside. Something black, all sharp angles and multi-jointed stood up through the gaping hole and tore more of the monster away as Iztar sagged down around it.

Someone drenched in green ooze backed out, dragging something else equally heavily coated.

Messenger ran up and helped. "Yuck, yuck, yuck."

The black thing sank into the ground.

Fair Morn ran up to them and lifted the limp figure in her arms and walked over to a clean area and laid her the grass.

Braidna joined them and watched as Fair Morn wiped the face clean. "Early Dawn." Fair Morn ripped Early Dawn's shirt open, leaned over, one ear pressed to the mostly clean chest, listening.

"Move away," commanded Braidna, dropping to her knees on the other side of the slack figure.

Fair Morn sat back. "I couldn't hear anything."

Braidna nodded, made a fist with her right hand and extended her forefinger, leaned, twisted, and stabbed it into the center of the exposed chest.

The body twitched, jerked, and thrashed. Early Dawn gurgled green stuff, coughed, and retched, splashing over Braidna and Fair Morn. And screamed, her head flying back, neck arching.

Braidna yanked her finger out and smoothed the wound closed. And nodded.

Early Dawn stopped moving, sucked in a deep shuddering breath, her eyes wobbling open. "It was horrible."

Suddenly the hill was surrounded.

Braidna leaped to her feet, calling in Great Death.

"HOLD IT!" Tinker charged over and grabbed her by an arm. "Hold it. Those are friends."

The demon set surged upward, covering all the slopes, eyes glowing red in the sunlight.

Ahamaezur barked orders. The set positioned itself and stood. Ready.

"Friends? Those things?"

"Yep." He pointed at the dead bodies. "Any more of them around?"

"No."

"Good. Then relax."

She waved away the stuff overhead. "Well, ummmmm, Consort," she smiled at him. "Why are you here?"

Fair Morn helped Early Dawn stand.

"Really a mess," observed Messenger. "Really really."

Early Dawn lurched over and wrapped her arms around Braidna. "Thank you." And kissed her. And yanked back. "Oh! Sorry." Braidna was covered with green goo.

"You are lucky that Iztar was distracted," said Braidna, waving away the stuff. From herself and Early Dawn. She looked at Tinker. "She is quite pretty." And smiled. "Now that we can see her. Clean."

He sighed and grumbled at Early Dawn. "I don't suppose that you brought an extra shirt?"

"No."

"Matters not," stated Braidna. "We are all . . . friends." She looked at Tinker. "I suppose."

Chicken hurried up to them. "Our Prince, we must a'home hurry. Fair Chantal does great medical care require."

"WHAT?" All the rest of himself jerked at the emotional surge.

"Cool it," rasped Chantal, turning her head and looking at him. "I'll survive." She glared from Early Dawn to him. "Damn well better."

Tinker dumped his pack on the ground and fished out the artifacts and handed them to Braidna. "Here! Gotta go! Come visit." Slapping the great sword onto his back, he hooked an arm through the pack strap and spun around. "Szart! Sha'gar! Let's go!"

Early Dawn tapped him on the shoulder. "I think that

I will stay here. I owe her a debt." She looked at Braidna. "May I?"

Braidna looked at him as he turned around and nodded and grumbled, "She'll explain everything." He charged over to where Chantal lay, Smoke sitting by her side, hand resting lightly on Chantal's shoulder "Let's go! Let's go!"

Everyone crowded around. Szart and Sha'gar held hands.

They swirled away. Braidna looked at Early Dawn. "How is this possible? I thought that none of his parts could be separated from the others."

Early Dawn smiled.

Braidna gasped

"I am not part of them. I was just visiting." Then she began to explain.

As she did, they watched the Tark pour back through the hole they had made.

Grandeville. Tinker's Place.

They swirled onto the rear deck in a cloud of twisting black.

"Hospital," whispered Chantal. "Get me to that damn hospital, Cowboy."

Smoke looked at Szart. "Now!"

Szart nodded and sent Smoke, Chantal, and Tinker.

Grandeville. Riverview Hospital.

They suddenly appeared in the driveway, just outside the entrance to the Emergency Room.

He shoved the door open and held it for Smoke as she carried her burden inside.

They walked over to the counter where the nurse stared at them with wide eyes.

Raj came running down one of the corridors toward them, Kartz at this side, dressed in whites, jacket and trousers.

"Szart told us," he said to Tinker. "Room two!" he snapped at the nurse. "NOW!"

She bolted in the right direction, throwing open the door, yanking various supplies from various drawers.

Raj indicated the examining table. "There." Smoke set Chantal there.

Two men in green garb rushed in and began to work over Chantal as Raj shooed Tinker and Smoke out of the room. "Wait outside, please."

Two more nurses raced into the room.

Tinker leaned on the wall and looked at Smoke, "Well?"

"Deep, ugly wound. We could call Dat."

Not yet. Don't what her changing things, snarled Chantal in their minds. *Prefer standard medicine.*

"Guess not."

Smoke leaned next to him.

He slid his arm around her waist. And sighed.

"I know," she said.

After a long time of silence, and hospital noises, she nudged him. "Fair Morn is feeling sad."

"Huh?" He returned to awareness. "What?"

"Because Early Dawn stayed with Braidna."

"Oh."

"We could go out and wait in the lobby."

"Why?"

"They just parked in the visitors area and are headed this way."

"O.K."

They walked out to the lobby just as the rest boiled in through the door.

"Come'mer, Moth." He wrapped her in his arms. "She'll probably come and visit."

She nodded. "Not the same."

Then they all sat, dozed, and thumbed through all the magazines available. Finally Raj walked over and joined them. "She will have to stay for a few days." He smiled. "As long as we were in there we removed her appendix. It looked mildly inflamed."

His face fell, his voice became carefully controlled whisper. "But rather bad news though."

Tinker jolted upright. "What?"

"Ahhhh, we had to remove her fallopian tubes. They were both badly damaged." He looked from face to face. "She will require quite a lot of care for a few weeks. I'll pop in on her everyday." Holding up one hand, he shook his head. "No visitors, just now. She is sleeping. Tomorrow. Two-o-clock."

It was two weeks and she grumbled at him as they sat on the rear deck admiring the flowers.

Actually she was admiring the flower beds, he was admiring her.

"I feel fine, John. I am going to work tomorrow. My partner can do the heavy lifting while I advise."

"Interesting scar," he said. She was wearing a two piece

bathing suit, a rather small one.

"Humpf."

"Rest is pretty interesting also."

She growled. "Won't do you any good, Cowboy. Raj said that I sleep alone for another week or so."

"We lucked out." He stared out at nothing, not the present, the just past past.

She nodded and gave him a poke with one finger, just to drag him back. "Yah, I know. That guy wasn't very smart."

He sighed. And mumbled, "I don't think that he knew what a gun was."

A shadow passed over head. And suddenly he was wet.

"Heh heh heh," cackled Fair Mom as she settled on the edge of the roof. "The Winged Warrior, Defender of the Innocent, zaps the Evil Lecher ogling our poor, wounded sister self."

"Bug nuts," he grumbled upward. Another water balloon burst nearby. "KNOCK IT Off!"

She laughed. "That one got away, slipped." And toppled forward, to coast silently to the deck, landing lightly next to where he sat. "Was that an invitation, Lech?"

"Huh?"

"Knock it off," she stated. "A slang term for. . . "

"All right! Everyone knows what it means. Sometimes."

"Heh heh heh." She stepped between them, wrapping her wings around them. "Guess who won The Ring because a certain person has to rest and heal?"

"Beats me. Who?"

"Heh heh heh heh."

Some Relaxation

Grandeville. Tinker's Place.

"DAMN IT, COWBOY!"

She leaned slightly toward him, a broad-shouldered woman, swimmer's shoulders she called them, hands balled into tight fists, jabbed angrily on her slim hips, also a family trait. She sucked in a deep breath, watched his eyes swing from her face to her corduroy shirt and back again, another trait she shared with her three sisters, small at the bottom, big at the top. And snarled at him, "Pay attention!"

"Sure." He stood loose, relaxed, and ready, just in case she decided to take a punch at him.

"It has been two months," she stated, daring him to disagree.

"Yep."

"And I am healthy and healed."

"Yep."

"Ask Smoke!"

"Don't have to."

"Then?"

"Sorry." He shrugged and held his arms out from his sides, palms facing her.

She crashed into him, arms flying out and around his chest. "Give us a hug, Simba Leader."

So, he did. Then he twisted her around until she could lean back against him, and folded his arms around her waist, One hand dropped and patted her lower abdomen. "Nice gut."

She laughed, "That all?"

He blew warm air into her hair, she was only a few inches shorter, and slid his hands upward. "Nope. Rest is pretty nice, also."

"Ummmmm. Stop."

"Uh?"

She grunted. "It is early morning. We are on the rear deck. And in a moment, if you keep that up, I am gonna yank off your clothes and get laid, splinters be damned."

He laughed, gently, and released her. "Definitely healthy."

Smoke walked out the side door and stood next to them by the railing and looked out across the flower beds, shrubs and first pasture, at the wooded slope stretching to the high forested ridge that ran north and south across that edge of their land. "A strong pouncer." She turned and poked Chantal with one fingertip. And smiled at the movement under the shirt. "Yum, yum, yum, yum."

Smoke nudged Tinker with an elbow. "Very healthy."

He nodded. "She told me."

"Everyone heard." Smoke poked her again.

"Smoke?" asked Chantal.

"I think that you lost some weight."

"Think so?"

"Yep."

"Thought so," he added.

Chantal laughed. "And here I thought that you were

just being your friendly best, not doing comparative work."

He sighed.

Smoke nudged him.

"What?"

"Wanna give me a quick check? Before breakfast?" Smoke began to unbutton her shirt.

"Merde," he grumbled. "Leave your shirt alone." She did.

The side door banged open and Messenger bubbled out, giggling wildly. "Next, next." She joined them, grinning widely.

"Grumble grump," mumbled Chantal.

"After you get done fondling Smoke," added Messenger, beaming at him.

"I am not fondling anyone," he growled at her.

"Gosh." She stared at Chantal. "Did you punch out his lights because he caressed you into quivering ecstasy?"

"We didn't get that far," sighed Chantal dramatically.

"Oh," said Messenger.

"Goofy," he suggested.

The clatter of cups as the tray was dropped onto a table and the dull thump of a full coffeepot announced the arrival of Fair Morn. "Fourth," she said as she filled the cups. "I brought coffee."

"Golly," gurgled Messenger. "You should be last."

"Here, grump." Fair Morn handed him a filled cup and then reached around him to hand one to Chantal. "Why? I got here before the others."

"Because," stated Messenger. "Once he gets his hands of your's, everyone else will be . . . "

"How about," he interjected, "we talk about something else?"

". . . second class," finished Messenger.

"I am not second class," grumbled Chantal. "Even if I lost some weight."

"Thought that we were going to town." He tried again to divert them away from their current topic of conversation.

"Oh, boy!" Messenger hastily buttoned her shirt and stuffed it back into her jeans. "I'll drive."

"Everyone going?" He stepped back and looked around, feeling pretty good at finally redirecting their conversation.

"Nope," replied Fair Morn. "Just us shirt fillers."

"I am going," stated Messenger firmly, looking up at the much taller Fair Morn. "Braggart!"

"As am I," added Smoke. "Quality over quantity." And headed for their van. "Let's go, kitten." She looked back over her shoulder as they walked away. "He can come and sit between the buxom pair. And drool."

Chantal spun around and headed down the deck, hooking her arm under one of Fair Morn's. "Probably a Pavlovian reaction. He can't help it."

"Maybe I will just stay home," he mumbled, trailing after them.

"Damn grump," grumbled Chantal, waving him along.

The van slid to a halt right in front of their destination. And they all piled out. And into the shop. Nan walked from behind the counter, smiled at them. "I put everything back in the dressing room."

They were inside **Nan's Clothe Worke**, a small shop just

off the main street in downtown Grandeville.

The four hurried away leaving him standing, idly looking at various racks of women's clothes. And wondering what was going on this time? And why was he here? Then he stood and stared out through the large front window, waiting patiently. A few people passed by and stared in at him.

He spun around as she walked from the back of the shop, wearing it. It was a powder blue shirt, a powder blue velvet shirt.

"Mouth's hanging open, Cowboy." Chantal slowly turned around and then faced him, smiling broadly. "Well? What'cha think?"

"I think," he rasped, "that you shouldn't wear something like that in public."

Smoke joined them. Her shirt was black. "Bet his fingers just tingle in anticipation."

"Clutch, clutch, clutch," giggled Messenger, bouncing up to them. Her shirt was a soft green.

"Stroke, stroke, stroke." Fair Morn's was a pale rose. "Pretty nice, huh?" She grinned at him. It was obvious that she wasn't wearing anything under her new shirt. Neither were any of the others.

Smoke ran her hand over her chest. "Reminds me of my long ago fur-bearing days." And grinned at him. "Of course, I didn't bulge like this, then."

Messenger giggled. "She ordered shirts for everyone. In their colors. Also."

"Who?"

"Me." Chantal winked at him. "I decided that we needed a treat, something new for our wardrobes."

Fair Morn stepped close. "Wanna feel my. . . material?"

Nan blushed.

He grumbled at Fair Morn, at them all. "Time to leave."

Chantal yanked a wad of bills from her jean's pocket and began to peel off the appropriate amount.

Fair Morn and Messenger took the stack of packages and headed out to their van.

Nan handed Chantal her change and walked with her to the door. "Have a nice day," she said.

"Heh heh heh," cackled Fair Morn as she dumped everything on the rear seat and clambered back to the second seat.

As they drove through town, Chantal nudged him. "Notice how the material shimmers?"

Then they shot out one side of the town and down the secondary road.

He nodded.

Fair Morn winked at him. "And tailored?"

"Think that was necessary?"

"And fuzzy on the inside," giggled Messenger. "Kinna tickles. In a nice sorta way." She steered them into the parking area and stopped. "Makes things pop out."

He sighed. "Now what?"

"Fair time," announced Chantal, sliding open the side door.

"Already?" He stepped down and looked at Entrance 'B' to the Fair Grounds.

"Yep," replied Fair Morn. "You can bring the rest, later. Smoke and I will get the tickets."

And so, they began to wander the fair grounds of the County Fair.

On the far side, near the stock barns, they met two gigantic men, wearing yards and yards of dark blue Grandeville Police Department uniforms. Two women strolled by their sides.

The cops, and their company, smiled at them.

"Wow!" said Janine.

Red looked at his partner and rasped, "There must be a city ordnance about things like that."

Sandy kicked her husband on the side of one booted foot. He didn't seem to notice.

Green looked back, over the tops of the heads of their companions. "Don't think so, partner. But maybe we could cite them for inciting a riot."

Janine jabbed him in the side with an elbow. And rubbed her elbow.

"Hi, guys," said Tinker. "Sandy, Janine."

Sandy looked at her close friend and secretary. "What do you think, Streak?"

Janine had a startling white patch of hair running along one side of her head, sharp contrast to the dark brown, a souvenir of an automobile accident that had almost killed her. She grinned broadly and looked at Chantal, one of her closest friends. "Where'd you buy those, Shooter?"

The nickname referred to Chantal's skill with her long-barreled revolver.

"Nan's. Special order."

"Any color?" asked Janine.

"Yep," bubbled Messenger. "Yep, yep, yep."

Janine smiled at Sandy. "I could get green and you could get red. For bowling."

Sandy laughed. "I like it. We can go after we are done escorting the T. Rex around."

Green looked at Red. "Your lawyer babe is gonna engage in psychological warfare. We already bowl bad enough."

Red nodded. "It was your secretary babe's idea." Then he smiled at Tinker and indicated Tinker's company. "They are really a bad influence."

"Corrupting the morals of the innocent," added Green.

"Who's innocent," demanded Janine.

"Me, babe," rumbled Green. "Red also."

"That's us." Red smiled at his partner. "Let's check out the fairway."

They strolled off, arms laid gently across the shoulders of their much smaller companions, who were not all that small except by comparison.

Tinker sighed. "Now you are infecting your friends as well."

"Let's get some cotton candy," suggested Fair Morn. "And maybe a few of those things on sticks." With her high metabolism she was always ready to eat.

"O.K., Moth Gut, lead the way." He walked by her side, watching the eyes pop open and swivel in their direction. He sighed. And wondered, not for the first time, why me?

Because you are lucky, stated Fair Morn inside his mind.

Big stud, added Smoke.

And finally, having visited every display and every booth, and after Fair Morn had eaten several slices of pizza, a "wonder burger" from the local service club food booth, three doughnuts, two candy apples, and a bag of popcorn, large, they made their way back to the van. Everyone else had a burger and fries.

"Home?" he asked.

"Yep," stated Messenger, backing the van out of the parking space, and heading them for that side of town.

They were met on the rear desk by the rest who took their packages inside the house. And shortly they returned, wearing their new garments.

Chicken wore yellow, Sgenn soft grey, Szart and Sha'gar had black like Smoke.

"Most comfortable, Me'Lord." Chicken ran her hands over the material and grinned at him. "Most lecherous a'look."

"Hum," said Szart. "Hum hum," agreed Sha'gar.

Sgenn glanced down, somewhat doubtful.

"Most beautiful," stated Chicken, winking at her.

"Hum," replied Sgenn, her soft half-smile, coming and going as she glanced at Sha'gar, her sister, who shrugged.

"He won't be able to resist," cooed Messenger. "Really really."

Chantal snorted. "When did he ever?"

Chicken poured from the pitcher on the table and handed him the glass. "Lemonade, Sweet prince?"

"Thanks." He emptied the glass. "Pretty good."

"Most ready," said Chicken.

"For?"

"For to most interesting fair a'go." She smiled at him. "Our Verra Own most Noble Escort."

"O.K., let's go." He headed back toward the van, escorted by the four.

As evening darkened, they bumped into Red and Green who were just arriving for their second shift. They would stay until the Fun Zone closed. Janine and Sandy had stayed at home. After shopping at Nan's.

Green nodded at them.

Red smiled. "Second shift."

"Yah, me too."

"Nice shirts," said Green.

Chicken nodded. "Indeed."

Red winked at her. "Well, keep him out of trouble, Princess."

The two monstrous cops wandered off to show their presence on the midway again.

"We would start at the food displays, We would," stated Chicken, who like to admire the cakes and the cookies and the bread. She was an enthusiastic cook, being able to make a mess in their kitchen equal to all the others combined.

So, that is where they started and finally ended up wandering around looking at the rides and the games.

And that was when Horace the Huckster made his big mistake.

He saw them standing there, looking around, this guy and his wife who was dressed in a very interesting yellow shirt, and the three others.

"Say there, young lady!" he called at Szart.

She looked in his direction.

He smiled. "You the little Lady, try your luck? Win a teddy bear!"

Szart stalked over to the booth and glared up at Horace. He was much taller. "How is this game played?" Calling her a lady was bad enough, but calling her little was even worse, if that was possible. Little was almost as bad as being called short.

"Two darts for a dollar. Bust three balloons in a row, pick what you want from the bottom row." He smiled. "Twelve darts for five dollars. Twelve busted balloons gets you your choice. Of anything."

She nodded and handed him a five dollar bill.

Horace blinked. He hadn't seen her take it from anywhere.

Sha'gar walked over to watch. She had felt the pulse of witch agitation building around her sister.

"In a row," said Szart.

"Right as rain," said Horace, setting twelve darts on the counter top in front of her.

Tinker sighed. And kept Chicken and Sgenn from joining them, hoping that nothing too extreme would happen.

And Szart tossed the first dart.

POP!

She nodded at Sha'gar. And threw the darts.

POP! POP! POP!

POP! POP! POP!

POP! POP! POP! POP!

POP!

A row of twelve balloon carcasses hung across the

middle of the display. She pointed. "That one. The silver grey with the blue bow."

Horace blinked. And stared down at her. He had never seen anyone do that so effortlessly. He took down the large bear and handed it to her. "How'd you do that, kid?"

"Magic," stated Szart, turning away, clenching the bear in her arms. It was close to three feet tall. She wasn't quite five feet tall. They made quite a pair. She walked back and handed it to Sgenn. "Here. For you."

Sgenn tucked it under on one arm and looked at Tinker. "Beat's me."

"Me'Lord," said Chicken. "Let us cotton candy get."

So they wandered in that direction. Behind them they heard what sounded like a batch of loud explosions going off. Every balloon had just burst.

"Heh heh heh," cackled Szart.

"Hum," replied Sha'gar.

Sgenn walked close to his free side. He bought them all cotton candy and suggested that maybe it was now time for them to head for home.

By mid-day the next day, Horace closed his booth, a very puzzled person. Every customer had won. No one seemed to be able to miss. He decided that this town was jinxed. But at the next stop he decided that it was the darts and bought all new ones. And cured his problem, such as it was. He puzzled over it for weeks as to how that could be.

Back at home, in the large living room, the others crowded around, admired Sgenn's bear and smiled at Szart.

Tinker dropped heavily into one of the couches. "Safe!"

Chantal handed him a cold beverage. And took a drink from her's, using the hand that wore the large ornate ring, making sure that he saw it.

"Night all." Chicken headed down the hall toward the large three-story open space that they called The Chamber, and her bedroom.

The rest slowly wandered in the same direction, Fair Morn and Smoke headed through the kitchen just to have a little snack first.

Chantal snuggled against his side and dragged his free arm up and over her shoulders. With one foot she kicked a small cooler sideways. It had been carried in from the rear deck. She leaned over and fetched out another cold can. "Brought lots." And sat, slumping so his arm could dangle. She set another in his lap."Here."

"Thanks." He took a swallow. "Those shirts are damned erotic." His fingers gently stroked over the soft velvet.

"Yaaah," she breathed huskily, setting her empty can aside, twisting around and tagging his shirt loose.

Some time later, she sighed as she sprawled all loose limbed, happily entwined around him. "The only good thing about that wound is that I don't have to worry about getting pregnant anymore. Sorta gives me a male perspective on things, so to speak."

He kissed her gently.

"Don't look so sad, John. I am just a little different than my sisters in the way I see the world."

"You sure?"

"Yep. I take my identity from the stuff that's between

my ears, not from the stuff that's between my hips."

He kissed her again.

"Well?"

"What?"

"Wanna go up to my room. My bed is bouncier than that thing that you sleep on."

"O.K."

They did.

Eventually.

Small Discoveries

Grandeville. Tinker's Place.

Sunlight slipped a finger in a high east window of The Chamber and poked a golden shaft into her room. It sprawled across them.

"Didn't realize that you were such a sensualist."

"Me?"

"Yep. Silk pajamas, velvet shirts."

"All your fault."

"My fault?"

"Yep. All your's. We all know it. You are absolutely tactile oriented. So, silk and velvet. Just for certain fingertips."

"Humbug."

She laughed."It is true. In the pitch black you can tell who we are. Just by touch."

"Poogle!"

"It is uncanny."

"It is bush wallah."

She sat up and grinned. "Oh." And glanced downward. "It seems that some fingertips just now are wandering around in a rather friendly manner even as we speak."

"Well. You are sorta right there." And tickled her ever so gently.

She twitched. "The prosecution rests its case."

In the kitchen, Smoke nudged Chicken as they finished preparing breakfast.

"Indeed," agreed Chicken, grinning wickedly. "T'will be jolly good fun." Their joined minds reached out and told all the rest. Except for him.

Chantal collapsed and smiled and gave him a friendly pat on the backside. And laughed softly "Maybe we ought to go down for breakfast. It is ready."

"Think that we should?"

"Yep. Morgan wants some new horses looked at. John Johnson has a sick cow. And Joanna Fry has a 4-H sheep that may need something. Busy day for a veterinarian."

"O.K." He rolled sideways and sat up. And looked at her. "Not much of a scar."

"Raj said that they tried to make sure of that." She sat up and pinched his side. "Shower!"

"OUCH! Sure."

They all gathered around the large dining room table for breakfast. And all through the meal, while they ate, they talked. He noticed the sly looks and nods and winks, passing from one to the other. And began to worry. There definitely was something going on and whatever it was they were keeping it from him. And, as far as he was considered, that was not a good sign. He sighed. "Now what's going on?"

"Naught," stated Chicken, reaching over, filling his cup.

He rolled his eyes.

She winked.

Which made him worry all that much more.

As soon as the meal was over, they scattered to do this and that.

Chantal headed toward town and out the other side, headed for her sister and brother-in-law's place.

Messenger, Smoke and Chicken drove into town to the grocery store to replenish their supplies.

Fair Morn took Sgenn outside to split more fire wood.

Szart and Sha'gar started cleaning the large living room.

Tinker walked upstairs, to his workroom. He had a backlog of editing and re-editing to do.

The day passed quickly.

He relaxed into his work.

And forgot to worry about them.

Smoke, Chicken, and Messenger made dinner. Roast beef, boiled potatoes, salad, and broccoli. It was a late dinner, starting at twilight, finishing in the grey black of early evening.

Then they drifted from the large living room, down the hall, and into the shower room while he sat slumped, reading, deep inside the large novel, somewhere around the midpoint. Finally, he realized that he was being poked. In the side. By Chicken.

"Huh?"

"Tis time, Sweet Prince."

"For what?" He looked up. They sat, looking at him, all wearing the heavy white robes from the tub and shower rooms. Fair Morn and Smoke stood and began fastening heavy blankets over all the large windows and the door connecting the breezeway to the Corporate Headquarters.

"What's going on?" He straightened up, marked his spot in the book with a ragged piece of newspaper, and set the book aside.

"Most noble experiment," explained Chicken.

"Oh?"

She nodded. "Indeed."

He frowned, just a little. "What kind of an experiment?"

"Ready," announced Smoke.

Chantal pointed. "You wait in the kitchen. Leave all the lights off. When we call, you come back here."

"What?"

"You get to identify us in total darkness." She grinned. "We all took a shower and used the same soap and shampoo."

He stared at her. "That's the experiment?"

"Yep."

"You guys are all goofy, mega-goofy."

"You'll see."

"No sweat, G.I.," said Fair Morn. "We are sure that The Vile Clutcher will have no problemo identifying his victims."

He sighed, yanked off his socks, and headed for the kitchen, snapping off lights as he went. In the kitchen, he stood, leaned back against a counter top and waited, in the dark, eyes slowly getting dark adapted.

All right, lover, any time. Chantal smiled at him. *Just announce who you think it is.*

He drifted soft, silent, into and through the dining room, and stepped into the large living room. "Blacker than black," he mumbled. He slipped forward, sliding each foot carefully.

One couch should be just ahead. He touched it, moved to the front, knelt and reached out, and touched soft skin and slid here and there, identifying ribs, then upward.

"Fair Morn."

Bingo, stated Chantal.

Standing, he headed around the couch. One foot nudged into warm flesh. He bent over and reached. The body twitched. "Princess."

Bingo.

Stepping carefully, he located the next couch. The body was lying face down.

"Messenger."

She giggled.

Bingo.

And immediately bumped into the next body. She was standing.

"Sgenn."

Bingo. Perfect score. Any doubts, lover?

"Nope." He laughed. "You win." He heard the rustle of the thick white robes being slipped back on and then someone switched on the lights, They all beamed at him.

Szart pouted.

"What?"

"Fondle one, fondle all," she grumbled.

He frowned at her. "It was your experiment, not mine."

"Riptik!"

He stepped over, grabbed her by the shoulders, spun her around, and yanked her back against his chest, sliding an arm inside her robe. "Satisfied?"

"Most brazen," observed Chicken.

"I did not fondle all," he mumbled, blowing warm air into her hair. She was a full head shorter.

"Let's have ice cream." Fair Morn headed for the kitchen.

"Pretty crude," suggested Chantal to Szart.

"Witches are nar nar," suggested Sha'gar, ordering the couches to rearrange themselves, so they all could sit on the floor in one space.

Messenger giggled and hurried into the dining room to fetch spoons and bowls.

"Ptar ptar tik tir!" suggested Szart to Sha'gar.

"Well, happy now?" he asked. "You have grossed out the Princess and Sha'gar and Chantal."

"Hum."

Bowls rattled and spoons tinkled as Messenger set them down. Fair Morn returned carrying a large number of cartons of ice cream. Chicken brought a large cloth and set it on the floor for the ice cream containers.

"MindMate." Smoke settled to the floor and began to open the containers. "When you are done caressing her, you could have some ice cream."

Szart nodded. He slipped his hand from her robe, turned and sat. "Chocolate, please."

Fair Morn grinned at him. "How many scoops?"

Chicken looked pointedly at Szart. "Me'thinks tis naught but two."

Messenger violently shook her head. "Oh, no, Princess. She is at least three."

Fair Morn handed him a heaped bowl and winked.

"You are only two," said Messenger to Chicken, who replied, "Et tu."

He stared at Messenger as she pulled her robe open and peered inside. "Maybe two and a half."

"I'll take strawberry," said Smoke, sitting next to him.

"Knock it off," he grumbled at them in general.

Messenger smiled at Sha'gar. "Five or six."

"Kitten," he snapped. "Eat your ice cream. We do not need another of you guy's rating scales."

She hastily grabbed the bowl shoved in her direction by Fair Morn, leaned close to her and whispered, "A baker's dozen."

He glared at Chantal. "Somehow it is your fault."

"Damn grump. Eat your ice cream."

They did.

Just sat around and ate ice cream, talking and laughing softly. And demolished their ice cream supply.

"Guess we'll have to go shopping tomorrow." Fair Morn began to collect the empty cartons while Messenger gathered up the bowls and spoons. "Again."

Then they headed for bed, snapping off the lights as they went.

In the dark, he sighed, and wondered how his life had ever managed to get this strange. He knew, of course, he just wondered why. And decided, once again, that it was definitely all the fault of Big Red. Somehow.

Day arrived.
Soft.
Quiet.
Unhurried.

He wandered through the kitchen, snatching a cup of coffee, and into the large living room, and slumped in a couch, facing one of the east windows. And watched dawn shift red into blue as the sun coasted up and over the far across the valley mountain range and began to flood the valley below with another late summer greeting.

He was thinking about getting another cup of coffee when she glided in, cup and pot in hand, filled his cup, and settled next to him.

"Mate'mer." The pot obediently returned itself to the kitchen.

"Ummmmmmm?"

She slumped and glowered at the bottom edge of her robe as her legs slid out.

"Nice legs."

"Eh?"

He slipped his free arm around her and tugged her closer. "Rest is pretty nice also."

"Szart was witch worried."

"Oh?"

"Yesssssssssssss."

"And you were not?"

"Witches are different than magicians."

He took a sip. "I suppose. And Sgenn?"

She twisted around and kissed the side of his face. "Theurgists never worry. About anything."

"I suppose."

"Including whether you slide your hands over them or not."

He sighed. "Thought that we killed that conversation last night."

"Just explaining." She ordered the pot to come back and held out her cup. The pot filled her cup. Then his.

He nodded. "Sure."

"Morning, morning, morning, morning," bubbled Messenger as she joined them. She looked at the pot, almost empty, hanging there. "I'll make another." She jumped up and headed for the kitchen. The pot trailed after her.

Right after breakfast, Tinker and Sha'gar, appropriately dressed for a short hike, small packs stuffed with fruit, a couple of sandwiches, water bottles, and a few cans of this or that. They headed out, across the first pasture and up the steep slope, following the trail up to the ridge. Turning south, they wandered along the trail headed that way until they reached a narrow spot, a low spot in the ridge, all grass meadow with a few trees. From here they could look east across the valley and see the far mountain ranges. Or to the west, at rank after rank of tree covered ridges. And far beyond them, the great snow-capped volcanos, white sparkling tops, some cloud capped.

"Hum." Sha'gar, walked over to the large dead tree, lying there, slowly rotting into the ground, just in the shade of the still living ones. She dumped her pack and fished out a sandwich, fruit, and something to drink.

He did the same and sprawled next to her, using the dead tree as a back rest. "One of the nicer spots up here." He squinted out and over the valley. "You can see forever and forever."

She handed him a sandwich.

"Thanks."

She nodded, yanked off her shirt and stuffed it into her pack. She was wearing a T-shirt decorated with a large, smiling dragon. Underneath the head of the dragon the lettering said

Chen's Chinese.

"Nice T-shirt."

"Braidna gave us all one. From Master Chen."

He grinned. "You guys aren't thinking of forming a softball team, are ya?"

She shook her head, opened two cans, and handed him one. "Still cold."

"Thanks." He took a swallow. "Always tastes good on a hot day."

She nodded. "Messenger means no harm."

He jerked. "Huh?"

She looked down at her tightly stretched T-shirt. "Making comparisons."

He laughed. "I know that. Just something in her cultural background, I guess." And grinned. "I gave up trying to get her to stop doing that. Just need to remind her every once in awhile, that's all." He winked. "Not bad. Five or six scoops."

"Hum hum." Her eyes flickered faint red. "My sister is more."

"Szaifeh?"

"Sgenn."

He cleared his throat. "Everyone is different."

"Hum."

He sighed. And stared up, watched a line of clouds march across the valley, south to north. "I keep telling everyone that it does not matter. To me."

"We know."

"Then?"

"Small game."

"Humpf."

"For you."

"Double humpf." He nudged her leg. "Want another? I put a bunch in my pack."

She nodded, and watched as he shed his shirt, balled it up and stuffed it into his pack, after extracting the two cans. "Still pretty cool."

She reached out, touched each can. He felt them go cold. And after sitting and sipping for some time, she said, "Szart fills with worry."

He jerked. "What?"

"About you."

He sat up and turned. "Now what? What's going on?"

She leaned forward. "Not out there. All here. You."

He stared into those deep black eyes and watched the faint flicker flame deep inside. "You gonna tell me?"

"It is a secret."

"Sure."

"All know except you."

"What? Some secret."

She snatched a handful of his T-shirt. "You must never say or do anything."

He nodded.

"Chantal was mother-bound until that ptar raz pak did that."

He stared at her and blinked. "She was pregnant?"

"Yessssss. Smoke knew, we all knew."

"Merde." His eyes unfocused as he fell inside.

She slapped him hard.

"OUCH!"

"That is why Szart worries."

"Ah." He laid back and stared up into the mostly blue sky. "She knew before?"

"Yesssss. It was to be a surprise after we returned." She laid a hand on his chest. "We are all fiercely protective of our mate. And of each other. You must understand."

"I do."

"Yesssss. Mother said that you would."

"Reep?"

"Yessss. She said that you were stronger than we believed or you understood."

"Ummmm."

"It is true."

"O.K."

Chantal stood on the rear deck and gazed up at the distant ridge and said to Smoke, "What do you think she is up to?"

Smoke shrugged. "Totally guarded before. Now they are out of range again."

"You ever figure out why that is not a problem, around here?"

"Nope." She slid her arm around Chantal's waist and patted her hip. "Must be because we are at home. So separation is not a shock." She tugged Chantal against her side. "It never worked that way in my elseplace. Maybe Big Red did something?"

"Smoke?"

"I think that you should tell him."

"Think so?"

"Yep."

The sun was way behind the ridge, the sky turning black blue black, when they came strolling across the first pasture toward the house. She was swinging his arm back and forth. He was smiling while she looked content and magician happy.

They all gathered in the large living room, settling here and there.

Chantal sat by his free side, grabbed one of his hands, and told him. The rest watched carefully.

But he took it calmly. And merely stated, "That is one more thing we will have to talk to Big Red about."

They could feel the deep anger in his voice.

Grandeville. The Bowl and Burger.

Ben Hanson had changed the name of the bowling alley again.

Red and Green had the weekend off, and, as per usual, were bowling, against their usual opponents. Augmented.

The two gigantic men had walked up toward their table and watched Tinker and Chantal walk down for their turns. Red had convinced them to join their game. So had Sandy.

"What do you think, partner?"

Green shrugged. And rumbled, "I think that Tinker's babe is as sneaky as your babe and my babe."

"Uh huh. Must be because they are friends."

They sat at the table, picked up their pitchers and took a sip. Janine and Sandy watched the action down on the lanes.

"Think that we ought to cite Tinker's babe for contributing to the delinquency of these babes?"

"Nope," rumbled Green. "Your lawyer babe would get her off on a technicality and we would waste a day sitting in court."

"What I thought," rasped Red, in his normal gravel tone of voice.

"What's the problem, moose meat?" asked Sandy, snatching the platter of fries from in front of her husband.

He reached out and gently ran a finger down her sleeve. She and Janine and Chantal were wearing the velvet shirts from Nan's.

Green looked at Janine. "You wander through the truck stop in that and the state cops will pinch you for soliciting cause the truckers will start a bidding war."

"That's a big uh huh," agreed Red.

Janine dumped catchup on her plate of fries and nodded. "That some sort of a complement?" And worked hard at suppressing her smile.

"Uh huh," replied Green, staring at her plate. He still couldn't figure out why anyone would want to do that to perfectly innocent french fries.

Janine and Sandy stood and headed down to take their turns as Chantal and Tinker walked up.

"Good game," stated Chantal. The men were ahead by five pins with only two frames to go in the second game. They had won by five in the first game.

"Uh huh," said Green.

Red looked at Tinker. "What do you think we go to Big Darlene's for chili afterwards. We'd take them to the Rail but that'd probably start a riot."

"Sure."

The men won the first two games and lost the last game

by a bunch.

On the way across town, Tinker sat, more or less, wedged between Red and Green in the front seat of Green's pickup while their opponents sat in the rear seat. The front seat rode in comfortable silence listening to the radio. The back seat held a low conversation and laughed a lot.

Once they were all settled in the largest booth, near the back wall, and had placed their orders, and had taken a sip or two, Sandy looked around the table, and stated in her best lawyer talking to the judge tone of voice, "You guys are cheating!"

Red's eyes shifted and looked at his partner.

Green looked at Sandy with his blankest cop expression, his voice rumbling from deep inside his chest, "Counselor?"

"You are cheating."

"I wouldn't do that! I am monogamous, even if I am not married." Green nodded at Janine.

"Better not be," she snapped, spinning a french fry around in some catchup. She had just received her order. "Cheating."

"The babes keep score," rasped Red.

"It is how you bowl," snapped Janine.

"How's that?" asked Green, rescuing some fries from a fate worse than death, from Janine's plate, before they were tortured to death in red goo.

So Sandy and Janine explained how Chantal had watched Tinker bowl and had suggested that as Red and Green were also well known for their athletic ability from their college football days, that the horrible way that they bowled had to be deliberate, and that, therefore, they must be cheating.

"Lawyer babe?" asked Red, gently laying his massive arm over Sandy's shoulders. "Does cheating also count point shaving?" He caught the quick flick of her eyes in Janine's direction.

"You noticed?"

"Uh huh."

Tinker grinned. "How long have you guys been bowling?"

"Awhile," rumbled Green.

Tinker laughed. "And they have been manipulating the game so you could win, ahhhhh, most or some of the time?"

"Uh huh," stated Green.

Sandy stared at Green and then at Red. "How long have you known?"

"Second game or so, babe."

Tinker laughed and laughed and laughed. Until tears streamed down his face.

"John?" Chantal frowned at him, just a little.

He waved a helpless hand at her and finally stopped and wiped his eyes with a napkin. And grinned. "It must he genetic, something in the female genes." And started to laugh again.

"Knock it off, Cowboy," grumbled Chantal, refilling her glass, and then his.

Janine nudged Green. "We thought that you wouldn't want to go with us if we beat you all the time."

Green looked at Red. Who nodded.

"Next time we play to win," stated Green firmly.

"I don't know, partner," said Red. "I've been bowling so badly for so long it might be hard to break the habit."

Green nodded, And looked at Janine.

"What?" she asked.

"Jock babe, you won't cry if we beat you too badly, will you?"

She wacked him in the gut with her elbow. He didn't blink. She rubbed her elbow. "Just try." She smiled. And then smiled sweetly.

"Duck!" snapped Red.

"Listen oversized," stated Janine. "If you think that you will be able to take us at bowling, or any other game for that matter, just go ahead and give it a try."

Green began to smile.

"What?"

"Let's play football. Full contact."

"Except that," said Sandy.

"Right," agreed Janine. "I am not being groped by two leftovers from the Jurassic Age."

"Take the fifth," rumbled Green.

"Uh huh," grunted Red.

Sandy looked across the table at Chantal. "Join us?"

"Sure."

Tinker threw his arm around her, yanked her close, and kissed her cheek. "And I thought it was just you guys." He started to laugh. Again.

New Experiences, New Friends

Paradise.

He smiled.

The sun peeked out from behind a large cloud and beamed down upon them.

His wife leaned against his side. "She is lovely, isn't she?"

His smile broadened. "Takes after her mother."

The slender young woman standing nearby, idly tickling a gigantic tiger under the chin, looked over at them. "Father?"

"Just complimenting your mother on her daughter."

The young woman's eyes narrowed as she looked into his face. "Father, what are you up to? Now?"

He laughed. "Can't hide things from wives and daughters." And waved his free hand, his other arm was curled around his wife's waist. "Sons, but not daughters and wives." She nodded at her. "Let's see, in John's calender system you would be, umm, twenty-seven, twenty-eight years old."

His wife bumped him with her hip.

"Oh!" he said. "Ah," he said, grinning sheepishly, not fooling either one. "I need you to deliver this." He held out his free hand. A blue ring appeared in his palm.

His daughter walked over and picked it up. "It is

disgusting."

He shrugged.

She held the ring in two fingers. The ring flashed blue fire. And subsided.

"It has been around," he explained. "For a long, long time." Then he patted his wife on the hip. "She should have traveling attire. Wispy robes just will not do."

"Trousers," said his wife.

He nodded.

"Shirt."

He nodded.

"Jacket."

He nodded.

"Sandals," said his daughter.

Her mother nodded.

So did he.

"Very nice," he said.

His daughter was now dressed in trousers with a slight bell at the bottom, a deep burgundy color. Her shirt was a light rose-tone while her short jacket was just a shade lighter than her trousers. Her sandals were close to the color of her trousers.

He released his wife, hugged his daughter, telling her who, what, and where, and kissed her on the forehead. And stepped away.

"Have a good time. And don't cause too much trouble."

She gave him a very daughterly frown. And disappeared.

"She will be all right," he told his wife. "She is my daughter too."

Grandeville. Tinker's Place.

It was mid-week. They had just finished lunch, put everything away, and were relaxing on the rear deck before going back to the various chores that always seemed to need doing.

He was sprawled in the hammock. Laughing, now and then, as he thought about that complicated bowling game that Red, Green, Sandy, and Janine were involved in.

Sgenn lay by his side, on her side, idly plucking at the buttons on his shirt, one knee propped over his leg, happy to feel his content.

Purple mist poured around everyone, quickly anchoring them all in a lavender fog. No one had time to react.

Bahn Duhr Tohr. The Quarters of The Royal Advisors.

It had her trapped.

In their bedroom.

On their bed.

And was taking liberties with her.

She twitched.

And shuddered.

And suddenly thumped the Dunzar on the snout.

"OUCH!" it said.

Hanred sat back and rubbed the end of his nose. "Midnight Love?"

Ripple waved her blouse back together and rolled over and stood, the air soft crackling around her.

"What?" he asked, recognizing the dangerous witch agitation starting to build.

"Husband, great danger."

"Here?" He leaped to the floor, fussing with his clothes.

She snapped her fingers, taking care of that.

He was dressed.

"No," she hissed. "I will need some help from those dusty tomes of your's."

He blanched. "Which ones?"

Magevern. Deep Below The Surface.

"We are armored many layers deep."

Sa'ar nodded at Aada. "Where are they?"

"In the common area in their section. Cazar and Bant are there. Moonda and Tinlee spin fair watch."

"He is going to be unhappy."

Aada shrugged.

Sa'ar, The Heart of the Vander, started out of the room, headed for the new area not long ago finished. "Come. We should be there when they awaken. It might help."

Grandeville. Tinker's Place.

Je'leel walk out onto the rear deck, a slender young woman, twenty years old, with a surprising narrow waist, a book held in one hand, her finger marking the place, and looked around. And wondered where they had gone. She turned and walked back inside the house.

Standing next to one of the several book shelves, she tapped her finger on the wooden surface next to a very ornate ring with a large jewel carved to look like a open eye. "Mother, wake up!"

After a few more taps of her finger, a tiny figure appeared, yawning and stretching. She smiled up. "Daughter?"

"They are gone. Father and the Mothers."

Dat jumped from the shelf, saying, "Tinker size," landed on her feet, and turned to her daughter, who was slightly shorter. "Let's make some cocoa."

She stepped back and ran her hands over J'leel's torso. And smiled. "You are becoming very indjinn. Narrow waist, soft rounded, lovely, full . . ."

"I know," interrupted Je'leel, starting for the kitchen.

"They are visiting Sa'ar," stated Dat, throwing an arm around her daughter, smiling happily, admiring her daughter. "Beautiful."

"Yes, Mother."

Magevern. Deep Below The Surface.

They stepped into the large central room and stopped. The bodies were laying on the floor.

"Him first," said Sa'ar. "Slowly."

Cazor nodded.

Tinker woke, looked up and saw them, standing, smiling down at him. And stood. "Now what is going on?"

Sa'ar stepped forward and kissed him. "First Greetings, Lord."

So did Aada, Bant, Tinlee and the rest.

Tinlee looked at Sa'ar. "Very calm, very curious."

Sa'ar nodded. Cazor woke them all.

Tinker watched as Smoke rose is one fluid movement. Tinlee stepped in front of her and kissed her, hands gently sliding here and there. "Warm welcome, Smoke Teacher."

Smoke smiled, slid into Tinlee's mind. *I doubt there is much more that I can teach you.*

I still have trouble with deep layers.

We will work on it.

Tinlee turned and stood close to Smoke's side, her arm sliding around Smoke's waist.

Smoke threw her arm over Tinlee's shoulders, her finger stroking through a small gap in Tinlee's costume. "There is a lot of Velvetmist in the Vander," she said to Tinlee. "I wonder if there is some connection between my folk and your's?"

"A frightening thought," grumbled Tinker.

"Elend the Archivist will search," said Sa'ar.

Sha'gar stepped close to him, fire flickering in her eyes, unhappy at being taken so easily.

"Ptar rak tak," growled Szart, edging closer to him. She was also very, very unhappy, which is a very dangerous state for a witch to be in. For others.

"Perhaps," said Sa'ar, waving one hand at the furnishings in the room. "If we all sat, had refreshments, I might explain. And you," her eyes flicked from face to face, "would, umm, relax."

When they settled, she did.

Explain.

Arktan and Moonda had been traveling many over, searching for information on a certain rare gem of special properties, something found in an ancient scroll that Elend had recently acquired that had ancient writings that dealt with the long ago of their Order.

While searching and conversing in an isolated elseplace, they heard a tale tell that the Fazmir had a Spell of Apprehension that they thought Andover the Farseer might find of some interest.

Moonda thought that it would be, so the pair of them

went two down to seek out the Fazmir, a small order that favored pale orange and white of a soft ivory. The Fazmir had specialized in feel-seeing.

Moonda had talked with them and in exchange for a certain Spell of Attraction, that could not be taught to any others, the Fazmir taught the Spell of Apprehension to Moonda who transferred it to Arktan.

Sa'ar smiled and explained that the Fazmir were on the verge of extinction as they were not gaining new members. But with the Vander spell they should now have no problem. It was group size limited. Over an agreed upon number and the spell became ineffectual.

Arktan has passed the spell to Andover who with Arktan had been testing it, first on themselves, of course, and then they had decided to see how the Vander Lord and all his were doing.

And that is why they had snatched everyone to Magevern.

"Andover saw great trouble coming your way," finished Sa'ar. She shook her head as he started to speak. "The spell doesn't speak what, only the degree of apprehension."

She stood, stepped over and yanked Andover's garment off her left shoulder, exposing soft flesh, badly bruised.

"Spell shock threw her across the room."

Andover nodded. "We are working on that aspect of the spell." Her eyes fastened upon his. "Vander Lord, Heart of Our Heart, there is great danger. We are layering protection many thick." She shivered. "But we cannot, yet, identify what it is."

He dropped back into his chair. "Merde." And looked

at the rest of himself. "We don't have any of our gear."

"Moonda, Cazor, and Galran will go and bring everything here," stated Sa'ar. The trio raced from the room.

"OOOOOF!"

Sa'ar smiled. "It has been too long since last I sat in your lap. We miss you, Imdar and I." And grinned. "As do all the rest."

He sighed. "You guys gonna behave?"

"We are always well behaved, Vander Lord."

"You know what I mean."

"Yes, dear," she said meekly. And then burst into laughter at his expression. "We wouldn't have done this if we didn't feel that it was necessary."

Andover stepped over and knelt in front of them. "The apprehension felt imminent. There was no time for discussion." She bowed her head. "You may do to me as you wish."

"Oh, no," he mumbled. "We are not getting into something like that again."

Imdar walked into the room and said to Andover, "Come. It time to treat your wounds." She walked over and kissed him. "First Greetings, Lord."

Eulin dashed into the room. "Father!" And quickly composed herself. "Mothers." And walked over and kissed him. "First Greetings, Father Lord." She turned and scanned the room. "Where's Je'leel and Dat mother?"

Sa'ar smiled at her daughter. "There is no threat to them. It seemed to swirl around him." She patted him on the stomach.

Eulin looked at her mother, something hard filling her eyes. "Well, let's kill it."

"Patience, Young Heart. We have not yet identified the cause."

"Oh."

"We must wait," said Sa'ar. And then in a firmer mother-to-daughter tone of voice added, "And behave properly."

"To hear is to obey," came the dutiful reply. Eulin walked over to kiss each of her mothers and to be hugged and kissed in return.

Clock Stop.

Arglo sat at the table, in front of the elaborate and elegantly prepared meal, shoved back the sleeves of his purple robe, the purple robe of The Dumart Guild, artfully trimmed in green and red. He had earned this meal for what he felt were just a few small tricks. And expected to enjoy it. After all, it had been quite a while since he had a good meal.

He wasn't bothered by the fact that, as far as he knew, there was no Dumart Guild. He was a little worried that the colors might belong to some real Mage Guild but had decided that the chances were very low, if not zero, that he would bump into anyone like that.

And besides, as soon as he strolled from this town, he would wear plain brown traveling clothes. In that garb no one would recognize that he was the Arglo, the cast out from the Njar Guild, cast out as an apprentice. The Guild Master hadn't appreciated the zeal that Arglo had put into promoting himself among the nearby town folk. Misrepresenting himself is what they said.

So, here he was, a rather poorly trained magician trying to get by on a few minor spells and a lot of gab.

Halfway through the meal, he suddenly worried about her. It wasn't something he did often, worry, but now he did. She had hired him to do a few simple things which he had yet to accomplish, after which he would return and give her the desired item.

He shrugged. He was only two out. Almost there. And, he told himself, he deserved a good meal. Now and then.

Lakelar.

She ordered the wall to mirror and looked at herself, standing there in the understated rose and pale yellow robe of the Cedinal Guild. She smiled. And agreed. You, Karlad the Sly Bronze, she thought, are a strikingly handsome woman. She had liked that description ever since Parquor the White had come lusting around her before he took a taste for witch. It was his expression.

She laughed. And looked what happened to him. Slowly she ran her hands up from her waist and over herself. "Much better than any witch. Parquor, your ego was certainly greater than other parts."

She brushed the rusty red hair back and admired the long line of her slender neck. And wondered why certain people were so hard to kill. It didn't seem fair, somehow.

Fartha Napnar.

Slinar Dar, known as The Swift, ran as fast as he ever had, living up to his nickname. He ran for his life, his career, and his fortune.

He had spent a full two moon cycle watching, planning, and inspecting every detail. In Martil's Shop of Things he had seen the object, remembered vaguely something about it, mainly in terms of value, and had decided to spend a little time finding out about that object.

Now he had it, a small, strangely shaped crystal sphere, deep green with a pulsating inner fire. To the right buyer, it was worth several fortunes. To a certain segment of society, it meant that The Swift was a Master Obtainer. And to Slinar, it meant success and health as soon as he zipped around the next corner.

Which he did, and leaped into a well planned and prepared narrow space, dark but not too narrow. Inside there he did several things, stepped back out, and calmly walked back the way he had come, no longer Slinar Dar, but Mazran ta'Nib, Traveler and Mystic. He stood in the idle crowd listening to the stories begin, the several versions already twining outward, of the very daring robbery, the theft of The Hapsta Var.

Some said that the Curse of the Var would rot the flesh from the owner's bones. Others said that would come from excessive enjoyment of the Pay-Play Ladies attracted to the object. Yet others suggested the wealth to be gained from selling the object would be worth it. And besides, suggested a few, Martil was as fat as ever and he had the thing for three years, on display, and who knew how long before that and nothing had happened to him.

Mazran laughed and wandered on down the street.

Magevern. Deep Below The Surface.

He woke, stretched, rolled from the bed and dressed. Then he wandered down the hall and into the room where he had been told a coffee pot would be waiting in the morning. Pouring a cup full, he settled into a small couch and slumped.

And sipped, eyes closing. And began to ooze into the day.

And, after some time, he realized that someone was in the room with him. He looked up.

She stood near, a rather slender woman, slightly taller than Messenger, dressed in the soft lavender garb of the Vander, but with a slightly different style than was the norm. Her trousers hung low and the blouse was cut high. Soft skin was exposed from her lower ribs to the lower abdomen.

Pale brown eyes watched him.

Realizing that he was awake, she jerked, popped forward, bent, and kissed him. "First Greetings . . . Lord."

"Morning," he mumbled.

She looked, snatched his cup from his hand, refilled it, and thrust it back into his hand. Then she sat in his lap. "I am Arboc."

"Hi." This close he noticed that her pupils were narrow slits, horizontal narrow slits, surrounded by a pale brown that seemed to have many golden specks and a slight violet tone around the outer edge.

"You the only one up?"

"Oh!" She shook her head, arching her back and her neck, her hands fluttering over herself. "Tinlee," she breathed, "wakens The Smoke with gentle fingers and caressing lips." Then she sagged, arms dropped to her sides. And stretched, twisting her torso, joints popping, and mumbled all sleepy tones, "Sa'ar, Our Heart, wakens." She smiled lazily at him. "She loves you greatly."

Then she sat up. "Soon many will rise for they now swim up from deep sleep." She peered into his face, pupils dilating, eyes going round, And stood, and sat down shoving her knees past his hips. Her fingers slid over her flushing cheeks. "Lord, my bodies readies itself for you. None will disturb us."

"Arboc, stop that!"

She sat back, stood, and sat back on his lap, legs thrown against the arm of the couch. "To hear is to obey. . . Lord." She smiled.

He sighed. And wondered.

"The Vander Lord commands The Heart. The Heart controls the body. We are your's." Her eyes stared back into his. "Am I not pleasing in form?"

"Comes with the territory," he mumbled.

"Lord?"

"All Vander," he sighed, "are pleasing in form. It is part of being Vander. Somehow."

She nodded. And began to unfasten the ties that held her blouse together.

"Stop that."

"You could inspect easier unclothed."

The sigh was long and loud.

Someone laughed, deep in her throat.

Arboc leaped up and hurried to her. And kissed her. "First Greetings, Our Heart."

Sa'ar walked over and sat. In his lap. Arboc dragged a chair close and sat.

"Just a seat cushion," he mumbled.

"I see that you have already met Arboc." Sa'ar grinned at him, took the offered cup from her, watching as she filled his cup and then sat back.

"Yah."

"She is new to us. Xanx met her while purchasing certain herbal supplies. And after some discussion. Arboc joined us."

Arboc nodded at him.

"She is called Arboc the Nar. Nar in her language means sense-too-much, a wild talent. She prefers Arboc."

Arboc pulled her chair closer until her knees touched his legs.

"We are working with her," continued Sa'ar, "to gain greater control."

Sa'ar kissed him. "First Greetings, Lord." She smiled, eyes twinkling. "And we are learning how she does what she does. All felt that it would be a valuable skill for the Vander to have." And whispered ever so softly, "She felt your, ahhhh, curiosity about her, ahhhh, attributes and merely thought to, ummm, satisfy her Vander Lord." She laughed.

He stared from one to the other.

"You guys are learning how to do that? Ummmmm, sense? Like that?"

"Yessssss."

Arboc blinked back a tear and slumped. Then sat up and smiled.

Chicken burst into the room. "Fair Morn, Sweet Prince, Fair Vander." She took a cup and managed to squirm alongside him on the couch. And kissed his cheek. And laughed.

"Don't start!" he warned her.

"Most grumpy." She smiled at Arboc.

Arboc began to fumble with her blouse.

Sa'ar cast control.

Arboc dropped her hands and nodded.

Don't mess around, he grumbled in Chicken's mind. *Most fair a'form.*

You guys leave her alone. She is in training. And I do not require distraction, either.

Smoke walked in, Tinlee by her side, stopped by Arboc and tapped her on the shoulder. "Stand up."

Arboc nodded and did.

Smoke grabbed her by the forearms. "This won't hurt." And said to Tinlee, *Follow me inside and watch.*

And they sank into Arboc.

Arboc heard someone humming a soft song and suddenly she felt different, somehow different.

You saw what I did? Smoke said to Tinlee.

Yes.

Then they were back outside.

Arboc raised herself on her tiptoes and kissed Smoke, and then Tinlee. "My body is your's."

"Already have one," laughed Smoke.

"Debt payment," explained Tinlee. *Now me.*

Smoke drifted in and made the small correction, And floated out again. *You fix Sa'ar. I will watch.*

Tinlee nodded and walked over. "Hold still, Our Heart." And slipped inside, Smoke trailing along. *There? And here? And here?*

Exactly. Smoke smiled inside Tinlee's mind. *You have all of them to fix. Be slow. Be careful.*

Yes.

Sa'ar smiled at them. And then at Tinker. And whispered to him, "No wonder Arboc did what she did."

"Huh?"

"Tell you later. In the privacy of my room."

He frowned. Just a little.

She kissed the tip of his nose.

Tinlee wrapped her arms around Smoke. *He doesn't know?*

Nope. It is why he is our's.

You saw?

Long ago. When it was just The Princess and I. She hugged Tinlee. *It is one of his endearing qualities.*

Tinlee laughed, a knowing Vander laugh.

Arboc smiled at him and at Sa'ar. "Now I am Arboc the Sensitive, not Arboc the Nar." She knelt in front of them. "I speak as Vander to her Lord. I speak as Arboc to the one called our Heart. To hear is to obey. To have is to give."

"Umm," he said.

"She has control now," explained Smoke. "And Tinlee and Sa'ar now have the Nar sensitivity as well." She grinned. "Under control." She looked at Tinlee. "I am hungry."

Sa'ar tickled him. "Well, Husband Lord, it seems that once again, you and your's, have aided the Vander."

"You guys keep messing around with weird stuff."

"We are The Experimenters of all the Mage Guilds. We seek new knowledge."

He sighed.

"Most true," agreed Chicken, poking him in the side.

"Gumpf. As long as the Vander do not start talking about their debt and how it needs to be satisfied." He glowered at Sa'ar who was smiling.

She laughed. "Some small trinket, perhaps."

"Sure."

Grandeville. Tinker's Place.

She stepped out and onto the rear deck and looked around. It was as it was shown. She nodded to herself. There really was a feel of comfort here. But it was more. It was comfort. It was safety. A glow of caring love. But now empty. She didn't think that the source was here.

A young woman stepped from the side door, holding a book in one hand. It was a young woman becoming a startling beautiful young woman, totally unconscious of her physical self. But she was something else as well.

"Who are you?" asked Je'leel, looking at this person.

"I am Ianna. And you?"

"Je'leel."

"An indjinn?"

"Mostly." She took a careful look at Ianna. "A pure force."

Ianna smiled broadly. "I am my parent's daughter."

"Who are?"

"Dancing-All-The-Day and Big Red. " She waved one hand. "Where are they?"

"Visiting. Would you care for some cocoa?" Je'leel headed down the deck for the side kitchen door.

Ianna walked by her side. "Mother named me Sun Song. But I like Ianna." She laughed. "Father grumbles."

Je'leel nodded. "Fathers do that a lot."

In the kitchen, Je'leel prepared the cocoa, set the pan on the stove to heat gently.

Ianna reached over and touched the pan with one fingertip. The cocoa steamed. She blushed. "Oh! Did I spoil your enjoyment?"

"No." Je'leel filled two cups. "Let's sit on the rear deck."
She headed that way taking the pan with her.

As they sat and sipped, Ianna smiled at her. "Interesting
stuff. Father told me to be careful about doing things like that."
She pointed at the pan. "He said folk wouldn't understand."

Dat strolled from the house, saw Ianna, and buttoned
her shirt.

Ianna smiled at her. "Pure indjinn. Very beautiful."

"Of course." Dat sat, filled her cup, and took a sip.

"Big Red's daughter," explained Je'leel.

"Beautiful," said Dat.

"Of course." Ianna laughed. "I am running a small
errand for my father. Where is John?"

"Visiting," said Dat. She didn't trust Big Red either.

"Where did he go?"

Dat looked at her.

"Tell me."

"No."

Lightening sizzled past Dat's head.

Dat took another sip from her cup. "Go home!"

Ianna disappeared.

"Think that I should go and tell your Father, My Great
Master, that Big Red is up to something? Again."

Je'leel shrugged.

"Beautiful," observed Dat. And smiled at her daughter.
"I will wait until they return."

Paradise. Another Lovely Day.

He stood and admired the deep valley with the deep
blue lake in the bottom and the soft sand beaches ringing it.

She was suddenly there.

"He wasn't at home."

"Too bad."

"The indjinns wouldn't tell me where they went."

"The indjinns?"

"Mother and daughter. They said that he was visiting."

"Daughter?" He laughed. "Oh yes, now I remember. Dat and Je'leel."

She nodded. "That Dat threw me here."

He threw a fatherly arm around her shoulders. "This is worse than I had thought. Things are moving, here and there. And he is off visiting."

She nodded.

Then he laughed, a rolling, hardy laugh. "John rarely visits out there. And when he does it is usually to one of three place. So try there." He told her where to go and which person to speak to. His arm hung in empty space for a moment before he dropped it.

Hahn Dohr Kahn. The Realm of The Dragon.

She stepped out and onto the scaffolding.

Workmen were everywhere working at a hurried but careful pace. This was the last section of the exterior wall of this wing. Eleven floors down, she could see people bringing and stacking materials for the roof. All the exterior walls but this one were finished as well as the interior walls and columns.

The Chief Builder had told his Queen that the roof would be on and finished before Ice Time descended upon them. So all the workmen where determined to make sure that this would be true.

They jerked and stared at this young woman who had suddenly appeared.

She looked at the dirty and sweat stained workers, men and women. Those nearby stared back. The others went back to work.

"I would speak to Queen Lurin," she said. "Please?"

A woman stood, shoved her hair back from her face, leaving a streak of grey stone dust on an already dirt streaked face, stared hard at her. An angry red abrasion ran across her left cheek. "Who are you?"

"I am Ianna. Can you tell me if John is here?"

The woman laughed and gestured with the tool she held. "Does this appear to be the place for Great Kings to while away their time? Begone! We have work to do and a building to finish."

Ianna nodded, healed the wound on the woman's face and stepped away.

Lurin grabbed the arm of the nearest artisan. "Quickly. Down and away. Fetch Our Brother's Queen to us. We feel that this bodes ill for Our Husband King."

Bahn Dohr Kahn. The Quarters of The Royal Advisors.

She stepped out and into the bedroom.

She gasped.

A multi-tentacled horror had pinioned a tall woman with moon-pale skin and jet black hair on a large bed and was attacking her.

She stuck the monster on a far wall and knelt next to its victim. "Are you injured?"

Snarling and hissing, the woman plunged a crackling silver wand into Ianna's chest as she rolled off the far edge of the bed, leaping to her feet, ordering her clothes on. She called in the vilest spell that she knew.

Ianna stared and grasped the wand at the end, withdrew it and held it out at arms length using only the tips of two fingers, her nose wrinkling. "Why did you do that?"

Ripple snarled and poured double death down upon this mate killer. Dark forms shifted around her. One stone wall began to crumble.

Ianna glared at her. "Stop doing things like that! It isn't nice."

Someone coughed.

Both heads snapped around.

Hanred, stuck diagonally across the wall, smiled at Ripple. "Midnight Love, that lovely woman is obviously not bothered by what you are doing. Please stop, before this section of the castle collapses and kills us all."

Ripple jerked back toward Ianna. "Release him! Instantly!"

Hanred thumped to the floor and lurched to his feet. "Thank you." He managed another smile of a rather bent sort. "I am Hanred. You have met Ripple. Who are you?"

"I am Ianna. Is John here?" She looked around the room. "Somewhere?"

"Cretin!" Ripple poured heal and all the protection that she knew over Hanred.

"Oh!" gasped Ianna. "Hanred the Illusionist." And blushed. "Many pardons." She waved him healthy. Then she stepped into the inbetween. Only one place left to check.

Hanred stared at Ripple. "What was she?"

Ripple frowned. "I . . . do . . . not . . . know." She sent

him to one of the towers, telling him first, "I must talk with The Old Aunts."

Magevern. Deep Below The Surface.

She stepped into the room and smiled at the young woman standing here, staring at her sudden appearance.

"Yes?" Eulin looked at the vibrant young woman and wondered who she was.

"Is John here?" Ianna looked around the rather large bedroom.

"John who?"

Ianna glowered at the far corner, at the Shadow Dragon now lurking there. "Why did you call him?" Then she smiled at Eulin "Oh, you are a Dragon Master."

Anamaxtor thumped into the room, filling half of it, thrusting his great head between the pair, huffing warning at Ianna.

She reached out and rubbed one hand lightly over his neck. "My, he is handsome. And very protective."

The golden dragon swivelled his head and looked perplexed at Eulin.

She told him to leave the room. "John who?"

"John Tinker, called The Chosen One. And a rather large number of other titles."

"Father?" Eulin cast soft binding around Ianna.

Ianna stared at her. "He is your Father?"

"Yesssss." She watched the spell slide off Ianna. "What are you?"

"Me?"

The door opened and Arboc slipped inside. "She is pure magic. FLEE!"

"Of course I am," agreed Ianna. "I am my Father's daughter."

"Who is your Father?"

"Big Red."

"He is your father?"

Ianna nodded.

Eulin sat on the edge of her bed and patted it. "Perhaps you will sit and talk with me. I think that we need to know what your father wants with my father."

Ianna walked over and sat next to Eulin. Arboc pulled over a chair.

"How did you know?" asked Ianna.

"I am a sensitive." Arboc's eyes wandered over Ianna. "How did you get to be?"

So, Ianna explained her father to Arboc. Then she and Eulin talked.

Far across the complex, in their suite of rooms, Tinker kissed Imdar and then Sa'ar. "We are going home. Let us know when you find out anything about whatever that weird spell saw."

Sa'ar and Imdar stepped away

"Be careful," ordered Sa'ar.

"Sure."

Szart took them out.

Moments later, Eulin, Arboc, and Ianna walked into the room.

"This is Ianna, Big Red's daughter," explained Eulin. "She is supposed to deliver something from Big Red to

Father."

"Big Red's daughter?" Sa'ar looked her over, and smiled. "That is news."

"This is my first real trip elseplace." Ianna looked from Imdar to Sa'ar and noted their calm watchfulness. "Certainly not as excitable as that witch."

"Ripple stabbed her and tried to kill her," said Eulin.

"She thought that I had hurt her mate." Ianna blushed. "I thought that he was a monster attacking her. In their bed." Then she explained her error there. And her errand here.

Sa'ar held out her hand. "Show me that ring."

Ianna reached out, plucked it from somewhere, and dropped it into Sa'ar's open palm.

"BrenBand!" Sa'ar's eyes narrowed, small wrinkles forming at their corners. "Why are you giving this lecherous thing to my husband?"

"Husband?" Ianna took a careful look at Sa'ar and another at Eulin. "Oh! I see." She grinned. "I think that Father has neglected to tell me a rather large amount about the person that I am supposed to deliver that ring to. Would you?"

Sa'ar laughed. "Sit here. And we all will."

Vander began to drift into the room.

An Interesting Daughter

Far Back Under.

Fam and Jonglar bounced and ran down the road headed for the small town called Isbin.

Actually, Fam was in an easy jog, one he could keep up for hours, mile after mile. Jonglar bounced and ran, which might be expected from a something that looked very much like a very large dog or wolf although Jonglar wasn't like the usual dog or wolf. Her thick fur was a very nice powder blue.

They had been traveling together for years, traveling widely. They had just come from Fartha Napnar where they had been hired by the merchant Martil. Now they were headed for their selected target to visit Mur Zinzar, a veritable fountain of information relating to folk who might do things such as that now causing Martil the merchant such unhappiness.

As they approached the edge of town, Fam slowed to a walk and Jonglar did the same, merely strolling by Fam's side. Fam was rather short while Jonglar was rather tall. This brought Jonglar's back up to the level of Fam's elbow. This was very handy for Fam as he could easily lean on Jonglar while standing and talking to other folk. It was very handy. It was very effective.

During these conversations, Jonglar cooperated by exposing rows of teeth and drooling. And staring at whoever Fam was talking to with her large, bright green eyes.

They were a team, were Fam and Jonglar.

Grandeville. Tinker's Place.

They stepped out.

From a faint haze of purple mist.

Fair Morn smiled at them. She was setting lunch on one of the large wooden tables, on the rear deck.

"Cannon ball," giggled Messenger as she hurtled into the swimming pool, swamping Chicken who had been quietly floating on her back in the middle.

"VILE WENCH!"

"Ooops." Messenger lunged toward the shallow end of the pool as Chicken lunged for her.

"Mother," said Eulin. "This is Ianna."

Fair Morn nodded. Her mouth was full. She had been sampling. Everything.

He came clumping down the deck with Chantal. In truth, she was clumping, he was not. They were carrying a large chest filled with ice and drinkables.

"Him?" asked Ianna, smiling at the man.

"Yes," replied Eulin. "Hello. Father, Mother." She stepped over as they dropped the chest and kissed him. "First Greetings, Lord."

"Hi, daughter. Have some lunch." Chantal wiped her hand on the front of her jeans.

Messenger ran past and into the house."Eeek, eek, eek, eek."

"CUR!" Chicken charged up and stopped, glowering all Royal Anger. Then she smiled. "Fair Princess. Be thee hungry?" She glowered again, this time at him. "Great Lord, thee must do something bout most vile kitten for she do Us attempt most watery a'demise."

"Oh?"

Messenger popped from the house, wearing one of the thick white robes, toweling her hair dry. "I did not! She is just exaggerating. Again." She grinned at Eulin. "I forgot to check first."

"Yum, yum, yum." Smoke walked up and set two large platters heaped with various food stuffs on the table.

"Hello. Mother."

"Yum, yum, yum," restated Smoke, nudging him, eyeing Ianna.

"Don't start," he grumbled at her.

Smoke kissed Eulin. "Turkey and ham and cheese. I was hungry."

Sgenn stepped from the house, looked at Ianna, and handed Chicken one of the thick white robes.

Szart and Sha'gar wandered around the far end of the house, stared at their visitor, and immediately poured protection over everyone.

"This is Ianna." Eulin smiled at them all. "She is Big Red's daughter."

"By George!" gasped Chicken.

Sgenn shrugged and began to make a sandwich.

"Hum," said Szart.

"Hum hum," replied Sha'gar.

Chantal joined Sgenn at the table and began to collect things to eat. "Think that I ought to get my gun? I don't like the look in her eyes."

Sgenn shook her head and grabbed a handful of pretzels. "Szart and Sha'gar watch her."

"Merde," grumbled Tinker. He sighed and nodded at Ianna. "What is he up to this time?"

Ianna shrugged. "He wanted me to deliver, this." She reached out and plucked it in. "You are really hard to find."

"What?" He stared at the small object nestled in her palm.

"Here." She held it out and dropped it into his hand when he held it out, palm up.

"Ga'zooks, tis most foul minded ring." Chicken stared at it.

You certainly have been busy in my absence. Lots of lovely new bodies. Heh, heh, heh, heh.

Quiet, commanded Tinker. He glared at Ianna. "Why does he want me to have this thing?"

Not nice, grumbled BrenBand.

"He did not say." Ianna looked at the table and the rest of them as they gathered around it. "May I have some? Lunch?"

He nodded. "Sure." And sighed. And wondered, now what is going on? He shoved the ring into his watch pocket.

Ianna stepped to his side as he stood at the table fixing a rather large sandwich. "A very dusty Queen looked like she wanted to throw me from the top of a very high structure."

"Structure?"

"And a very nasty witch tried to kill me."

"What?"

Ianna yanked her shirt front down and over. "She stabbed me right here."

He sighed. Heavily. "Stop that! What?"

"And then some very friendly mage had their hands

inside my shirt before I could even blink."

"Vander?" He was getting totally confused by her story.

Eulin frowned. "I will speak to Mother about that."

Ianna shook her head. "Please don't. It wasn't unkind, just unexpected." She nudged him sideways so she could reach one of the platters. "Father said that I should experience the elseplaces but I am not sure if that is what he really meant."

Chantal laughed. "Probably not."

Smoke reached over and tapped Ianna on the shoulder. "Pull your shirt closed."

She did. "Father said that he enjoyed that." She looked at Smoke. "Will he take me inside the house and caress me?"

Chantal snorted root beer across the deck.

Messenger giggled and clamped her hand over her mouth.

His glower grew darker and darker.

Ianna stared at his glower. "Father said that you do that a lot."

"GO . . . HOME!" He spun away, stomped over to a chair, dropped into it, tilted it back and shoved his feet against the top railing, and frowned at the distant forest, the one out beyond the first pasture. "GO . . . HOME!" He took a great bite from his sandwich and mumbled crumbs into his lap. "That rotten S.O.B. is meddling again."

Ianna looked back at Smoke, holding a sandwich in her hand. "Father didn't mention behavior like that."

Chantal wiped her chin with a bunch of napkins. "How old are you, toots?"

Ianna blinked. "I think that I am approximately twenty-seven of your annual cycles."

"Where have you been living?"

"On Paradise, of course."

Chantal looked at Smoke. "That explains that."

Smoke nodded.

"Of course," said Ianna. "I was on Hahn Dohr Kahn, then Bahn Dohr Tohr, and then Magevern, briefly."

"And got threatened, stabbed, and grabbed," stated Smoke.

Ianna nodded and grabbed a handful of chips. "Are all the people that he knows so strange?"

"Certainly not," snapped Chantal. "Mostly."

He stood, walked around the table, glared at Ianna, and made another sandwich. "Finish your lunch. Go home. Tell your Father that you delivered BrenBand and that we fed you." He took a few pickles. "Why didn't he send Silly?"

"My brother and his wife are visiting her family." She watched Fair Morn make another large, multi-layered sandwich. "After lunch will you show me your wings?"

"Ummmm," said Fair Morn. Chewing slowly.

Ianna looked around at the group. "Where's Early Dawn? Father said that you stole her also."

Messenger banged her cup on the table top. "We did not! She wanted to be real. So we, ah, freed her, ah, so she could be. Be real."

"She do visit elsewhere." Chicken made another sandwich, wiping hot mustard on everything.

"You are not going to go home, are you?" grumbled Tinker, starting to worry about whatever was going on this time.

"Father said that if I looked properly doe-eyed and sad

that you would let me stay." She tilted her head to one side and pouted, a little.

He sighed, loudly and slowly. "I give up. Your old man is up to something again which I am sure we are not going to like and that for some reason he is sticking you right into the middle of it."

"Three yums at least," observed Smoke.

"I am going upstairs and work," he growled, stomping into the house.

"He is really grouchy," observed Ianna. "In a nice sort of a way."

Chantal looked at Smoke who shrugged.

Dat stepped from the house, followed by Je'leel. And looked at Ianna. "You again?"

Ianna nodded.

Dat looked at Smoke. "Shall I sent this female pest person home before he gets a chance to play with her body?"

Ianna looked at Eulin who shrugged.

Sgenn walked over. Deep down something growled.

"Mothers?" Eulin looked around.

"If My Great Master does not want her here, then I shall send her home," stated Dat.

"No," snapped Ianna. "You will not."

"Ianna," hissed Eulin, stepping sideways. "If you fight with my Mothers, I shall aid them."

Sgenn smiled at Ianna, a soft half-smile. "I do not care what you are." And something dark rose up beside her, its yellow eyes glittering.

"STOP!"

Big Red stood there. And laughed. "Can't have you

ripping the fabric of the universes." He hugged his daughter. "Which is what would happen if you decided to resist." He looked around. "Where's John?"

"Upstairs," snapped Chantal. "And you had better damn well explain what is going on."

Releasing his daughter, he cringed dramatically. And grinned. "Sun Song has no idea, don't blame her. I will talk with John." He disappeared.

Messenger looked at her. "Sun Song?"

Ianna frowned. "I do not like that name."

Messenger giggled. "It is pretty. Really really." And grinned broadly. "Like you." She glanced sideways. "And really really like Dat."

"Kitten," softly warned Smoke, knowing Messenger's predilection for starting conversations about comparative anatomy.

"Don't be angry with my daughter, John. She hasn't seen much of the elseplaces. Yet."

As he swung around, his swivel chair squealing loudly, he snapped, "YOU!"

"In person," laughed Big Red, sitting down. On something. Just floating in the air.

Tinker spun away, exited from his work and shut everything down, turned back to his visitor, and glowered at him. "O.K. What are you up this time?"

"Me?" Big Red worked on looking innocent. He failed.

"Go away," hissed Tinker. "And take your daughter with you when you go."

Big Red grinned. "She needs adventure, excitement,

travel, to meet interesting beings." His smile faded as he leaned forward, his arms on his knees. "And to learn her limits."

"Send her on a tour."

Big Red leaned back and crossed one leg over the other. And shook his head.

"Send her to work with Mirf. She fits the bill."

Big Red nodded sagely. And then shook his head again.

"Merde," grumbled Tinker, slumping in his chair, glowering. "Go bother someone else."

"You owe me," stated Big Red.

"Oh?"

"Yes. I fixed your little Faan witch agitation problem. I returned BrenBand to you. And you stole Early Dawn from me."

Tinker's frown darkened. "Right. Right. And you manipulated Messenger into that!"

Big Red laughed. "Well two out of three ain't too bad."

"Take it all back and go away."

"Can't. Terrible forces are loose in the universe of universes and I need your help. Again."

Tinker sighed. "Go find another pigeon."

"It threatens Braidna and her folk."

"You go."

"You know that I cannot do that. Not directly."

This time the sigh was even louder, And longer. Tinker stared at the floor and grumbled, "It just never stops, does it? Do I ever get to be just me, and not something that keeps getting beat up?"

Big Red slid close and said gently. "John, I don't make the universes what they are or the individuals running loose in them, intent upon doing terrible mischief. When the fabric is threatened then things must be done."

"And I, we, are one of those things that get to do that, do the things that must be done, right?"

"Please, John, don't do that." Now it was Big Red's turn to sigh. "You know that you are one of the forces that can effect events directly. You need to do that. Now!"

Tinker looked up at him through lowered eyebrows. "So, we are stuck, aren't we? Again?"

Big Red nodded. "You might consider yourself drafted, again. And you will get help, of course."

"Like?"

"I gave you BrenBand. And Sun Song will be with you for awhile."

"Who?"

"My daughter."

"That is it? One ring with a very gross set of values. And your daughter?"

Big Red shrugged. "I can't interfere too much you know."

"Merde!"

"Your have to do it, you know."

"Why?"

Big Red leaned forward and began to explain.

Chantal stood. "Guess we had better get things packed and ready." She crooked a finger at Ianna. "Come on, toots. I'll get you some proper clothes, etc."

Ianna followed her into the house wondering why Chantal wanted to do that.

Eulin looked at Smoke. "Mother?"

"Big Red is sending him out there again to stop something terrible from happening to Braidna." She smiled. "We'll be careful."

Eulin hugged her. "Please do, Mother. All of you." And stepped back.

And was gone. Soft violet mists drifted away on the mild breeze.

Rimlee. The Dark Lands.

Dpart stared deep into the well, fingered the amulet hanging from her neck, and slowly let out a ragged breath. Someone was meddling in her design, her carefully crafted design. As her eyes flowed from point to point, she could see that very little had been affected. Whoever it was, they didn't seem to understand.

Waving the well away, she walked from the room, radiant purple green robe rustling soft sigh. For now she would just watch. It was much too soon to take action or to change anything.

The door closed itself behind her.

All the light faded from the room.

It Just Never Stops Happening.

Fartha Napnar. Late Afternoon.

They banged in, a whirl of black and confusion.

Szart wobbled to the edge of the street, bent over, and spewed her last meal into the gutter.

Sha'gar gasped, staggered, and dropped to her knees, gasping for breath.

Weapons jumped into hands as the rest spread out. Encircling their members, staring around, looking for the danger.

"What's going on? This time? Why are we here?" He looked up and down the street.

Messenger gently slid her arm around the short witch as she straightened up. "Are you all right?"

"Par rak dak dak," snarled a very angry witch.

"Nar nar tak pak," growled Sha'gar, struggling to her feet, helped by Ianna.

Tinker joined them. "What happened? You all right?"

"Yesssssss," hissed Sha'gar, her eyes red fire, the air crackling wildly.

Szart lurched over to them. "Some narnak kak ptar twisted us here from inbetween." Black seeped out and swirled around her. "That ptar zik tik needs to die! Piece by piece! Slowly!"

"Who?"

Szart shrugged and looked at Sha'gar who shook her head. They both looked at Ianna.

She stared back at them. "I didn't do anything."

He sighed and flapped the great black sword back onto his back. "Less than one minute and things are already fubar." He glowered at their surroundings. "A new World's Record and the Gold Medal Winner in the Messed Up Category. Merde!"

He looked around. The folk were crossing the street to avoid approaching their small group. Then he looked up and down the street and at the buildings.

"Certainly doesn't look familiar to me. Anyone have any idea?"

Ianna quickly walked across the street and stopped a man carrying some sort of pet. And talked with him. Then returned. "This elseplace is called Fartha Napnar."

He looked at Szart and Sha'gar.

"No," said Szart.

Sha'gar shook her head.

"What if we just go home and try again?"

Szart frowned and sent something black. It crashed back, gurgling wildly. And vanished.

"Not that way," she stated.

Ianna looked puzzled at him. "Father was correct. Being with you will be an adventure."

His frown darkened. His weaponkin sang soft murder song. The jewel set in the hilt pulsed yellow.

Chantal stomped over, shoving her revolver into its holster. "Cool it, Cowboy. How about we just start walking around and take a look. Maybe we will see something useful."

He nodded. "O.K. Let's walk around a little, find someplace to stay, and things like that there."

Szart nodded. So did Sha'gar.

The group started down the street.

Magevern. Deep Below The Surface.

Eulin found her sitting in a small meeting room talking with Aada and Tobtz. "Mother, they have disappeared."

Sa'ar nodded. "Who?"

"Father and them."

"Disappeared?"

Eulin sat at the table. "I sent a tiny blue-green to Braidna's place to watch. They didn't appear. And are not at home either. Father said that is where they were going."

Sa'ar laid her hand over one of her daughter's. "Perhaps they decided to go elsewhere?"

Eulin shook her head. "Big Red visited and told them that terrible forces were after Braidna."

The air shimmered around Sa'ar. She looked at Aada. "Go to Fandor's Dan and ask Sedeem to come. Please?"

Aada nodded and stood. "To hear is to obey." And disappeared

Sa'ar looked at her daughter. "Your sister is three-layered magic." She touched Tobtz on the arm. "Ask Galron to travel to his elseplace and speak to Faan witch Reep. See if she can track them down."

Tobtz stood and hurried from the room.

"What is Big Red up to?"

"No idea, Mother. But Father is very upset."

The body thumped to the tabletop and crawled toward Eulin. She carefully held the tiny dragon in her hand, her head close to its head as it rasped something and went home.

"Daughter?"

"It tried to follow them through the inbetween. A vile twist in their path did that. We must warn Reep."

Sa'ar stood and sent a hard call to Galron, telling her about that. "Come, we must all gather and discuss this. Whatever Our Lord has gotten into this time must be approached with great care. It appears to be very powerful and very treacherous."

Eulin stood. "And evil."

"Yesssssss," hissed Sa'ar. "And very evil."

They hurried down the corridor to the Council Hall gathering all in to plan.

Dol Spar. Monetary Control Headquarters.

"OI VAY!"

Mirf dropped heavily into her chair. And reread the short message again. Then she stared at The General. "Such a pain in the tuchis this will be."

He nodded. And cleared his throat.

"VAT?" She hissed at him. "A look in your eyes like that makes my skin give a crawl."

"Maybe we shouldn't get involved in this."

She stared at him. "Meshuggener, if not us, who?"

"It might be beyond our capabilities."

Her eyes glittered with a sparkling light. "So who got hob-goblined and survived?" She threw her arms wide. "Ta Dah! Me, that's who?" She leaned toward him. "And who has some very interesting scars in some very interesting places from that super nasty that tried to destroy the Faan clan?" She grinned, a grin that would have frightened most folk into a heart attack. "Bingo-rooney! Me!"

The General leaned forward and grabbed her hands in his. "Don't want to lose you."

She nodded. "You making a pass at me after all these years?" And grinned broadly.

"MIRF!"

"Ho ha, much better." She freed one hand and patted his hands. "So do me a favor."

He hesitated, carefully checked her expression, winced, and asked, "What?"

"Let me in the special vault in the armory."

He leaned back, slowly freeing his hands. "You don't use weapons."

"My assistants, my poor, underpaid, low-ranked assistants do."

He nodded.

"And," she grinned, a pure hob-goblin grin. "My lowly clerks, ah, clerks, dash, prime, should be graded as clerks, dash, investigator."

He nodded. "All right. Everyone gets a raise and a grade change. But!"

Her eyes squinted into the narrowest of slits. "Vat?"

"Be careful."

She laughed, a rolling boisterous laugh. "It's a deal!" She banged a spot on her desk. "Quan, wake up Fred and go get Nema and Rema. Hurry, hurry, hurry!" And jerked her hand up, grabbed and wiggled that sheet of paper at The General. "This is all we know?"

"So far."

She waved one arm, one seemingly disjointed arm.

"Why this time of night?"

He moved his chair around, close to her, and told her, very carefully, in a very low tone of voice.

Raztur Plaz.

"It is a trading village," said $1.98. "The shop that we need to find has a yellow door and a red roof." He was reading from the scroll as they walked along the narrow street. They had just passed through the town gate.

"Dear, I think that these directions are not going to be very much help."

The scroll, released, snapped shut. "Duff?"

She gestured at their surroundings. "Look."

He did, and stopped walking. "I see."

Every door in sight was painted bright yellow. Every roof was red, red tiles glowing soft tones in the sunlight. Most of the structures were low, one-story buildings, all round corners and gently curving walls.

"Maybe we came to the wrong town."

She turned and stepped in the way of a woman walking in their direction. "Can you tell us the name of this town, we think that we made a mistake."

The woman smiled gently at her. She gestured grandly. "This is Byar, elseplace Raztur Plaz. May I help you?"

Duff smiled back. "We are trying to find the shop of Nif, The Trinket Trader."

"Nif?" The woman frowned and stared into nowhere. Then she laughed and pointed. "That way. Two corner, turn." She gestured. "Two more corners." She held up three fingers. "Twap on this side." She patted her left shoulder, bowed and pushed past Duff. "Buy clever, stranger."

Duff smiled up at $1.98 and pointed. "That way, Dear."

They walked deeper into Byar. $1.98 wondered how anyone could keep track of where anyone lived.

"Let's stay here tonight."

He nodded. "If we do find Nif, we can ask him where the local inn is located."

Far Back Under.

The place was more tavern than inn.

While the establishment had three rooms upstairs for travelers, the main activity was in the large, pleasantly furnished gathering room on the main floor. The Wonder Inn was well known among the inhabitants and out to the nearby smaller villages as a pleasant place to visit, lounge, and talk.

Fam and Jonglar sat at a small table in one corner, mostly by themselves, and were finishing their meal of ample but rather plain servings. The various customers had paid little attention to the pair and had appeared even less interested when they were served their meal.

Mur Zinar, a rather nondescript citizen in ample but plain robes, was just finishing her dissertation. She had started before the food had arrived and had been talking in a very quiet way ever since. Most of her story was filler and wanderings to this point and to that point. But, finally, she stopped, and in one long swallow emptied her cup.

Fam gestured for a refill. "You are sure that it was The Swift?"

"Hm ooto," stated Mur, taking a careful sip from her mug now that it was full again. "He was spotted fast footing from that establishment, looking proud."

Fam laughed. "Sounds like Dar to me. Any word on

why he chose that object?"

"Nar noto." She casually looked around the rooms. "There are words floating that deep treachery is involved."

"Epm'ah! That sounds not right for Dar. For a quick thief, he was always top right."

Mur shifted in her chair, causing waves of motion inside her many layers. "Fam, on this one worry much. There is more than one bad stroller tangled in it. Lesser folk are," she snapped her fingers, making a loud POP!

Fam nodded, and wondered, and then doubted that Martil The Merchant was capable of anything like that. So, something other than a simple theft was involved. "Who would buy if this is so?"

Mur leaned forward, lapping over the edge of the table. "There are note three." And from somewhere she produced a writing tool and material. And listed them. Then she shoved the list at Fam and lifted up. "Worry much, Fam, worry much." She smiled. "You also, Jonglar." She turned and surged toward the front door and outside.

Fam looked down. "We are not paid sufficient for this. Should we seek something else?"

"Neh," gurgled Jonglar. "Not yet."

Fam smiled. "What if we should happen to visit Dol Spar and slip inside and take a peek at some of the M.C. files?"

Jonglar curled one lip exposing a row of sharp teeth. "Mirf will turn you into tarna food."

"We could be more careful this time."

Jonglar hiccuped laughter.

Fam nodded, left the correct amount of coins on the table top, and headed for the door, and the outside to find the nearest node.

Jonglar walked sedately by his side, ears up.

Fartha Napnar.

Arglo stepped out and looked around. Up and down on this road there was no-one in sight.

He called on the robes of a Semtia mage, all pale green with dense green trim. He doubted one of them would be wandering this far across the universes from their elseplace. And headed around the bend toward the town.

Grandeville. Doc's Place.

Galron dusted into the room, soft violet sparkles. And froze in place. Two great deep black eyes were watching her, intently.

"Cross-tied," gasped Galron.

Reep drifted close and reached with one fingertip, gently touching the small orange dot of Galron's cheek. "Hum," sighed soft shadows.

J.C. stepped into the room and hastily swirled a large towel around his hips and tucked it in. "Ooop! Didn't hear anyone come in." He looked at Reep.

"I am Galron of the Vander." Galron bowed her head and relaxed. "Our Heart wishes for help." She jerked and gasped, "OH!" And stared at them and whispered, "Great danger." She quickly regained her center. "It is vile beyond vile."

Reep pointed at a chair and waved clothes onto J.C. He winked at her and said to Galron, "How about we sit and talk about it?"

Lakelar.

Karlad strode aimlessly around the garden, deep in thought, pondering things. Then she stopped and called in a small disc, held it up, and peered at what it showed her.

And there he was, walking down the road, dressed in fancy robes. She sighed. His choice of clothes was a disaster waiting to happen. She smiled. He was of little concern, His pretensions were of little concern. After all, his chore was quite simple and straight forward.

Her smile broadened. His chore was such a subtle thing to do.

She faded away.

Fartha Napnar. Early Evening.

The inn was nice, their rooms pleasant, and the meal, very enjoyable. Now they were just wandering around, playing tourist.

"Most pleasant, Me'Lord."

"Yep." He winked at her. "If we ignore the fact that we don't have the foggiest idea of what is going on, of where we are, and of little things like that there."

"Hum," said Sha'gar. She was walking on his other side.

Ianna spoke softly to Chantal as they walked in the rear of their little group. "Is he always this grumpy?"

Chantal laughed. "You ain't seen nothing yet."

"Snack time," announced Fair Morn. They were just passing a street vender pushing a bright green cart. She pointed at the steaming containers.

"Karpush?" asked the vender.

"Show me."

He whipped off the lid, grabbed a large tong, and

snatched one from the cooker, and slammed it between two thick slabs of bright yellow.

She paid him, took the offering and a big bite. "Yum yum." And wiped her chin. "Sorta like a polish sausage. Only different."

They started down the street again. They went one way, the vender another.

"Spicy," said Fair Morn. "Gonna need something to drink. In a bit."

"G.G.," mumbled he.

"What?

"Garbage Gut."

"Pookle," replied Fair Morn, popping the remainder of her snack into her mouth.

"Gosh." Messenger nudged Szart. "She pookled him."

"Heh heh heh," cackled Szart.

Two people just passing them suddenly began to hurry. Cackling witches could be dangerous to be around.

"Decision time," he announced. They were at an intersection. Roads headed away in five directions. "Which way?"

So, they walked from corner to corner, peering down each street, trying to decide which way looked to be the most inviting.

"Well?" he asked. And laughed. Arms were pointing in as many directions as there were streets. "Par for the course."

"How can you do that?" Ianna watched the arms changing directions as various conversations started up.

"What?"

"You are a single entity. How can you have five

different opinions at the same time?"

"Let me explain." And Chantal did.

And shortly thereafter.

They had almost decided.

Which direction was best.

Almost.

When the sky ripped open.

Dol Spar. Early Morning Hours.

They slipped silently along the corridor, two vague shapes sticking to the darkest patches of shadow in the empty feeling upper floor of the large building.

On the lower levels, clerks worked, sorting and filing all the information that constantly flowed in from all the elseplace offices.

Others, Analysts, read and produced whatever was new, and old, in their assigned section. And held conversations with higher level Analysts. Information, that caught the important sense of events, worked its way ever upward.

The pair paused by a closed door, at the end of a long hall, breathing as softly as they could. And waited.

For many long moments, they waited. And then slowly opened the door.

"GOTCHA!" boomed a loud voice, yanking him inward, strong fingers clenching the front of his shirt.

He laughed.

The lights snapped on.

She released him and dropped into her chair behind the large desk. "SO, everyone knows everyone?"

Nema shook her head, answering for her sister and

herself.

"He," stated Mirf, waving everyone to sit, "is Fam Inderlil." She smiled. "And his companion is Jonglar the Wertha."

Jonglar sat and looked at everyone.

"My clerks, Nema and Rema," explained Mirf. She leaned back. "So, gonifs, what's the occasion?"

After a long silence, she hissed, "There is an interesting lockup on Pon Dubda. If you like ugly."

Fam told her.

"Ho boy, bad news like that I don't need. Slinar Dar?"

Fam nodded.

"Think that you could find him?"

Fam nodded.

"You're hired! Again!" Mirf yanked open a drawer, grabbed, and threw a sack at him. "Coin! Of the realm." She shoved a small thin object at him. "Don't leave home without it." It was an Monetary Control I.D. of a special type. The bearer could ask for anything and expect to get it. From any M.C. office. No questions asked.

Fartha Napnar. Evening.

She tumbled from somewhere, snarling and growling, cursing angrily. And trailing smoke and fumes of strange colors and odors. And thudded into a disorderly heap right in the middle of the intersection.

Interrupting the flow of traffic, light as it was.

Interrupting the flow of conversation, chaotic as it was.

They had pared down the choices to three and had been in the midst of a great debate as to the merits of each direction chosen when she appeared.

He had been sitting on the curb stones and watching whatever happened to pass by, waiting for them to come to a decision.

Sgenn and Ianna had joined him and were sitting on either side of him.

Then they were running out to help whoever it was. Making all those vile noises, colors, and odors.

She sat up, ordered the local strangers away, and glared at the trio as they raced up. Banging away their helping hands, she lurched to her feet. "Whatever nirl nahnix is responsible for this is going to die a'na!"

"Are you hurt?" asked Ianna as the rest of the group rushed over.

"Some." She looked from face to face. "A na'stra group is this one." She had recognized one witch and one magician. The rest of them felt different but not in that way.

"Well," said Tinker. "If you are all right, we will be on our way."

"I require directions."

He shook his head. "Sorry, we are strangers here ourselves. Just arrived a short while ago."

She looked down and banged one hand flat on her tattered robes. And looked puzzled. "Strange."

Sha'gar stepped closer and stared at her, red flame flickering in her eyes. With one careful fingertip she touched this person on the side of the face, and jerked her hand away. "Ptar ptar baz rarta!"

"Vile vile," hissed Szart. "You sure?"

The woman's eyes traveled up and down both of them.

"Eh quata, Faan? Both black, one Faan coarse."

"Hum," said Szart yanking in a golden wand.

"Hum hum," echoed Sha'gar, a purple wand crackling in her right hand.

"It is so." The woman nodded. "No other clan hums like that." Her eyes fastened on Sha'gar. "What did you see, Faan magician?"

Sha'gar stepped back, one step. "Magician, you have been spell burned and spell dampened. Sorry sorry."

Szart hissed and cast protection over them all, dark seeping out around her feet. "Someone hates you much."

The woman gasped. "Spell dampened? I am helpless?" She looked at the stuff that she had ordered away.

Sha'gar nodded. "Sorry sorry."

"Gosh," gasped Messenger. "No wonder."

"Shhhhh," said Smoke.

Don't start, he grumbled in Messenger's mind. And turned and headed for the sidewalk.

"WAIT!"

"Huh!" He turned back.

Her eyes jumped from face to face, from body to body.

"Oh, oh," he mumbled.

"Whish, My Lord," said Chicken. "Tis naught but fair and helpless magician."

"Ummmmm," he mumbled to Chicken. "What?" he asked the fair and helpless magician.

She plucked at her garments. "These are ruined. I have no currency, local or elsewhere. And." Her voice dropped to a near whisper. "I am helpless. Help me."

He sighed and nodded. "O.K."

Szart looked at Sha'gar who looked at the woman. "What kinds of robes, magician?"

The woman pointed at Chantal. "I would dress non-magician like that."

Sha'gar cast clothes. The tattered robes became a corduroy shirt, blue jeans and comfortable hiking boots.

Szart shoved a bulging sack at her. "Coins."

"Many thanks. Mage debt." She smiled. "Hopefully." And looked at him. "One more . . . favor?"

He frowned. "What?"

"May I do wander with this group? For some small time?" Her shoulders slumped. "I feel most uneasy being this way."

"Merde," he mumbled.

"You may," stated Chicken. "What do be your name?"

"I am Zamir, once of the Gnaral Guild."

Old babe magnet is still cooking, laughed Chantal.

I do not like this, he grumbled.

"What are the colors of the Gnaral Guild?" asked Sha'gar

"Midnight blue and sun bright yellow."

Fair Morn walked over, grabbed one of his arms, and tugged him into motion. "Let's stroll."

"Sure." *Something wrong here. Bad coincidence.*

She nodded and agreed.

They wandered down the street, just being tourists.

Zamir walked in the rear of the group, accompanied by Sha'gar and Szart.

Surprise, Surprise

Ord Increase.

"He is in there, eating a meal."

Fam stepped away from the corner of the window and looked up and down the street. None of the locals appeared to be wondering why someone would be peering in through one of the windows of the inn. He looked at Jonglar. "He will bolt the moment he sees me."

Jonglar nodded and arched her back. And began to swell and flow. Fam could hear the bones crackling. Then with a long drawn out hiss of breath his companion straightened up. She leaned close and kissed him on the cheek. "I do not think that he will recognize me." And quickly took the garments Fam handed her, hastily yanked from his pack, and slipped them on. "Now." She spun and walked into the inn, paused, located Slinar Dar and walked over and sat at a nearby table. When the inn-keeper came by, she pointed at the food on Dar's table. "I will have a serving of that. It looks good." And slid a gold coin across the table to him.

He hurried away. This customer paid well, very well.

Jonglar noticed Dar looking at her. She smiled. "It is good, is it not?"

He nodded. "Care for a sample?" She nodded back, stood and joined him at his table, sitting across from him. She took a small morsel from his platter. After some chewing, she smiled. "It is edible."

Dar laughed, then stared at her.

"Yes?"

"One hardly ever sees eyes of that color green."

"Is it all that different?"

"Such clear green certainly is."

"Runs in the family."

Dar shoved aside his platter and the dishes as the inn-keeper hurried up and set down her serving. She ordered a flask of the local beverage and two glasses. The inn keeper hurried away, headed for the correct barrel. Dar smiled. At her.

"I am Er Atzar. Who are you?"

Dar smoothed the front of his robe. "Mazron ta'Nib, Traveler and Mystic."

Er filled her dish. "Can you future tell?" And began to eat.

"Not well. I am still traveling and learning much."

A dull thump announced the arrival of the ordered flask. Er filled both cups. "Would you palm look? For a suitable fee?"

"I might not see anything."

"I will pay, either way." She set a stack of gold coins in front of him.

"I will need to hold your hand."

She stood, walked around the table, sat very close to him, and laid her arm on the table top, palm side up. Dar leaned forward and peered at her hand, frowning dramatically.

"What do you see?" she whispered.

"Very, very vague," he mumbled. His hand crept near and then with light fingertips began to stroke her palm. And gasped.

Her hand had snapped around and fastened strong fingers around his wrist. "What are you doing?" he rasped.

"Merely holding you." She smiled. "Relax, Dar, relax. You will not be harmed."

He stared at her. Then his eyes jumped up as someone walked into the inn and over to their table. "Fam?"

Fam sat next to Dar. "Relax, Dar. But listen carefully." Fam told him of the concern expressed by M.C. over Dar's most recent activity. "So where is it?" asked Fam.

"Under the table. Side pocket."

Fam leaned sideways, took something from a side pocket of the pack, put it into a grey sack and straightened up as he dropped that sack into his pocket.

Er released Dar's wrist. "We will pay you whatever you thought you would get for selling it."

He looked at her and rubbed his wrist, A blue bruise was forming where her fingers had clamped around it. Then he fell his fingers begin to tingle as the blood flow returned. He stared at her. "What are you?"

"As I said."

His head swiveled the other way.

Er pushed some food onto a dish and slid the dish around to Fam. "Have some. It is not too bad."

She smiled."Dar thinks that it is good."

"Kah." Fam took a spoonful and chewed thoughtfully. "Actually it is pretty good."

"Fam?" Dar frowned at him.

"Oh." Fam nodded. "She is Er Atzar. Now. Usually she is Jonglar. A very good friend."

She patted Dar's hand. He jerked. "I am," she explained, "Wertha. Botser Sib. Understring Pao na." And began to eat. To reform took lots of energy.

Fam nudged Dar. "Travel with us, Dar. M.C. believes others will be hunting you to acquire that artifact."

Dar nodded. "M.C. pays?"

Fam laughed. "We have unlimited funds."

Dar grinned. "Where do we travel?"

"To a far corner."

"Let us pass through Zin Par Nik. There is a certain fine golden neck plate there."

Fam nodded. "We can do that." He looked past Dar at Er who had just finished her meal. She nodded.

Fam stood. "Let's go. Where's the closest node?"

"Follow me," said Dar, heading for the outside door, swinging his pack into place.

Raztur Platz.

Nif the Trinket Trader smiled at them. It was the practiced smile of a seasoned dealer in interesting artifacts. He was a short and wide individual dressed all in shades of soft brown, seated behind a long and low counter top. His face carefully didn't show his curiosity. He had never seen a pair like the pair that had just entered his establishment.

"You are Nif?"

"Absolutely." And wondered how he could not be.

"We require information and were told that you were the individual to speak with."

Nif sat up. A little. "Interesting." And cleared his throat. "What kind of information do you seek?"

Duff stepped close and smiled at Nif. "We have some

items and wish to know about them."

"Appraisal?"

"No. Function and purpose and ownership."

Nif sat absolutely straight and pushed a spot on the counter top. The door locked and the window shuttered itself closed. "Privacy." He looked at $1.98. "Costly."

Duff dropped a leather sack on the counter top. It clinked loudly. "All your's."

"Show me. We are open for business." Nif smiled.

$1.98 fished the items from his pockets and set them on the counter top in front of Nif.

And watched Nif's face go pale as he gasped for air.

Dol Spar. Mid-Morning.

"So, Darlinks, we ready?"

Mirf rolled her eyes dramatically at her two clerks. She had ordered sturdy clothes for them and then had shooed them out of the room to dress. They had just hurtled back into the room.

"Yes," replied Nema. Rema nodded.

So did Quan.

"Chirp," said Fred.

"Ho boy, it's unanimous." She bounded toward a door. "And you all do work hard at staying alive. It's too hard to get and keep good help."

Fartha Napnar. Evening.

Ianna nudged him with her elbow.

"What?" He had been walking along deep in thought, wondering why they always seemed to get stuck doing the things that they always got stuck doing. And wondered how and why Big Red was involved. The rest of himself stayed away from his mental turmoil.

Ianna wondered why he was frowning so darkly, again.

"What are we doing?" she asked.

"Wandering around."

"Wandering around?"

"Yep."

"That is it?"

"Wandering and wondering. Poor lost travelers far from home."

She looked past him at Chicken.

"Most ferle," observed Chicken.

"That's me," he mumbled. "Bug nuts."

Ianna looked at the shops and at the stores and at the other businesses that lined this street. "You really want to go home?"

"Sho nuff," he grunted

Ianna looked back at Chicken.

"Most true." She nodded.

Ianna popped her hands together.

Once.

Grandeville. Tinker's Place.

They stood on the rear deck.

"Done," said Ianna.

"Morning, Father, Mothers." Je'leel smiled at them. So did Dat.

Someone hurled curses.

"Your new houri," observed Dat, looking at Zamir, "sounds very unhappy. Did you kidnap her?"

"Merde!" he snapped. "What is she doing here?"

Zamir leaped away from them, crouching and snarling. "What manner of Panna are you?" She pressed her back against the wall of this strange looking structure and wondered how she was going to defend herself.

"She looks very upset to me." Dat looked at him. "I thought that you had better taste than that." She smiled. "Of course, it looks like a very nice body to play with."

Zamir growled loudly. "I will die first!"

"I'd give her back," suggested Dat.

"QUIET! She isn't supposed to be here."

"Sorry, John Tinker." Ianna shuffled one foot. "I took the group and she was inside it."

"You did?"

"Yes."

Zamir turned and ran down the deck and out into the parking space and around the far end of the house.

Smoke charged after her. *Won't get far.*

"FUBAR!" He dropped onto a wooden bench. Je'leel shoved a cup in his direction. And filled it with cocoa. He took a sip. "Again. Per usual."

The rest dropped their gear and settled here and there.

Lost her, reported Smoke.

Fair Morn stepped onto the table and unfolded and unfolded and unfolded her great butterfly wings. She floated upward and over the roof of the house. *The Winged Warrior joins The Great Predator in the hunt for The Lost Wench,* she intoned in their minds.

He sighed.

"Panna are devious and nasty," grumbled Dat. "And most unkind."

"Huh?"

"Panna."

"What is that?"

She hitched closer to him. "She is. Most unkind. Panna are weird magic users. Very rare."

"Bad bad," hissed Szart.

"Eh?" asked Sha'gar.

"Nar nar Sorceress things," growled Szart.

"Eh?"

"They use hard to feel twisted bent magic, called strange," explained Szart.

"Ummmmmm?" said Tinker.

Then they were all looking down from Fair Morn's eyes as she floated in a gentle glide along their long driveway. Zamir was running down it, toward the county road. Smoke was charging at an angle down and across the slope. It appeared that they would meet right at the mail box.

Hard to touch her mind, stated Smoke.

Zamir noticed the strange shadow on the ground as it passed by, skidded to a halt, spun around and looked up. From somewhere she yanked out a blade and plunged it into her chest.

And slowly crumpled to the ground.

Fartha Napnar. Mid-Afternoon.

Arglo drifted casually down the street and into the shop. He was now dressed in the garb of a wealthy merchant from Fartha Agnar, the sister place of here. That should convince the owner of the shop to treat him with the courtesy and the respect that he deserved.

Martil beamed, rubbed his palms together and then on

the sides of his jacket and walked over, carefully not too fast. It would not do to appear anxious. "Something, Maz?" He used the most formal greeting one used to a High Merchant.

Arglo nodded. "I am only interested in the most rare of the rare, anymore."

"A narrow thing," replied Martil, mentally reviewing everything he had in stock. Maybe one or two items at best would fit that desire.

Arglo lowered his voice. "It was heard that Martil has a certain rare among the rare. I would buy that."

"What thing?" Martil wondered how many times he might multiply the value and still make the sale.

"The Hapsta Var," whispered Arglo.

Martil gasped and staggered sideways, clutching the display case.

"I will pay. Most much," purred Arglo.

"Stolen," grunted Martil. "'It was stolen."

"Haz, naz paz!" Arglo felt the blood drain from his face. She would be furious. And probably blame him for being too slow. He whirled around and ran from the shop.

"I hired the very best," wheezed Martil at his vanishing customer. "To get it back."

Grandeville. Tinker's Place. Late Afternoon.

"Any idea what her problem is?" grumbled someone.

Her eyes fluttered open and focused. Then jumped from face to face.

"Massive fright," replied Smoke. "Hard to know about what. This mind is strangely closed."

"What are you?" she rasped.

"Cool it!" snapped Chantal.

Zamir blinked. She had never heard such a peculiar spell cast. But apparently nothing happened. She checked herself. She was still magic numb. Hard to tell if that unusual spell had been effective or not.

"Fierce Prince, we do frighten her muchly. Praps t'would be best did thee and Our Dark Sister only a'speak with her."

He nodded. "Ummm. O.K."

"If she comes out of that room without permission," growled Chantal. "I'm gonna knock her on her butt."

They all left the room.

He carefully sat on the edge of the bed. "You wanna tell us what's going on?"

"Ne?"

He sighed. "Look Zamir, we want to know why you tried to kill yourself and what the excitement is all about."

She struggled with the covers and sat up, staring at him. Then she yanked these strange clothes open and stared at the scar. And at him.

"Button it up," he ordered.

"Yum, yum, yum." Smoke winked at him.

"Knock it off."

Zamir's eyes jumped from face to face. "I am alive?"

"Sure are. Button your pajama top."

"This thing that I have been put in?"

"Yes."

She did. "How is this possible?"

"We will explain that later. Why did you do that?"

Her eyes carefully searched the room. "How did you keep the Terle away?"

"The what?"

"The winged soul destroyer. I saw it as she," Zamir pointed at Smoke, "ran at me. It was swooping from the sky." She shuddered. "You must be a mighty warrior to face and kill a thing like that." She pointed one quivering finger, she pointed at Smoke. "I have never met a tame Avataz before."

"Ummmm." He glanced at Smoke.

Tightly guarded, MindMate.

What is she?

Smoke shrugged.

"O.K." He sighed. "Zamir, you have to believe this. Because we can't keep chasing after you and, ahhhhh, keeping you alive."

Her eyes watched his carefully.

"There is no Panna, no Terle, and no Avataz either."

She laughed. "Fool with me, not! We were moved. I saw it." She jabbed her finger at Smoke again. "And I felt it!"

"Stubborn," observed Smoke.

Fair Morn, you and Ianna come in here. Please.

In a moment they stepped into the room, closing the door behind themselves.

"One?" asked Fair Morn.

"O.K., what do you see?" he asked Zamir.

"Two females. Nicely formed."

"You sure?"

She nodded.

He looked at Fair Morn and Ianna. "Touch Zamir, please."

Frowning slightly, they did, laying their hands on either side of Zamir's face.

"As I said," snapped Zamir.

"All right." He waited until cautious hands were withdrawn. "This is Ianna. And Fair Morn."

"I remember."

"Ianna moved us here."

Zamir's eyes flew wide. "Her?"

Ianna smiled.

"And Fair Morn is what you saw, flying." He leaned forward. "Be quiet!" And looked at Fair Morn. "Show her."

"Not much room in here," grumbled Fair Morn as she began to unfold and unfold and unfold her great butterfly wings. She curled one around him and one around Ianna and began to fold them down as they pressed against the ceiling.

Zamir gasped and looked for some way to run.

"Don't!" ordered Smoke, ready to grab her if she bolted.

Fair Morn folded and folded and folded her wings. And smiled at Zamir. "Just me."

"What elseplace is this? What kind of elseplace is this?" Zamir shook her head. "Never has such been told. Never!"

"They are not from here." He tried a small smile. "Now, tell us why you did what you did."

"I thought that I had been captured by nether demons. It is better to die swiftly than to allow them to do things. I was bare, unmagic'd. No defense." A tear ran down one cheek. "But I did die. I felt it going."

"Close," stated Smoke, handing her a handkerchief. "Very close. You were almost successful."

The door opened and Dat stepped into the room, and looked at Zamir. "Pretty nice."

"Dat?" He frowned at her.

"I didn't do anything. Except repair her. I left the scar as a memento." She nodded. "Really ought to sent her back. She calls people nasty names."

"You?" Zamir stared at her.

"Yes."

"How?"

"Indjinn simple." Dat smiled.

Zamir nodded as she checked Dat's teeth, eyes and hands. "I see. How is it, Indjinn Dat, that you obey this male with the strange companions?"

"He is My Great Master."

"Him? You?" She stared at Tinker. It didn't seem possible. He wasn't what a Great Master was supposed to look like.

"Yep," replied Dat and Tinker.

"May I please be left alone?" Her eyes pleaded with them.

"Sure." He stood. "But no more running away, right?" Zamir nodded.

They left.

And she thought deeply.

She had never heard of such a group. And wondered what manner of beings had befriended her. She had never before felt so completely helpless. Or so confused.

Baz Longa.

Zimmit the Sun Sprite sat up, stretched and yawned, and looked at the bright sky, and puzzled as to why The Queen held such a deep down grudge against him. He reached over, picked up the order scroll and reread it .

And snorted. It was the same message as last night. He was to journey from here, far from here, and provide assistance to one of those large folk. It was hardly ever done. His folk preferred not getting involved with them. They were rarely rational and often overly excitable.

Ah well, the sooner started, the sooner finished.

He stood, dressed, polished his crystal clear wings, very carefully. One must look their best after all, and shot straight into the sky becoming nothing more than a bright flash of sunlight.

Grandeville. Tinker's Place.

He sighed.

A long sigh, a loud sigh.

They had all settled in the large living room, on the couches, in various of the chairs.

Reading the newspaper.

Holding small discussions.

Chantal was slumped in a chair going through a backlog of professional journals, her Veterinarian journals. Somehow she never quite seemed to get caught up with her reading.

Messenger sat on the small of Fair Morn's back as Fair Morn sprawled face down on the floor. Messenger was massaging Fair Morn's upper shoulder muscles, her upper back muscles, her flight muscles.

"Wonderful," mumbled Fair Morn.

"Me'Lord?" Chicken was sitting by his side. She looked up from the wire puzzle she had been studying. It was a new one.

He nudged Ianna. "Sit up." She had been leaning against his side. He looked at Chicken, who batted her bright blue eyes. "What's going on, slim?"

"Naught." She held up the twisted wires. "Most bothersome a'puzzle, this one." She indicated Ianna. "Most demure, most well-behaved."

He looked doubtful.

"She said that I should," explained Ianna.

Chicken nodded. "Most true."

"Huh?" Now he looked puzzled.

Ianna poked him in the side with a finger. "She said that I should, ummmmmmm, cuddle. A little."

Chicken nodded. "Most true."

Chantal snorted and glared at them and grumbled, "Better be all she does."

"So?" he hissed at Chicken.

"She does do this thing." He received another nod and a smile.

"Why?"

"Experiment." Ianna leaned, just a little closer. "You really are nice and warm and comfortable feeling."

Chicken nodded. "Most true."

"Maybe I will just go camping," he grumbled, slumping a little lower, reopening the novel he had been reading. "For a year or two. By myself."

"Piffle," suggested Chicken. Then she sucked in a quick breath and gasped, "By George!"

"I loaned her a pair of mine," explained Fair Morn, looking sideways across the rug at Zamir as she stepped into the room, dressed in pajamas. "Pretty good fit."

Zamir pulled a chair around and sat down, facing Tinker. Her face flushed. "Many apologies." Her eyes dared him to not accept it. "I have never encountered such before."

"Ummmmm. O.K."

Dat, sitting on Chantal's shoulder, back to her usual indjinn size, leaned close to Chantal's ear and whispered, "She must have indjinn in her line. Yum, yum, yum, yum, yum."

"Shhh," whispered back Chantal, opening another journal, taking a quick glance at Zamir, then reading the Table of Contents to see if there was anything of interest in this issue.

Zamir frowned at him.

Chicken looked up. "He do mean most humbly accepted."

Zamir nodded. One short quick nod. She fingered the material of her pajama top. "And nothing like this. Ever."

He nodded. "Looks nice."

She stared at him and smiled. One glacial inch of a smile.

She is used to being in control, explained Smoke to them all.

"Explain yourself," Zamir said to Tinker. It wasn't exactly an order. But it was close.

Eyes snapped in her direction from all around the room.

His book popped shut as he lurched upright, a little. Chicken carefully set her puzzle on the arm of the couch.

"What?" snapped Zamir.

"What" he echoed.

"I want to know what sort of a person you are." She sat back, very straight, arms dropped on the arms of the chair, feet planted flat on the floor. "What is this elseplace? Is it hidden?"

So, he did.

Explain.

A very little.

She nodded.

"Your turn. Who are you? Really?"

"I am," she stated firmly, "who I am." Fingers lightly touched the collar of her pajama top. "And what you see."

Hiding something, said Smoke.

"Not exactly," he replied.

Her eyes narrowed, tight wrinkles forming at their corners. "Not exactly?" she said, noticing all those staring eyes. Except for the one. She merely looked curious.

"Right. You are being very careful and hiding who or what you are. And we would like to know." He smiled. "What sort of a person you are."

"Ahhhhhh, I see."

"Hope so."

"Zamir," she said.

"Ptar ptar nar," snapped Sha'gar as she disappeared. So did Zamir. And the chair.

"Now what?"

Szart stood and headed for the kitchen and the cookie jar. "Took that zar nak mage to her dar space."

Zamir's eyes jumped wildly. Something held her in the chair. Something held the chair to the floor. That tall magician dressed in black stood and stared at her, red flaring in her eyes.

"You will tell me," hissed Sha'gar. "False mage." She called in a long, thin silver wand. Angry red crackled up and down the length of it.

"False?"

"I asked for a list from Ah'ander. There is no Gnaral

Guild." Sha'gar stepped close, her wand crackling softly. "Tell easy, tell hard."

"I am Zamir."

Sha'gar gently touched. Smoke puffed up as a patch of pajama flashed away. Zamir screamed.

"Small lesson," hissed Sha'gar.

Zamir sucked in a deep breath and looked down. A coin sized patch of her pajama top was missing.

"I could put a matching one on the other side," suggested Sha'gar. "For symmetry."

"NO!"

"Speak tell!" Red seeped across the floor and up one of Zamir's legs, tickled past her ankle.

"STOP!"

"Speak tell."

Suddenly they were there.

Sha'gar nodded at him. "Mate'mer." She sat next to Szart. Szart handed her the cookie jar and cackled softly.

Zamir sat in the chair, slumped, face sweat glistening. One pajama leg was shredded. Her top hung in tatters. She stared at him. "She," one arm wobbled up, one finger pointed at Sha'gar, "is narbu." And glared at him. "Say nothing, do nothing."

His eyes jumped to Sha'gar who shrugged. Szart took the cookie jar back.

"I am," rasped Zamir. "Karlad." She cleared her throat and glared at Sha'gar. "I am Cedinal magician Karlad, called The Sly Bronze."

Szart growled, black billowed around her. "You!"

Karlad winced.

"What?" He looked from face to face.

Szart jabbed the black wand at Karlad. "She was associated with that paz ptar rak Parquor the White."

"He deserved what happened to him," hissed Karlad. "That was zin dar par!"

"Hum," said Szart, sending her wand away.

"Hum," agreed Sha'gar.

He looked at Sha'gar.

"She was," her eyes flicked to Karlad, "unwilling to speak tell." She cast. Karlad's clothes reformed back to new.

"Why?" He looked at Karlad.

"Spell dampened frightened."

"And," probed Sha'gar.

"Something twisted the inbetween. For you. For me. Knowing that was bothering. I thought," she cleared her throat, fingers gripping the arms of her chair tightly, "to steal the, emmm, Hapsta Var." She slumped. And then jerked her head in Sha'gar's direction. "It is powerful. I did not want it to fall into hands not mine."

"Why?"

Karlad pressed herself tighter into her chair. "I will not tell until I stand in its presence."

"She is death oath bound." Sha'gar slipped one arm over Szart's shoulders.

"Strange strange," said Szart.

"Mate'mer," explained Sha'gar. "She will die if she tells. Horribly."

Karlad nodded. "Mage true." She nodded at Sha'gar. "Your guana ba may do what she wishes to me but I will not say." A muscle jerked in her cheek.

He sighed. "O.K. How about we all relax." He glared at Sha'gar. "And nothing is going to happen to Karlad."

Sha'gar shrugged. A half-smile coming and going, looking very much like her sister, Sgenn, for a moment.

Beginning To Twist

Sky Clar.

The bright shaft of sunlight flashed through the open window and into the room.

Early Dawn grabbed it.

It squeaked.

Holding it not too far from her face, she stared at it. "What a strange looking bug."

"I," stated Zimmit with as much dignity as he could muster given that she was now holding him by his wings, tightly clasped between her thumb and forefinger, "am not a bug. I, Zimmit, am a Sun Sprite."

Then it was his turn to stare. At her teeth. And her wings. "What are you?" He knew that he had never seen anything like this before. And decided that his Queen really held a deep grudge against him.

Early Dawn smiled, pointed teeth glittering in the sun light, the real sunlight streaming through the window. "I am Early Dawn, Zimmit. I haven't seen one of your kind around here before. Where did you come from? And why are you here?"

"I am on an important mission which is none of your business. Release me!"

Laugh lines crinkled around the corners of her mouth. "Do you taste good?"

"NO!"

"Really?"

He nodded. "Absolutely. It is known far and wide. Eating Sun Sprites causes diarrhea and intense gastro-intestinal cramping pain."

"Oh." She released him.

And caught him again.

"Mzzpir!" He glared at her. "Let me go!"

Someone walked into the room and walked over to look. "What do you have there?"

"A nasty bug."

"I am not either."

"Foul mouthed," added Early Dawn. "Do you have a large jar?"

Braidna held out her hands and a large object appeared. "I used to have one of these when I was a child. It's called a Bug Zoo."

"I will not be put in prison," yelled Zimmit. Then he stared at Braidna. "Ahb ler nee! You are the one that I came to protect. I can see the glow."

"I am honored, kind Sir Bug." Braidna smiled at him. "If you are released will you, um, behave?"

"Of course. I am Queen ordered here." He pointed at Early Dawn. "Tell your thata to stop grabbing me. I am not a bug!"

"Stop grabbing him," said Braidna.

"Sure." Early Dawn released him.

Zimmit shot sideways, a flash of sunlight, and hovered on the far side of Braidna, away from Early Dawn.

"How could you catch it?" asked Braidna. "I could only

see a flash of light."

Early Dawn grinned. "Bats can always catch bugs."

Braidna held up her left hand, forefinger extended. Zimmit sat on it. "I am Zimmit, a Sun Sprite," he told her. "I was sent by my Queen to protect you from great and horrible danger. I am not a bug!"

Braidna nodded and sent the bug zoo into nowhere.

Zimmit curled his wings and began to inspect them for damage and glowered at Early Dawn.

"Could have announced yourself instead of sneaking in through the open window," suggested Early Dawn.

"Besrup," he grumbled.

"What danger?" asked Braidna.

Zimmit shrugged. "The Queen didn't say. But I will know it when it gets here." He nodded vigorously. And popped into the air. "Tell the rest of your thatas to leave me alone, please?"

"I am the only one," replied Early Dawn. "You are safe."

He flashed out the window, searching for nest material.

"I wonder what Sun Sprites are," mused Braidna. "And what they think is dangerous." She smiled at her companion. "Lunch is ready."

"Good. I am really hungry."

They strolled from the room.

Moments later, Zimmit flashed in and began to build a nest in a high corner.

Zin Par Nik.

They strolled into the store and looked around, one group among many: Fam, Er, and Dar. Fam headed them toward a display of clothes. He had decided Er required something nicer than the plain brown garments that she was wearing.

Dar scanned the immense interior. "Fam?"

"She needs finer clothes," he explained, smiling at her. Then he carefully explained to the woman standing by the place of clothing what he wanted and waited for Er to return. Then he sent her and the woman back and forth until he was satisfied. Dar sat and watched and waited.

When Fam was really satisfied, he paid the woman and smiled at Dar. "Isn't she beautiful?" And winked at Er.

She smiled broadly at Fam. Dar thought that it was a rather wolf looking smile. She purred at Fam, "I'll bet you say that to all the Wertha you know." And laughed, knowing that almost none ever met a Wertha and that fewer than that had ever traveled with one.

Fam looked stern at her. "It is true."

She stepped close, nose not quite touching nose, and murmured, "Then I guess that I will stay in this form for awhile. Is that it?" Her tongue flicked out just brushing his lips.

He grinned widely. "That is also true. After all, we are just traveling, spending M.C.'s money."

She stepped back. "Then you and Dar should also have new clothes." She called the woman back.

Eventually they left, Fam and Dar also dressed in new clothes, sturdy, not too plain, not too fancy. Just the sort of clothes that no-one really noticed or ever remarked upon.

Dar smiled at them. "Think that I could get a position with M.C.?" It had been a long, long time since he had enough money to buy new clothes.

Fam shrugged. "Perhaps. Mirf is always looking for a few rare talents. Her's is the only office where you could get away with what we are doing."

"Mirf? Office?"

Fam nodded. "She works for the General. And is the only totally independent one in M.C. Totally independent of all the rules and regulations that govern M.C. everywhere." He laughed. "And she has probably broken every one of those rules and regulations at some time or other. Her office is called Special Investigations. Her crew is small and select. And mostly invisible to M.C. at large."

Dar smiled back. "Sounds like my kind of place."

Fam nodded slowly. "High hazard. High mortality."

"High pay?" Dar's eyes sparkled.

Fam nodded again. "Lots of cash." He held up one hand and waggled a finger of caution. "Mirf is a one-time employer. You will never work for anyone else." He shrugged. "Most of the time."

Dar shrugged. "You work for her, correct?"

Fam nodded back. "I am one of her many broken rules. So, yes and no." He smiled, a small wane smile. "And do not ask because I will never tell you. It is much too complicated to explain."

Dar's eyes flicked to Er and back again.

Fam grinned. "Yes. That is how I met her."

Er pointed at the shop they were approaching. "Do we buy or steal?" She smiled.

Buy," said Fam.

They wandered into the shop and found the artifact that Dar wanted and bought it, shocking the owner into speechlessness. He had never had a customer do that, just walk in, point, and pay. Not when the price was that high.

As they strolled further up the street, Dar nodded to himself and then said softly, "Can you arrange a meeting with this Mirf person for me?"

Fam looked at him. "You sure?"

"I am."

"Then we will do that."

Dar pointed across the intersection at the large, ornate structure. "We'll take rooms there and rest and eat."

That is exactly what they did.

And as the three of them relaxed after dinner at their secluded table, a small group approached them, grabbed chairs, and joined them, without so much as asking if they could.

"So, gonif," boomed the woman in the gold suit, all uniform severe cut. "How's by you? And your Wertha chickee?" She waved grandly at the waiter. "Drinks! For everyone. Here. We are not buying for the whole town." After urging the startled waiter away, "GO! Rush off! Shoo!" she leaned forward a little and stared at Dar through a narrow squint. He knew that he had never seen eyes like those before. "Soooooooo," she hissed at him. "You the sticky fingers with the fast feet that bagged that thing?"

"This is Dar," said Fam. "And this is Mirf." He suppressed his smile as Dar just sat there and stared at Mirf and then at the woman wearing the great cape draped over herself from the neck down. This person's eyes were silver and multi-faceted, light reflecting colors from them.

"And Fred, the suk-dragon. Quan is her, um, husband.

And Rema and Nema."

"Mirf?" gasped Dar.

She flopped back in her chair, yanking her coat open, relaxing. "You bet your booties, bubee. It is I, every luscious inch." She grinned. "And I won't mind if you drool."

The waiter arrived, set out the glasses and poured. Mirf grabbed a glass and belted the drink down. "Not too bad. Bring some more." She shooed the waiter away again. And looked at Dar. "Soooooo, boychick, you done admiring my bod? Where's that artifact?"

Fam tapped the tabletop with one fingertip, one sharp tap. "I've got it."

"Vunderbar! Keep it! Here's what you are going to do with it." She carefully explained the next step to him. Then she leaned back. She had been leaning intensely forward. "Need anything? Money?"

Fam shook his head.

Mirf looked at Er. "How about you, cuddle curves?"

"No," replied Er. "I have all that I require."

Mirf leered at her. "So, let him rest tomorrow, or the next day. He has to be alert." She grinned. "I hear that the beds in this joint are big and soft."

Dar choked on his drink.

"What'sa matta, G. I?" She laughed. The sound bounced all the walls. And looked sideways at her clerks. "Either, or both of you hard bodies, want this guy? You can have the night off."

Nema shook her head. Rema said, "No."

"Toooo bad," boomed Mirf at Dar. "It would have been a treat like you never had before, if you'll pardon the pun."

"Mirf," said Fam.

"Vat? So speak already. I'm all ears." Then she shrugged. "Well, not anymore. Vat?"

Fam nodded at Dar. "He wants to work with us, ahh, for you."

Mirf grabbed a bottle, took a long drink, and stared at Dar. "So you are a crazy, a Messhuggener? Soft in the kopf? You have a death-wish? You want a short but strange life, right?" She rummaged in a coat pocket and dragged out a rumpled piece of paper. "So O.K., if it's O.K. by you, it's O.K. by me."

She shoved the paper and a writing instrument at him. "You're hired, boychick. Sign somewhere on that. And welcome to the club, such as it is." And sighed dramatically. "Ho boy, such a crew this is."

Snatching back the paper and writing instrument, she stuffed them into her pocket and bounced to her feet. "Don't call me, I'll call you." She tossed Dar a small badge. "Keep this in your pocket. You'll need it." And stalked from the room followed by her assistants.

Dar picked up the medallion. "What is this?"

Fam smiled at him. "License to steal."

"What?"

"That identifies you as one of Mirf's staff. Any M.C. office shown that will do what ever they can to do whatever you ask them to do." He stood. "See you in the morning. Get a lot of rest while you can." He turned, walked from the room, Er at his side.

Dar sat for a long time, turning the small medallion over and over in his hand. And began to wonder what he had just done. Then he began to wonder how Mirf had known that they would be here. He had picked this elseplace to visit.

Kran's Danle.

They were sitting around the table.

They were relaxing.

They had completed several short missions.

They were several elseplaces away.

They had enjoyed a very expensive dinner.

They were waiting while Mirf terrorized the desert menu.

The waiter, hovering just the correct distance behind her right shoulder, was trying not to stare.

"Ho boy," she gurgled, "lots of hard choices." She dropped the mangled remains on the table top, head swiveling in the direction of the waiter. "Just bring us whatever is the best thing on the menu." He snatched up the tatters and hurried away.

Nema looked at her sister. Rema nodded. "Mirf," said Nema quite sternly.

Mirf eye's popped wide. This was something new, that tone of voice. "Vat?"

"We do not think that it is appropriate for you to offer us to some male person or other that is around."

"So who's we? You got a mouse in your pocket?"

"Us," stated Rema, equally sternly.

"Ho ha!" Mirf looked contrite, and failed, totally. "So I'm sorry. Mea culpa and all that." She scratched one thumb nail across the table cloth. And stared at the cut mark. "So it'sa frail cloth." And looked up at her clerks. "You going to resign?"

They shook their heads.

"Vunderbar! Never again!"

The waiter arrived and carefully placed a desert in front of each of them.

"So," gurgled Mirf. "Vat's this?"

"Chef's Special," gently announced the waiter. "Whipped Farza Cloud Ears."

"So fetch us something to drink." She made shooing motions with her hands and spooned a large piece into her mouth. "So it's all right," she mumbled around her mouthful. "Glad that I ordered it."

"But he was rather handsome," stated Nema, carefully tasting the desert.

Rema nodded.

Mirf choked. "Who vas?"

"That male person with the dark grey hair," replied Rema.

Mirf's eyes narrowed as she squinted at them through the thinnest of lines. "You are not related to those Faan witches by any chance?"

"No," said Nema.

"You suddenly having lust attacks?"

"No," stated Rema.

"Sooooo?" hissed Mirf.

Nema shrugged.

So did Rema.

Mirf's eyes slowly opened as she carefully searched her clerk's faces. "So, eat your desert. It'sa good for you."

Everyone did.

Mirf sizzled quietly to herself.

Mac's Pit.

Arglo revised his robes for the ninth time, let his hair and beard grow, and had moved from small elseplace to small elseplace, and now felt somewhat comfortable, somewhat sure that he might be safe. Well, more or less safe.

At the moment, he was strolling down a side street in the mountain village of Rinet looking for an out-of-the-way place to stay. Then he smiled to himself for there it was, just a few doors ahead.

Hurrying inside, he quickly arranged for comfortable lodging, all meals, and other amenities, all paid for in advance. Then he smiled warmly at one of the serving girls, young woman actually, and strolled up to his rooms, on the third floor, feeling rather satisfied. She had smiled back.

Later, as he stared out the open window of his rooms, admiring the softening colors of the fading day, he heard a soft feminine voice, a throat clearing actually.

Arglo slowly turned, smiling warmly, gasped and backed into the window sill, the blooding draining from his face. If he jumped, he'd die for sure. For a fleeting moment he considered it as being a better choice than being in an empty room that had cleared its throat. Something pinned him in place as the vague blackness slipped closer.

"Greetings, Arglo. You are one of Karlad's, aren't you?" It was a very pleasant, somewhat deep voice, but definitely female.

"Who," he gasped, "are you?"

It drifted up to him and stopped, very close, very very close. "The one who thinks that you should answer her questions."

He stared hard at that blackness and thought that he could almost see a face inside. And nodded.

"Speak!"

He cleared his throat and found that he had to do that a few times before he could speak. "Yes. Arglo. Karlad's. Not quite. She hired me."

She laughed, a soft sound. "It appears that Karlad is not receiving good value for her investment."

"No," agreed Arglo, willing to agree to anything.

"What did you do with the artifact?"

He stared even harder. That stuff had to be a her. "Nothing . . . nothing." And violently shook his head. "It was gone. Before I got there." He whispered, "Someone took it, stole it from that shop."

"Well," the voice said. "That is news." And laughed. "And I thought that you had bought it for Karlad." A slender hand reached from somewhere and gently patted the side of his face. "A word of caution, Arglo. These folk are all Slarana." She laughed. "I can see from your expression that you have heard of their, ah, how shall we say it, um, unusual sexual practices. You might cast your glances at females elsewhere."

She was gone.

Arglo slowly sank to his knees and leaned back against the wall. He decided to go to Quazel. It would be much, much nicer and much safer, for him.

Fandor's Dan.

Aada misted in, a soft cloud of violet, and looked around. She stood in a large open area.

On all sides of the clearing were gigantic heaps of

rubble. The way she was facing she could see a large multi-storied building, which appeared to have been recently repaired. Roads ran to the left and to the right.

She strolled over and into the building and stopped at the only desk and smiled at the woman seated behind it.

"I seek Sedeem," stated Aada. "The mate to the Silver Ranger head. Can you give me directions?"

"Do you have an appointment?"

Aada smiled even more warmly. And cast lightly.

A soft blush burst across the clerk's cheeks as she felt warmth settling here and there. She blinked and whisper purred, "I am off duty in a few short and live not far."

Aada nodded and said gently, "I really do have a need to visit with Sedeem."

The clerk stood and gently took one of Aada's hands and tugged her toward the staircase. "Up two," she murmured and slowly licked her lips.

Aada nodded and kissed her. "Many thanks."

The clerk wobbled slightly and whispered, "Hurry back."

Aada hurried up the stairs and as she passed out of sight the spell faded.

On the third floor, she stood and looked up and down the wide corridor. At the far end a door opened and Sedeem called, "This way, Aada."

As she walked in, Sedeem smiled at her. "I felt you cast. Is there something here that the Vander seek?"

"No. Not in the sense of your question."

"Then?"

"It is The Vander Lord."

Sedeem grinned, turned, and walked over to the great window and looked out.

Aada joined her, standing close.

"What? Now?" laughed Sedeem. "What is my Father involved in this time? Has he taken another Vander?"

"It is not that." Aada smiled. "You know that would cause us no problem. The Vander Lord may do as he would wish."

"Then?"

Aada began to explain.

Hazl Back.

She sat up, turned and rapped him on the sternum with one sharp knuckle, "Well, Dear?"

His eyes flew wide. "WHAT?" Then he smiled. "Even more beautiful than Marz An'ad."

She smiled back. "That was not my question, but thanks, Dear."

"Oh. What?"

"You have slipped us, twisting and turning, through a dozen elseplaces in rapid around motion. I think that it is time to talk about those things."

"I'd rather not." His thumb gently brushed over velvet smooth skin just above her hip.

"We said that we would deliver them."

"That was before we knew about them."

"If we do not deliver them, what will we do with them?"

$1.98 stared past her face at the ceiling. "We could wrap a bind spell around them and send them to Hog Nap Nar."

Her face moved closer, filling his vision. "And what do

you propose to do if the rightful owner finds out and comes to us demanding their return?"

He gazed into her large, soft eyes. Soft hiding hardness beyond measure. "I do not know."

Her eyes seemed to grow and to swell ever larger. "And what do we tell Hog Nap Nar if the owner tries to do things to her?"

His answer was barely audible. "Flee."

Duff sat up, her expression shifting. "Dear, I am not fleeing from my home." The hardness began to flow into her face. "And I am not going to allow any harm to come to you."

"I do not think that those things should be delivered."

She smiled. "I propose that we do this." She slid her leg over his other hip. "Then we will discuss that problem."

Grandeville. Doc's Place.

Reep stood and waved on her robe, all flowing dark shadow material. She turned and kissed J.C. "I will go see this twist point," whispered the softest of shadows. And disappeared.

Grandeville. Tinker's Place.

Reep appeared on Tinker's rear deck, found the appropriate magical strand, and followed it into the inbetween, caution beyond caution. It was a unique skill, following a magical strand anywhere.

Szart's eyes popped wide. Then she relaxed. She had felt her Aunt appear and disappear. She nudged Sha'gar, stood, and headed for the rear deck.

Sha'gar followed. Karlad as Zamir carefully watched Sha'gar walk by.

They stood and looked around the empty rear deck.

"I wonder what Aunt is doing?"

Sha'gar shrugged. One never really knew what witches were doing, or why they were doing it, most of the time. This was even more true when it was her Mother.

"Pik tik," suggested Szart. She had picked up Sha'gar's thought about witches.

Sha'gar shrugged.

The short witch carefully checked, searching, seeking some touch to explain why Reep had passed quickly in and out on their rear deck. She carefully, ever so carefully searched, until she felt the disturbance.

Whirling around, she leaped and shoved Sha'gar violently away, sending the startled magician stumbling back and into the house wall.

The air suddenly twisted, folding in upon itself, a hole into the inbetween. A dark figure hurtled out, crashing and tumbling across the wooden deck, violent magic crashing and crackling around her. Two lounge chairs and half of one of the large wooden tables crumbled into dust.

Szart cast protection over herself and Sha'gar and the rest of the household, as deep as she could. And approached the heap between the house wall and one of the large planters at the north end of the rear deck. The black wand she clenched in her right hand hissed angrily.

Sha'gar danced near, red fire seeping from her, eyes blazing.

The side door banged open and Sgenn walked out and strolled over to them and peered down at the crumpled form. "Who causes all this?"

Szart leaned over and poked at the person with her wand and then looked at Sha'gar. She nodded, knelt and helped Szart pull and roll the body onto its back.

"AUNT!" Throwing the wand somewhere, Szart ripped open Reep's robe and poured healing into her.

"Mother?" said Sha'gar and Sgenn.

The rest boiled from the house.

"Now what's going on?" demanded Tinker, hurrying over.

"Cool it, Cowboy," snapped Chantal, pushing past everyone, kneeling next to Szart, checking Reep for obvious damage, her pulse, and anything else she could think to do.

"Careful, careful, careful," hissed Szart. Reep's eyes had just fluttered open.

Chantal grabbed Reep's face with one hand. "Talk to me, Reep."

"Twisted ugly pooz nar kak ptar!" hissed the soft sunlight.

Szart gasped and stared at Reep. "Vile beyond vile, Aunt."

"Not nice, Mother," added Sha'gar.

Sgenn looked at her sister and nodded. "Most witch vile."

Dat stared past Sha'gar's shoulder at the sprawled figure and bare torso. "Not to bad for a slim person. Hard to tell that she suckled three off spring."

"Quiet," growled Tinker. He looked at Chantal. "She all right?"

Chantal shrugged. "Far as I can tell. Szart?"

Szart nodded. "Aunt?"

"I am mostly uninjured," sighed soft shadow. She looked at Szart. "Call my mate and the Vander here."

Szart stood and reached out.

"Whoa." J.C. turned and looked at the group. "Hi, guys! What's up?"

Chantal stood. "Over here, J.C." She beckoned.

He walked over, knelt, tugged her robe closed. "You showing off?" Then he scooped Reep into his arms and stood. "What have you been doing?"

"No," whispered soft. "It was Szart done." His eyes jumped sideways.

"I poured heal into Aunt," explained Szart.

"Ah." J.C. glowered at his wife. It wasn't much of a glower. He walked over and sat on one of the benches. "O.K., silent sneak, what have you been doing?" He brushed the hair back from her forehead. And whispered, "You all right!"

She nodded, the faintest of faint movements at one corner of her mouth came and went.

"Stop laughing," he demanded, kissing her forehead. "And tell me."

So she did, and the rest.

About the evil twist in the inbetween. And that it appeared to be targeted. And that she had followed a back trail, and down, and around, and located the origin. And had run back inbetween. And had fought her way through a three-layer trap to get back.

Her eyes, fastened upon them all through the tale, seemed to swell and grow ever larger and darker. "I killed that trap." Her eyelids sagged. She was fast sleep.

He looked up. "Tinker?"

"No idea."

Sha'gar spun on one heel and looked at Karlad, who winced, and stepped closer to Tinker, using him as a shield.

"You?" Sha'gar frowned death.

"I am ruined because of that thing," snapped Karlad. "And not suicidal, narnip!" He stared at Galron. "A Purple Mage?"

"I am that," stated Galron. She indicated Reep. "Was she badly injured? I warned her but she insisted." She looked at Szart. "May I aid?"

"Unnecessary."

Galron looked at him. "Lord?"

"Beat's me. This is way out of my league." He turned and pointed. "The corner bedroom is free, J. C."

"Thanks." J.C. stood and headed into the house, carefully stepped sideways through the open door.

Tinker dropped onto one of the wooden benches. "How did you know, Galron?"

"Our Young Heart sent a tiny blue-green to find you. It returned and told her."

"Nothing else?"

"No, Lord." She stepped over and sat, next to him. "Who is that one, the damaged mage?"

"Karlad. She is visiting."

"I could take her to Magevern. Perhaps something in our archives would help us restore her talent?"

"Not my decision."

"May I speak with her."

"Sure. She is a free agent."

Galron kissed him, stood, and walked down the deck,

beckoning Karlad to come with her. They stood at the far end and talked. And disappeared.

He looked up and sighed. "Certainly would like to know what's going on this time."

Chicken sat next to him. "Fret not, Our Love. Me'thinks t'will all work out."

"Suppose."

She faded in. "Hi, Dad, Mothers." And bent and kissed him on the forehead, and then Chicken. Then she hugged and kissed everyone else, and finally sat by his side. "So, what are you doing this time?"

"Worrying."

Chicken nodded. "Most true."

"Dad?"

"Daughter?"

"Aada told me about that twist that Eulin found. It takes a lot of power to do something like that."

"Guess we will have to stay home then."

"Father?"

"Oh, oh."

Sedeem laughed at his expression.

"What?" he asked.

"How did you get home?"

Ianna joined them. "I did it."

Sedeem smiled and nudged him.

"No. Ianna, this is my daughter, Sedeem."

Ianna smiled at her. "Father told me all about you."

"Big Red," said Tinker.

"Really?" asked Sedeem.

"Yes," said Tinker and Ianna.

Sedeem looked at him. "Big Red's daughter? Here?"

"Visiting," he mumbled. "Just visiting."

Ianna pulled a chair close and sat. "Your Father wanted to come home."

Sedeem nodded. "So you did it?"

"Yes."

"And you are just visiting?"

"Yes. And traveling with them. Father said that I should. As part of my education."

"Learning much?"

Ianna leaned toward her. "Being around your Father is really different than I thought it would be. And his friends really are."

Sedeem looked from her to him and then Chicken and back again. "Different?"

"Yes. A Queen threatened me from the top of a tall and very large structure. Then a witch stabbed me with a wand." She yanked her shirt open and over and pointed. "Right here. And then those Vander grabbed me." Ianna smiled. "Of course, they were just being friendly. Then Karlad fell in, her magic dampened. And I brought us home again."

"Pull your shirt together," he grumbled.

Ianna did.

"Very pretty," said Sedeem.

"Thank you." Ianna nodded at her and said, "Father said that he likes pretty women."

Sedeem laughed as he frowned darkly at Ianna who turned to Sedeem and said, "I really don't think that Father understands him very well at all.

"Dad?" Sedeem looked at him. "What are you involved

in this time?"

He shrugged. "Usual problem. Things just keep happening to us and we don't have the slightest idea of why or what." He smiled and indicated Ianna. "Like her."

"Hum," said Sedeem.

Ianna stared at him. "I am not happening to you. Am I?" And frowned darkly at him.

Chicken jabbed him with her elbow. "Not nice, Our Prince."

"OOOOF!" he replied to the elbow. "No," he said to Ianna. "It was a joke."

"Better not be thinking of happening to him," grumbled Chantal to Smoke. "Get her butt shot off."

"Probably wouldn't work," suggested Smoke. "Given her lineage."

Nothing But Surprises

Sky Clar.

They were sitting in the sun filled room enjoying their meal when the Agnat bounded in.

It eyed the remains of their meal, them, snarled, and advanced toward Braidna.

Early Dawn leaped up and over and punched it in the side of the neck. It tossed her through the window crashing into the ornamental shrubbery.

Braidna cast.

It brushed the spell aside and licked its lips.

"Halt!" ordered a small voice as a flash of sunlight snapped into the room. Zimmit hovered in front of the monster and shook a finger at it. "Go back!"

It grabbed at the Sun Sprite.

There was a sharp, sizzling crack. The Agnat collapsed, a steaming hole blown between its eyes and out the back of its elongated skull.

"Many thanks," said Braidna, waving the carcass away as Early Dawn hurtled back inside through the shattered window. "What was that thing?"

"An Agnat," stated Zimmit, soaring around Braidna, checking for damage. He halted in front of her face. "I must go see my Queen. You are in greater danger than she supposed." He frowned at her, then at Early Dawn, and ordered both of them, "Stay out of trouble." And disappeared, a streak of sunlight out the window hole.

"He killed it," explained Braidna. "It just brushed off my spell cast."

"What is an Agnat?"

"I think that I had better go visit my Grandparents and talk with them. Maybe they will have some idea?"

Early Dawn nodded. "Do they live nearby?"

"No." Braidna grabbed one of Early Dawn's wrists and yanked her into the inbetween.

Magevern. Deep Below The Surface.

The archives had been ransacked, every scrap read and re-read, as everyone searched for something that might shed light on the problem. But now, hours and hours later, they sat in one of the gathering rooms, talking quietly, drinking beverages, a smudged and rather dust marked group. They hadn't found anything.

There was a soft pop of purple mist as Galron swirled in, one arm around the waist of a woman whose eyes flickered over them, cautious but unafraid.

"This is Karlad." announced Galron. Then she explained everything that she had learned.

When she was done, she introduced Karlad to each of the Vander.

"Totally gone?" asked Sa'ar.

Karlad nodded. "It happened inbetween."

Aada lightly touched Sa'ar who nodded.

"What?" asked Karlad.

"That twist is of great concern to us," stated Moonda.

Karlad nodded.

"It is not selective," stated Aada.

Karlad gasped. "I thought that I was the target."

Eulin shook her head. "It tried to damage a small dragon seeking my Father."

Karlad dropped into a chair. And then looked up at Sa'ar. "Perhaps it is elseplace linked?"

"No," replied Eulin. "It tried to attack a witch that passed near."

"Horrible." Karlad blinked. "Worse than worse."

Arboc stood, walked around, and stood behind Karlad. "This is a deeply hidden mage."

Karlad jerked. "Hidden?"

Arboc's hand slid down, palms gently caressing the side of Karlad's face. "Yes. Strong magic, sly magic, hidden magic." The hands feather stroked the sides of the throat. "Yessssss. Seething. Tightly bound."

Karlad looked upward, tilting her head back. "I am not . . . dampened?"

Arboc shook her head. "Not dampened."

"Help me," murmured Karlad. She reached up and grasped Arboc's hand. "Forever debt."

Arboc looked at Sa'ar.

Karlad followed her gaze, and then looked at the rest, one by one by one. "Any price. I will not live so crippled."

"Leave the Cedinal Guild," breathed Arboc. "Rise above the Sly Bronze."

"Who are you?" rasped Karlad.

"I am Arboc the Sensitive." She yanked her hands free. And snarled. "Mistrust. Deceit. Manipulating." Arboc stared from Karlad to Sa'ar and Eulin. "Guard her well." And slowly collapsed.

Moonda leaped over and grabbed her before she hit the floor.

Karlad hunched over, hands covering her face, and began to sob. "How can I not be meeeeeeeeee?"

Shorz To Adag.

Not long ago they had stepped from the node: Fam, Er, and Dar.

Now they were strolling along a rather wide, dirt road that edged a vast open field of some sort of cultivated plant. None of them recognized what it was. But it was pretty. Deep green growth topped by spikes of bright red flowers swaying and rustling soft sounds in the slight breeze.

"Pleasant place," observed Dar.

"Something comes." Er pointed down the road at it. A large thing was coming, hopping and bouncing rapidly toward them.

"Maznar," cursed Fam. Fighting monsters was not one of his well developed skills.

Dar slipped a long blade from his boot.

The thing lurched to a halt, blocking their way. And glared at them.

Dar edged closer to the edge of the road.

"Can't run faster than something like that," said Fam.

The thing's head swivelled back and forth and finally settled its gaze on Fam. "I smell what I seek on you. Give it to me."

"What?" asked Fam.

"The Hapsta Var. It is my mission."

"Are you a magic user?"

"No. Give. Or die."

Er stepped forward. "Leave us. Go back to your owner."

"I will eat you first. Then the thief. Then the one who holds." It stepped toward her.

Er shuddered, and sighed, and expanded, her clothes bursting at the seams, then tearing into shreds, falling to the soft road surface.

The monster managed to bellow before the Harzar ripped its throat out and disemboweled it with long, razor sharp claws.

Dar leaped into the field and ran as hard as he had ever run. An arm sailed past and thumped into the vegetation.

"STOP!" shouted Fam.

Dar slithered to a halt and spun around. And stared. Fam was wildly waving his arms and yelling at the Harzar as it ripped and tore the monster into smaller and smaller pieces, tossing the remains in all directions.

Suddenly the great thing hunched over and fell into itself.

Dwindling.

Dwindling.

Dwindling.

Fam dropped to his knees and threw his arms out and around it.

Dar hurried back toward the road, his curiosity swelling. As he approached them, he could see that Fam had his arms around a dog of some sort and was whispering to it.

"Fam, what is happening?"

Fam looked over. "She is very tired. We must find food and lodging soon."

Dar stared at them.

The dog looked up. And winked at him.

Dar looked at the mess covering a sizable section of the road. "She?"

Fam stood. "Yes. This is the Jonglar phase." He waved an arm. "Let's go. I will tell you about the Wertha as we walk. You wouldn't happen to have something to eat on you, would you?"

Dar nodded and fished out a flat, thick wafer from one pocket. And handed it to Fam who held it out to Jonglar. She gently took it from his hand with her teeth and then chewed it and swallowed.

Fam began to tell him his tale.

Sky Clar.

Duff whirled around and stared up at him, surprised and startled.

"What?" he asked.

"Why did you travel us by node? Dear?"

He walked over to a low, broad stonewall that ran some distance along the edge of the rock road they now stood upon. A large structure was not too far away. And sat down. On the top of the rock wall, and beckoned her over. She stepped over, turned, and jumped up, to sit right next to him.

"Dear?"

Slipping one arm around her shoulders he gently hugged her. "Duff, I felt something wrong with the inbetween. But I do not know what it is. Just something bad." His arm tightened, a little. "We must be ever more careful than we have ever been before."

She leaned against him, very, very worried. She had

never heard such a hollow tone to his voice. "Let's go home, Dear. Let's go home."

He twisted around and swung his other arm around her. "Just up there, ahead of us, is our destination. I want you to pour all the protection you know on yourself. Any type, Any form. Any spell."

She nodded. And kissed him. "And you?"

He stared into her eyes. "I learned a spell long, long ago while traveling and training. And was told to use it only in the most extreme of extreme situations. I believe this is that extreme situation."

"You sure, Dear?"

He nodded.

She kissed him again. And slipped from his arms and jumped down to the road, calling in a clear crystal wand. She swirled in and down and around and around her, layers and layers of protection. Then she turned and smiled at him. "I am ready. Do be careful, Dear."

$1.98 stood, whipped a long, slender black wand from his left sleeve and said the words.

The sky crackled and shimmered.

"Is that safe?" she whispered.

"Yes." He stepped close to her. "Our errand is almost done." And frowned at the road. "We are never going to do this again."

She nodded. "Shall we finish it?"

"Yes."

They started walking along the road. Toward the large structure not all that far away.

Grandeville. Greater Downtown. Early Morning.

"What'ya think, partner?"

Red tromped on the gas pedal, snapped their patrol car around a corner, and headed toward the location of the problem that had come crackling in over their car radio.

"Don't think that we are properly equipped for something like this."

Green grabbed the doughnut bag as it slid from the dash. And fished another out. "Different all right." And took a large bite from it.

"Not a wooden stake or bottle of holy water in the trunk," said Red.

"So what do you think it really is?"

"D.T.'s. It was sighted just down the alley from The Rail."

Green nodded, eyes watching everything at once.

Red eased their patrol car up to the curb just far enough back from the mouth of the alley that anyone down there couldn't see that they just drove up.

Dispatch had told them that a Vampire had been spotted down the alley, clutching its latest victim.

It was 2:45 a.m.

The monster had been spotted just around the corner from The Rail, *The Railroad Bar and Grill*, a noted hangout for that layer of the local heavy drinking culture that often saw things that were not there.

Red and Green had been called to check out such matters, every now and then. They knew most of the denizens that saw things of various types.

The two gigantic men, dressed in the midnight blue uniforms of the G.P.D., eased from their rig, walked around to the trunk. Red popped it open. They both took out a shotgun, loaded and ready to go.

Red gently shut the trunk. "Wonder what we will find?"

"Last time it was a small bear that had wandered from the edge of town."

They walked to corner of the building. Red crouched and carefully peered around and down the alley. He whispered, "Well, partner, there is something way down there, about two-thirds of the way from here." He slowly pulled back and stood.

Green nodded. "Five minutes." And turned and jogged off and around the block.

Red carefully opened their rig and took a doughnut from the bag, walked over and leaned by the corner of the building, chewed thoughtfully and watched the minute hand on his wristwatch slowly move.

Then the doughnut was gone, the five minutes were up. Holding the shotgun by his side, down next to his leg, one finger close to but not in the trigger guard, he stepped around and began to slowly walk down the middle of the alley, watching the vague shapes ahead of him. One seemed to be watching him.

Halfway there he began to wonder exactly what was going on, here in the alley. The person holding the other person up, looked like they were wearing wings on their back. It was the wrong time of the year for Halloween. He cleared his throat. "Do you need help?"

She nodded.

"Is your friend dead?"

She shook her head.

Now he was only ten teet away. And could see that both of them looked as if they had been in a very bad accident. Tears were running down the face of the one watching him.

"Set your friend down please. And step back. Then I will check her out. And then we will get both of you to some medical help. All right?"

Slowly she gently eased the limp form to the pavement, then she wobbled to her feet and lurched backward, a few stumbling steps.

Red watched her as Green stopped not too far back, and watched them. Then Green carefully walked around them, scooped the limp form into his arms and stood. "Red, bring the other one. It's Braidna." He hurried back toward their car.

Red stepped closer. "Do you have a name? Miss?"

"Yes," she rasped. "Early Dawn."

"Indian?"

"No. Where are we? How did your friend know Braidna?"

"Grandeville," he replied, edging around her back. "Green worked with her when she was a cop." He stared at the wings. They certainly looked real.

"Grandeville," she mumbled. "Can you call John Tinker for us, please? We need help."

"Do you know John Tinker?"

She nodded.

The patrol car rolled into the alley. And stopped in front of them. Red opened the door.

"Get in, please."

Braidna was slumped in the back seat. The radio was crackling conversations as dispatch talked with Green.

When she was settled, wings and all, Red shut the door and climbed into the front seat.

Green snapped on the flasher and shot down the alley, headed for the hospital.

"How is she?" asked Red.

"Pretty beat up."

Red grabbed the mic and told dispatch to connect him to Tinker's place.

They were starting up the long drive to the hospital when Red glanced into the rear seat. "This is going to be really hard to explain."

Green twisted around to look in the back. "That's a big uh huh."

The rear seat was empty.

Green headed them around the block and turned into the adjacent residential area, snapping off the lights on the roof. "The Chief is gonna put us on medical leave."

"Let's head for Tinker's place," said Red as he snatched up the mic and told dispatch that the emergency had turned out not to be one. Then he turned off the radio.

Grandeville. Tinker's Place.

A phone call at three in the morning had brought them all awake. And they listened to the phone call as he listened to it.

"Merde," he said, hanging up.

Smoke and Fair Morn headed for the kitchen to start coffee makers and pots of cocoa.

Chicken and Messenger started making breakfast. Szart and Sha'gar ran for the rear deck.

The rest went to their bedrooms to prepare for the arrival of Braidna and Early Dawn.

Finished in the kitchen, Smoke and Fair Morn hurried out to the rear deck and arrived just as the two bodies tumbled in, pulled by Szart and Sha'gar. Smoke scooped up Braidna and hurried inside. Fair Morn hurried to Early Dawn who was barely standing, wobbling from side to side.

"Hi," rasped Early Dawn as she slumped into Fair Morn's arms.

Fair Morn looked at Szart. She shrugged and headed inside.

"Fold your wings." Fair Morn gently stroked Early Dawn's hair. "I can't carry you into the house with them getting in the way."

Early Dawn nodded. The wings snapped shut. "Dusty. Itchy."

Fair Morn lifted her in both arms and stood. "We can shower everything in a little while."

Sha'gar looked into the still dark night. And cast every protection spell that she knew around the house

Fan's Dangle. Mid-Afternoon.

Arglo suddenly lurched and staggered. A sharp pain had just jolted through his body. Then it was gone, leaving behind only the fine sheen of sweat on his face and body. After checking his surroundings, he spun and hurried into the nearest food place, selected a table in a quiet corner, sat and carefully checked himself. He didn't feel different. And, as far as he could tell, he wasn't injured.

So he sat and puzzled on this strange event all through his meal. Then, over a rather smooth and nice tasting after dinner beverage, a small remembrance surfaced. He would travel to Karzanoga and seek The Bindar Kar.

He stood, paid for everything, tipped the server two over, and went forth to seek a comfortable inn. He would rest for a few days first

Grandeville. Tinker's Place.

He walked down the hall to peer inside the bedroom to check on Braidna. He couldn't see anything. The room was filled with black.

Sedeem stepped out. "Stay out, Dad. Szart is calling great dark." She looked into his eyes. "Have I met, ummmmm, Braidna before? I felt a different magic on her. And a touch of you."

He led her into the large living room and dropped into one of the couches. And then told her all about Braidna. Chantal and Messenger joined them, bring cups and a coffee pot.

"The Princess is preparing breakfast," stated Messenger as she hurried away to finish setting the dining room table.

"A Grandeville cop?" Sedeem smiled at him.

"Chen's Head Cook's daughter."

"She looked like she must be very pretty."

Chantal laughed. "You betcha."

"Dad?"

He nodded. And sighed. "We just got caught up in a Big Red scheme to keep a Wizard Guild alive."

"Both of them?"

"Nope," said Fair Morn, joining them, thumping down into the couch next to Sedeem. "Early Dawn is, ahhhh, was a magical jest. One of Big Red's."

Sedeem looked at her and then at her father who nodded. "Messenger freed her. After being manipulated by Big Red. She stayed with Braidna in Braidna's elseplace."

"So what is going on?"

This time the sigh was very long and loud. "We do not know that." He glared at nothing in particular. "But I am really sure that we are being messed with again and that B.G. is responsible."

"My Father?" Ianna had slipped silently in and had sat in one of the chairs.

"Damn right," snapped Chantal.

"Karlad also?" asked Sedeem.

He shrugged.

"Aada told me. The Vander are worried."

"Worse and worse," he mumbled.

Someone thumped on their front door.

Smoke hurried over and threw it open. "Come in."

"Now what?" He watched Red and Green come in and sit in another of the couches.

"We gotta talk," rasped Red is his normally raspy tone of voice but a shade lower than normal.

"Hi, Sedeem," said Green.

"Hi, guys." She smiled at them.

Green looked at Tinker. "We need a little help, Tinker. Otherwise The Chief is gonna put us on extended, unpaid leave, to put it nicely."

"Huh?"

"We picked up two babes," explained Red. "In the alley next to The Rail. Both beat up. One with wings. One without."

"And," added Green. "They disappeared from our rig

on the way to E.R."

Tinker looked at Smoke who had pulled a chair over. "Szart took them," she said. "Braidna is stable, now."

Green leaned forward. "Tinker, we gotta take a beat up babe to E.R."

Tinker sighed.

A door banged open.

Someone yelled. "PTAR RAK RAK!"

She lurched into the room.

From the hallway.

Smoke leaped up and threw her arms around her.

"I'll go," mumbled Braidna, managing a very crooked smile at them. "Quietly, Officers."

Green lunged up and over to Smoke. "Really beat up, partner."

"Thanks, Green, Let's hurry."

He picked her up, cradling her in his arms. "Let's go, Red." And started for the door.

Red stood. "We'll phone as soon as possible." He yanked the door open and followed Green and his burden outside.

Smoke looked at Tinker. "She will be all right."

"Calm down, Cowboy," snarled Chantal. "Braidna knows what she is doing." She frowned at him. "I hope."

Fair Morn stood and headed into the hall and into another of the bedrooms. "Hi, sis."

Early Dawn smiled up at her. "We made it."

"Certainly did."

"How's Braidna? Something tried to kill us."

Fair Morn sat on the edge of the bed. "She will be all

right. How do you feel?"

"Hungry. Dirty. Hungry. Itchy. Hungry."

"Feel like a shower?"

"Yessssssss. Scrub my wings?"

Fair Morn yanked the blankets away. "I'll scrub anything that you want." She slid her arms under Early Dawn and picked her up. "I think that you lost some weight." And headed down the hall and into the shower room.

In the kitchen, Smoke began making large amounts of additional breakfast, mostly for Early Dawn.

Grandeville. Riverview Hospital.

The patrol car rolled up to the entry port to the Emergency Room. Red slid from behind the wheel, stood, and opened the back door.

Green slipped out, Braidna still in his arms. "Hang on, partner. We're there," he rasped.

"I recognize the place, Green. And it is not as bad as it looks."

Green looked at Red. "Sounds like someone I know."

As they entered the lobby they were met by Raj. "This way, chaps. An examining room is waiting. Tinker phoned."

Inside the room, Green gently laid her on the table. "We'll be right outside."

As soon as the door closed, Raj leaned forward and peered at her. "So, my dear, what happened to you?" He began to check and began giving instructions to the hovering nurse.

Finally, he straightened up. "First things first. You require a bath. Then a few pictures, x-rays actually. A little blood workup. And a few more pokes and prods." He waved vaguely in the direction of the outside door. "Be right outside, talking with those two." As he slipped out the nurse began to open Braidna's clothes and sponge away some of the stains.

"Right," he said closing the door. "What happened to her?"

"Accident," rumbled Green.

"How is she?" asked Red.

Grandeville. Tinker's Place.

Chantal walked into the dining room and dropped into her chair. "Raj says she is doing all right. He is going to let her come home the day after tomorrow. Said that she looked worse than she was."

"Heh heh heh heh heh," cackled Szart. She and Sha'gar had dumped heavy heal spells on Braidna just before she was taken to the hospital.

They looked at Smoke who smiled back. "Early Dawn will be all right." She winked at him. "She is getting everything scrubbed clean."

Steam flowed in soft billows from the shower room into the tub room, long streamers drifting across the ceiling.

Fair Morn knelt next to Early Dawn and finished scrubbing the last spot on the front of one wing. The back had already been done. Water pattered down upon them from all sides. She grabbed the plastic bottle, dribbled green across Early Dawn's chest and gently began to wash her.

"Ummm. That is very nice."

"You were really filthy." Another glob of green was squirted on her stomach and gently massaged around.

"Ummmm."

"Stop wiggling."

"Your fault."

Fair Morn stood, reached down and lifted her to her feet and watched her wobble into the tub room.

"Lay on the deck and I will dry your wings." She walked out and opened the walk-in closet and grabbed a stack of thick white towels.

Early Dawn flopped on her face and hummed as Fair Morn began to dry the surfaces of the leather wings, then her torso, arms and legs. Finally, Fair Morn picked her up, turned her over and waited until she lay back.

"I am almost done." Shaking out another towel, she dried the front.

"Ummm." Early Dawn smiled up at her. "I think that you are being overly friendly."

"As he would say, there's nothing wrong with that." She stood and lifted Early Dawn to her feet. "Fold them."

The great bat wings snapped away. Fair Morn handed her one of the thick white robes and gently helped Early Dawn put it on, then she yanked on one herself and tugged the belt tight. "Keep it closed. Or he will start grumbling."

Early Dawn nodded. "How's Braidna?"

They started for the dining room. "She'll be back in a couple of days," said Fair Morn.

As soon as they sat down, Early Dawn next to Fair Morn, Chantal shoved some platters in their direction. So did Smoke. "There's lots."

The platters were heaped with pancakes, sausages, and scrambled eggs.

Fair Morn served them both.

As she started on her second helping, Early Down leaned sideways and whispered in Fair Morn's ear, "Who is she?"

Shielding her mouth, Fair Morn whispered in return, "You don't know?"

"No."

"Big Red's daughter."

Early Dawn jerked and hissed sharply, "I will not go back!"

"Relax." Fair Morn grabbed her thigh and squeezed. "She is just visiting."

"Is he?"

"Nope. She is just visiting." Fair Morn released her grip and dragged over a basket of toast. "Have some."

As she chewed, Early Dawn murmured, "She looks like she wants to."

"Shhhh,"

"What?" He looked down the table at them.

"Nothing," replied Fair Morn. "Nothing at all."

He looked at Early Dawn.

"Much better," she said, taking a few more sausages.

"Good. We'll talk about it later." He looked at Smoke.

She nodded. "We'll go grocery shopping today."

It was early evening.
　　Dusk turning into night.

They were swooping around and over the house.
　　Just having a good time.
　　　　Fair Morn and Early Dawn.

It had been a few days since the incident inbetween and Early Dawn had felt the need for some exercise.

So there they were, soaring in wide circles, searching for victims. They both held a water balloon in each hand.

Then they saw it. A small sports car turning into the long driveway that led up to the house. It was Chantal.

They circled higher and drifted to one side, planning to glide down, over the top of the garage, bomb, bank away, and coast down behind the house and out of sight.

The pair drifted over the garage and up, waiting for the car to approach, pull into the parking space. They started down, on their bombing run, watching the driver door open then the other door. Two victims!

The bombs fell.

"DAMN!" snarled Chantal.

Her companion laughed. "Don't ever remember being greeted that way before."

"Oooops," said Fair Morn as they settled to the parking lot, having recognized the second victim much too late.

Chantal grumbled at them. "She needs resting, not drenching. Dinner ready?"

"About," replied Fair Morn as she folded and folded and folded her wings "We were just getting some exercise."

Early Dawn's wings popped away. "Really hungry."

Braidna hugged her, then Early Dawn.

Chantal and Braidna followed them inside.

As they all settled around the large table, Smoke, looked at Braidna, and winked at Tinker. *Mostly healed. Pretty healthy. Relaxed. Wet.*

He nodded. "Pass the spuds, please." Braidna certainly

looked recovered. After dinner they would talk about whatever had happened. Nothing seemed to be making sense. But people kept getting beat up.

They were in the last stages of demolishing two large chocolate cakes when a flash of light popped across the room.

Early Dawn snatched something from the air.

"Armmmm nap!" squeaked a small voice.

"What are you doing here?," asked Early Dawn.

"My duty. Release me!"

Braidna looked over. Early Dawn did.

"What is that thing?" He and all the rest were staring at the hummingbird tiny being, now hovering in the air in front of Braidna.

"Zimmit, the Sun Sprite," said Braidna and Zimmit.

Chicken nodded. "What manner of bird do be this?"

Zimmit shot across the table, hovered, and glowered at her. "I am not a bird. I am a Sun Sprite."

She smiled. "Indeed." And sat straighter. "Pray tell, Noble Zimmit, why for be you here?"

"My Queen has ordered me to protect her, The Lyral Princess." He crossed his arms over his chest and frowned. "Why is she here in this place?"

"We will speak soon pon this matter. Would have cake?" She pointed.

"Very kind." Zimmit zipped sideways, settled on the edge of the cake dish, cut a piece and carefully nibbled. "Strange stuff. But very tasty."

Tinker looked at Smoke. She shrugged.

Braidna laughed at their expressions. "Zimmit is my

protector. He is very, ahhh, effective."

"Then how come you got so heat up?" grumbled Tinker.

"That was different."

Zimmit flashed up, over, and around her. "What?" Light popped in various directions.

"Simmer down, bug butt," growled Chantal. "Or I'll get the fly swatter."

Zimmit spun and glared at her. "I am not a bug!"

"Have some more cake," suggested Chantal.

"Wellll, maybe I will." He slipped over and did.

Tinker looked around the table and mumbled, mostly to himself. "No one would believe it if I told them."

"Pish tosh, Me'Lord." Chicken nudged the side of his foot with one of her's.

"Right. Let's sit in the living room and talk."

They did.

Sit in the living room.

He slumped in one of the couches. Braidna slumped next to him. Messenger snuggled against his other side. Zimmit hovered in front of them and stared at him

"What?"

The Sun Sprite pointed at him. "You are the one."

"The one, what?"

"You triggered her magic."

"Oh. That."

Zimmit nodded and headed up to a high corner of the canted ceiling to check out some interesting looking corners.

He nudged Braidna. "How'd he know?"

"Sees the mark."

"Oh."

Fair Morn winked at him.

"O.K." He sighed. "Tell us what happened."

So she did.

Szart pushed at Sha'gar, just a bit.

"We met a mage," stated Sha'gar. "That was also attacked by that twist inbetween. She was spell drained."

"Who?" Braidna sat up.

"Karlad the Sly Bronze."

Braidna shrugged. "No one that I know. Or have ever met."

"Any idea why you were attacked?" he asked.

"No. It was a surprise. We were going to visit my grandparents, were attacked and I thrashed us out, seeking safety." She smiled, a soft gentle smile. "This is a very safe place."

He sighed.

Smoke nudged Chantal. *She wants her magic triggered. Again.*

Chantal frowned.

He glared at them, and grumbled, "How about we just take it easy and rest and relax."

They did.

For two days.

"All right, all right, all right." He strode into the large living room, cookie jar under one arm, cup in his free hand. "Does anyone have any idea what's going on this time?"

He sat in his chair, took a sip, then set the cookie jar on the floor beside to his chair, and fished out one, chocolate chip. "Other than people getting beat up out there."

A sea of blank faces stared at him.

It was the evening of the second day of two days of taking it easy and resting and relaxing.

"What I thought," he mumbled. "Same as every other time." And leaned sideways and took several cookies this time. He had left the lid in the kitchen.

"Damn grump," grumbled Chantal, standing, walking over, and snatching up the cookie jar. "Stop hogging the cookies." She took a few and handed the jar to Fair Morn and dropped back onto the couch.

Zimmit drifted down from the high corner of the ceiling that he favored and stared at Tinker. "Someone doesn't like her."

"Her who?"

"The Golden Princess."

"Huh?"

"Me?" Braidna sat up and looked at the Sun Sprite.

He snapped over to her. "Yes. It is why my Queen sent me to protect you."

"Why?" asked Braidna and Tinker.

"We do not know. Just that it is so."

"Who?" asked Tinker.

"We do not know that also."

"Double gumpf," mumbled Tinker. "Worse and worse."

Soft black fog filtered into the room and spoke to him. "I know who?"

His head snapped around. "Reep?"

She stood there dressed in her black robe, hood pushed back. "It is an ugly twist. And very selective in target but very protective of itself." She pointed. "The piztik is correct."

Zimmit soared up to the ceiling. "I am not a piztik! I am a Sun Sprite." He glowered down at her. "Witches are mamble ibel."

Reep ordered over a chair and sat, next to Tinker. "The twist," sighed soft shadow. "Is twice ordered ugly laid. I followed the anchor down and around and in. I saw her, carefully, in her place of control. She is a Necromage, a dark spinner of catch webs."

Szart growled.

Sha'gar gasped.

Braidna looked stunned.

Sgenn looked at Tinker, blank-face, calm, grey eyes asking their unspoken question.

"Let's talk about it," he grumbled. "First."

Basrak Nipnarl.

It was a rather small, in terms of population, rather out of the way elseplace.

The scattered hamlets were occupied by a pleasant folk, a mixture of human-appearing types and the indigenous Birmar. Few folk traveled to here. Because of these factors, Arglo thought that it had been a great plan to come here to rest and relax. In fact, he felt quite safe.

After a number of days, he felt very, very safe. Especially after he visited the Monetary Control Office. It was a two person operation, a man and his wife. So it was obvious to Arglo that this elseplace was of little interest to anyone.

He wandered around and visited here and there. Not once did he meet anyone from elsewhere. So, satisfied after long days later, he decided that it was truly a good place to be. But, it had one drawback. He couldn't find appropriate companionship. Perhaps he would travel out and back to solve that problem.

And then it happened.

He really wasn't sure where it came from.

An urge.

A very strong urge.

He felt the need to travel.

An urgent need to travel.

Finally he couldn't stand it any longer.

So he did.

Magevern. Deep Below The Surface.

Sa'ar looked across the bed at Imdar, across the still body lying there.

"I do not know," stated the Healer. "It is very strange."

"Who or what is she?"

Imdar shrugged. "A puzzle. No more or less."

"Then," stated Sa'ar. "This puzzle will be very well guarded. Have Bant and anyone else who wishes multi-layer this room in wards and bindings. This person is not to leave this room. Alive." She spun on heels and headed down the hall. She would sent Aada to speak with The Vander Lord.

Sky Clar.

Fam, Jonglar, and Dar stepped from the node and looked around. On a distant hill they saw it, a large sprawling structure.

"Almost done," said Fam, idly running his fingers through the thick fur on Jonglar's neck.

"Careful," she gurgled. "It all feels uneasy."

Dar jerked and stared at her.

She looked over and said, "Woof." And laughed, deep gurgling, deep in her throat.

Interesting

Sky Clar.

It was obvious that something had happened to or in this room. A large window, the remains of a large window, were scattered over the shrubs and grass in front of the building. But it was also obvious that no one was here.

"It is strange, Dear."

He nodded and stared out the hole that had been the window and the stain on the floor that had been something. "We cannot leave those artifacts just lying about, unattended."

"Absolutely correct." She nudged him. "Locate the owner, Dear."

"Duff?"

She walked away and sat on a chair. "I will wait here while you do."

He stared at her. "Duff?"

"I know that you can do it." She smiled at him. "I want to get rid of those things as much as you do."

He sat on the floor, tossed his hood over his head, and tucked his arms inside his sleeves.

She leaned back in the chair and waited.

Rarare Nindle.

The small group stepped from the node and looked around.

"So it's a nice place."

It was. A small village perched on the gentle slopes of a great mountain, one of the many poking up all around them. The air was warm, but not too warm. All the buildings that they could see were neat, constructed from stone of a soft brown color. Doors and windows stood open and the people strolled here and there, apparently on business, but in no rush to do whatever it was that they were doing. They nodded and smiled at the small group of visitors.

"Also interesting," added Mirf, taking another look around. She nodded her choice of directions and headed that way.

The group headed towards the bigger structure, the one with the tan roof.

"The troublemaker that we want to see is supposed to live in there." Mirf sizzled quietly to herself. "So let's give a hope that she is reasonable. And at home."

Grandeville. Tinker's Place.

He appeared on the rear deck, looked around, and wondered where he was. It wasn't where he thought he ought to be. Maybe there was someone inside this strange building, someone who would know. So he opened the side door and walked inside. It was night in this elseplace.

Sky Clar.

Fam pointed up the slope, at the building not all that far away.

"As soon as we deliver the artifact, we can go on our own ways."

He grinned at Dar. "Don't worry. Mirf will let you know

if and when she needs you for anything. Just stay out of trouble, travel around, enjoy yourself."

Jonglar looked at structure and gurgled softly, "Hurry! Something is happening up there!"

Fam started to run. She trotted by his side. They heard Dar thumping along behind them.

Blue smoke was drifting from the structure.

Rarare Nindle.

She looked into the well and nodded to herself. The main problem was incapacitated and the one she sought, while not dead, was less of a worry than before.

It was now time for a direct approach. Everything would be in one spot and her's for the taking. The web had been complicated but ever so effective.

Suddenly she felt great danger.

And jumped elsewhere.

Sky Clar.

Duff watched the two young men and their pet run into the room, skid to a halt, and stand and stare at her and $1.98.

$1.98 sat slumped, just a few traces of blue smoke still seeping from his robe. "This is terrible," he mumbled. "Terrible."

Casting a warning glance at the men, she jumped down from the chair, walked over and nudged him. "What is terrible, Dear? Tell me."

He shoved his hood back and looked at her. "She is at his home, in his elseplace.."

She nodded. "That is a surprise."

He stood, slowly he stood. "It is always terrible when

they are involved. Somehow."

"Can you travel?"

"Yes." He looked sideways. "Who are you?" The air crackled around him making sharp popping sounds.

Fam bowed to them. "I am Fam. He is Dar. And she is Jonglar."

"Bad coincidence," stated $1.98, sliding his right hand up his left sleeve.

"Careful, Dear," cautioned Duff, knowing how destructive things became when he started waving around that black wand of his. She looked at the trio. "Why are you here?"

Fam smiled and leaned on Jonglar. "We are merely delivering something to the person who lives here. Who are you? What happened here? Where is she?"

Jonglar stared, curled her lip, exposing sharp, glistening teeth. And drooled.

"I am Plum Duff and he is the $1.98 Magician. We are also delivering something to the person that lives here. We do not know what happened here. We just arrived."

Fam laughed. "But you know where she is."

"Most clever," hissed Duff, plucking a thin, gleaning golden wand from somewhere.

"Oh ubta," muttered Dar, eyeing the doorway.

"Do not move," cautioned Duff. She nudged $1.98. "What do you think, Dear?"

He looked at the pair and stared at Jonglar. "Behave, Wertha, behave. We mean no harm to your Amaranered."

Duff swirled protection over $1.98 and herself. "A Wertha?"

"Yes," gurgled Jonglar, sitting on her haunches. She

smiled a wolf-smile at $1.98. "Few know or recognize my kind."

"Kar hamar za tmada," replied $1.98.

Jonglar looked at the startled Fam. "He is a friend ta'an. Perhaps these magicians will aid us?"

"What aid?" asked Duff

"Take us to wherever the occupant of this house is so we may fulfill our mission. We will be most grateful." Fam bowed again and smiled at the magicians.

"Dear?"

$1.98 relaxed and looked at her. "Should we?"

"Yes. Dear."

He nodded.

And did.

Rarare Nindle.

Mirf stared as the explosion blew the building into the air and over the small village.

"HO BOY! Such a bunch of bad news that was." She ducked into a handy doorway and watched her crew doing the same thing as stone, roofing material, and pieces of furnishings rained down and bounced off the street and roofs of nearby buildings.

Grandeville. Tinker's Place.

Smoke bounced to her feet. "Visitor. Strange visitor." She stepped into the hallway. And returned leading a very confused man wearing elaborate robes.

Tinker stood and stared at him. "Who are you?"

"Arglo," he gasped, eyes jumping around, trying to watch all the eyes staring at him. "I am Arglo." He dropped heavily into an empty chair. "And I seem to have gotten lost somehow."

"Lost?"

Arglo nodded. "I really do not understand. I was traveling. And came out here." He slumped. "But I do not know where here is. What is the name of this elseplace?"

Tinker thumped down into the couch. "Earth."

"Never heard of it," mumbled Arglo.

Chicken nudged Tinker. "Most strange, Our Prince."

"Certainly is."

"Relax, damnit," growled Chantal.

Tinker looked at Braidna. She shrugged. "A barely trained magician of some sort."

Rarare Nindle.

Mirf stepped into the street and looked one way, then the other, and at all the debris. "So who or vat did this?"

"I did," said the soft breeze.

Mirf bounded across the street and spun around, crouching, fingers curling, and stared. And straightened up. "Oi vay! It's you!"

Reep drifted over to her. "Yessssssssss."

Mirf's crew hurried over and stood around them.

"You are making my life difficult," stated Mirf. "I wanted to talk not destroy part of the town."

Reep shrugged. "She escaped."

"Difficult," hissed Mirf. "More difficult. Most difficult."

"I will find her," breathed the sunlight.

"So take us with you."

Reep nodded, turned and drifted up the street in the direction of the column of smoke rising from the place where the building had been.

Mirf hurried after her, waving one arm wildly, calling over her shoulder at her crew. "So let's give a go, we have a witch to follow."

"Necromage," hissed Reep.

"Oi yoi yoi, so it is something I never heard of before." She strolled alongside the rapidly moving witch. "Is it bad?"

"Yessssssssssss," hissed Reep.

"Such a life I lead," mumbled Mirf.

Grandeville. Tinker's Place.

They faded into the large living room.

"Merde," growled Tinker, not liking the arrival of all these people, all at once. It was getting late and he was ready to go to bed.

"Hi," bubbled Messenger, beaming at Duff and $1.98. "My, what a pretty dog thingy." She stood, walked over to the startled Fam and Dar and ran her hand through Jonglar's fur.

Duff looked at the faces staring at her. "Which one is the wizard?"

Braidna stood. "Who are you?"

"I am Plum Duff. This wreck is the $1.98 Magician and mine. We are delivering some artifacts to you." She waved one arm in the general direction of Fam, Jonglar and Dar. "So are they."

$1.98 reached into a deep side pocket and removed the blue things, stepped over and handed them to Braidna. "These are your's." He stepped back, slid one arm around Duff's shoulders and looked at Tinker. "We will visit some other time."

He took himself and Duff home, glad to be done, glad

to be rid of those things.

Magevern. Deep Below The Surface.

Moonda shoved the man into the room, startling Sa'ar, Eulin, and Imdar. The trio had been sitting and discussing what little they actually knew about their strange visitor.

The man stared at them, eyes round and wild. Soft lavender twined around his neck and mouth. A large lump was rising on one side of his forehead, turning mostly dark blue and black.

"This person," snarled Moonda, "was in her room and she was gone."

Sa'ar stared at him. "How did he get in?"

"Know not," snarled the very angry Vander warrior, fastening the man to the floor.

"Release his voice, we would question him."

Moonda did. Eulin gently touched her mother's arm. The Shadow Dragon that she had called filled the dark space under the table. This man was one twitch from death.

"Who are you?" asked Sa'ar.

He blinked and stared at them. "I am Arglo. Who are you? And where am I?"

Grandeville. Tinker's Place.

She twisted in.

Szart and Sha'gar instantly cast protection.

The woman smiled and pointed, casting a clear net across one corner of the high ceiling, trapping Zimmit in place.

"My! What an interesting assortment of beings." She casually examined the room and its furnishings and the beings in it.

She pointed at Jonglar. "Do nothing na'beast or he will die instantly, horribly."

"Oh my gosh!" gasped Messenger. *She is surrounded by black strands all twisting around.*

Braidna stared at her. "Who are you?"

"The one that will keep you from attaining."

Tinker lunged to his feet. "All right, that is just about enough." His eyes leaped from Arglo to Fam and jumped back to this most recent visitor. "Whatever is going on, it is going to stop! I am tired of it out there and really tired of it coming here."

He pointed at her. "You! Get out of here! Take your argument elsewhere."

She laughed. "I like spirited beings. Sit down!"

Sgenn rose to her feet, stepped next to Tinker, grey eyes fastened on this person. "I am Reep daughter Faan theurgist Sgenn. You are not welcome here." Deep rumbling came from under their feet. "Who are you?"

The woman nodded at Sgenn. "One of them?" She looked at Tinker. "More than you seem, it seems. I am Dpart." She pointed at Tinker. "Even protected, he will die, if you try anything, theurgist." Then she looked at the rest. "Arglo, what are you doing here?"

Alglo wobbled to his feet, a muscle jumping in his cheek. He recognized that voice, the one from the darkness. "I do not know. I am lost."

Dpart's eyes jumped to Fam. "I will have that artifact now. Please. Just take it from your pocket and throw it over here. Now!"

Chantal headed for the hallway. "I'm gonna get my

gun." And was frozen in place.

"Give her the object," gurgled Jonglar.

"Do it, Fam," whispered Dar. "We can steal it back, later."

Fam nodded, dragged it from his pocket, unwrapped it from the gray sack, and looked at it. "This?"

"The very thing." She held out her hand. "Throw it here."

Fam did

Arglo snatched it out of the air. "The Hapsta Var!"

"Arglo, what do you think that you are doing? Bring that thing here! Now!"

He looked at her, smiled, and began to shimmer. She smiled at Dpart. "Surprise."

"Karlad!"

"Yessss," hissed Karlad, releasing the power of the gem. The bolt snapped forth and threw the necromage back against the far wall.

Karlad watched the body slide down the wall, the hole in her chest flickering deep green and blue flames.

Karlad stepped over to Braidna and held out the artifact. "I believe this is your's, Braidna, Lyral Princess." She dropped it into Braidna's lap, turned, and walked over to Tinker.

"All apologies, Chosen One, for everything bothering that I have caused. But there was no other way. That necromage had to be believe that all her web weaving had worked." She bowed her head.

Chantal stalked over, released from the spell, hands balled into tight fists.

"Hold it!" snapped Tinker, throwing his arm up,

keeping Chantal away before she could punch Karlad.

Sha'gar stepped over, flaming red wand held in her right hand.

"Careful," cautioned Karlad. "That was Arglo that you maltreated, not I."

"Gosh," gasped Messenger. "She swirls bronze."

Karlad nodded. "True. I am not spell dampened."

Fam cleared his throat. "Could someone tell us where the nearest node is located. We would like to be on our way."

Karlad turned around. "There are no nodes in this primitive elseplace. Where would you like to go?"

Dar cleared his throat. "Doth Lamax. We need a good place to rest."

Fam nodded. So did Jonglar.

Karlad smiled. "Step away from them, Messenger." Messenger did.

The trio was gone.

Karlad smiled at Tinker. "Perhaps I will visit some other time when everyone is more, umm, relaxed. But for now I have to visit those Purple Mage, rescue Arglo, and make apologies there as well." She stepped close, very close, leaned forward, and kissed him, murmured to him, "Very tasty." And disappeared.

"Most brazen a'wench," observed Chicken.

"Very sly," hissed Szart.

"Hum hum," agreed Sha'gar, tossing her wand somewhere.

Black swirled into the room, crackling angrily. They stepped out.

"Aunt?" gurgled Szart.

"Mother?" asked Sha'gar.

"Ho boy," boomed Mirf. "So who's been leaving carcasses laying around?"

"Now what?" grumbled Tinker.

"Hayou, Mother," said Sgenn as Reep slipped over to look at the dead necromage.

"Strange spell," sighed the darkness. She straightened up, turned, eyes traveling over them all. "This was the one that built the twist inbetween. It should be gone now that she is dead. Who killed her before I could?"

"Karlad the Sly Bronze," softly hissed Szart. "Aunt."

"Hum," breathed the quiet.

"Hum," replied Sha'gar. "Karlad, and that ptar nak kak, were many twisted around this one." She pointed at Braldna.

Braidna watched Sha'gar's finger carefully and relaxed as she dropped her arm. Braidna held up the now deep purple gem. "This is called The Hapsta Var." And held up the strange blue artifacts. "And these are part of the totality." She slipped the things into the gem, one by one, watched it shimmer and change. Taking more of the blue things from her pockets, she fastened them here and there.

The room filled with golden light which vibrated and then went calm. She fastened the circlet it had become around her neck. "This is the true property of The Wizards of Trefil. It settles our power and guards our boundaries."

Lifting her hand, she beckoned with one finger, and smiled as Zimmit settled there. She gently touched him with a finger of her other hand. "Your Queen will now see that Zimmit is a brave one and ennobled by us. Tell her that we owe debt for your aid."

Zimmit smiled and snapped away, a bright flash of sunlight.

Braidna turned to Reep. "Do you wish to spell take from that necromage?"

"I have no need."

Braidna nodded. The body disappeared.

"Ho boy," mumbled Mirf. "A skill like that I should have."

Braidna looked at her. "True?"

Mirf's eyes glittered hob-goblin wild as she pondered the offer. She shook her head. "Thanks, but no thanks. Such a temptation like that I don't need."

"Home?"

"Vunderbar!" She stepped over and hugged Tinker and laughed. "So don't hold back, big guy, they won't mind."

He hugged her and whispered, "Not bad for Monetary Control." And laughed.

So she kissed him. And laughed, all loud boisterous laughter. "Better than that." She stepped away and looked at Braidna. "So O.K., Beauty Bod, home!"

Braidna nodded. Mirf and her crew disappeared.

Reep walked over and kissed Sha'gar and Sgenn on their foreheads. And faded away in a soft glow of black

Braidna winked. And started to sag. Early Dawn grabbed her. "What?"

"Tired. Very very tired. I need healing rest."

Early Dawn scooped her up and headed into and down the hallway.

"Whoosh." Chicken tugged him back and into the couch.

"Oooof!" He looked at the rest of himself. "Things just keep getting stranger."

Chantal joined them and frowned at Szart. "That ward needs improving. Too many things slipping in."

Szart grumbled, but nodded and nudged Sha'gar who nodded. They headed for Szart's bedroom to discuss this problem before going to sleep.

Early Dawn walked into the room, yawning widely. "Can I sleep with you, sis?"

"Sure. It's a big bed." Fair Morn winked at her.

Then they all headed for their respective bedrooms with Tinker grumbling at them as they walked into The Chamber that no one needed to get up early.

Early Dawn nudged Fair Mom and winked at her.

He slipped under the covers and bumped into a warm body and sighed loudly into the darkness. "Now what's going on?"

"I wouldn't have allowed that necromage to hurt anyone," she said.

"I didn't see you anywhere."

"I was being discrete."

"Oh."

"How did you trigger her magic?"

"Huh?"

"That wizard. I heard the Sun Sprite say that you had triggered her magic." She nestled against his side. "You are really nice and warm. Just like they all say you are. And comfortable feeling."

"Go to bed."

"I did."

"Your . . . bed. Go to your room."

"Did you know that you radiate?"

"What?"

"Calm and security."

"Huh?"

"Strength and male purpose."

He rolled onto his side and stared into the dark where he figured her face ought to be. "Exactly what are you talking about?"

"You."

"Merde."

"That is not very nice."

"Then how about not being so cryptic and just state, in plain English, whatever it is that you are talking about. In nice and plain straight forward simple terms so I can go to sleep."

So she told him.

He flopped onto his back and frowned darkly into the darkness. And grumbled.

"The Thought merely enhanced what you already were. Way back at the beginning."

He sighed.

"Now you know why things happen around you the way they do."

"Poogle," he mumbled.

"Now," she stated firmly. "You must do something for me."

"What?" It was a very cautious question as he began to worry a whole bunch.

"Hold me."

"What?"

"Don't be so cautious."

Sighing loudly, he rolled onto his side and reached out.

Heh, heh, heh. Shall I stimulate her for you?

BrenBand?

Nice body. All your's.

"I am wearing the ring," she murmured.

"Take that damn thing off!"

"It can't do anything to me."

Tickle, tickle, tickle.

Something flashed blue and popped in the darkness.

OUCH!

Ianna laughed. "See?"

"Then why do you wear it?"

"I would experience life as a non-magical being. Like them."

"And?"

She is blushing.

Quiet! He ran his hand over her hair. "No one needs BrenBand to do that."

Don't do it, cried the ring.

"I sent it to the book shelf next to The Eye of Dat."

"Good."

"May I kiss you?"

"Sure."

She did and sighed in his ear. "Leaving in the morning."

Chantal slipped into Smoke's room, her small flashlight guiding her way.

"Don't grumble." Smoke sat up.

Chantal sat on the edge of the bed. "Think that it will

ever stop?"

"She will go home in the morning."

"Not what I meant."

Smoke slipped her arm around Chantal. "He can't keep it from happening." She laughed gently. "He even has that effect on female demons. And now a pure magical force."

She massaged the tightness out of Chantal's shoulder and neck. "You worry almost as much as he does."

"Uh huh."

Peace and Quiet. Sorta.

Grandeville. Tinker's Place.

The gentle breeze drifted by with pleasant mild warm touch and gently ruffled the jet black hair. It was a soft caress. one female to another.

She didn't notice. Her eyes were locked predator tight on her prey who was, at this moment casually strolling across the open grass and would pass very close to where she was crouched, muscles tight, ready to pounce.

"Oooof!"

Flat on his back, he stared up past her head and admired the clear blue sky. And wondered, once again, what was going on this time.

Raising herself up, forearms crossed over his chest, she grinned down into his slowly beginning to frown face. "I gotcha!"

"Yep."

She wiggled, just a little.

He sighed.

"Give up?"

"I gave up a long, long, looooong time ago."

"What?"

"Trying to understand you guys and what you are up

to."

"We are not up to anything."

"Oh?"

"That is your job."

"Huh?"

"Being up to things."

Well, he thought to himself, it is worse than I thought.

"TA DAH, TA DAH, TA DAH!" Someone made trumpet-like noises.

And they thudded down.

Well, they didn't exactly thud.

Half a dozen, large, water-filled balloons burst. Drenching both of them. Two burst off to one side.

"Ooooopsie," giggled someone.

"Me'thinks foul predator and innocent prey do be both a'killed."

"Well, Princess, think we ought to drag the bodies away or just let them lie out here and rot?"

"Ugh, ugh, ugh." Messenger peered down at him. "We were hunting that terrible creep beast but she got you before we could save you." Messenger grinned at him. "That is her, sprawling on top of you."

"Oh."

Chicken nodded. "Most true, Our Lord."

"How about dragging the body off so I can go in the house and get some dry clothes?"

His attacker sprung to her feet and scooped up the short young woman in her arms. "Your aim is terrible, kitten." And tickled her.

"EEEEEEEEEK!"

He headed for the house, hooking his arm around the waist of the slender woman who had joined him. "O.K., Slim, what's going on?"

"Naught, Me'Lord."

A tall woman joined his free side. "Right!" She nudged him with an elbow. "That monster wanted to rip your clothes off but we got her before she could."

He sighed.

"It is her animal nature."

"Knock it off," he grumbled.

"Exactly. Need any help?" She leered at him.

"Wench," hissed Chicken.

"That's stacked wench," corrected Fair Morn.

Smoke trotted past them, Messenger slung over one shoulder, stopped, and tossed. Messenger landed in the deep end of the swimming pool. And surged to the surface, giggling wildly.

"Weirder and weirder," he mumbled.

"Damn grouch," observed the woman setting lunch on one of the large wooden tables on the rear deck. It was a new table.

"Not you that got jumped on and drenched," he snarled at her as he walked up and onto the rear deck.

The short woman standing by the table rolled her jet black eyes dramatically. "He is just being unhappy because he didn't have time to rip Smoke's shirt off."

He stomped into the house, slamming the door loudly. Then he flung the door wide and snarled at them, "POOGA!" And slammed it shut again.

"Pooga?" asked Chantal.

Szart shrugged and began to fill the glasses with orange juice. "Some arcane spell perhaps?" She shook her head. "Not witch."

She walked around the far corner of the house and headed down the deck toward them, carrying baskets of bread. "Not magician either." Sha'gar began to place baskets in strategic positions amidst the various heaped food platters.

"Just a John grump." Chantal dumped a jar of olives into a bowl.

"Must be." Fair Morn tried one of the olives. "Yum yum. Doubt that word is in the dictionary."

Messenger dashed past and into the house trailing water.

In the bedroom she handed him a large white towel as he dropped his shirt on the floor.

"Thanks, Princess."

"Fret thee not, Sweet prince."

"I am not fretting."

"Pish tosh."

"I was just enjoying a solitary stroll until that Big Cat jumped on me. Then you guys drenched us." The towel dropped on top of the shirt.

"We do naught but cool thy ardor."

"Wasn't me leaping on anyone." He yanked his trousers on. "And I didn't need cooling down either." He fastened his belt.

"Be that most fair inducement, Handsome Prince?" She smiled slyly and batted bright blue eyes at him.

He grabbed her by the shoulders. "O.K. Slim Sneaky,

what are you guys up to? This time?"

"Naught. Tis time a'lunch."

"Not talking, huh?"

Sgenn joined them as they headed for the rear deck. "Lunch time."

"I know."

"Most grumpy," explained Chicken to Sgenn.

She nodded, grey eyes carefully checking his face.

"I am not grumpy," he grumbled, stomping out the door and across the rear deck.

Smoke grinned at him from the far side of the table and took a big bite from her sandwich and mumbled at him, "Roast beef."

Messenger nodded and waggled her sandwich at him. "With horse radish."

"Any ham?"

Fair Morn handed him a thick sandwich. "Here, Big Stud!"

"We've got orange juice and orange juice." Chantal handed him a full glass. "It's good for you."

"Thanks, mom."

"I am not your mom, Oedipus."

"Oh, dear," gasped Messenger. "If he works his wicked ways on her, he will have to tear his eyes out."

He sat on one of the benches and grabbed a handful of olives and popped one into his mouth. And decided that it would just be best if he ignored that remark. And hoped that they would.

They all settled around the table and had lunch.

"It is Wednesday," he observed, chewing on his second sandwich.

"Yep." Chantal reached past him and grabbed a bag of potato chips. "Took the day off. Carlos can handle whatever comes up." Carlos Vera was her partner in her veterinarian clinic. As she poured the chips onto her plate the ornate ring she wore flashed bright colors in the sunlight. She winked at him. And took another sandwich.

They were joined by their house guests.

"Pretty slow," observed Fair Morn.

"No one told us, sis." Early Dawn sat and began to assemble two thick sandwiches. The other guest sat by his free side.

She beckoned a platter over and made her own sandwich. "It has been two weeks. And is time for me to return to my own elseplace."

He hastily swallowed. "You sure?"

"Yes." Braidna slathered mustard over her ham and added pickles. "I am healed, rested and healthy. Thus, there is no reason to stay." She laughed. "Other than your company, of course." And smiled at all the others seated around the table. "That includes all of you."

He nodded and washed the remains of the sandwich down his throat with orange juice. "So I got pounced upon because you are leaving?"

Smoke grinned. "Just keeping you distracted."

"Humbug!"

"Can't have you grumpy, Stud Butt." Chantal grabbed another handful of the potato chips.

Early Dawn made another pair of sandwiches and

winked at Fair Morn who was doing the same thing. "You mind if I stay?"

"Nope." Fair Morn grinned at her and shoved the bowl of olives in her direction.

"Better go grocery shopping," he grumbled. "Buy a cow or two."

Early Dawn grinned at him. "I'll sleep with Fair Morn."

"And don't smile at anyone we don't know," he stated firmly.

"He is mad," suggested Fair Morn. "Cause you are sleeping with me."

"Pish tosh," he mumbled.

"Heh, heh, heh," commented Fair Morn.

"Chantal has the ring." Early Dawn emptied the chip bag onto her plate.

"Damn right." Chantal stood and began to collect dirty dishes. "You can help." She nodded at Early Dawn. Who did. Help.

The pair headed down the deck toward the kitchen.

"Where's your daughter and Dat?" asked Early Dawn.

"Dat is still sleeping in her ring and Je'leel went on a camping trip with J.C. and Reep."

"For two weeks?"

"Just a short nap for an indjinn."

They loaded the dish washer. And Chantal decided that they should make cookies. A new activity. For Early Dawn

Braidna went home to her elseplace.
And the household settled down.
As much as it ever did.

Individuals Of Note

Grandeville.

Tinker's Place
John Tinker -- the individual used as an intermediary by Big Red in his ongoing activities to maintain the balance of the universes. During his initial time on Mirk Wild Weald, Tinker was told by The Thought that he is The Chosen One of legend. Now merged telepathically into an entity with the rest following the cultural values of Smoke's people.

Smoke of the Velvetmist - a gigantic, telepathic carnivore, now transformed into a human shape by Big Red. She was selected from her home, a hidden and never visited elseplace, to be one of the original companions to aid and journey with John Tinker. Now MindMate to Tinker, Chicken and the rest.

Princess Chicken - an Easter Season fluffy chicken toy from an Easter basket, transformed by Big Red and placed as a traveling companion and aid for John Tinker.

Messenger - Once "The Messenger" of her people but joined with Tinker and the rest when she began to fold inside herself believing Tinker and crew were monsters and demons from her folk's mythology come alive.

Fair Morn - a one-time mythological jest created by the magical force, Big Red. Messenger severed her magical bonds changing Fair Morn from a jest into a real person.

Ferrelden - of the Risshar, a Night Runner from Zhorndar'h. (Deceased).

Flar - one time owner of a Magical Items Shop. (Deceased.)

R-Bar - a witch of The Faan clan, joined into the polyorganism of Tinker and the rest by Smoke. (Deceased).

> **Sedeem** - her daughter, a magician.

> > **Farth** - Sedeem's mate-for-life, a Silver Ranger.

Chantal Baire - a Veterinarian with a clinic near Grandeville.

Ranfer - witch of the Tanpak clan. Preferred to be called Ran. (Deceased).

Sha'gar - Faan magician, daughter of Reep and J.C.

Sgenn - Faan theurgist, daughter of Reep and J.C.

Dat - an indjinn, gifted to Tinker when the group bought a ring, The Eye of Dat.

> **Je'leel** - her daughter by Tinker.

Szart - Faan witch - chosen by R-Bar to be Tinker's mate-for-life.

Chantal's Friends

Frederica Hensler - "Freddie" - lives in Portland.

> **Ralph Andervante** - her husband

Sandrew Sherl Sandermeyer now **Anderson** - "Sandy" - Tinker's Attorney.

> **Red** - her husband, a member of the Grandeville Police Department.

Janine Teacate - "Streak" - Sandy's secretary.

Chen's Chinese - The Building.

Adam Lieu Chen - Master Chen owns and operates *Chen's Chinese,* a restaurant located in Greater Downtown Grandeville. He also trains Tinker in the martial arts.

Dragon Ranch - not far from Tinker's Place.
Prince Goose - a windup plastic toy transformed by Big Red into a traveling companion for John Tinker. He is a brother of Chicken.
Chen Gum Lung - The Golden Dragon of the House of Chen. A sometimes amulet gifted to Tinker by Master Chen, now the consort of Goose.

Doc's Home
Kappa "Doc" Heckmann - anthropologist and adventurer. A friend and neighbor of John Tinker's.
J. C. Smith - one of Tinker's close friends. He works for Doc in many capacities.
    Reep - of the Faan witch clan, married to J. C.
    Szaifeh - her daughter, a witch.
    Sha'gar - her daughter, a magician.
    Sgenn - her daughter, a theurgist.
Membrane - one of Doc's "associates." He run Doc's stores, *Cactus Spine*, specializing in cacti and succulents.
Badnews Treefalls - another of Doc's "associates." He is Doc's constant companion.

The Hardcastle Residence.
Alandale Fredrico Hardcastle IV, known as "Hard" by all his friends.
    Ramp - of the Faan witch clan, a magician, his wife.
    Sa'ar - her twin daughter, a magician.
    Shem - her twin son, a magician, also known by his parents and grandparents as **Alandale Fredrico Hardcastle V. Tajaar** - his wife.

Grandeville Police Department (GPD)
Red and **Green** - two very large men who once played football together on the local college team. They function, usually, as the late night patrol. They are good friends of Tinker, J. C., and Hard.

The Elseplaces

Paradise.
Big Red - a pure force of magic personified. He is primarily concerned with maintaining the balance and order of the universe of universes. And, more often than not, has some influence over the events that plague Tinker.
> **Dancing-All-The-Day** - Big Red's wife.
> **Silly-All-The-Day** - their son.
> **Treena** - the wife of Silly.
> **Ianna** "Sun Song" - their daughter

Various - depending upon mood.
Dram - an individual often called The Evil One. He began life on Murk Wild Weald as a magician-in-training. But after long and secretive study in The Library of Arcana he slowly was transformed by his knowledge and his ambitions into one of the few pure forces in the universe of universes. Dram has a tendency to work at living up to his title.

Stumpf.
The-Mountain-That-Walks - an individual most often addressed as Mountain by his traveling companions. He is one

of the original companions selected to aid John Tinker.

A Place Unnamed.
Macabre - who specializes in killing things. He is usually accompanied by his pets: The Vipers, and the Sparkling Tigers.
Gyre - his female companion, created by his vessel, Gyreship.

The Six Lands.
Sorrowful Mistidings - a professional Teller of Tales, selected from The Six Lands, as one of the original companions to aid John Tinker. He lived with his wife and sons. Now deceased.
Tears Trimblechin - his grandson, a growing Teller of Tales, trained by his grandfather.

Clear Bandler - The Land of Magicians
The $1.98 Magician - trained by Big Red and told to aid Tinker in whatever manner he could.
Plum Duff - a magician and consort to $1.98.

The Old Lands - Bahn Duhr Tohr.
Willawa, The White Warrior, Queen of all the lands, New and Old.
Toucan, The King - he is the brother of Prince Goose and Princess Chicken and once was Tinker's advisor.
Hanred, Ripple's mate-for-life - he is a Master Illusionist who once traveled widely through the universe of universes and is also known by many of the folk as "Old Hanred."
Ripple, Advisor to the Royals - she is the Clan Head of the Faan witch clan.

The New Lands - Aahn Duhr Tohr

> **Frinda** - son of Willawa and Toucan, now King of Bahn Aahn Tohr.
>
> **Sook** - a Faan witch, now his Queen.
>
> **Lurin** - daughter of Willawa and Toucan, now Queen of Hahn Dohr Kahn, The Realm of The Dragon.
>
> > **Frahn** - her son by Tinker.
> >
> > **Nadarl ca Irinl** - his wife.
>
> **Daish a'an'Nald ca E'Nilt**, The Swordpoint of the Victorious.

Dol Spar - Headquarters of The Monetary Control and Mirf's home.

Mirf - The Special Chief First Inspector, often sent on special assignments by The General, the overall director of The Monetary Control and her boss.

> **Fred** - a suk-dragon, her Assistant.
>
> **Quan** - Fred's mate - Mirf's Assistant.
>
> **Rema** and **Nema** - her clerks (sisters).

Magevern - home of the Vander mage Guild.

Sa'ar - the Heart of the Vander, who made Tinker The Lord of The Vander.

Clans, Guilds, and Other Organizations.
(known individuals listed)

Anaza sorcerer Phylota - located in Far Corner.
    Netanada -- Elixa (Clan Head), Sorceress.
    Abadoda -- Three Rank Sorceress.
    Hatopa -- Three Rank Sorcerer.
    Important Artifacts.
        The Ancient Book of Songs.

The Divineal of Thantala - located in Murklan Obscuratan. A Place Never Visited.
    Lady Grimtouch - The Glimmer (Clan Head) of The Divineal of Thantala.
    Lady Fairdeath - traveling with Sluba mage Ransapal.
    Lady Dawnmort
    Lady Softtouch
    Lady Nightreaper
    Lady Final Kiss
    Lady Lastgift
    Clan robe color - forest green almost black; carry a short gold staff.
    Important Artifacts
        The Book of Death.

Potri witch Clan

Turintor

Clan robe colors - grape and green design.

Faan witch Clan - scattered widely throughout the universe of universes.

Ripple - Clan Head - The fifth Born.

Hanred, the Illusionist, her Mate-For-Life.

Shitar - their daughter, a witch.

Mantara - Grenzanr warlock - her mate-for-life.

Santar - their daughter, a witch.

Sook - their daughter, a witch.

Sepanix - their daughter, a witch.

Szart - their daughter, a witch - mated to Tinker.

Ranna - The First Born

Anjan - her mate, Death Warrior

Adarlak - her mate, Hacto mage.

Riz - The Second Born.

Rekel - The Third Born.

Ap Kar - a Hinta warlock, her mate-for-life.

Rbat - The Fourth Born. At one time thought by many to have gone far.

Reptar - The Sixth Born.

Rumtah - The Seventh Born. Known as The Lucky One.

Reep - The Eighth Born. Known as The Silent One.

Married to J. C.

Szaifeh - their daughter, a witch.

Sha'gar - their daughter, a magician.

Sgenn - their daughter, a theurgist.
Rotak - The Ninth Born.
Raft - The Tenth Born. Known as The Fast.
Mrrinar - a Catfolk Healer, her mate.
R-Bar - The Eleventh Born. (Deceased).
Tinker - her Mate-For-Life
Sedeem, their daughter, a magician.
Ramp - The Twelfth Born. A Magician.
Married to Hard.
Sa'ar, their daughter, a magician.
Shem, their son, a magician.
Important artifacts.
An immense collection of volumes dealing with the arcane collected by Hanred during his many travels through the universe of universes.

Talair witch Clan - located on Tanadra.
Motaiss - a warlock
Mendurra - a witch.
Clothes colors - black with just a hint of faint grey in an ornate design that runs down the outside of each sleeve.

Sluba mage Guild, one member located in Three Trees Town.
Ransapal- studied the Dark Under and ancient witch history. Traveling with Lady Fairdeath.

Vander mage Guild - located in Magevern.
Sa'ar - the Heart of the Vander.
Eulin Dragon Force - her daughter by Tinker, a mage and Dragon Master.

Tobtz - the Soul of the Vander.

Cazor - mage warrior.

Moonda

Aada

Bant

Andovar - the Farseer.

Imdar - the Healer.

 Rorx - Vander warlock - her son by Tinker.

 Szaifeh - a witch, his Mate-For-Life.

Imten - the Artificer.

Tinlee - the Adept.

Xanx - Apprentice Healer.

Marl - the Seeker.

Galron - The Bent.

Zulan - The Brave.

Arboc - The Sensitive.

Clothes color - they are always dressed in garb of the faintest purple. It is from the color of their garments that folk often call them "The Purple Magicians."

The Wood With - located in Newlar, relocated from Blurratha. Hidden. In Plain Sight.

 Fairlan - Cluster Head

 Ringlan - Cluster Head

 Clearlar - Cluster Head

 Faerlar - Cluster Head

 Flerlan - The Observer

The Wood With are always accompanied by their beast. When the Wood With are present one might notice the smell of blooming flowers on the air.

The Garden Gnomes - located in Growing Green.
Phineas Grass
Hiram Toadstoll
Franny Waxflower
Franelken Vetch
Tiny Rosebud - the emissary
Rose Perrywinkle

Monetary Control - located on Dol Spar.
The General - Head of Monetary Control.
Mirf - Head of the Special Investigations Office.
 Fred - a suk-dragon - First Assistant.
 Quan - Fred's mate - First Assistant.
 Rema - First Clerk.
 Nema - First Clerk.

The Nagar
 Kartz - Head
  Raj - a Medical Doctor - her mate.
 Reslar - youngest sister.

The Silver Rangers - located on Fandor's Dan.
Farth - Tindar (General) of the Silver Rangers.
Sedeem - Faan magiwitch - his wife.

The Wizards of Trefil - located in The Guarded Lands.
Ragnok - grandfather
Bizl - grandmother
  Braidna Chin Lee, Lyral Princess, The Enchanter
  - their granddaughter.

Bits and Pieces of Cultural Data
(From the files of Monetary Control)

The Garden Gnomes.

The Garden Gnomes are a small folk, perhaps the smallest of all the folk. As their name implies they are fascinated by gardening and frequently visit those gardens that they recognize as being above the average in terms of arrangement and care, whether ornamental or functional.

At some point, in their past, one of them had been seen while visiting a particularly well designed ornamental garden. This kind of happening was not something that they liked to happen nor did they like to talk about it. This garden, as things seem to happen to this folk or that folk over their histories, belonged to a sculptress of some skill and very fast eyes. She made a statue of what her eyes saw as just a fleeting glance and set this statue in and among a artfully organized patch of flowers.

And as things so often happen, a visitor saw this statue and asked the owner to make one for him. And so it went. And so it went. Much to the consternation of the Garden Gnomes.

And eventually an entire industry sprang up around these statues and their production. People even wrote fanciful books about the culture of these things. They were all wrong, of course. None of the authors had ever talked with one of these small folk or had ever visited a Garden Gnome village.

The end result of all this was that the Garden Gnomes retreated deeper and deeper into areas where they would not, or could not, be observed.

Young Garden Gnomes, every once in awhile, on a dark, a particularly dark night, would steal one of these statues and hide them away.

Of course, this had no effect on the overall population of these fake garden gnomes. That industry was to well intrenched.

The Divineal of Thantala.

In time before time almost before memory it is told that the Divineal were there, passing through the universe of universes upon business that none dared ask about and few would dare challenge. The few that did, died. This rare occurrence, challenging one of them, and the result of that challenge, was told one to the other, and thus was the tale spread, and The Divineal were left to pursue their own interests. Most of these interests appeared to have something to do with Death. Death as a being, not merely as the end of something.

All the folk of the elseplaces recognized them as none else would dare to wear a deeply hooded robe of dark forest green that was almost black. And none else would presume to carry a short gold staff.

It is said among the many cultures in the universe of universes that few have ever seen the face of the individual hidden in the blackness of the deep hoods. It is also said that to see that face is to die. But, if one had ever done so and survived, none had ever so stated.

It is known and understood by most folk that one does not approach one of The Divineal and start a conversation. One does not watch one of The Divineal closely. One tries as much as possible to ignore their existence. One hopes to stay alive. It was this understanding that brought into being the label used far and wide for them, "The Sisters of Death." But it never, ever, was used when of them could hear it.

None knew where their elseplace, their home place, was located. None knew which of the many elseplaces, numbers beyond counting, would be the one wherein they resided. And even if one could find out, in some mysterious way, none would dare chose to go to such an elseplace.

The Divineal were polite and very soft spoken, if and when they might chose to speak to someone. And all, but the foolish and soon to be dead, would do all that they were capable of doing, if asked to do something. That is what the folk in the universe of universes believed. And none knew of anyone that had been asked and who had refused and survived.

None knew how many Divineal there were. None knew why or what they were about and most folk felt that the best place to be when one of them was around was to be somewhere else.

The Divineal were like a pebble dropped into a still pond whose action caused ripples to flow out in all directions. And like that pebble, they were totally unconcerned about those ripples.

The Witch Clans.

The Potri witch clan came into existence, as did all the witch clans, during what all the clans call "The Great Migration." From where this migration came is a great matter of debate and argumentation, but not why.

The ancestral clan, or clans, also a matter of intense

debate and argumentation, had, through arcane knowledge, come to understand that a disaster beyond the control of any user of magic was about to happen to their homeland.

So they fled out into the universe of universes and over time the witch clan, or clans, splintered and grew into the myriad of clans that are now present.

The long ago seen disaster happened in a single violent explosion that removed their homeland as their sun erupted and ate everything within reach.

Some thing, some event, during that long ago migration and scatter brought into the witch culture a sense of authority coupled with a powerful magic that each clan cultivated. Each clan developed their own clan interests and evolved their own unique concept of magic. The end result of this was a somewhat provincial sense of proper witch attire and proper witch behavior. The pairing of these beliefs with their sense of authority meant that the folk living in the many elseplaces in the universe of universes knew that any witch tended to be rather short-tempered and had a predilection toward violent behavior when the behavior of other folk, witch, magician, or non-magical user, was felt by the witches to be engaged in improper behavior, undesirable behavior, or were just plain irritating.

Most witch clans dressed in wardrobes of midnight black, the exact style of their clothing varying widely. Some of the clans, in the long before before, had, for reasons they chose not to reveal, settled on wardrobes of other colors.

The Faan witch clan is unique. Among all of the witch clans scattered across the universe of universes, they are the only one that does not maintain a clan house. And, unlike all the other clans, the members are all and only generationally linked. The magic of the Faan flows down the female line from mother to daughter.

The Faan clan, unlike the other clans, are trained almost exclusively by their female relatives, mainly by their mother and their aunts. But if a sister has learned some new and unique twist, it may be shared, sister to sister. It is due to this multi-generational sharing and training that has made the Faan noted throughout the witch clans as being the most powerful clan and to be avoided if at all possible. And some few understand that at some point in the long ago long ago, in their mating with their chosen mates-for-life, from other witch lines, that something unusual happened that twisted and transformed their genetic material.

The result of this event was that, at times, their offspring are born with new and unique abilities. This tends to explain why the Faan do not maintain a clan house. Members of their clan, most often, prefer to wander mostly by themselves and to study and collect magic and magic spells. And other things.

The Mage Guilds

The mage Guilds apparently came into existence in the long ago long ago in a manner none understand or thought to record as this event was in a time when such occurrences were not seen as being important enough to warrant special note.

Magicians are, in one sense, at the opposite end of the magical spectrum from the witches. That is why the magicians and the witches tend to avoid each other whenever possible, especially physical contact. The magic of each tends to be unstable in contact, often resulting in fatal results. However, there is the fact that, at times, in a manner none truly understand, that magicians and witches may have close association, even mates of the others, without dire affects.

The Vander mage Guild, as written in the Histories of the Arcane, was once a sub-Order of the Fanderlaine mage Guild. Little is known of the Fanderlaine and what they thought to specialize their skills upon. The Vander sub-Order eventually split away from the Fanderlaine and pushed deep into the arcane knowledge that was of particular interest to their members. The Vander became the most radical of the experimenters of the mage Guilds and explored many areas of interest to them. This was considered most strange in the mage communities as the Guilds tend to be extremely conservative in their outlook and mage knowledge. Unlike most Guilds, the Vander are almost exclusively female, each member carefully selected for skills and aptitude.

The Anaza Sorcerers.

The Sorcerers were, and are, a small clan and have forever lived in small isolated elseplaces rarely relocating. Small isolated elseplaces were more common in the universe of universes than most of the folk realized. And that suited the Sorcerer clan quite well.

Why they preferred to live this way is lost in the dim reaches of an ancient history begun in a time almost before time itself. Various of the First Sorcerers at numerous points in time in their long, long history had searched their book of lore and learning, The Book Of Songs, for clues as to why this was the way it was. But each had failed. None of them realized, or knew from the oral traditions of the clan, that the Book Of Songs had come into existence long past the time when the reason why could be remembered.

So, as these things happen, the Sorcerer clan has

remained reclusive and unknown to the larger universe of universes, not really hidden so much as just being very remote and private.

There was one piece of information known to the clan, a piece of information never allowed to be transmitted to anyone not a member of the clan. And similar to the reason for their preferring small, isolated elseplaces, the acquisition of this piece of information, the how and the when and the why of it did happen, was lost in the time long before before.

Someone, way back then, had learned to recognize the presence of a folk never seen and poorly understood. This recognition was not visual but rather a matter of odor, the odor of blooming flowers. With such an olfactory clue, this small clan of magic users, the Sorcerer clan, knew when the Wood With were around. They had never seen one but the delicate and pleasant odor told them when these folk were about.

The Wood With knew of this strange thing. So they tended to keep a watch on this small group more from a matter of curiosity than of any fear of what that clan might do.

The Sorcerer clan, of course, knew when these other strange folk came and went so they, the Sorcerers, tended to keep Sorcerer business very carefully hidden from these others. And in some strange and subtle way, the clan felt that the Wood With were not to be trusted. It was a cultural tradition, never to be questioned. The reason for this was also lost in the dim historical past. And, of course, they would never attempt to affect the behavior of the Wood With. Tradition also stated that this was not to be done.

The True History of the Magic Users as Discovered by the Divineal.

Many of the witch groups, whether the Witch Clan, the Sorcerer Phylota, the Nagar sort, or the Divineal, have a tale from a time long before long before, and long before written records, of fleeing their homeland before it was destroyed by an event that no magic could prevent. This tale was passed member to member as an oral tradition and eventually was written down. It appears that this event happened.

But, as the magic users scattered into the universe of universes, their knowledge and identities became unique, group to group, and most felt that they were different than all the others.

However, all the groups so far mentioned are witch, even though some felt that others were not and needed to be hunted down and destroyed.

What none of them knew, or understood, is that the magicians were also from this same single event. Witch and magician fled from the same homeland, although, in some manner not understood, the magicians lost the remembrance of that past happening.

The witch and magician groups on that homeland attempted to cast a great spell of prevention. It failed and they fled. None knew that the failure of that spell caused a great change in their magic, with witch and magician forces becoming polar opposites of each other, hence the great danger, now, of mixing, one with the other, magic or personnel, most of the time.

The Wood With.

The Wood With are a small folk. If anyone saw one of

this secretive group from a distance, an event so unlikely as to be in the realm of never, it might be thought that what was seen was a very young human child of ten or twelve years of age. Of course, few human children are accompanied by a beast as tall as they are.

The Wood With, from a time before forever, have remained unobserved and unknown, which is exactly what they wish. As a group they are, for the most part, uninterested in the affairs of other sapient beings in all the universe of universes. But, every so often, there occurs a one that attracts their attention. This event is a rare, but not unusual, happening.

The Wood With prefer to live in and among the big trees, taking comfort one from the other. They and the environment blur together where ever they might be. This skill, this cultural attribute, is the main reason, but not the only reason, why they remain unseen and unnoticed.

Their beasts are as unique a species as the Wood With. From an early age one finds the other and from that instant the pair are inseparable. The beasts blend into their surroundings with the same ease as their constant companions.

It is a peculiarity of the Wood With that their presence leaves a faint odor of blooming flowers in the air. In all the time of their existence only one small group have ever realized this fact. But that group's mythology and cultural values are such that the fact that they know this is all that they know. Every thing else they believe, everything else are tales from antiquity with all the error that derives from that.

The Kingdom and Kingdoms of Bahn Duhr Tohr.

The Kingdom of Bahn Duhr Tohr had been, until its most

recent merging into a whole, a series of large and small kingdoms, each with a unique name and a unique color scheme. These color schemes were relegated to their Royalty and to their armies. It was very useful to combatants to be able to recognize friend from foe in the chaos of massed combat.

Many of the kingdoms, but not all, could trace their existence back into the dimly remembered past. Some even argued that they existed long before written records came into use. The kingdoms large and small, frequently merged, or broke apart, as the normal political intrigues and royal wheeling and dealing created large kingdoms out of smaller ones, or as so often happened, smaller kingdoms out of larger.

But, in spite of the usual turmoil over boundaries and royal household alignments, all the kingdoms were dependent upon each other as no single one had all the resources necessary for true self-sufficiency.

The bonds between the rulers and the ruled are tight and mutually advantageous. Rulers who did not keep the needs of their folk foremost did not last long. Of course, the occasional battle with a neighbor was accepted as just part of life. Battles were, for the most part, short. This was due to the usual approach to warfare that assumed that most of the fighting would happen between the royalty of the houses in contention. The knights and lessor troops often suffered nothing worse than broken bones. Most of the time this occurred during the first melee and charge.

Grandeville.

Grandeville is a small, rather isolated, rural community of 8,000 population (more or less) tucked away in the mountainous corner of northeastern Oregon. It survives in a provincial unawareness of many things, being overly conscious of the ancestors who settled the place long after the westward migration brought California, Washington, Oregon, and Idaho into statehood.

The town sprawls down from "The Bench," a shallow bench along the edge of the next door mountain slope, to The Blue River, named after the color it has after the first snow melt surges from the canyon and out across the valley proper, always threatening to jump its banks and flood the surrounding farm land.

There are two newspapers published in town, a weekly and a daily (except for Sunday). The Daily, The Grandeville News, tends to ignore anything happening outside the edge of town. The weekly, The Mountain View, tends to ignore anything happening in Grandeville and prints whatever the publisher happens to feel like publishing.

There are a number of local establishments of note:
- The Two Bags Full - a grocery store.
- The Railroad Bar and Grill - also known as The Rail.
- Big Darlene's Bar - the home of the Annual Chili Cookoff and Arm Wrestling Championship Event, All Comers Invited.
- Johnson's Everything Shop.
- Chen's Chinese Restaurant.
- Leonard's Outdoor Supply Shop.
- The Always Open Gas Pump.
- The Romp and Stomp Motel
- Randy's Truck Corral.
- Dave's Soup and Salad Bar.
- Nan's Clothe Worke.

About the Author

George R. Mead began to study anthropology in 1962 after being discharged (honorably) from the U. S. Army, Combat Engineers. He eventually received a B.A., M. A., and Ph. D. in his chosen field. And many years later an M. S. W. in Clinical Social Work. He was worked in aerospace, taught at the college and university levels, worked in a community action agency, ran a restaurant, been unemployed, and worked for the U. S. Forest Service. He is now retired from the work-a-day world but does a certain amount of consulting, writing, and research. He lives seven miles outside of the small town of La Grande, Oregon, with his wife, one cat. A new dog joined the house as an eight-week old puppy found under some brush in the middle of the American Southwest desert. Rez is now four years old and weighs 107 pounds (some puppy).

www.ingramcontent.com/pod-product-compliance
Lightning Source LLC
Chambersburg PA
CBHW071340020726
47502CB00001B/185